AVATARS

BOOK ONE
SO THIS IS HOW IT ENDS

TUI T. SUTHERLAND

AVATARS

BOOK ONE
SO THIS IS HOW IT ENDS

An Imprint of HarperCollinsPublishers

Eos is an imprint of HarperCollins Publishers.

Avatars, Book One: So This Is How It Ends
Copyright © 2006 by Tui T. Sutherland
All rights reserved. Printed in the United States of America.
No part of this book may be used or reproduced in any manner whatsoever without written permission except in the case of brief quotations embodied in critical articles and reviews. For information address HarperCollins Children's Books, a division of HarperCollins Publishers, 1350 Avenue of the Americas, New York, NY 10019.
www.harperteen.com

Library of Congress Cataloging-in-Publication Data
is available.
ISBN-10: 0-06-075024-3 (trade bdg.)—ISBN-13: 978-0-06-075024-4 (trade bdg.)
ISBN-10: 0-06-075028-6 (lib. bdg.)—ISBN-13: 978-0-06-075028-2 (lib. bdg.)

Typography by Christopher Stengel
1 2 3 4 5 6 7 8 9 10

First Edition

For Adam,
the person I'd want with me at the end of the world

and for Kari,
because they all are, really.

ACKNOWLEDGMENTS

With a million thank-yous to Alix Reid, Abby McAden, and Ruth Katcher for being absolutely brilliant editors and friends.

AVATARS

BOOK ONE
SO THIS IS HOW IT ENDS

Beginnings

Nine years ago . . .

By the time he got there, the hair salon was a smoking hole in the ground. Flames darted toward nearby buildings and then back as if they were alive. Strangely, nothing else nearby had caught on fire. It was as if the salon had spontaneously combusted inside a bubble.

Officer Bill Nichols pushed back his hat and rubbed the bridge of his nose with a sigh. A contained fire was good news, certainly, but it was going to be tough to explain in the report.

"Where's the girl?" he said.

The fire chief pointed to a small shape huddled near one of the ambulances. The area was crawling with activity—people shouting, stretchers rolling, emergency lights flashing. Around the girl, however, was an island of empty space. The emergency workers were giving her a wide berth, whether deliberately or subconsciously, Nichols couldn't tell.

"Why isn't someone taking care of her?" he asked angrily.

The fire chief shrugged, his face pale. "She didn't need taking care of," he said.

"A nine-year-old survives a fire like this and she doesn't need taking care of?" Nichols shook his head and walked away before the other man could answer.

All he could see of the girl was a long curl of dark hair snaking out from under the orange blanket.

"Hi there," he said, crouching beside her. "I'm Police Officer Bill."

No response.

"Can you tell me something about yourself? What's your name?"

Still she said nothing. The poor child was clearly traumatized.

"Listen," he said, "we're going to take care of you. You don't have to be scared."

Slowly her head lifted, and he felt a chill run through him. Her eyes were deep pools of darkness.

Shock, he told himself. *She's in shock.*

"I'm not scared," she said. "My mom is coming."

Was her mom on one of the stretchers? On her way to the hospital right now? How could he begin to explain this tragedy to a nine-year-old?

"Sweetheart," he started.

"There," she said, pointing.

At that exact moment, a panicked voice called, "Kali! Kali!" Nichols turned and saw a woman fighting her way through the crowd. "My *daughter* was in there!" she screamed, shoving two of the perimeter officers aside.

He stood up as she stumbled over to them. She was petite, blond, and delicate, nothing like the wiry Indian girl in the blanket. But she seized the child and clung to her with a gasp of relief. Something about the woman made him want to protect her, even more than her daughter.

The girl wrapped her arms around her mother's shoulders. He barely caught the words as she whispered, "They were mean. I told you I didn't want a haircut."

"I know, darling, I'm sorry," the woman said, stroking her daughter's hair. "I came right back, didn't I?"

Kali buried her face in her mother's neck and nodded. The tiny woman lifted her as if she weighed nothing and turned to face Officer Nichols.

"Thank you so much," she said, her eyes huge and blue. His heart did a strange little backflip. "Thank you for taking care of Kali."

The fire chief's words popped into his head: *She didn't need taking care of.*

"I'm afraid we're going to have to ask your daughter a few questions," he said. "Once she's had time to recover from the shock, of course."

"Of course," Kali's mother said, smiling. "But I'm sure she doesn't remember much. And we wouldn't want to make her suffer through it all again. She's so young."

There was something oddly rehearsed about the words, as if she had said them before, but he barely registered it. He felt like he could dissolve in the blue of her eyes. *Cheesy metaphors now,* he thought. *I wonder if she's single. I wonder if she would date a cop. I wonder how long I have to wait before it's appropriate to ask.*

"Could I take her home now?" she said. "I could give you our phone number, and you could come by to talk to her anytime you wanted."

It wasn't quite protocol, but it *was* the opportunity he'd been hoping for. He could talk to the child later, find out what she saw, and also see the mother again.

As the two of them walked away through the smoke, he caught a glimpse of dark eyes watching him over her mother's shoulder. Uneasily, he turned back to his job.

It was time to count the dead.

SIX YEARS AGO . . .

The tray of instruments clattered to the floor, and Dr. Harris let out a frustrated sigh.

"Vicky, go find Tigre and have him come in here."

"No, Dad, I can help, really I can." She crouched and began picking up the scalpels, but one slipped out of her hand again with a crash. The patient on the table whimpered.

"Vicky." Dr. Harris gently took her shoulders and moved her aside. "I need Tigre."

"Fine," she spat. She slammed out of the operating room and stomped down the stairs as loudly as she could. She didn't care if she woke the whole place up. It would serve her dad right. And that stupid kid who helped him. Tigre (and what kind of name was that?) was only eleven too, just like her. He wasn't *smarter* than her or *better* than her. He was just the first kid they'd met in Chile, and now he got twenty bucks a week to help translate into Spanish for the clients.

"TEEEEE-GRAYYY!" she hollered, banging into the back room. Sure enough, all the boarders leaped to their feet and started barking. Stupid dogs. She didn't even like animals. She had to be, like, the worst veterinarian's daughter ever.

At the end of the rows of cages she could see Tigre lying on the couch, snoring away. The two feral cats that had been brought in yesterday were curled around his head and on his stomach, purring contentedly. She hated those cats. They had been wild, hissing, snarling beasts just a day ago; one of them had left a long scratch on her arm, not that her father cared. And here they were snuggling up to Tigre as if he were made of tuna fish.

"No people," he mumbled. "All gone."

"Tigre!" She badly wanted to grab him and yank him off the couch onto the floor. It would serve him right for sleeping through this racket. But she didn't like the look the cats were giving her, so she settled for picking up a packet of dog biscuits and throwing it at his head. "TIGRE!"

He blinked at her with blurry eyes. "Vicky?"

"Dad wants you," she said curtly. "Now."

"Okay." He yawned and stretched. The cats protested with *mrrrrs* of disappointment as he sat up. "I was having this weird dream."

"Let me guess," she said. "About animals." *Bo-ring.*

"Sort of," he said. "Except you could see through them—what is the word?"

"Obvious," she said. When he didn't get it, she rolled her eyes and said, "Transparent."

"Transparent," he repeated. "And there were no more people. And I'd done something very bad, but nobody knew."

"Maybe it was a vision of the future," she said sarcastically. "A future where you finally go live in the woods with a bunch of wild, furry, slobbery creatures, the way you've always dreamed."

He shrugged and pulled on his sneakers. "I don't like to think about the future. I guess whatever happens will happen," he said. "There's nothing we can do about it anyway."

She smacked his shoulder, hard. "I *hate* it when people talk like that," she snapped. "There's always *something* a person can do."

"Not always."

"*Yes* always!"

"You don't believe in fate?" he said, standing up. "That our lives are all planned out ahead of time?"

"I know what fate is, dumbhead," she said. "And I think it's stupid."

"You think a lot of things are stupid," he said with a little smile.

"And you think you're pretty smart," she shot back. "Now go, before my dad freaks out."

She met his eyes for a moment, and images of jungles and fierce toothy creatures flashed into her head. She shivered, and he turned and left the room.

Outside, thunder rumbled, and rain began to fall.

· • ● • ·

THREE YEARS AGO . . .

"I always feel like I'm split in two
There's the part that likes me
and the part that likes you. . . ."

"Who are we listening to?" Gus asked. The girl's voice was ethereal, like one of the elves from *Lord of the Rings*.

"You're kidding," Becky said, twisting around to look at him. "You don't recognize Venus?"

"She's on the radio *all* the *time*," Lisa said petulantly, kicking the back of her sister's seat. "Becky *loves* her."

"I've heard of her," Gus said. Who hadn't—fourteen years old (his own age), two albums, about a million music awards. But he didn't pay much attention to pop music.

"You just have to see her in concert, Lisa," Becky's boyfriend, Mark, said, slowing down for a traffic light. "She's got this crazy magic. Everyone falls in love with her."

"I said a year ago that she was going to be the next big thing," Becky said. "Didn't I, Mark?"

"Yes, sweetheart. As usual, you are right about everything."

Becky swatted at him and the car swerved a little.

"Hey!" Lisa protested. "Careful, it's icy out there."

"Worrywart," Gus said, poking her in the ribs. She giggled.

"Want to borrow the CD?" Mark said. "Becky and I like converting people to our cults."

"Sure," Gus said. Becky ejected the CD and handed it to him as they pulled into his driveway.

"Looks dark in there," Mark said. "Don't your parents usually wait up for you?"

"Yeah," Gus said, leaning forward to peer out the windshield. "And Andrew never goes to bed before midnight. That's weird."

"Maybe they went somewhere." Lisa shrugged.

"Want me to wait?" Mark asked.

"No, it's okay," Gus said. He sort of did, but Mark was three years older, and Gus didn't want to look like a scared kid in front of him. "I'll see you tomorrow, Lisa." She leaned over and kissed him on the cheek, and he blushed.

"Good night," she whispered.

Gus shut the car door and walked toward the house. Where was everybody? Why was the house so dark and quiet? He unlocked the door and turned to wave at Mark and the others as they pulled away.

Inside, the house was cold. He crossed to the thermostat, banging his knee on the coffee table and swearing in the dark, and turned it up.

"Hello?" he called. "I'm home!"

Were they asleep?

"Mom? Dad?"

He switched on the living room light, then the light over the stairs, and climbed up to their bedroom.

Empty.

Down the hall, Andrew's bedroom was empty too.

He walked from room to room, switching on every light in the house.

Don't think about what might have happened. Don't think about murderers and kidnappers and accidents and abductions and burglars with guns.

The more he tried not to worry, the more images crowded his head.

When he'd left earlier that day, his dad had been cleaning the gutters. Gus had laughed at his floppy fisherman's hat and oversized gardening gloves, and his father had joked that he shouldn't have to do these backbreaking chores with two teenagers in the house. In *his* day he'd had to— "Walk barefoot in the snow to school? Uphill both ways?" Gus had guessed, and his dad had grinned and muttered something about respect and kids these days.

Now Gus couldn't stop himself from picturing Dad slipping on the ladder, crashing to the ground, his arm twisted under him, Mom and Andrew rushing him to the hospital.

Or maybe Mom had cut herself making dinner—he always thought she chopped things too quickly, too carelessly—she'd been putting out carrots and potatoes for stew, her red-brown hair, like his, falling into her eyes and her SO MANY MEN, SO FEW RECIPES apron coming untied.

Then there was Andrew, his room a tangle of wires and dismantled computers. Perhaps he'd electrocuted himself, reached for the wrong thing at the wrong time, blue fire shaking his body. Gus pressed his hands over his eyes, trying to stop the images.

Wouldn't they have left a note if they'd had to go somewhere? Even if they were rushing to the hospital, wouldn't there be a note or a message?

The answering machine light was not blinking, and the magnets on the kitchen fridge held nothing more than the usual shopping list and report cards. Andrew's cell phone went straight to voice mail.

He crossed back into the living room and put the Venus CD into the stereo. Her voice curled through the room, chasing the pictures out of his head, calming him down. He huddled on the couch, wrapping a blanket around himself. There was an explanation. They would be back soon. Everything was okay.

The album was on its third time through when the doorbell woke him up.

"Hey, Gus." Shannon, Andrew's girlfriend, was standing on the porch, leaning against the railing like she needed it to hold her up. She looked like she'd been crying. He shook his head, trying to wake up. What was she doing here in the middle of the night?

"Gus," she said with a tremor in her voice. "Gus, there's been an accident."

"Where's Andrew?" he asked. He tried to focus on Shannon, but the tears spilling out of her were too surreal. She seemed to be floating away from him.

"He's at the hospital. He asked me to come get you." She reached toward him, and it was like her hands were moving in slow motion and the air around them was turning to water. He couldn't breathe. He felt like he'd been sliced across the chest and everything below his ribs was falling away, vacuumed into darkness.

"Do I have to choose," Venus sang. *"Between being loved and being free, or in the in-between of you and me is there a space for both to be."*

He didn't remember getting into Shannon's car, but he found himself there, staring at his feet, realizing he'd put on Andrew's boots instead of his own. They were so large. Such big feet. There was a dent in the toe of the left boot where Andrew had dropped a piece of scenery on it.

"There was a man in the middle of the road." Shannon was talking, nervously; she always talked, that's what made it funny that quiet Andrew was dating her. "They were coming back from the video store and they swerved to avoid him—they were saving his life, Gus—he came out of nowhere."

Gus closed his eyes and she stopped talking.

"*It's not okay.*" Venus's last song was still playing in his head. "*It's not okay and it won't be okay and if there must be good-byes there still shouldn't be lies but I'll hold you for now anyway.*"

ONE YEAR AGO . . .

The sun beamed brightly overhead, sending shoots of light through the hole in the temple roof like vines.

Professor Emerson sighed.

"I can't explain it," she said. "The guards were patrolling the site all night. We've had problems with vandals and grave robbers before, but this isn't like anything I've ever seen."

She could tell that the Egyptian policeman wasn't following her English, but her knowledge of languages was limited to the ancient kind. She turned to her translator impatiently; the teenager was gazing around in curiosity.

"Tell him nothing was taken." Mostly true. One gold

amulet was nothing compared to the rest of the treasure in the temple they were excavating. "I only called to report *that*." She pointed to the new hole in the ceiling, where a block exactly one foot square had been removed and the sun now poured through merrily.

The translator started talking to the official in their language. Professor Emerson rolled her eyes at her partner. "We're going to have to speed things up," she muttered to him. "Everything in here will decompose faster now that it's been exposed to sunlight."

"It's such an odd thing to do," Angus said in his lilting Scottish accent. "Where did the block go? If it was removed so a thief could get in, how small would that person have to be? If someone came in and out, why didn't they take more? It's the most peculiar crime I've ever heard of."

"Lucky us," she snorted. "Well, we'll have to start by hiring a whole new set of day laborers. Obviously these can't be trusted." She started to leave, then turned back. "Oh, but keep the cook. His food is great, and his son is a good translator."

Angus agreed, but uneasily. There was something about the boy that he didn't trust . . . but perhaps he was just imagining the sly look in his eyes and the flash of gold under his shirt.

Now . . .

THE DAY BEFORE

FRIDAY, DECEMBER 21, 2012
NEW YORK, NEW YORK, 6:02 A.M.

There were eyes watching her from the darkness.

A shaft of moonlight slid through the leaves, illuminating a darker patch of shadows among shadows, where something gleamed, like a silver knife in folds of black silk. . . .

Kali started awake just before her head hit the cereal bowl. The tree outside the window—the last tree in Brooklyn, her mother called it—rustled like it was laughing at her. It didn't even *have* leaves at this time of year.

Across the kitchen table, a small face regarded her curiously.

"Hey, Amy girl," Kali said, rubbing her eyes almost hard enough to press them through her head. "If you must be up before the sun, shouldn't you help keep me awake too?"

"You tired," her little sister said. *Half-sister*, Kali reminded herself, and they didn't look even a quarter related to each other. All three of her half-sisters were delicate and blond, like Mom, although Amy had Bill's quiet temperament, Beth had his light brown eyes, and Josephine seemed bossy enough that she might easily become a cop one day. They'd been named after the March sisters in *Little Women*, but their personalities were totally mismatched to the characters from the book.

At least Kali wasn't named Meg. There wasn't anyone less like a Louisa May Alcott character than she was. Kali liked to imagine that she looked like her own father, who was out in the world somewhere: tall, with skin the color of dark honey, strong features, and large almond-shaped eyes. All she knew about him was that he'd come from India, but her mother refused to say anything about how they'd met or why he'd disappeared before Kali was born. The only thing he had left them was the bone pendant Kali always wore around her neck, with her name carved on the back.

Amy was suddenly at Kali's knee, putting her tiny hands on either side of Kali's face in an uncanny imitation of Mom.

"You go back to bed," the five-year-old said solemnly.

"*You're* the one who should be in bed," Kali said, standing and scooping Amy up in one swift motion. "*I* have to go to work." She carried Amy down the hall and into the bedroom the little girls all shared. At least Kali had her own room, even if it was more like an attic crawl space in their Brooklyn brownstone apartment.

Kali dumped Amy in her bed, but quietly, so as not to

wake the other two. Amy caught Kali's hand before she could walk away.

"Maybe you can stop working soon," Amy said. "Maybe today Daddy'll come home."

Kali scowled. She was never going to forgive the idiot babysitter who had told Amy that Bill was on a business trip the last time he went into the hospital. Now, almost a year later, Amy still asked every morning if this was the day Daddy was coming home, no matter how often Mom and Kali tried to explain "dead" to her.

"No frowning," Amy said, poking at Kali's forehead.

"Go back to sleep," Kali whispered. "Before you wake your sisters."

"Will you be home early tonight?" Amy asked as Kali tucked the comforter around her. "Maybe we could go back to the pet store." With Christmas four days away, visions of puppies were clearly dancing through her head.

"We'll see," Kali said, knowing already it wasn't possible. "I have a lot of work to do." *And the stupid subway I normally take isn't running after 11 P.M., so with all the transfers and rerouting, it'll take me an hour longer than usual.* She dropped a quick kiss on Amy's forehead and left the room, closing the door behind her.

The girls were sweet and she wanted to take care of them, but she always felt so large and scary around them. Big, scary, dark sister with eyeliner and piercings and a room they were not allowed in. She couldn't help feeling sometimes like a dragon living amidst a flock of chickens.

When Bill was alive, Kali hadn't been responsible for them. Back then she either hid in her room (in case Bill noticed anything else weird about her) or tried to run away. Back then her earnings were hers alone. All the money she'd made had gone into her savings for India, where she planned to find her own father and not deal with any more oafish law-enforcement types trying to take over her life and be her pal. Back then there was always at least the chance of freedom.

But after Bill got sick, she couldn't run away anymore. Mom would never be able to support the kids on her own. Who could have guessed that Bill's presence was a kind of freedom after all?

Well, he was gone now. Mom watched the girls; Kali earned the money. Maybe one day there would be enough for her to travel, or—crazy thought—go to college. Right. Maybe when the girls were old enough to support themselves. Jo-Jo was eight now, so, in ten years, if she was lucky . . . twenty-eight wasn't *so* old for college. But ten years of waitressing and typing and filing and taking messages for people who couldn't remember or pronounce her name would make her much older than twenty-eight by then.

Don't get mad, she told herself. Breathe in. Breathe out. Like it said in all those self-control books her mom kept leaving around the house. Nice and subtle, Mom.

There were two ways to deal with the peculiar things that kept happening around Kali. That's what Mom had said seven years ago when she gave Kali the Notebook of Strange Events she'd been keeping since Kali was two. Kali pasted in the relevant articles now, and made sure Mom never saw it.

One way, Mom had told the eleven-year-old Kali, was to be so charming that they could get out of anything.

This was an act Mom had perfected: a wide-eyed innocent air that helped deflect attention from Kali—a "goodness, my poor child has suffered so, the little angel, can I take her home now?" flutter that won over cops, firefighters, private investigators, and anyone else who might have become suspicious about how many fires and accidents seemed to happen around this particular kid.

But there was no way Kali was going to pull off charm, so the only other option was to stop the strange events before they happened. This was how Kali ended up with *Anger Management and You* on her bedside table. Not that it was working all that well.

She had to get out of here. She had to get to India and find her dad. Her dreams were full of jungles and tigers and emeralds and flashing knives in the dark.

New York was clearly driving her insane.

LOS ANGELES, CALIFORNIA, 8:14 A.M.

Gus got bored about fifteen minutes into Andrew's argument with the lot attendant. What do you mean I can't park here, why not, who else is using the lot right now, I'll show you rules, buddy, I need to park here, we have lights to unload, do you want to take this up with . . . yada yada yada. Finally Gus slid open the door at the back of the truck, grabbed two lights, and jumped down.

"Hey Andrew, I'll just start taking these inside," Gus said, and took off before anyone could stop him.

"Gus!" Andrew shouted. "If she's there, don't talk to her! Are you listening to me?"

Despite everything Andrew had told him about Venus,

Gus found it hard to believe there was a celebrity so compelling that he wouldn't be able to resist talking to her. Gus didn't talk to strangers if he could help it. Which meant he hadn't made many friends since moving to California last year, but that was all right, since he preferred hanging out with Andrew anyway.

Especially when he could get paid for it, like now. All he had to do was cart around a few lights and avoid talking to this pop-star princess. Not that she was likely to be here this early in any case.

Gus shouldered open the side door and found himself in the dark. Backstage? Didn't they have to leave a ghost light on? He blinked, his eyes adjusting. Oh. There was a black curtain in front of him—keeping the daylight from shining through onto the stage. He fumbled with it for a minute before he found the way through into a space that seemed vast and smooth compared to the backstage of his school theater.

He looked around in awe. Everything was clean and bright. The levers for the flies had red plastic covers and bright metal rings, instead of being rusted in place. The weights were all neatly labeled and stacked to the side. But it still smelled like a real theater. Gus set his lights down next to the wall and ran his hand along the ropes.

He knew he should go back out and get more lights, so that they'd all be unloaded by the time Venus's roadies showed up. But first he wanted to try and find his way up to the catwalks. You could tell how expensive a place was by how nice the catwalks above the audience were. The ones at his school were more like crawl spaces, covered in asbestos and just waiting for a teenager to set a foot wrong and plummet through the flimsy boards.

Gus had heard that this place had catwalks you could actually stand up in. He wanted to explore them before the others arrived, in case they got all macho and grown-up and wouldn't let him up there for safety reasons.

But there were so many doors and hallways leading away from the backstage. He didn't want to run into any security guards, or worse, walk in on the pop star preening for her performance. Andrew would *never* forgive him for that. Andrew had tried to talk to her once, backstage during a rehearsal last time she came to L.A., and she had shut him down so fast and yet so politely that he said it was like having a ton of shining gold bricks dumped on your head.

Sure, Gus loved her music. But that didn't mean he wanted to meet her, or talk to her, or find out how shallow and boring and stuck-up she really was. Despite Andrew's stories, he didn't think she'd be nearly as interesting in person as she sounded in her songs.

He peered down a hallway on the side of the stage, looking for ladders, but saw only more doors. One of them had to lead to a staircase, or some way up to the catwalks. He saw that one of the doors had a poster taped crookedly to it. Upon closer inspection, it turned out to be the cover image from Venus's first album, *Birth of Venus*. He'd had an argument about it with Andrew just last week.

In the picture, Venus was half leaping, half flying out of a giant seashell, waves crashing on either side of her. Her eyes were closed, and her head was back as if she were leaping straight from the ocean up to heaven. Her arms were out to either side with her hands in fists. She was dressed in black leather, wound in strips around her arms and legs and fitted around her body, with her hair flying out behind her like a golden cape.

Andrew had picked up the CD during his halfhearted monthly cleaning of the living room. Gus, as usual, was lying on the couch watching DVDs of science fiction shows that had been popular before he was born.

"Dude," Andrew said, peering at the cover. "What's with the Jesus imagery?"

"What?" Gus said.

"I thought Venus was a Greek goddess," Andrew said. "So why's she in this cross position?" Andrew believed that one of his responsibilities as Gus's guardian was to talk about what he was studying at school. This semester he'd picked Gus's art history class as the one for discussion, since calculus and American Classics hadn't gotten them very far. Usually Gus could steer him back to more comfortable topics like Tolkien and Alan Moore.

"It's not Jesus imagery," Gus had replied. "It's like that painting, you know, by that Italian guy. Vermicelli or Botticelli or something. *Birth of Venus*, like the name of the album."

"Really?" Andrew tilted his head. "So . . . shouldn't she be, like, you know, naked or something? I thought the chick in that painting looked all sweet and innocent and, uh . . . naked."

"Man, no superstar is going to be naked on the cover of her album. Not to mention she was, like, thirteen years old when that came out."

"Okay, now I feel gross," Andrew said, putting it down.

"I think the point is that she's like the Greek goddess of love, but more empowered. You know? All her album covers are based on these famous paintings of naked women, but instead she's wearing cool clothes and doing something rebellious. So here, instead of just being born and floating around on a shell, it looks like she's actually bursting out of the shell and flying up into the sky. See? Like she's creating *herself*, I think. It's, you know, symbolic. And there's another one where it's, like, Adam and Eve being cast out of the Garden of Eden, like the Sistine Chapel painting. Only, on her album cover version, she's walking away like she *wanted* to leave. Here I go into the world, see ya, God."

"So in that one, she's, like, Eve?"

"Well, yeah."

"But I thought her name was Venus? Does she change it for each album?"

"No, moron, it's always Venus. That's her *name*. The album covers are just to make a point."

"I guess it's lucky for her there's a genius like you to appreciate it, then," Andrew had said, and moved on to Swiffering around the furniture.

Gus was about to try opening one of the doors when he heard an almighty crash from behind him. He ran back down the hall and found that both the lights he'd brought in had been knocked over. A very short girl about his own age was sitting on the floor next to them, clutching one shin and cursing like a sailor.

"Oh!" Gus said, shocked into speaking to her. "I'm sorry—are you okay?"

She looked up, and as their eyes met he actually felt his

breath catch in his throat, which was something he'd thought only happened in the novels that Andrew's girl-friends read. It wasn't that this girl was beautiful, exactly. She was wearing jeans and an oversized flannel shirt with the sleeves rolled up above her elbows. Her red-gold hair hung in tangles like she'd recently gotten out of bed, her face was freckled, and her nose was sunburned while the rest of her was pale as the moon. But there was something about the green of her eyes that made him feel like he was floating in the ocean—somewhere between blissfully serene and relatively certain he was about to be eaten by sharks.

"Did *you* leave those there?" she snapped.

"Guilty as charged," he said. "I'm really sorry."

"Didn't it occur to you that people might need to walk around down here?"

"Nah—the regular crew usually doesn't show up until 9 A.M., which is why we come early to bring the extra rented lights. And I was looking for the catwalks. Do you know how to get to them?"

She stared at him for a bewildered minute. He'd assumed from her outfit that she was another techie who might know the layout of the backstage area, but from her expression he could see she had no idea what he was talking about.

"You know—the catwalks where the electricians hang the lights?" he explained.

"I thought catwalks were those things models walk on," she said.

"No, these are much cooler and higher up," he said, and then, before he knew what he was saying, he added,

"Want to help me find them?"

Her expression was skeptical bordering on I-think-you're-a-psycho. He offered his hand, feeling shy but strangely brave at the same time.

"Come on, I bet they're off this way. If you've never been up above a stage, you really should check it out."

She hesitated, still looking confused.

"Quick, before the superstar or her security team catches us," he added.

She accepted his hand and let him pull her to her feet. Her hand was tiny in his, with slender, manicured fingers. If he'd noticed those earlier, he would have known she wasn't a techie. He wondered if she was related to Venus. She did look a bit like the girl on the album covers, but shorter, paler, and less perfect looking, with curlier hair and a more crooked nose. Maybe she was a younger sister or a cousin or something. It would probably be weird to ask, and he didn't want to scare her away.

Feeling braver with someone alongside him, Gus tried the first two doors in the hall. One was a makeshift dressing room and the other looked like an office. But the third door revealed a spiral staircase.

Soon they were standing on a narrow wooden walkway with only a thin railing between them and the flaps that formed the ceiling of the auditorium.

"Isn't this cool?" Gus whispered. Something about the darkness and the space made him want to keep his voice down. "I love seeing what's behind the scenes of things. I keep getting in trouble for going through closed doors in museums and stuff."

"Maybe they know you'd be hazardous to the art's health," she whispered back, and he grinned at her. She added, "I had no idea it was like this up here."

"See those pipes? That's where we hang the lights," he said.

"Really?" She sidled closer to him to peer over the railing. He felt her arm brush against his and smelled something like lilacs. This was bizarre. He'd never reacted to a girl like this before, not even his one and only girlfriend, Lisa, who'd broken up with him after his parents died because it was too depressing to be around him—not that she'd admitted that was why. Luckily Andrew got the job in L.A., and they'd moved the next year.

And now he was getting all light-headed about a girl whose name he didn't even know—a girl who probably wasn't allowed to associate with techies in case they sold stories about her sister to the tabloids.

"How do you reach those pipes over there?" she asked. "Or are they too far away?"

"Well, I haven't worked here before," he said, "but I imagine we'll get down on our stomachs and reach out as far as we can. That's how it works at my school." He knelt down on the catwalk and walked his hands out onto the false ceiling, stretching until he could reach the bar she had been pointing at.

"Careful," she whispered as he tipped a bit too far forward and caught himself.

"Usually we have someone to hold us down," he whispered back.

"Like this?" she said, kneeling to lean on his legs with

a smile he could just make out in the dim light.

"Exactly," he said, hoping that if she could see how red his face was turning, she'd think it was because he was upside-down. "And then that guy usually gives us a hand to get back on the catwalk."

"Too bad there isn't a guy like that here," she said, ignoring his flailing hand as he tried to pull himself back up. "Nope," she continued, looking around at the labyrinth of empty catwalks, "no nice burly guys to help you out. Maybe this is why tech people aren't supposed to wander around backstage on their own."

"Are you teaching me a lesson?" Gus wheezed. He really was starting to get dizzy now. Finally he managed to find a solid vertical post of the railing, but couldn't get to the right angle to pull himself back.

"Oh, all right," she said, releasing his legs and seizing his arm in one quick gesture. "Lucky for you I'm not a big fan of rules either." She heaved him back onto the catwalk with surprising strength for such a small person.

He lay there for a moment, catching his breath, and she sat cross-legged next to his head. Even with his eyes closed, he could sense her studying him.

Just when he thought he'd mustered enough courage to ask her name, a shrill, tinny noise blared right next to his ear. The girl jumped and then scrambled for her pocket, and Gus recognized the sound as a Venus cell phone ring tone. He wondered how she felt about being reminded of her sister's celebrity every time her phone rang.

To be fair, he planned to download them too, just as

soon as Andrew bought him the cell phone he kept promising.

"What?" she snapped into the receiver.

A distant yapping sound came from the phone. It sounded like she was talking to a convention of Scottish terriers.

"Are you kidding me? Doug, that's the worst idea I've ever heard," the girl said.

More yapping. This time she interrupted before it paused.

"Seriously, Doug, use your brain," she said, her voice rising. "This is *me* we're talking about. You know what I'm like when I'm not onstage. Do you really want to share that with America? I don't want to be one of those celebrities who's always in people's faces."

If he hadn't been lying down, Gus was pretty sure he would have fallen off the catwalk right then.

This was Venus. *The* Venus. He had been talking and joking and flirting with—and falling for—Venus, pop superstar, queen of the *Billboard* charts.

"Doug," Venus said into the phone. "Tell them absolutely no. I'd like to pretend I still have a shred of privacy, please."

She stood and started pacing the catwalk. Gus slowly sat up, and then pulled himself to his feet, watching her sideways and trying not to stare too obviously. How had he not recognized her? Her face was on the cover of every other magazine. But without any makeup, without the fitted fashion and spotlights and airbrushed photography, she looked like an ordinary girl. She looked so *real*.

Andrew was right after all. There was something about her that made you want to talk to her. Something that had made Gus want to believe she wasn't who she was.

"I know . . . okay . . . Doug, I get it . . . I *know*. Yeah, that's what my mom said too. But—listen, I'll think about it, okay? Fine. I'll talk to you later."

She snapped her phone shut and looked at Gus.

"I hate reality television, don't you? How high up do you think we are?" she asked.

"Um," he mumbled, tongue-tied now. "I—I don't—"

"High enough," she said, and tossed her phone out through a gap in the fake ceiling, casually, like she was flinging a Frisbee.

There was a pause as they both listened, and then a satisfying cracking sound.

Well, Venus thought, *that was a nice vacation in Surrealville.* It had been a long time since someone honestly couldn't recognize her. She looked at the techie boy, who no longer had on the friendly, open face that had gotten her up here in the first place.

He was probably older than she was, or maybe her age. His hair was straight and brown and flopped in his eyes. Dark green eyes, behind glasses, watched her now with wary confusion.

She ran her hands through her hair, then wrapped her arms around herself. It was so damn cold all the time. She felt like she'd been freezing every minute of the four years since she became "Venus, International Superstar."

This wasn't how it was supposed to be. This wasn't what *she* had planned for her superstardom. This wasn't making a difference, and reaching people, and music all the time. This was politics, and acting charming when she didn't feel like it, and agreeing with people she didn't really like, and having her own mother push her around constantly, even though Venus's money supported the two of them, plus most of her mom's extended family.

Venus had liked the early days, when she was just starting out and people still seemed to like her for her own self, not for her image. She did like being adored. She loved the feeling of having a thousand people cheering for her, of being the most special, beloved, popular girl in the whole arena.

But she also liked being alone. She liked her gigantic impersonal hotel suites, where she could shut the door on her mother, her manager, her bodyguards, and her fans, and stretch out into the empty space around her, knowing that for a short time no one was watching her, that she could wear anything she wanted and eat anything she wanted and make up songs in the shower. It didn't make sense to her that she could be turned on by the attention of thousands of people, but also love being completely alone. She would probably fail the are-you-an-introvert-or-an-extrovert part of any personality quiz.

The thing she never got to do was hang out with only one person—pretending to be a normal girl, getting to know a new guy who just thought she was cute.

Well, so much for that. This guy looked like he would have bolted down the stairs by now if she weren't standing in his way.

"Okay," she said, trying to sound brighter and airier

than she felt. "Time to go back to the real world, I suppose."

"I didn't—" he stammered. "I didn't realize—"

"I know you didn't," she said. "I couldn't have come with you if you had recognized me. It would have been 'how do you do' and 'how terribly lovely to meet a fan' and 'I *do* so love my fans' and 'off you go now, dearie' and that's it." She shrugged and headed down the staircase. After a long moment, she heard his boots clomping on the steps behind her.

As they reached the backstage area where she'd tripped over the lights, they heard a door slam and footsteps running. Andrew and one of Venus's bodyguards, a big German guy, pushed through the curtains onto the stage.

"Gus, man," Andrew groaned as he saw them together. "I'm really sorry, miss. I told my brother not to disturb you."

"Oh, it's all right," Venus said, turning on her thousand-watt smile. "He was a perfect gentleman. And Ivan should have been keeping better watch . . . isn't that right, Ivan?" She wagged a finger at him in mock disapproval.

Ivan just looked surly. All Venus's bodyguards spoke very little English and disliked Venus immensely—those were the number one qualities her mom apparently looked for when she hired them. Venus suspected that this stemmed from an ill-advised viewing of that old Kevin Costner-Whitney Houston movie.

Guys this hostile were hard to come by, since most people seemed to like Venus as soon as they met her, but her mother could make their jobs very disagreeable if they were ever friendly or did anything wild and crazy, like smile.

"Would you boys like an autograph?" she said. "I'm afraid I can't be in any pictures right now, but if you have one of my albums in that backpack, I'd be happy to sign it for you."

"Sure," Andrew said eagerly, and Gus winced. There went any chance he might still have had of seeming cool.

Venus took the album from Andrew's hand, pulled out the liner notes, and signed her name in thick black ink across the acknowledgments section, like she always did. It was her personal secret "Take that, Mom" gesture for all the people her mother had forced her to include, even though Venus didn't think they deserved acknowledging at all. She handed it to Gus with her brightest smile.

"There you go. It was *great* meeting you—" She paused, realizing she hadn't gotten his name. What had the other guy said? Pete or Amos or something? Breeze past it. "I'll leave you to your lights." She turned to walk offstage in the other direction. It was frustrating that she didn't feel comfortable with the stage yet, which was the whole point of being here this early in the first place. But sweet, lovable Venus would *never* pull a diva move like throwing people out, not if she wanted to avoid any more gossipy Internet stories about her "attitude."

"Venus, I'm sorry," Gus said.

Something about the way he said her name made her shiver. He said it like he really did know her. *Well, he wishes he did,* she thought. *But so far he only knows the nice version of me, and we should keep it that way.*

"Don't worry about it, honey," she said. She snapped

her fingers at Ivan and stalked away.

"Gus, man," Andrew said. "Do you want to get me fired? I got you out of school for this because I could use the help, but didn't I tell you she's weird about people talking to her? I know other guys who've worked on her shows. They say it's like night and day—she's either a furious diva ice queen, or she's so sweet it makes your teeth hurt. It's safer for techies not to talk to her." Andrew snorted. "Some goddess of love. And her *mom* is even *scarier*—"

"She wasn't scary," Gus said. "She was . . . normal, for a little while."

"Yeah, right," Andrew snorted. "No one who's been a celebrity since the age of thirteen can possibly be normal, Gus."

I wish I could have talked to her, Gus thought, *to find out what's going on in her head. I want to know how she always knows exactly the right thing to say in her songs.* But more than anything, he would have liked to spend more time with the girl he'd thought she was before her cell phone rang. What an idiot he was, falling for a huge celebrity just like any other dweeb.

Andrew patted his shoulder awkwardly.

"Come on. Let's unload some lights."

SANTIAGO, CHILE, 12:07 P.M.

"Hey."

Tigre flinched as Vicky kicked his sneaker, harder than she needed to to get his attention. She looked mad. What had he done now?

"We need to talk," she said.

Normally he'd be more nervous, but lately she said this every other week or so. After two years of dating her, he had finally realized that those four words could lead to anything from "this relationship is a disaster" to "I've decided to stop eating grapes," and there was no way to predict what it would be, so he shouldn't even try.

"Okay," he said resignedly, rolling up the rest of his sack lunch and stowing it in his backpack under the table. He followed Vicky around the courtyard wall to a bench in one of the school hallways, deserted while everyone was at lunch. Here he made the mistake of sitting down before she did, and she stood in front of him, crossed her arms, and glared.

Should he get up and wait until she sat down? That might make things worse, if she was actually glaring about something else. He shifted awkwardly and looked up into her face. He was so tall, he rarely looked up at anyone. Vicky looked pretty in a sophisticated way, but also meaner.

"*What?*" she snapped.

"What?" he said, startled.

"What are you staring at?"

"Uh. Nothing."

She huffed angrily. He waited, figuring nothing he could say would help. Sometimes he wondered if these conversations would go better in Spanish, his native language, but Vicky hated Spanish, and the rules said they were supposed to speak English during school hours anyway. He could handle it—he should, given all the

American television he watched—but it didn't feel natural, and maybe that was part of their problem.

"I think we should break up," Vicky announced.

Tigre blinked, reactions crowding through his head too fast to process. Did she mean it this time? What was the right thing to say? How did she expect him to react? He stared at the curl of blond hair she was twisting around one finger.

"Tigre? Did you hear me? I'm breaking up with you."

He nodded, thinking that was what she wanted, but it only seemed to make her angrier.

"Aren't you going to say anything?"

"What do you want me to say?"

"It's not about what I *want* you to say," she cried in frustration. "Aren't you feeling anything? After two years?"

"Sure, of course." She raised her eyebrows, like *yes, and?* "I mean, I'm—I'm sad. But if that's what you want . . ." He trailed off, his fingers absently tracing the lines on the wooden bench, carved with hundreds of pens by eons of students before him: THIS SUCKS in jagged blue capitals.

"So it's okay with you."

"If that's what you want," he said again.

"You're not going to fight for me or anything?" she said, her voice rising. He winced, thinking of all the kids in the courtyard beyond, probably listening in. Were they thinking it was about time she dumped the weirdo animal-obsessed freak? Were they laughing at him?

"TIGRE!" she yelled, and he jumped.

"What?" he said defensively. "It's not like I can stop you, right?"

"So you're not even going to try?" Now she looked like she might cry. He didn't know what he should do if that happened. "That is *so typical* of you, Tigre. It's like you don't even care about anything."

"I do care," he protested. "It's just—if something's going to happen anyway and there's nothing I can do . . ."

"You might as well give up," she finished.

"I wouldn't call it giving up, exactly," he mumbled.

"I would," she said, pulling off the earrings he'd given her and throwing them at his feet. "Well, see how you like it, because as of right now, I'm giving up on you."

As she stomped away, thunder rumbled in the gray sky, and he wondered if he should have asked her why.

Not like I can't guess.

Vicky wasn't into weird, and Tigre was getting weirder all the time.

She also liked to be the center of attention, and for the last two months, ever since the night of the really bad storm, he'd found it impossible to concentrate on anything, including Vicky. She'd start gossiping about some celebrity's love life back in the U.S. and he'd inevitably find himself thinking about the old man and the slashed raincoat, wondering again and again what had really happened, and trying to push the images out of his head.

It wasn't his fault. It couldn't have been. It wasn't like he had secret foot-long claws hiding under his skin. (Yeah, he'd seen that movie—Vicky hated science fiction, but she had a huge crush on Shawn Ashmore and insisted on watching all his early work.)

Here he was, back to thinking about it again. His girlfriend had just broken up with him, and he still couldn't focus. Tigre's skin prickled, and he realized he was feeling something more than upset. *Weird. Restless. Something wrong.* Like something was coming, and he knew how it would start, at least.

This had never happened in school before. And considering how it might end—he had to get out of here.

As he stood up, the end-of-lunch warning bell rang and Ms. Roseman appeared in the door of her classroom, her mouth drawn down into stern, disapproving lines. Other students started drifting into the hall, and he guessed from their whispers and sideways looks that the breakup news was already spreading.

"Señor Montenegro," Ms. Roseman said. "Were you planning to join us for English today?" Her face was pale and scrunched up in a frown, so her wrinkled face looked as carved up as the bench. He suddenly caught himself wanting to fill in the lines with his pen, making them deep and blue like the letters on the bench.

A prickling wave of resentment surged through him, and another rumble of thunder sounded from outside.

"I'll be right back, Ms. Roseman," he said, ducking his head and heading down the hall.

"You have one minute, young man!" she called after him.

He turned the corner and started to run. He could feel something building in his chest, like a pelican trying to beat its way out. What did it mean? Strange things happening. Nothing he could do to stop it. Outside—he needed to be outside.

Ignoring the shocked and amused expressions of the

faces he passed, Tigre flung himself through the nearest double doors into a courtyard, then rounded the walls into the parking lot. Guards stood at the gate, as always . . . supposedly to keep the students safe, and sure, maybe some kids, the embassy kids, needed that. But not him; he was the type they were there to keep *in*. Luckily, they weren't very good at it.

Staying close to the walls, under the trees, he took a running leap for the iron fence, scrambled over it, and dropped to the ground on the other side. Something about the restlessness made him able to do things he normally couldn't.

Like kill people?

NO.

He was across the road and into the park before security could blink. And here he could run and run, wind rushing past him, free in the outdoors, or as outdoors as one could get in this city. Rain started to fall as he blocked out the thoughts of what his dad would say, how his mom would look at him, the detention he'd probably have for the next month, Vicky's smug face. Now was all there was, and he was flying, exploding, free.

ALEXANDRIA, EGYPT, 6:22 P.M.

Twilight. Dark alleys, marketplaces lined with carpets, lamps glinting off bronze statues, blue hippos, green scarab beetles . . .

There! A lean figure in white, running, scrambling over walls, into the shelter of a cool mosque silence . . . gone again.

Temples lit by the setting sun, ancient, waiting.

HE IS THERE. BUT THERE IS SOMETHING . . . WRONG ABOUT HIM. HE SHIELDS TOO WELL . . . ALMOST LIKE HE KNOWS TOO MUCH.

BUT HE IS ONE OF THEM?

YES.

AND CAN HE BE—REMOVED?

HE CAN BE EXTRICATED WITH THE OTHERS, YES. BUT WE DO NOT THINK IT IS WISE. HE IS TOO DANGEROUS. THEY SHOULD BE MADE TO CHOOSE ANOTHER.

IT IS TOO LATE. WE MUST ACT NOW, AND THEY CHOSE MANY YEARS AGO, IN ACCORDANCE WITH ALL OUR RULES.

BUT IF WE CANNOT MONITOR HIM, HOW CAN WE KNOW—HOW CAN WE JUDGE—

IT DOES NOT MATTER. HE IS NECESSARY. COMMENCE EXTRICATION.

EXTRICATION

FRIDAY, DECEMBER 21, 2012

LOS ANGELES, CALIFORNIA, 8:50 P.M.
TEN MINUTES FROM EXTRICATION

"Venus, honey, would you mind waiting offstage for a second? We want to try something with the lights, and you're a little . . . distracting." Carl's disembodied voice came over the headset in her ear. He was out in the audience with Doug and the lighting designer, making the decisions she wanted to be making.

Venus raised an eyebrow at the dark seats.

"Well, I hope I don't *distract* too much attention from the lights during the concert," she snapped.

"Aw, sweetie, you know—" She cut him off by switching off her microphone and earpiece, pulling them over her head and dropping them on the nearest chair in the wings. That should give her about three minutes' peace, until someone decided to come looking for her. Then she'd probably get yelled at. Again.

She rubbed her temples, standing close to the curtains, out of the way of the flurry of backstage activity. Her roadies were trained to stay out of her way as much as possible, and they kept their voices down whenever she was offstage. Here, surrounded by the dark velvet, she could almost pretend this was all the world there was— nobody out there waiting for her, no demands, no fans, no managers, no publicists, no unending phone calls and flashing cameras. She was just herself for a moment, not Venus, this imaginary love goddess of song.

A movement over by the back wall caught her attention. It was that boy—the one who'd taken her to the catwalks that morning. What was his name? Maybe . . . Gus? He'd obviously been put in a corner and told to keep out of the way. She wondered how he would react if she talked to him. *Which would be a bad idea, Venus. This is how stalkers get started.*

Oh, he's not that bad, the other half of her brain chimed in immediately. *He seemed sweet. He was fun to talk to. And he clearly liked you. Don't you want people to like you?*

No.

Yes, you do. So be nice.

She could pretend she didn't see him. He looked like he was trying to melt into the wall as it was. And what would she say anyway? "Thanks for the trip into the ceiling. Sorry I'm not allowed to speak to you ever again."

She reached up to run her hands through her hair and remembered the stupid elaborate silver headdress she was wearing. Leila and Bruce would flip out if she messed up their carefully constructed hairdo. Why did she care? It wasn't as if there was an audience tonight. Nor would there be any cameras, hopefully. But her mom and Doug preferred to do her rehearsals in full costume, to plan out the whole effect.

When did that happen, anyway? Wasn't *she* supposed to be in charge? *Nice fantasy, "Venus."*

Gus wished he could think of something to say that wouldn't make him sound like an idiot. He wished Venus didn't look so intimidating now, in silver chains and black leather with her hair twisted into a sunburst over her head. He wished she'd stomped off to the other side of the stage instead.

Mostly he wished he'd found someone else to like this much.

There wasn't a single scenario he could think of that might result in him getting any closer to her. In a few hours, the rehearsal would be over. Tomorrow he'd be one of the anonymous fans in the concert audience, and then she would be gone.

He'd just have to get over it. He had barely spoken to her, so this couldn't be anything serious. Only a loony fan-boy crush.

At least there were enough techies moving around the backstage between them that he ought to be able to stay out of her sight.

"Hey, kid."

Gus jumped. While he'd been staring at Venus, an enormous bald man with tattoos of coyotes up and down his arms had materialized in front of him. The giant jerked his thumb over his shoulder. "Need a pair of eyes here."

He didn't wait for Gus to respond. Clapping a meaty hand on Gus's shoulder, he steered him through the other crew members to a spot with a clear view of the stage— a spot only a few feet away from where Venus was standing. Was it his imagination, or did she glance at him?

"Watch the large pieces as they fly in," the giant said. "I'll be back here operating the ropes, so you holler before anything hits the floor. Or, you know, a person." He made a scary rumbling sound that Gus realized was a chuckle. "Got it?"

"Yes, sir."

Rumble, rumble. The guy lumbered back to the panel of levers and pulleys. Gus watched him, trying not to turn and look at Venus instead. But she was *right there*. He could at least tell her he liked her music, couldn't he? Or would that be lame? Better not to say anything.

And yet here he was, speaking to her again before he could stop himself.

"Seems kinda—"

"Listen," she said at the same time, and they both broke off, flustered.

"Sorry, you go," he said.

"No, go ahead," she said. "What were you saying?"

"Just that it seems kinda rough out there—I mean, don't those guys drive you crazy?"

Murderously so, she thought, but didn't say. Instead, she shrugged. "Oh, I'm used to it. They are the experts, right?" *Smile. Keep to yourself anything that shouldn't be printed in a magazine.*

"HEY!" the giant bellowed from the back wall. "Watch the seashell!"

A large pink scallop shell, like the one on the cover of *Birth of Venus*, was descending from the ceiling into the center of the stage. It still had several feet to go before it would be fully visible by the audience. Gus signaled to the giant to keep lowering it.

"Anyway, I'm sorry," he said to Venus. "I didn't mean to bother you. What were you going to say?" He tried and failed to keep the hopeful look off his face.

I was going to say: "Listen, honey, I hope you don't think I'm a terrible person, but I can't really talk to you right now." But that wasn't what she really wanted.

"I don't know," she said, wondering how she could ramble on and on to folks like Jon Stewart or Dave Letterman, but when it came to this perfectly ordinary guy, she had no idea what to say. "Maybe . . . thanks."

"Thanks?"

"For showing me the catwalks. They were a lot more interesting than the models' kind."

She *had* to be making fun of him. She'd probably seen a million things and places more interesting than one California theater's lighting grid. He covered his embarrassment by looking back at the seashell. It didn't seem to have moved from where it was before, except that now it was swinging back and forth slowly like a pendulum. He signaled to the giant again, who was wrestling with a pair of ropes.

"I'm serious," Venus said, and took a step toward him. He wished he could pull the stage curtains around them and shut out the rest of the world.

"Um . . . anytime," he managed, and winced at how dopey he sounded.

Venus fingered her headdress, looking up at him, and wondered what the heck she was doing. She couldn't be friends with him. She shouldn't let him think they could be. Venus did not have friends in the regular world . . . to be honest, Venus did not have friends.

"I should get back to the rehearsal," she said. See, look at how his face fell. She ignored the instinct to "stay and be nice" and moved quickly back onto the stage, hoping that Doug and Carl wouldn't order her right off again.

"Yeah, okay," Gus said. There wasn't any reason for her to stay and talk to him. She had to—wait—a lurching motion in the corner of his eye—he looked up and yelled, "Watch out!" as the seashell began plummeting to the ground.

Without thinking, Gus leaped forward and grabbed Venus's arm, yanking her back toward him. The corner of the seashell hit the stage where Venus had been standing and the whole thing tilted dramatically forward, knocking over a low platform with a crash. All the roadies backstage started shouting, and several of them ran past him to try and untangle the scenery.

"What kind of crap theater is this?" Venus yelled. Gus noticed that she kept holding on to his arm with shaking hands. He glanced over his shoulder, but the enormous, bald, tattooed man had vanished.

Suddenly the ground buckled under them, then heaved wildly to the side. Venus was thrown into Gus, who braced himself to keep her from falling. The whole theater shook and rumbled, the floor underneath them pitching from side to side like a ship in a high wind. Onstage, the shouting intensified and the techies began to scatter out of the way of all the things hanging over their heads.

"Doorway," Venus yelped, but as they tried to get to the nearest door, the ground tilted again, and they were knocked sideways into the wall.

Earthquake, Gus thought, and then *isn't this the stuff of stupid fantasies, me and Venus trapped together by an earthquake . . . we've got to get out of here, all those weights and lights above us, everything could come crashing down, we have to get outside, have to get her somewhere safe. . . .*

Suddenly he felt a strange piercing sensation shoot through him, like nothing he'd ever felt before, as the lights went out and the ground shuddered. It almost felt like what he thought being struck by lightning would feel like . . . but in a moment it was gone, leaving a sick churning feeling in his stomach, and then the ground paused for a moment and Venus struggled to her feet, pulling him with her.

The roof above them groaned ferociously. Gus plunged his free hand into the black curtains, looking for the door he'd come through earlier that day. The floor started shaking violently again, and Venus stumbled toward him as he found the handle and they burst out into the night.

"Doug's in there—my manager—" Venus tried to say, but Gus yanked her away from the building.

"Yeah, my brother too, but I bet they'll go out the back exit," he panted. "We have to get away from the walls . . . it isn't safe, this building. . . .'"

As if in confirmation, they heard a huge crash from inside. They took off running, still holding hands, into the open parking lot, where there was empty space. . . .

Far too much empty space.

NEW YORK, NEW YORK, 11:56 P.M.
FOUR MINUTES FROM EXTRICATION

Kali often felt like she spent her whole life in the subway. Standing on trains, waiting for trains, walking from one train to another. What a gray, claustrophobic way to live. Here she was again, for the fourth time today, just trying to get home before the whole cycle started all over again.

A train was waiting as she came down the stairs. And from the looks of it, it had been there for a while. She had time to walk to the end and get in the last car, which, if she was lucky, would be blissfully empty.

Kali glanced at the people in the cars as she walked past, her boots making that satisfying *clok-clok* sound that echoed off the walls like it was coming from somewhere much farther away. Everyone in the station looked exhausted, suspicious, pale, and fearful. One couple was arguing, voices too sharp in the almost-midnight subway quiet. Friday at midnight—where did all these people come from? Why weren't they at home?

She reached the last car and slipped inside, onto one of the cool, pale blue seats. Perhaps the fluorescent hum, the expectant buzz of the train, would drown out the noise in her head. There was only one other person in the car—an old guy, all in black, slumped over in the far corner. At least he was quiet.

This had not been a good day. New York did not make it easy to stay calm and serene. Everyone was pushy and aggressive, and most days she wanted to kill them all. Today had been exhausting to start with, and then she'd had a run-in with the kind of person that aggravated her most.

It was on one of her interminable subway rides, where she'd been thinking about why she hated so many people—which, to be fair, was not something the anger-management books recommended.

She hated stupid people, who slowed things down for everyone else.

She hated oblivious, selfish people, the ones who had to get onto *this* subway car *right away* before anyone else.

She hated slow people the most, especially the large ones. Large, old, sluggish bubbles rolling ponderously down the streets, taking up the sidewalk, weaving and ambling and chattering in their nasal, angry way. She wanted to seize them by the hair and scream. "Do you *know* how *slowly* you're going? Is there any need to be *so mind-numbingly slow?*" She wanted to sink her nails into their shoulders and fling them out of her way, hurl them into shop windows, run them into walls. She wanted to yank their cigarettes out of their hands and stamp them out on their toes with her boots.

For a specific example, she'd thought, she hated the woman sitting across from her, and Kali had only had to listen to her for two stops.

"So I told her," the grating voice said, "I told her, why don't you go back to your *own* country, since you're obviously too incompetent to work here? And guess what happened. No, guess. Okay, I'll tell you: she started crying! Come on, if you can't handle being told what customers actually think of you, then *customer service* probably isn't the right field for you, is it?"

The woman speaking had flat, pale blond hair, almost colorless eyes, and folds of flab around her chin. She kept eyeing Kali's tattoo and piercings disapprovingly, as if they represented all the world's problems. She was taking up two spaces on the bench, between her expansive self and her giant brown leather purse, which she had plunked on the seat next to her. Her friend was squeezed on the end, nodding tiredly, not even trying to get a word in edgewise.

Kali checked her watch. Late again, thanks to the ten-minute stop in the tunnel. She'd have to run once she got outside.

The subway screeched to a stop and the two women got up, shoving their way to the front of the crowd. The blond woman kept talking loudly, ignoring the glares she was getting. Kali tried to dodge around them, but people blocked her way and she wound up trapped right behind the blond woman as they climbed the stairs. At. The. Speed. Of. *Grass. Growing.* Kali felt fury building up inside her. If they would just let her in front of them, she could have been out of the subway station by now. But no, they were both huffing their way up one step at a time, side by side so no one could get by.

Just then the mousy friend fell back a step and a space opened up on the blond woman's left. Kali darted through, brushing against the giant purse, and started to take the steps two at a time.

All at once something stopped her with a jerk, and she nearly fell back. Incensed, she turned around to discover the blond woman clutching the strap of her backpack to hold her in place.

"Ex*cuse* me," the woman sneered, "did you just *push* me?"

Kali yanked her bag out of the woman's claw, noticing the gridlock of people starting to pile up behind them. *Don't engage. Don't get involved.* "No," she said, turning around again.

"WELL," the voice rose behind her. "I'm pretty sure you *pushed* me." Kali felt her seize the backpack again. "Why don't you go back wherever you came from—"

I wish, Kali thought, whipping around with such speed that the woman let go and fell back a step, the words dying on her lips as she saw Kali's expression.

"Hasn't anyone ever told you," Kali hissed, leaning forward, "that it's dangerous to talk to strangers?" With one swift movement, she yanked the giant leather purse out of the woman's hands and threw it in a smooth arc over the side of the stairs. Makeup and pens flew in all directions as the purse spiraled around and landed with a *whump* on the train tracks below.

Both women's jaws dropped simultaneously. Kali was up the stairs and out of the station before they could react.

Several hours later, and she was still fuming. *So much for keeping my distance,* she thought now, rubbing her eyes. *So much for those self-control exercises.*

Well, remember, it could have been much worse. At least I didn't make the entire station collapse on her. Or her head burst into flames. Hooray for me.

Kali liked to imagine the city empty of people. She pictured vast open streets free of trash, of cigarette stubs, cleansed of the slow-moving herds. She dreamed of thunderstorms sweeping through, rivers rising to flood the streets. She liked to imagine stepping out of a subway and finding everything clean and empty at last.

But she was usually careful not to imagine it too intensely . . . just in case.

Shrieks of laughter came rioting down the tunnel, followed by gleeful half screams and high-pitched voices competing for attention. Oooh, teenage girls who had the time to be teenage girls. Kali closed her eyes, wishing they would disappear.

"Look! A TRAIN! THERE'S A TRAIN! Quick, RUN, we're going to miss it!"

"EEEEK, wait, don't leave us, wait!"

"C'mon, Katie! The train's going to leave!"

"God, you guys, it's just sitting there. JEEZ, you're such babies."

"Shut up!"

More high-pitched giggling and squealing. Kali's head was throbbing. She visualized them all vaporizing into particles of shiny dust. It was a beautiful, calming thought. Her frustration collided with her exhaustion, and she let herself imagine a wave of energy washing down the platform, evaporating everyone in sight.

Suddenly the noise stopped. Kali opened her eyes suspiciously as the lights in the car flickered and went out, the humming sound of the subway shutting down with it. For a minute she couldn't stop the thought that her wish had come true, but she scolded herself for being stupid. She didn't have *that* kind of power. And trains did this all the time.

Was the train out of service? They could warn people, couldn't they?

Then the fluorescent lights on the platform started to blink out, too, one by one. A few stayed on, flickering, up and down the platform. Now that was something she'd never seen before.

She noticed that the old guy in the corner was gone. She hadn't heard him leave, though . . . weird. She got up to peer out the door and noticed through the window that the next car was empty too.

Hadn't there been people in there when she walked past?

She stopped in the doorway and listened. Everything was eerily quiet. Even this far underground you could usually hear street noises, or other subways rumbling around. But now there was just silence—the kind of loud silence left when noises you don't usually notice abruptly disappear.

Something else was different. She stepped hesitantly out of the subway car, her boots sounding even louder now. What was it?

Wait.

The graffiti?

Had that been there before?

Emblazoned across the far wall, glowing in the dim light from the few remaining fluorescents, in huge silver letters: THE END HAS COME.

And on each pillar of the platform were silver symbols,

like a figure eight with the bottom circle flattened out.

How had she not noticed that before?

She caught herself thinking irrelevant thoughts, like *Silver paint? Isn't that kinda expensive for your average graffiti artist? And why "the end has come" instead of "the end is coming"? If the end had already come, who would be left to write about it?*

That was something she really didn't want to think about.

Kali was about to turn around and go back into the train, when movement farther down the platform caught her eye. There was something on the ground, something small, jumping . . . flashing in the faint light.

What . . .

Maybe she should investigate. The train didn't seem to be going anywhere.

She walked slowly down the platform, in and out of the dim, flickering lights, half expecting something to jump out of the shadows at her. There was no one in the next car either . . . or the one after that.

Where had everybody gone?

Had she fallen asleep?

Could she have slept through everyone leaving the station?

She checked her watch. Midnight. Still. No time at all had passed since she sat down in the train. She lifted her wrist to her ear and listened. Her watch seemed to be working fine. So whatever had happened had happened as suddenly as she'd thought.

She approached the small, jumping thing slowly.

It looked like . . . well . . . it looked like a fish, actually.

It *was* a fish. A real fish, flopping and gasping on the platform, sparkling like it was still wet.

This triggered a realization: The painted figure eights were not figure eights. They were fish, standing on end. Upright fish.

Was this a joke?

Perhaps it would be funny if it weren't quite so creepy.

Well, no. There really wasn't anything funny about a random dying fish on an empty subway platform. This seemed too weird even for those old TV shows of the *How Stupid Can We Make You Look for Money* variety.

Kali suddenly felt a new sort of rumbling below her. It sounded like a train coming, but different somehow, fiercer. Wind tugged at her long hair, pulling it loose from its clip. She looked up as a drop of water plopped down from the ceiling, then another.

That's what was different about this wind—it roared, like ocean waves, and it felt wet, heavy with spray.

A sudden, sinking feeling of panic gripped her. The roar was getting closer. The drops of water from the ceiling were speeding up, and now she could see puddles forming on the empty track across from the train, streams pouring in from the dark tunnels.

She turned and ran for the stairs.

SANTIAGO, CHILE, 1 A.M.
EXTRICATION COMPLETE

Rushing, ripping, tearing. He was huge, massive, powerful. He leaped forward with a ferocious roar, felt something cave in below him . . . a crackling, booming sound . . . then blood, blood everywhere. . . .

Whoosh!

Pitter-patter pitter-patter . . .

Tigre woke up with a start. Strange noises. Or had he dreamed them?

Everything seemed quiet now.

He lay still in the leaves, listening, but all he could hear was the dark rustlings of the trees and the loud, triple-time beating of his own heart. Just a dream, then. Another dream.

The long run and accompanying blackout weren't a dream, though, as much as he wished they were. He rolled over and sat up, groaning. His whole body ached. He felt like he never wanted to move again. Last time it had taken him two weeks to recover, but then, almost overnight, the pain went away. That's how it always worked.

The forest around him was soaking wet, the trees quivering as if in shock. The air had that heavy, just-rained-might-do-it-again-soon feeling, and the sky still seemed electric with barely contained power. Everything around him screamed that a thunderstorm had just gone through.

And yet he was completely dry.

He rubbed his head and tried to remember. There was an empty part of his memory in between vaulting the school fence and now. He wondered where he'd run to this time. He wondered who he could call now that Vicky had given up on him.

Was it the weather that did this to him? There had to be a connection. The restlessness, the sudden bursts of energy, the gaps in his memory . . . and each time he'd wake up, far from home, in the aftermath of a storm but somehow mysteriously dry.

The first time it happened, when he was twelve, he'd tried telling his parents, but it just confirmed their opinion that there was something wrong with him. It was bad enough that he never measured up to his perfect older sister—and *she* was the adopted one. Then he spent all his time with animals instead of people, and he had weird attacks like this. So they handed him off to a shrink for a year and then basically tried to know as little as possible about his life.

After that, the only person he told was Vicky. He had to; he needed someone to come get him when he ran too far, and she could talk her dad into anything, no questions asked. She'd been supportive at first—okay, "supportive" was the wrong word. She'd been *interested*. She liked the unpredictability of it, and it made him less boring than she'd probably expected.

But then, a year ago, the attacks had gotten much worse. The change in him had coincided with a wave of freakishly intense storms that had been sweeping across Chile for the last year. His memory gaps were longer; the distances he ran were farther; the places he ended up were scarier. No wonder Vicky couldn't handle it anymore. Of course she resented his mood swings and the difficulty of finding her boyfriend when she wanted to do something normal, like go to the movies. And he hadn't even told her what happened two months ago, during the biggest rainstorm Santiago had ever seen. . . .

The shredded raincoat. The bus shelter. The old man.

Tigre shuddered. He knew what he'd seen. He just didn't know what he'd done. He needed to stop thinking about this.

He was climbing to his feet when he heard it again: *Whoooooosh!*

Pitter-patter pitter-patter . . .

He ducked into the shadow of a tree and waited, listening. The whooshing came from overhead, but the pattering was all around him. And yet he couldn't see anything, even with the moon shining its ghostly light on the forest. How the heck had he found an actual forest? He was definitely somewhere he'd never been before.

There! Something . . .

Gone.

No, wait, there was something.

Something small and alive crouched in the tree across the clearing from him. A hint of eyes glinted in the moonlight.

It looked half human, almost. But it was too small for a human, and too large for any South American monkey.

Suddenly a piercing shriek ripped into the night from the forest off to his left. Another answered immediately from his right. They were spine-chilling and completely inhuman. It felt like freezing needles plunging into him from all sides. He pressed himself back into the tree, terrified. Should he run? Which way? He could hardly tell where the sounds were coming from—what if he ran straight into them? Whatever "them" was.

A dark shape leaped into the clearing, larger than a

man, larger than a lion. From his not-nearly-hidden-enough spot, Tigre could only see that it looked like an enormous panther. But then it reared up onto two legs, and from its back a pair of jagged, leathery wings unfolded. They beat the air rapidly, as if straining to take off, but they were obviously too thin and flimsy to support a creature as massive as this.

The panther clawed at the air for a minute, snarling. Then it dropped down to all fours, folded in its wings, threw back its head, and shrieked that piercing, enraged scream again. Tigre felt the scream in his bones, like his own inner demons howling to be let out.

He was so awestruck by the bizarre creature that he nearly forgot to be afraid. How had no one ever discovered this animal? Who could possibly miss hearing that sound if they were within ten miles of it? That gave him an extra chill. What if there *was* no one within ten miles? Surely he couldn't have run *that* far from the city. The farthest he'd ever run before was twenty-four miles, but Santiago was larger than that.

The winged panther bounded off into the trees. Tigre almost wanted to follow it, to find some way to approach it and study it. Animals were much more understandable than people. But the logical part of his brain, the part that was pretty keen on survival, prevailed.

Tigre waited a full minute before moving. The shrieks had moved farther away by then, away into the darkness around him. He slowly edged out from the shadow of the tree into the moonlight.

He'd forgotten about the monkey creature.

ALEXANDRIA, EGYPT, 6 A.M.
EXTRICATION COMPLETE

Amon knew before he woke up. In his sleep he felt the change flowing over the earth around him. He smiled and stretched.

In the morning he would prepare for his journey. America was far, and he had never been there . . . but the winds would take him. They always responded to his power.

First he would return to the temple where he had stolen the amulet—where his new partners had first spoken to him a year ago. Before he did anything, he wanted to be sure promises would be kept and rewards would be granted. *They may think they're in charge now,* he thought as he slipped back into sleep. *But we'll see about that.*

NEW YORK, NEW YORK
EXTRICATION COMPLETE

There was no one in any of the subway cars Kali passed as she ran toward the stairs. The wind was getting stronger, the roaring louder, and the platform seemed endless like it did on days when she was late. At least there weren't hordes of people in her way now. . . . *Where was everybody?*

A gust of wind tore down the tunnel, nearly knocking her over as she reached the stairs. She scrambled up them two at a time, clutching the railing, as the roar grew louder, closer, and all at once a huge wave of water came pouring through the tunnel, over the train where she'd been sitting moments before, rushing furiously up the stairs and lifting her off her feet to crash into the tiled wall on the landing.

Gasping for air, she scrambled through the water and started up the next set of stairs, slipping and splashing and nearly sliding back down. The water continued to pound through the station below her, rising up the stairs as she ran.

At the top of the stairs there was an exit—she could escape that way. There had been a man in the booth as she went through; she could tell him about the freak flooding. But maybe he already knew . . . maybe that's why everyone else had been evacuated. So why not her? Had she missed one of those weird garbled PA system announcements?

There—the turnstiles! She leaped the last couple of stairs and ran, the water hissing and gurgling behind her.

No the gate *when did they lock the gate?* the gate was down blocking the turnstiles, the light was out in the deserted transit booth, and *I'm going to kill someone* she could see another gate down over the stairs that led up to the street *gates everywhere, stupid stupid stupid, if they knew there was a flood wouldn't it make more sense to leave them open so people could* escape, *it's not like the gate is going to stop the water it's just going to* trap me *here.* . . .

She could see that gates were down over the exit at the other end of the tunnel too, dimly lit by the few fluorescent lights still flickering. Wasn't the subway always open? Wasn't that the whole point of "the city that never sleeps"? There was always an open exit somewhere. *What is going on?*

Through her panic she noticed the same graffiti up here, silver fish and THIS IS THE END blazing in the dark shadows along the wall.

Not the most comforting thought right now.

Could she fit through the bars? Not likely. The water was rising steadily toward her, lapping at her ankles. Within minutes, the whole station would be submerged and she would drown.

She looked around frantically. Wasn't there another exit nearby? She thought she had seen one . . . or maybe it was being closed up . . . something here, where this wall was now.

She ran her hand over a wall that she was almost *sure* hadn't been there a week ago. Had they blocked off an old exit here? If she was remembering right, maybe there was a staircase behind this wall . . . and it felt pretty flimsy, for a wall. . . .

She remembered everything her mom had said about being a normal girl, about controlling her anger.

Well, being a normal girl would be nice, but not if Kali had to be dead in the bargain. She'd choose weird and alive, thanks very much.

Time to destroy something.

She knocked over the nearest garbage can and wrestled off the lid. She slammed the metal into the wall furiously, focusing as hard as she could on the mental image of the wall crumbling, space behind, a staircase appearing. The water was up to her knees now.

Cracks splintered along the tiles. There definitely was a

section here that was newer and thinner than the rest. She slammed the lid into the wall again, and some of the tiles snapped and broke off. She felt a weird spasm of guilt about how they'd have to rebuild this, but then she thought, you know, if they wouldn't lock people in the subway when *the tunnels were flooding*, people wouldn't have to resort to destructive escape methods, so it served them right.

She picked up the mysteriously empty garbage can and threw it at the wall with all the strength she could muster, praying there would be stairs on the other side.

A whole section of tiles caved in, revealing a dark hole behind the fake wall. She scrambled through with a rush of water and felt about in the dark. Yes—stairs! There *were* stairs here. She felt her way up them as fast as she could, the water building and rising behind her as if it were angry that she was escaping, tugging at her hooded sweatshirt, her hair, her backpack. At least it wasn't cold water; in fact, it was creepily warm.

Starlight! There was a grate above her, a heavy metal grille laid down over the old entrance to the subway. *Please don't let it be welded in place*, she thought, reaching up and shoving it with her hands. It shifted slightly, but refused to lift. *Come on, come on.* She turned and backed up the stairs, watching the water rise, covering the steps and her way back down, as she pressed her back into the metal bars and forced all her weight and strength and anger into it.

The metal protested loudly, squeaking and clanking as it lifted an inch . . . two inches . . . *come on* . . . she closed her eyes and concentrated as hard as she could.

With a huge creaking sound, the section of the grille rose up, twisting and crashing to the side.

Kali overbalanced, slipping backward and smashing her arm into the concrete. Pain ricocheted up into her shoulder, but she climbed to her feet and scrambled out of the water onto the cold New York sidewalk. Now someone would help her . . . someone would realize what had happened . . . she had jumbled, fleeting thoughts of being on the news, suing the city, money for college . . . she sank to her knees, looking around for help.

The streets were deserted and dark.

Most of the streetlights were broken, the lightbulbs missing or smashed.

All the buildings were dark and silent, wind whistling through broken windows.

A glowing almost-full moon lit up the empty side-walk.

Gone. Everyone was gone.

Just like in her dreams.

Kali crawled to the shelter of the nearest wall, away from the subway. This wasn't happening. There must be some sort of power outage. Probably all the people were inside waiting for it to pass. She would just find a phone somewhere, yes, and she would call her mom and figure out what to do, and everything would . . . everything would be okay. Yes.

She curled up on the doorstep and passed out.

• • ● • •

Los Angeles, California
Extrication Complete

Gus stopped running so suddenly that Venus crashed into him.

"Ow," she yelped, pulling her hand free.

"The cars—" he stammered, "where did all the cars . . . why isn't there . . . weren't there buildings over there?"

Venus looked around. The earthquake was fading, just small tremors in the ground now, like a giant's footsteps stomping off into the distance. It hadn't felt as big as the 8.7 earthquake of 2009. But he was right. All the cars were gone. The parking lot was completely deserted. And across the street, where there used to be office buildings, were lonely mounds of rubble.

She decided to sit down.

"What the—?" Gus said. "Did the earthquake do that? Wouldn't we have heard something? I didn't hear anything as loud as buildings falling down. Did you?" He went back and tried the door, but it had locked behind them, so he returned to where she was sitting. "And where's Andrew's truck? Earthquakes don't make cars disappear. Car thieves? In the middle of an earthquake?"

"You talk when you get nervous, don't you?" Venus said, pressing the balls of her hands into her eyes, hoping that when she opened them again, everything would be back to normal. Nope. A little fuzzier, but still quite, quite wrong.

Gus looked down at her, distracted and worried about

Andrew. She got to her feet and touched his shoulder lightly, and even through his anxiety he felt himself shiver at her touch.

"Come on. Let's go see if everyone else got out the other door. We might have to call an ambulance or something."

He let her lead him away from the parking lot and around the building, but he had a feeling she didn't realize how strange everything was. She was much too calm. Whereas he felt kind of sick, like boiling lava was cartwheeling around inside him.

They reached the front of the theater, where two of the six spotlights were working, and discovered large chunks of concrete scattered across the courtyard. With a puzzled frown, Venus started climbing over them. The building itself seemed intact from the outside. Although it did look darker than he remembered, like it was covered with a layer of soot. And the courtyard had been rearranged somehow, even apart from the concrete blocks.

"No one's out here," Gus said.

"They must still be inside," Venus said in her airy voice. "It probably wasn't that big an earthquake after all. Let's go check." She scrambled over another pile of concrete, heading for the door.

"Wait," Gus called after her. "What if the building isn't safe? It could fall down any second."

"All the more reason to get people out, right?" she called back.

Okay. That was a pretty good point. He watched the

silver chains of her stage outfit swing as she climbed and found himself thinking *smart, determined, proactive,* as if cataloging Venus's good qualities would make her his.

It was eerily quiet. He hadn't heard any crashing or falling sounds. He hadn't seen any other people since they came out of the theater. He couldn't even hear cars or sirens. Everything was still and dark, except for the area right around the building.

He shivered. This was not quite what he'd imagined when he'd wished he could spend more time alone with Venus.

As he had that thought, she came scrambling back over the concrete, looking furious.

"Some idiot chained the door shut! Can you believe it? They're probably trapped in there! There's a huge gate down over the front."

"Really?" Gus was relieved. Here was a perfectly normal explanation for why everyone else wasn't outside in the courtyard too.

"Yeah." Venus was looking around, hands on her hips. "There must be something around here we could use to smash it down, don't you think?"

"Smash it down? Are you serious?"

"Is that a new statue over there?" she asked, pointing. "I don't remember seeing it earlier today."

"Uh . . . me neither," Gus said. "We probably just didn't notice it." But he felt uneasy. He didn't remember seeing it either, and yet there was something familiar about it.

Venus clambered over to the statue and started clearing

away the shrubbery around its base. Gus was about to kneel beside her when suddenly Venus gasped and leaped back. Instinctively, Gus jumped back too, but nothing happened. The statue continued to stand there, looking ordinary and nonthreatening. Yet Venus was staring at it in shock.

"What? What is it?" he asked, managing to stop himself from adding: *I won't let anything hurt you.*

"Is this some kind of *joke*?" she cried angrily. She whirled around, eyes searching the darkness. "Are there cameras hiding somewhere? Is this for a stupid TV show?" She seized Gus's arm, pulled him down to her level, and whispered, "Can you see anyone out there? Any cameras?"

"No," he said, squinting into the dark. "Why do you think there would be?"

"That," she said, pointing at the statue. To his surprise, Gus saw that she was near tears. *Of course celebrities cry,* he chided himself. *She's only seventeen, like me.* But it made her seem more like the girl he'd met this morning, despite the black leather and silver headdress, and he wished he had the nerve to hug her.

He took a closer look at the statue. The pose was amorphously triumphant, but the marble was worn down and dilapidated, so it was hard to see anything about it clearly, especially in the dim light. He noticed that the shrubbery around it nearly covered the base, so it couldn't be that new, after all.

He knelt and moved the leaves aside, pulling his flashlight out of his pocket to read the plaque better.

HERE LIES
VENUS
BELOVED SUPERSTAR
AND DAUGHTER
THE EARTH MAY HAVE SWALLOWED HER
BUT HER MUSIC LIVES ON.

Then there was a date. *Today's* date.

He stood up quickly, tripped, and fell over backward.

No wonder Venus was freaked. Now he recognized the statue: it was the pose on her first album, *Birth of Venus*, fists clenched and everything.

He looked over at the real Venus, who was touching her hair like she wanted to run her hands through it. He felt a surge of unfamiliar anger that made him want to find whoever was doing this to her and rip their throats out, violently, bloodily.

Gus blinked. He didn't know where *that* impulse had come from. Violence wasn't normally one of his problem-solving strategies.

"Maybe this is some kind of test," Venus said, more to herself than to him. "Maybe it's, like, a really warped *Candid Camera* or *Punk'd* or something. Or a publicity stunt. Maybe Doug did this."

"No," Gus said, shaking his head. "Look at those ruined buildings. Something much bigger than a publicity stunt is going on."

Venus shivered, rubbing her arms. Her video for the song "Lost" had been about the end of the world. The crew had closed down a few city blocks and cleared all the people out, so it looked like she was wandering in an empty universe. For some of the shots they had put up backdrops in a warehouse, green-screening her into computer-generated scenes of destruction and ruins. This felt as unreal as those had—fake and glossy and distant. She couldn't wrap her mind around any of it. Her thoughts kept circling back to her own memorial.

"Let's get out of here," she said. Whatever was happening, she wanted to get as far as possible from that statue. And she wanted to stay with Gus (that was his name, right?). *Don't get too friendly,* that part of her brain warned, but she thought under the circumstances she could ignore it for a little while.

"Maybe I should go back to my hotel," Venus began, then stopped with a gasp.

"What is it?" Gus said.

"My hotel . . . it was right over there. It was close so I could go back and forth easily, but I just realized it . . . it's *gone.*" *Along with all my stuff . . . my ID, my credit cards, the photo of Dad I keep hidden in the secret pocket of my suitcase . . .*

The fact that all the tall buildings in sight had fallen was only starting to sink in for Gus, too. The silence made it hard to believe. If something terrible had happened, wouldn't there be screaming and sirens?

"I—I think I should try going back to my house," he said. "Maybe we blacked out or something, and everyone went home . . . or somewhere. . . ." He trailed off. He couldn't imagine Andrew abandoning him here, but maybe in the confusion of the earthquake . . .

Venus turned and looked at him, shivering. The cold she always felt was creeping through her now stronger than ever. It was a reasonably warm night in Los Angeles, but then again, she wasn't wearing very much. More than anything, what she wanted to do was get out of these stupid leather pants and wrap herself in flannel. And if her hotel was gone—her hotel with all her things—where could she go now?

EAST! a voice suddenly said in her head, clear as church bells. She jumped.

Had she really heard that? She frowned and shook her head.

"No, of course," Gus said, misinterpreting her gesture. "You shouldn't come back to my house. You should probably go to, like, a hospital or something, make sure someone knows you're not really, um, not really . . ."

"Dead," Venus said. "Right." She shook her head again. She was feeling pretty dumb for throwing away that cell phone now. She knew she should try to find some sign of civilization and connect back to Doug, but she was so mad about the statue, so convinced that it was a publicity stunt he'd arranged, that she didn't particularly *want* to find him right away. *I'd rather stay with Gus,* she realized. *At least I believe he's not part of any plan to trick me.*

"I want to go back to your place with you," she said impulsively, taking his hand and then dropping it quickly when she realized how that might sound. "I mean, so I can use your phone to call my mom, if that's okay."

"Sure," he said, smiling at her. *She's coming to my house!*

Even if ambulances and limousines showed up to cart her away as soon as they got there, he'd get to spend the whole walk with her.

"Don't worry," she said. "I'm sure there's a reasonable explanation for everything."

He nodded. "Okay, then. Um. This way. It's not exactly normal walking distance, but it shouldn't take us that long."

Venus was already wishing she had her sneakers. These boots were comfortable enough for dancing, but they weren't meant for long-distance treks. As they headed out of the parking lot, she reached up and started dismantling her headdress. It was beginning to seem less and less likely that anyone was going to see her in it anyway.

SANTIAGO, CHILE
EXTRICATION COMPLETE

As Tigre stepped into the moonlight, something heavy flew out of the trees, knocking him to the ground. He found his arms seized and twisted behind him. A series of thuds signaled the arrival of more animals.

He struggled, kicking and swearing, but tiny hands pinned him down, many tiny, fearsome, elongated hands. They looked like a child's hands stretched to a creepy alien extreme, glowing blue and green in the moonlight, with black pointed fingernails. He saw flashes of brown and gray fur, sharp teeth, and large cloudy eyes, but they moved so quickly he couldn't get a clear look at them.

"Ceassssssse thiss squalling, sstrange thing," a voice hissed in English from the trees above him. Tigre stopped struggling, every movement still a fierce agony, and looked up at the speaker.

It had the face and body of a baboon, except the legs were longer and thinner. He could see now that the pack of animals around him moved on their hind legs alone, instead of using their arms like regular monkeys. They were constantly moving, even those who held him down. They kept switching places with each other and running off into the trees and back, making the *pitter-patter* sound he had heard earlier.

Their eyes were also larger than an ordinary baboon's, gigantically out of proportion with the rest of their face—black eyes with a strange cloudy film over them. They didn't look especially frightening until they smiled . . . if you could call it smiling.

The speaker in the trees grimaced down at him. Its mouth was full of bristling, sharp teeth, almost too many to fill the space. Tigre could see now that the creatures' mouths were bleeding, teeth sticking out every which way and tearing up their faces. They spoke with serpent-like tongues darting in between the teeth, hissing even when they weren't speaking.

He had never been so terrified in his life.

"Who are you? What—what happened to you?" he stammered, not sure if that was quite the question he meant.

The one holding his arms hissed directly in his ear.

"*We* are assking the quesstions, weirdling. What are you?"

Was there a wrong way to answer this question? Did they not know about humans?

"Me? I'm a human being . . . you know . . . just a guy. . . ."

The hissing around him intensified, and a few of the animals drew back as if he might be contagious. But the speaker in the trees laughed, a frenetic, cackling sound.

"That iss imposssible. All the humanss are gone."

Tigre felt that eerie chill down his spine. A gust of wind whipped through the trees. The storm was coming back.

"What do you mean, gone? Humans aren't gone. Humans have been around for ages—they're everywhere. Maybe there aren't any around here, but—"

"We can *sshow* you," the one behind him growled.

"Yess, sshow him, sshow him," the others echoed.

He felt himself lifted, twisted like a pretzel until he was wrenched into a contorted position, arms pinned under him. The creatures lifted him over their heads and ran, whisking him through the trees, *pitter-patter pitter-patter*. He thought about trying to wrestle free, but they were moving so fast he was afraid he'd go flying off into a tree—and they felt strong enough to hold him harder if they wanted to. He might as well see where they were taking him.

They swept down a hill and out onto a stretch of open space. He tried to lift his head and saw tall buildings ahead of them, not too far away. So he hadn't gone that far after all.

This looked vaguely familiar, but somehow wrong. There was no extensive forest this close to Santiago, and certainly not one with hybrid monsters living in it. Someone would definitely have noticed gigantic creepy talking monkeys.

All of a sudden the hands on him pulled away and he went crashing to the ground. Bright pain lanced through him. The thundering inside got louder and faster, and an answering rumble shook the sky.

"Ssee, weak intruder?"

He climbed to his feet unsteadily. They were in a suburb of Santiago he knew—he had cousins who lived here. But this was not the same place he had visited last Sunday. All the houses were dark, some with their roofs torn off, some with huge cracks down the middle. Windows were shattered, and strange plants were writhing through the gaps—plants he had never seen before, huge and vibrant. It looked like they were growing as he watched, creeping over the town, tearing it down.

He stared around him, openmouthed.

How had this happened? He cursed the gaps in his memory that wouldn't even give him a hint as to how much time he'd lost. This didn't look like something that could have happened in a couple of hours, or even a couple of weeks.

Had Santiago been attacked? Or had the people all left suddenly? Could they have been evacuated for a volcano warning? There was something horribly orderly about the emptiness. If there had been a sudden attack, wouldn't there be cars abandoned along the road, or something that indicated an unexpected interruption? But the remaining cars were parked neatly in garages. Doors were shut, everything quiet, as if one day the people had all simply decided to walk away.

"There are no more humansss, creature. Thiss place is ourss now."

Lightning crackled in the sky, and he could feel the pressure building inside him. Could he stop this storm from controlling him?

Did he want to?

Maybe he should let it overtake him. Maybe he could do to these animals what he'd done to that old man. He wouldn't be able to remember it, but that wouldn't necessarily make it less satisfying.

"What is this?" he demanded. "What have you done with all the people? Where are they?"

The monkey creatures closest to him stepped back, perhaps sensing danger.

"We did not do thiss. It iss thiss way."

"What do you mean? What happened?"

The first speaker bristled, baring his teeth. "We are not here to ansswer your quesstionss."

"Well, you'd better—" Tigre stepped toward him and suddenly felt something explode. It was a ferocious, screaming sensation, and he realized he wasn't willing to be overtaken that way. He didn't want to wake up hours from now covered in blood, confused and mysteriously deadly.

Better to run. Better to run and keep running.

He turned and took off down the street, leaving a chorus of howls and hissing behind him.

His last thought came out of nowhere, a foreign voice in his head: *NORTH. GO NORTH. RUN.*

EXTRICATION COMPLETE.

THERE IS A PROBLEM. AN UNANTICIPATED PARTICIPANT.

NOTHING THAT CAN'T BE TAKEN CARE OF.

SO YOU SAY.

WE WOULD LIKE TO LODGE A COMPLAINT THAT HAZARDS DISPROPORTIONATE TO THE EVENT HAVE ALREADY BEEN ENCOUNTERED BY OUR ENTRANT AND EXPRESS THE GRAVE CONCERN THAT NOTHING LESS THAN HER DEATH WAS INTENDED BY THE MANIPULATORS OF THE SITUATION.

NOW, NOW. WE ALL KNEW THE RISKS.

THE BALANCE IS DELICATE.
DID YOU THINK THIS WOULD BE EASY?

COMPLAINT DULY NOTED. AS NO DEATH ENSUED, WE SHALL PROCEED AS PLANNED.

SO NOW WE WAIT.

YES. WE WAIT.

THE DAY AFTER

NEW YORK CITY

"her"

  "her"

  "she-who-"

  "she-who-"

  "creates"

  "destroys"

  "creates"

  "destroys"

  "she-who-creates-destroys-escapes-tears down-"

Kali drifted awake to the sound of whispering voices. Images of empty streets and flooded subways flashed through her mind. Maybe the whole thing had been a nightmare. Maybe she was lying in a hospital bed right now and her mom was next to her and—

Except the voices didn't sound like doctors.

And the cold, rough surface below her didn't feel

like any kind of bed.

She shifted and rolled over, trying to sit up without opening her eyes. Pain rocketed down her left arm and she collapsed again. The whispers skittered around her, too many of them, like a hundred mice racing in circles.

"must go"

"must hide"

"time"

"hurry"

"hurry"

She opened her eyes and immediately closed them again. The sun was coming up directly in front of her. She covered her face with her right hand, trying to will the pain in her other arm to go away. What was going on? Had she been asleep for hours? Why hadn't anyone helped her?

Well, silly question. This was New York, after all.

But she couldn't ignore the silence around her. No sound of cars. No people walking, talking, arguing, except for the whisper-voices, which had suddenly disappeared. Just the rustle of the breeze sweeping trash through the streets in circles, a slow, thoughtful sound, as if it had a thousand years to clean up and no need to hurry.

She shoved herself into a sitting position, blinking. There was no sign of anyone who might be attached to the voices. The city was exactly as it had been last night.

Abandoned. Empty. The streets were completely bare, windows broken, doors barred and barricaded. Nothing but her, the wind, and the rising sun.

And, she noticed, it was strangely warm for December, which explained why she hadn't frozen to death sleeping outside all night. The air felt more like early fall or spring. She squinted at her watch, which, mysteriously, read 5:39 A.M. That couldn't be right. The sun wasn't supposed to rise for ages yet. Her watch must have been screwed up by the water, which meant the city owed her another watch in addition to emotional damages and hospital fees.

Her backpack was lying in a crumpled heap next to her. Kali checked inside and everything was still there— her wallet, keys, sunglasses, everything, including the Notebook of Strange Events, which she always carried with her. She touched the border of flames on the cover, checking to make sure it wasn't water damaged. She'd never thought about what might happen if someone ever saw this, but since apparently no one had, she wasn't going to worry about it now. She climbed to her feet gingerly, readjusting her backpack so it didn't knock against her injured arm.

What happened?

Okay. Phone. Find a phone, call Mom, make sure she and the girls were all right.

There was a pay phone, if she remembered correctly, about a block away. They used to be everywhere, before cell phones made them virtually obsolete. She wished— not for the first time—that she could afford a cell phone.

She walked down the street, searching for signs of life. A whole city of people didn't just *disappear*, did they?

Only in my dreams, a voice inside her said. She shuddered and walked faster. No way could she possibly have had anything to do with this.

She reached the pay phone and picked up the receiver,

cradling it on her shoulder as she fumbled one-handed through her bag for change. There was no dial tone, but maybe that only came once you put money in.

She shoved in her coins and waited, pressing the phone to her ear. Nothing. No sound at all. She tried pushing some buttons, but nothing happened. She smashed down the lever and got her coins back, which was the only good surprise so far today.

What could she do now? Were any of the subways working? She'd rather decapitate a goat than go back down there.

WEST, a voice suddenly commanded in her head, so loud and confident that she was sure it had come from behind her.

She spun around.

Nobody there.

Was she hearing things now? What the heck did that mean?

Maybe New York City had finally driven her completely around the bend. Maybe she was really standing on a crowded street corner right now, and people were walking past her, averting their eyes from the crazy, mumbling, hearing-voices girl. Maybe this whole situation was one horrible hallucination.

Well, one thing was real: the pain in her arm. She should probably find a hospital. But what she really wanted to do was get home and check on her family. Then she could take care of her arm, once she knew they were okay.

Kali took off her sweatshirt and looped it awkwardly into a makeshift sling, cursing the difficulty of doing it all one-handed. At least her arm felt better once it was supported.

She headed east toward Brooklyn. There were a few other subway entrances on this street; she'd check them as she went by to see if any of them were not flooded. She could try another pay phone, too, if she found any. If not, well, she'd walked all the way to Brooklyn before. The Williamsburg Bridge would take her pretty close to home.

The sun was above the horizon now, shining down the street. It was strange to watch a sunrise here, in Manhattan. Usually she was too rushed to notice, or there were too many people in the way.

Everything seemed much bigger and cleaner without the people or cars. The streets stretched glittering around her, vast and clear and deserted. It really was exactly as she had imagined it. What could cause something like this? It was almost too tranquil to be scary, although she felt guilty for enjoying the peace.

She had walked about four blocks when she heard the sound. It began with a sudden shift in the wind. Kali froze in the middle of the street. The wind whooshed past her and then back, tossing her hair in her eyes.

At the same time, she heard something like thousands of crystal bells tinkling, or wind chimes in a hurricane. It started faintly, in the distance, but got louder and closer very quickly, with the speed of a train rushing toward her.

She darted over to the nearest office building. Its doors were still intact, although the walls around it were shattered, the glass lying in shards on the ground. She almost used the doors anyway, but forced herself to go through the skeletal walls. Inside was a vast marble lobby, lined with cold elevator doors, serene and silent. *Like a crypt*, she thought before she could stop herself.

Now the tinkling noise was right outside. A huge shadow moved over the street, spreading from one sidewalk to the other. Kali leaned forward to look out and up, and found herself staring openmouthed, the pain in her arm forgotten.

Some sort of giant bird was soaring overhead, its wings stretched across the street. Its claws flexed as if it were grabbing for something. Its head twisted back and forth, eyeing the empty sidewalks. Its beak was long and pointed, with tiny sharp teeth catching the light as its mouth opened and closed. In fact, the whole bird sparkled and glittered in the sunlight. It looked like it was made of glass, of hundreds of tiny particles, shining and reflecting.

It was beautiful.

It was terrifying.

Kali froze, hoping it wouldn't notice her. Was that the best thing to do? Or should she run? How well could birds see? Was it dinosaurs that could only see you if you ran? Were there any rules for dealing with enormous glass hallucinatory creatures? She tried to remember some of those Discovery Channel documentaries she used to watch with Bill, but as details frantically flicked through her mind, the crystal bird passed overhead and disappeared down the street, wheeling around a tall building and flying away.

She sank to her knees on the cool marble floor, clutching her arm.

What was going on?

LOS ANGELES

"So," Venus remarked, "when you said 'not that far,' I take it you meant 'no farther than *New Zealand*, that is.'"

Gus turned to apologize and noticed that she had goose bumps on her bare arms. Freed from the headdress, her hair was a disheveled mess around her face with a few silver wires still tangled in it. It made her look less like an intimidating superstar and more like the superstar's younger sister who he'd thought he'd met in the first place. He felt a stab of guilt, especially since a good chunk of the three hours they'd been walking had been an accidental forty-five minutes going the wrong way, thanks to his terrible sense of direction.

"I—I guess I didn't realize it was this far. I always forget how big Los Angeles is because we never walk anywhere. Um. Are you cold?"

She gave him a look that either meant *obviously* or *bite me.*

"Here," he said, unbuttoning his shirt. "I don't need this, and it might help—I mean, if you don't mind that I've been wearing it." He winced, thinking about how that must sound. Luckily the T-shirt he was wearing underneath was plain black and didn't say anything dorky like "How far to Alpha Centauri?" or "My other shirt is made of mithril."

"Oh," Venus said, shying away as he started to hand it to her. "I probably shouldn't . . . if anyone saw . . ."

"Who's going to see?" he said.

They'd been walking for hours and still hadn't found anyone else. Venus guessed that it was past midnight by now. Everything was dark and creepy, with no lights in any of the houses. Most of the streetlights were either out or fizzing and sparking. At least in this area there were still buildings standing, although they all looked dirty and cracked. It didn't feel like the aftermath of an earthquake.

It's sweet of him to offer, her brain argued. *You should say yes.*

Wearing his shirt? Doesn't that qualify as inappropriate flirting?

Not if it's in the interest of self-preservation.

The tabloids would have a field day.

But think of the sacrifice he's making—you can't reject it.

"Please take it," Gus said as she still hesitated. "I'm sure your manager wouldn't want you to freeze to death for the sake of fashion."

You clearly don't know Doug, Venus thought. "Okay," she said. "Thank you." She held out her arms so he could slip the shirt over her chains. It was huge on her, but still warm from his body, and she hugged it to her for a minute, feeling her chills fade away.

"It suits you," Gus teased.

Part of Venus loved the way he was looking at her, like wearing this big rumpled flannel shirt actually made her more attractive, but the rest of her was unsettled. She looked away, running her hands through her hair.

"What is *that?*" she asked, trying to distract him. She crossed the street and hooked her fingers into a chain-link fence surrounding a park.

"The La Brea tar pits," Gus said, coming up beside her. It was this oddball park in the middle of Los

Angeles with tar pits where scientists had found lots of old bones from prehistoric times. He'd been here a couple of times, because he and Andrew lived close by, but normally he went right past it without remembering it was there.

Venus gave him a puzzled look.

"Are those *mammoths* in there?"

For a moment he thought she meant real mammoths. Then he remembered the statues in the park: one mammoth in the tar pit, drowning, with two mammoths watching from shore. They were all dimly lit in the glow from a nearby street lamp, which made them look sort of alive, in a completely creepy way.

"Oh yeah." He squinted through the fence. "I read the sign once. I think that's supposed to be the mother who got stuck in the tar pit, and the father and their baby are the other two. I guess this probably happened all the time, in, you know, prehistoric days. They found a lot of bones here," he finished incoherently, feeling like he hadn't explained that very well.

"Hmmm," she said, leaning into the fence again. After a moment she said: "That's really sad."

"Sad?" Gus said, amused. They were statues in a tar pit. Not even very realistic statues.

"I mean, say you're the person in charge of tar pit tourism. You think, okay, let's have a prehistoric scene with mammoths. What on earth would make you pick a mother drowning in tar while her baby watches? Seriously."

"Well . . . maybe they couldn't think of any happy prehistoric tar pit stories."

Venus looked at him suspiciously to see if he was teasing her.

"Okay, granted," she said. "But if you're going to create something, shouldn't it be uplifting or beautiful in some way? This is so 'Nothing Escapes the Tar!' And that baby's going to have to stand there forever watching its mother die. And you know what else, the dad doesn't even look upset. Big jerk."

Gus had never spent this much time looking at mammoth statues. He'd never spent this much time looking at *regular* statues, like, ones that were supposed to be artistic and stuff. He leaned into the fence, trying to think of a response. She was kind of right: the dad mammoth looked practically smug.

"Maybe . . ." he said slowly, "I mean, maybe it has to be sad like this because it *is* sad that all these animals are dead now. Maybe it's supposed to stir our subconscious guilt about endangered species, so we come away from the museum thinking, heck, I don't want the animals in *my* world to end up as frozen statues."

"Or us," Venus murmured, and he felt the weight of all the empty streets they'd walked through hit him like a physical blow. He kept talking, trying to get away from the subject of extinction.

"Also, maybe it's saying you can't ignore or avoid the sad stuff—it's always going to happen, but the important thing is not to go jumping into the tar as well. The baby all determined to live on *is* kind of uplifting. It's like your music, sad and happy at the same time.

"Or," Gus concluded, "maybe the father actually pushed the mother in, and this is a reenactment of the world's very first crime scene."

She laughed.

"Okay, smart-ass," she said. "Serves me right for trying to find a moral in a mammoth diorama. Are we almost at your house?"

"Yeah, we're only a few blocks away. I promise."

She smiled a little, and they started walking. The rolling, violent feeling inside Gus subsided while he was talking to Venus but came back whenever they were quiet. It made him edgy; he kept thinking there were things moving in the shadows. He wasn't ready to deal with the disappearance of all the people yet. He figured he'd get home and find Andrew, and then things would start to make sense.

At least he wasn't alone. At least he was with *her*.

"Here we are," he said finally, turning onto a side street and bounding up the front steps of his apartment building. "It's kind of small," he admitted as he dug out his keys, "and it's probably a huge mess . . . sorry about that. Hey, I know: blame it on the earthquake."

"Whatever." Venus shrugged. She'd gotten quiet again while they walked, and he hoped she wasn't regretting coming with him.

In fact, she was thinking about her mom and wondering if she should be more worried about her. They'd had yet another enormous fight two days earlier, this time about Venus wanting to take a mini-vacation from touring and recording after Christmas. Her mother was convinced that any break in her schedule would mean the end of her career, and she didn't seem to care about how tired Venus was. The next day Mom had flown out to

Tennessee to visit her uncle, and Venus had been hoping not to see her again for at least a week.

Surely whatever had happened here hadn't affected Tennessee. Mom was probably fine. Venus knew intellectually that she should be panicking and trying to get in touch with her mother, but the emotion wasn't there. Her mom treated her more like a lucrative trained seal than a daughter, and had for years. Maybe after the shock wore off, Venus would be more upset.

Gus shoved open the front door and led the way up the dark steps to his third-floor apartment. He couldn't help thinking that Venus probably hadn't been anywhere this shabby in her life, or at least not since she got famous. She didn't seem bothered by it, though; she looked around as if it was interesting.

They got to his door and he fumbled with his keys, grateful that he carried everything with him in his pockets. His heart was suddenly beating faster. Why did he think Andrew would be here, if the rest of the city was deserted? *Because we promised we'd always keep track of each other. He'll know I'm looking for him.*

Gus swung open the door.

"Hello?" he called, reaching in to switch on the light, which, miraculously, worked.

No response.

He stepped inside and froze in shock.

"What is it?" Venus said. "What's wrong?" She peered around him into his living room.

His completely empty living room.

All the furniture was gone, the couches gone, the rug gone, the tile floor bare and cold. Everything was empty like the city, missing like the people, all still and empty and gone like Andrew, gone *with* Andrew, his brother's *Star Wars* and *Lord of the Rings* and *Spirited Away* posters missing from the pale vacant empty walls.

"Um . . . I'm guessing it isn't always . . . like this?" Venus said.

Gus shook his head numbly. This was about the last thing he had expected. Andrew being gone could perhaps be explained somehow—people evacuated, a sudden emergency—but their stuff? Their furniture? Why? How?

Venus moved farther into the apartment, looking around.

"You're sure this is the right apartment, though, right?"

"Yeah," he said. "Definitely. See that hole in the plaster? That's where Andrew decided one day that punching the wall would cheer him up."

"Did it work?"

"Not so much."

She brushed her fingers over the dent. "What was he so mad about?"

"Nothing." Financial stuff, tax stuff that came up long after the funeral, after they'd moved, when the sympathy had waned and no one cared to help, but she didn't need to know that. Venus tilted her head at him, but didn't press it. She moved on, peering into their tiny (empty) kitchen, opening the door to their even tinier (empty) bathroom, and then the door to Andrew's (also empty) room. That was almost more than he could bear, seeing his brother's room like that. He stood in the doorway, trying to breathe normally.

"So was this your parents' room?" she asked, gesturing around.

"No, this is Andrew's. It's just me and my brother. My parents are—my parents died—a while ago. Andrew was old enough, so he takes care of me," he said, trying to sound casual, although it was hard to talk at all.

At least she didn't give him the pity look. She nodded instead, turning to the final door and pushing it open.

"Oh!" she gasped. "Gus, look!"

Over her shoulder he saw his room. His stuff was there! In this crazy-stupid upside-down empty world, somehow, by some miracle, his room was intact, exactly the way he had left it this morning.

Or—not exactly.

He crossed to his desk and ran one finger through the dust that had collected in the empty space on top of it.

"My computer is gone," he said, puzzled. The first thing he always did whenever he came into his room was sit down and check his e-mail. But now the humming, clunky desktop that Andrew had built for him had vanished. The books and schoolwork Gus had been working on the day before still surrounded the space where it had been, but there was a gaping hole in the middle of the desk. Gus traced a spiral in the dust absentmindedly, feeling lost. Why would Andrew have taken his computer when he could always build a much better one for himself?

"Is that the only thing missing?" Venus asked. She was trying to find out, diplomatically, if his room was usually this empty. The walls were bare—not a single poster, postcard, tapestry, frame, anything—and the top of the dresser held only a stereo and a neat pile of CDs, three of which, she noticed, were albums of hers. Books were piled haphazardly around the desk, and there was a construction of wood in the corner that looked like a halfhearted attempt at making a bookshelf. The tiny window didn't even have curtains or shades. She realized, sadly, that that was the sort of thing a mother would put up; two teenage boys would probably not think of it on their own.

"Yeah," Gus said. "Otherwise it's just like I left it."

"What about that?" Venus said.

Gus turned and saw that she was pointing to a rectangle of white lying on his pillow.

A letter.

A letter labeled GUS.

SOMEWHERE IN CHILE

Tigre felt like he'd been running for years, but he couldn't remember any of it clearly. His head was full of nightmare images: monkeys with teeth, panthers with wings, other twisted animals that spiraled away into the dark around him as he ran. His heart was pounding wildly, dangerously fast.

He woke to the feeling of water on his face. Rain? He shook himself awake and sat up slowly, realizing that half of him was soaking wet.

Ah. Ocean. He was on a beach, and the tide was coming in, lapping around him where he was lying in the sand.

He must have escaped the monkey creatures, then. But a *beach*? How far had he run?

Aaargh. Just once he would like to wake up and not have that be the *first* thought in his head.

This was a very different awakening from the jungle night, though. The sun was just peeking over the mountains in the east, and the Pacific Ocean to the west shone peacefully in the morning light. Waves brushed gently against the sand. Everything was pearly and quiet and shining. It felt like waking up to a brand-new world.

A world cleansed of people, their violence, pollution, and noise.

He forced the thought away. It couldn't be true. Nothing bad could happen to his normal, boring parents. They were probably sitting at home right now, watching soccer on TV and complaining about how their disappointment of a son had stayed out all night again. They rarely wasted energy worrying about him when they could spend it on getting angry instead.

He wished he were with them right now, getting yelled at, instead of sitting on a beach wondering if he was the last person left on Earth.

Tigre rolled onto his knees and tried to get up, but his legs gave out under him and he collapsed to the sand.

Okay. Perhaps he'd just lie here for a while, *not* thinking about the monkeys or abandoned Santiago. It wasn't real. It couldn't have been real.

His legs felt weak and numb, like they were barely there. If he'd really been running for several hours straight—at the flat-out pace he'd started at—he'd be pleasantly surprised if they ever worked again. His heart was still racing, sending the rest of his body frantic signals that didn't match his tranquil surroundings.

He lay still on the beach, feeling himself sink into the sand as he watched the sky lighten and small clouds waft around overhead. No planes. No boats. No sound of people at all. The only noise was the sea, and he felt his pulse start to calm down. He closed his eyes and started sinking into a real sleep.

SPLOOSH!

A sudden enormous wave of water crashed over him, soaking him completely. He sat up with a yell, tried to stand, and fell over again. He scrambled up to his elbows and crawled away from the ocean, sputtering salt water.

Whooooops. Sorry, a resonant, bubbling voice said in his head.

Tigre spun around and found himself facing a giant eye, black as ebony and the size of a television. It was surrounded by brilliant green feathers. He froze. Slowly, it winked at him. He scrambled back another few feet, wishing his legs were working properly.

Calm doown there, tiger. I dooon't bite. Noot unless you're fish flavored. The huge feathered head rose out of the water, sending waves splashing in all directions, and he realized it was some kind of bird—but the most enormous bird he'd ever seen. The eye studied him thoughtfully.

Are you fish flavooored? The bright yellow beak parted slightly as the creature grinned at him. At least, that's certainly what it looked like it was doing.

"What are you?" Tigre demanded. "I should warn you I—I'm a lot scarier than I look."

Hee hee, the voice said. *Of coourse yoou are. Although maybe not in this particular physical state. Can't yoou tell what*

I am? It arched its back and rose above him so he could see more of it, revealing a blindingly red underbelly and three-toed claws that seemed too small to support its size. It looked like a super-parakeet the size of a whale. A super-parakeet with shimmering blue-green wings and a big goofy grin.

Tigre moaned and covered his face with his hands. There was nothing normal left in the world. The planet had obviously been taken over by strange hybrid monsters. He should just give up and let Super-Tweety eat him.

Yes, yes, toooo beauuutiful for mortal eyes, I know. There was a sploosh and another wave of water crashed toward him as the creature resettled itself, shaking its wings. *It is my eternal burden, this dazzling beauuuty of mine. I am cursed! Cursed, I say!* It bobbed in the shallow water, looking giddy. Every other sentence sounded like a giggle—a watery, burbly giggle. Tigre realized that he couldn't tell if it was speaking English or Spanish; he could just understand what it meant, like it was bypassing the language parts of his brain. And it understood his Spanish just fine. The thought crossed his mind that this would be a useful skill to have, say, when interacting with girls like Vicky.

He sat up and stared at it.

It *was* kind of beautiful. The sun reflected off the bird's feathers in bright jewel tones, and its tail was two flowing, emerald green feathers that were twice as long as its body. The bird lifted these out of the water and wafted them through the air like banners, sending sparkling showers of waterdrops in all directions. He noticed that its feathers had an iridescent sheen that helped the water roll right off.

Yoou're not quite what I imagined, huuman.

"Well, I can't say I ever imagined you, either," Tigre responded. This set the bird's tail into whirling pinwheels of glee.

Huumans are funny. I didn't know that. Hey, let's goooo somewhere! Do you like to travel? I doooo. I've seen just about everything.

"Okay, hang on." Tigre pressed his hands to his head. "Just let me think for a second." It was weird enough to be sitting on a mysterious beach hearing a gigantic bird's voice in his head. But the mention of travel had reawakened the urgent feeling inside him, that he had to go north as fast as possible. And that didn't make any sense. What he should be doing was looking for his parents. If they had evacuated Santiago with everyone else, had they left him a message somewhere? Maybe they had gone to his grandfather's ranch: that was far enough from the city that it probably wasn't affected by whatever had . . . happened.

Had Vicky and her father gone back to America? Back to Connecticut? *Don't think about Vicky,* Tigre told himself sternly. *She wouldn't care what happened to you.* He flinched, knowing it was true.

Vivid images from last night flashed through his head. Monsters and empty streets and jungles of plants growing over everything. He had the impression he might have run through other deserted cities as well.

But maybe it was only Santiago. Or maybe it was only in Chile . . . they had relatives in Argentina, too, so maybe his parents had gone there. He rubbed his face, trying to think. What he needed was a telephone or e-mail. Claudia was in the States, at Columbia University; she could tell him where their parents were.

He looked at the bird again, who was ducking its head in the water and making odd shapes with its tail, trying unsuccessfully to be quiet.

"Um, hey," Tigre said. The bird popped up and hopped toward him. "I'm kind of—kind of confused. Can you— do you know what's going on? Where everyone is?" The bird tilted its head at him and blinked through a starburst of green feathers.

First, introductions. I'm Quetzie. She—the bubbliness of her voice made him think it was a she—pronounced it KETT-zee. I *am a neoquetzal, the most advanced and beauu-uuuutiful species ever knooown. Resplendent quetzals were quite loovely, too, once upon a time, but they were too tiny and squash-able.*

"Okay, Quetzie," Tigre said. He'd heard of quetzals, the national bird of Guatemala, but he was pretty sure they were usually more like two feet long, and he wondered why she talked about them in the past tense. "Nice to meet you. I'm Tigre."

Tigre? Hmmm. That's not what I was tooold. Tigre, really? That's your name?

"It's a nickname—wait—what you were *told*? What do you mean?" Tigre pushed himself farther away up the beach. He didn't know whether to be frightened or angry or both.

Well, Quetzie burbled. *"Told" is such a strong word, you know . . . soo oopen to misinterpretation—*

"Tell me what you know about me, Quetzie," Tigre said.

Ooh, noothing. Unless your name is really Catequil, of course. The super-bird gave him a mischievous look.

"It is!" Tigre cried. He hated the name his parents had given him, and since no one could pronounce it, he'd gone by his sister's nickname for him for as long as he could remember. "How did you know my name?"

Whoo knows, Quetzie said good-naturedly. *Isn't it a funny world? I got a message to look for a huuman named Catequil on a beach in Chile and take him wherever he needed to goooo.* Very *impressive of me to have found you, if I doooo say so myself. I mean, talk about ambiguous. I could have spent months gallivanting up and doown the shoreline. This beach? Nooooope! How about this beach? Nooooooope! Ooonly five hundred to gooo! I'm quite a busy neoquetzal, normally, and whooo would think I have that kind of time to look for tiger boys? It's lucky your energy sticks out so much. You're a spiky one!*

"Stop, stop, hold on. A message from *who?* And how?"

The neoquetzal let out a dramatic sigh, unfurling her tail to its full length. *Ooooooh,* I *don't know. Sometimes I hear things in my head. You know? And I figure I should dooo what they say. Doesn't that happen to everybody?* She widened her eyes innocently at Tigre.

"I'd say not. So you really have no idea who sent you here?"

Is that bizarre? Maybe it's bizarre. But I figure, if the voices are in my *head, then I proobably ought to listen to them, don't you think?*

NORTH! boomed a different voice in Tigre's head, as

if on cue. He flinched. That was definitely not Quetzie. Was it the same voice that had sent her here? He shook his head furiously. No way was he going north just because a voice in his head said so. Not until he knew what was going on here.

Doon't you want to go somewhere? Quetzie asked hopefully, extending her wings with a loud flapping sound. *I haven't tried carrying a huuman befooore, but I doon't think it'll be hard. I can fly oor swim anywhere you like. Neoquetzals have evolved to be happy in the air, on land, or in water. We're the most adaptable, agreeable creatures on the planet. And there's lots of places to see!*

"Can you—can you take me to the nearest place where there are other humans?" Tigre said. For the first time, Quetzie looked solemn. And a little guilty.

Ermmm. You know, I doon't think that's a very good idea, really. Wouldn't you rather see some waterfalls? Oor Iceland's got loovely geysers this time of year, and we could stop by Panama and pick a fight with some pterodolphins on the way, or—

"No," Tigre interrupted firmly. "I really need to find some other people. If you don't want to come with me, that's fine, just point me in the right direction."

Hesitantly, Quetzie raised a wing and pointed. North. Tigre nearly laughed.

"How far that way? Peru? Are people evacuating from Chile for some reason?"

Quetzie looked horribly uncomfortable now. Her tail feathers swooped back and forth in unhappy curves.

Noooo. Not exactly.

"Quetzie? What aren't you telling me?"

The neoquetzal flapped its wings nervously. *Ooooo, I'm*

noot noot telling you anything. I thought you knew.

"Knew what?"

There aren't *any people. Here. On this continent. Just youu.*

Tigre's jaw dropped. "Just *me*? That's not possible! Yesterday there were millions of people here! They couldn't have all disappeared!"

Now Quetzie looked puzzled. *Little tiger man, maybe your brain needs a rest. I'm sure you'll find answers to your questions by traveling. And speaking of traveling! Did I mention the hot springs?*

"Quetzie," Tigre said.

Okay, okay. I can tell you what I dooo know. There aren't any people on this continent. And there weren't any last night, either. Or the night before. There haven't been any people on this continent in years. It's moostly jungles full of strange animals—unnatural *animals. Animals that were never meant to be.*

Not like me, of course! I am the culmination of evolution's starward ascent, Quetzie concluded cheerfully. *Did I mention our adaptability? And to think my ancestors came close to extinction.*

"*Years?*" Tigre felt the awful struggling sensation in his chest. His breathing was getting ragged and his pulse was speeding up. At the same time, dark clouds were starting to roll in and lightning crackled over the distant mountains. Quetzie rolled her eyes to the sky with a worried expression.

"You must be wrong. You have to be wrong. I was in school yesterday!" Thunder grumbled overhead and he tried to get up again, but his legs were still too weak. "This isn't happening. It isn't. It isn't happening."

All right, cut that out right now, Quetzie barked. She hopped up the beach and firmly knocked Tigre onto his back with a wing, pinning him to the sand. *Breathe! Right now! Breathe deeply. You absolutely may not spoil this lovely day.*

"Wha—hey! Stop! Let me up!"

Breathe!

"It won't help!" Tigre shouted. Rain was starting to fall all around them. He wanted to run, *needed* to run. If not, something terrible might happen. "Let me go! When the storm gets worse, I'll just go berserk, I swear, I can't help it! It makes me do things, I can't—"

Noooo, Quetzie chuckled. *Are you kidding? The storms don't do this to you. It's you making the storms, tiger boy. Haven't you ever noticed that when you get upset or excited or emotional, it starts to rain? Coincidence? Nuh-uh. It's part of your spikiness. I could tell that right away.*

So if you can call the storms, you can make them go away. Just calm down and breathe. I'd like my sunshine back. And besides, how far do you think you'd get on those legs? Now shut up and think happy thoughts. She covered him completely with her wing and spread out on the beach next to him, humming quietly.

Tigre could hardly think, so much was running around in his head. He lay still in the tent of Quetzie's wing, trying to steady his pulse. Happy thoughts? Like that his parents had disappeared? That he was alone on a continent of monsters? That his only companion was a crazy giant quetzal who clearly had no concept of time? That voices in his head were telling him to do strange things?

Or how about the notion that *he* caused the storms instead of the other way around? The storms didn't *make him* do things. It was all him. Meaning the old man—might really be his fault ... this wasn't calming him down. The rain was pouring down outside.

He focused on the way the light still came dimly through the feathers on Quetzie's wing, casting emerald and azure shadows over him. He focused on the sound of raindrops overhead. It reminded him of camping trips with Dr. Harris and Vicky, when he was a kid, before everything started. Tears started rolling down his face and since there was no one to see him, and no Vicky to make fun of him, he let them flow until he finally fell asleep in the tear-stained sand.

LOS ANGELES, CALIFORNIA

Gus sat down on the edge of the bed and picked the letter up, shaking off the dust with a bewildered frown. As he opened it, Venus crawled over the bed and knelt behind him, peeking over his shoulder. She was so close he could feel her hair move when she breathed, and he wondered how someone could walk halfway across Los Angeles and still smell like lilacs.

The handwriting was Andrew's.

"Dear Gus" was crossed out, and underneath that was written "Hey Gus man" and then that was crossed out too. The letter started right below that.

Okay. I feel kind of stupid writing this. I'm not sure why I'm bothering. I know what people would say. I mean, they've already said it plenty of times, when they see I've left your room exactly the way you left it. Okay, sure, it's stupid. I just keep thinking you'll come back. Isn't that crazy? I just can't believe that you're dead. I mean, surely there's been a mistake, Guy in Charge of Everything, 'cause don't you remember you just took Mom and Dad? You can't possibly want Gus too, not right now, not already. It's illogical.

I have this feeling, see. I have this feeling that one day the keys will click in the lock and you'll come walking through the door. Like you're hiding somewhere, and one day you'll decide to come home. So I want your home to be here for you, even if I can't be.

I would stay here and wait, but we all have to leave L.A. It's getting too dangerous, between the earthquakes and the hunters. At least I can keep this place without having to pay rent on it. No one cares about property in L.A. now. Or anywhere, I guess. So I can leave your room here, like it is, in case you do come back. Are you coming back? Gus, man, I hope so.

Everything's been awful since you disappeared. It's like the whole world's gone crazy. And it keeps getting worse, and nobody knows why. There's no way to explain all the bad stuff that's happening. I feel like we did something wrong and we're being punished. I mean . . .

well, that's how I feel. Like I screwed up, and I let Mom and Dad down by losing you, and now I'm being punished for it, but it's on this huge global scale. Yeah, it sounds stupid.

Anyway, I wanted to leave you a letter, just in case. I want you to know that I didn't just leave. I stayed as long as I could, but I have to go now. Ella left months ago. You would have liked her. But she couldn't deal with me waiting for you. There's almost no one left here. So I don't know why I think you'll ever come here, no matter where you are now, but I can't think where else you would go. And I remember our deal, don't you? Always leave a message, no matter where you're going. Keep everything sorted out. Like Mom and Dad would have wanted.

I wish I'd never taken you to that stupid theater. Sometimes I imagine that you weren't there when the earthquake happened. I had this fantasy for a while that maybe you and Venus fell in love backstage and ran off together to get married in Vegas or Aruba or something. Celebrities do that kind of thing all the time, right? But I know if that were true then you would have come back by now, or at least e-mailed me. I made a big fuss, man, you would have been proud, trying to get a memorial to you, too. I mean, why should she get a statue and they don't even mention you? But no one listens to the guys backstage. You know that.

Anyway, I think of your room as a kind of memorial, I guess. And I think about you all the time, believe me. More than anyone thinks about her, I bet.

I'm going to this place in Kansas. It's supposed to be safer in the middle of the country. I know, who ever pictured us in Kansas, right? But there's a community there of some folks who haven't totally lost their minds, and some of my crew said they'd be there, too. So, if you do get this, somehow, come find me there. I just want to see you again. I just want to know you're alive. Please be alive, Gus.

The last few sentences were an almost illegible scrawl. At the bottom, in a different color like an afterthought, was an address in Kansas and a hastily-drawn street map.

Venus found herself on the verge of tears. The poor guy, losing his parents and then his brother. She wished Andrew were there right then so she could give him a hug. *Like that would fix anything.*

She could tell that she'd finished reading the letter before Gus had, because he gave a little jump when he got to the part about running off with her to Vegas, although he didn't say anything. At least now she knew she was right about his name. Gus. She wondered how long ago their parents had died; this letter made it seem like only yesterday. Maybe it always felt like only yesterday, when it was your parents. Her dad was still alive, but he'd cut off all contact with her in the last four years, and she missed him terribly. She wondered if her mom did think of her or miss her as much as Andrew missed Gus. *She probably misses the parties and ninety-thousand-dollar award-show gift bags.*

Gus lowered the letter to his lap and stared at it for a long moment. Venus wasn't sure what to do. Should she try to console him? She wasn't used to the people around her having real emotions, ones that actually meant something and weren't for the benefit of cameras or reporters.

Finally he took his glasses off and swiped his eyes with the back of his hand, then put them back on.

"Do you think we're dead?" he asked without looking at her. "I thought Mom and Dad would be here, but maybe this is what it's actually like."

"Silly," Venus said, trying to keep her voice light. "Dead people don't get letters from living people. Listen, it'll be okay. At least you know where to look for Andrew."

He nodded, folding the letter over and then unfolding it again. "Hey," he said, "do you mind if I do something that might seem kind of weird?"

"Oh, and I was having such a normal day," she tried to joke. "What is it?"

Gus got up and crossed to the dresser. "There's a song of yours that I listen to whenever—well, it calms me down." He shifted his shoulders in a half shrug, looking embarrassed. "If it'll make you uncomfortable, just tell me."

"No, go ahead," she said.

He turned on the stereo, picked up the remote control, and returned to the bed. Venus realized that her CD was already in there, and she wondered how often he listened to it.

Gus scrolled ahead to the fifth song, "This Is the Way the World Ends," and closed his eyes as it started, so he missed the look of surprise she gave him. This was her favorite of all her songs, but she'd never met anyone who liked it as much as she did. "Too sad" said the teen magazines; "sounds like it's about divorce or something." *Rolling Stone* had said: "melodically intriguing but overly wistful, out of character for this young, normally starry-eyed singer." Not a single reviewer had mentioned the T. S. Eliot poem she'd taken the title from. Doug had forbidden her to perform it in concert anymore after one audience in Boston ended up too mournful to buy any merchandise.

She watched Gus and felt all of the reasons she loved music come back to her. He had on exactly the expression she hoped for when she wrote it: sad but understanding, at peace with the loss of everything.

"I haven't told anyone this before," Gus said haltingly as the chorus came on, "but this is the song I was listening to when my—when I found out about my parents—about the car accident." He opened his eyes and met hers, and she felt a strange shiver run through her, like looking under the bed for a pair of shoes and coming face-to-face with your favorite teddy bear who's been missing for years.

"Want to know a secret?" she said impulsively.

What are you doing? Logical Half of her brain screamed. *You can't tell him that! The newspapers! The magazines!*

"A secret?" Gus repeated.

"Venus isn't my real name."

"Really?" He looked puzzled. She could almost see him mentally flipping through the dozens of interviews where her mother went on and on about how she had thought Venus was such a lovely name for her baby girl, and how she'd always known Venus would be a superstar, with a name like that.

"Talk about a well-kept secret, huh?" she said. "Not even my—" She stopped herself just in time from saying "crazy stalker fans." "Not even my management company knows. Except for Doug, of course. He's the one who came up with Venus." *And he's going to kill me for telling,* she thought, and then, immediately, *no, he's not. He can't. He's probably dead by now, whenever "now" is.*

"But all the—I thought your dad said—"

Venus laughed, a short, sarcastic sound. "Mom offered to pay him to keep my real name a secret. This was about two years after the divorce, when Mom and Doug were putting my 'image' together. Dad got so angry, he stopped talking to us both." She shrugged, playing with her fingernails. "I was named after his mom, so I guess that's why he was so mad. I see his point. I hate the name Venus, too." *Too much information. This could be worth a million dollars to some stupid tabloid.*

Then again—what tabloids? Maybe there is an upside to the end of the world.

"So what *is* your name?"

"It's Diana. There you go. Now you can be the only person in the world who calls me by my real name." *Maybe the only person in the world, period. Maybe that's really*

*why I told him. I don't want to be "Venus," imaginary pop god-
dess, to the only other person left on the planet.*

"Diana," he said. "Okay. Nice to meet you, Diana."

No one had called her Diana in so long. It felt like a
puzzle piece snapping into place.

They half smiled at each other. "Listen," Diana said, "I
know it sounds crazy, but I think that we've somehow lost
a whole bunch of time. Maybe you were right before, that
we blacked out in the earthquake and didn't realize it.
Maybe we both got amnesia, and we got lost for a while,
but then we got our memories back and didn't realize
time had passed."

"But how much time?" Gus said. "That letter said . . .
how could we possibly have lost *months*, maybe even
years? Where have we been? What did we do? Why
wouldn't someone have noticed *you*, at least?"

"Okay, I don't know," she said. "But I'm sure there's a
reasonable explanation. I'm *sure* of it."

"Time travel," he said.

"No. I said 'reasonable.' Time travel is impossible.
There's no such thing."

"How do you know? Because it's never happened to
you? Oh, wait, it just did."

She slid her fingers through her hair, considering. If it
wasn't time travel, what was it? And if it was time travel,
could *this* be the future? Was this what was in store for
humanity? Los Angeles ruined and abandoned?

"The question is how far forward did we go," he continued, as if this were a perfectly normal subject.

"Can I use your phone?" she asked.

"Sure, of course." He untangled the phone cord from

the bedside table and set the phone on the comforter between them.

"We'll figure this out," she repeated, lifting the receiver. "Hey, there's a dial tone." He realized he hadn't expected there to be one either. She punched in a number and listened.

"Who are you calling?" he asked.

"My manager. Oh," she said, frowning. "It says his cell phone has been disconnected." She listened for a second, her expression shifting from frustrated to puzzled. Then she hung up with a worried look.

"What happened?"

"It's that annoying computer voice you get when a phone is disconnected. But it doesn't say 'this number is disconnected'—it says *all* cell phone service has been halted and the company is shutting down and not to try any more of their numbers because they will no longer be doing any business ever again. Oh, and thank you for using Sprint PCS."

"I'll try calling Andrew's cell—I think it's AT&T."

"Yeah, okay. Try that."

He dialed the number, feeling optimistic again. It rang once and a computer voice picked up—pretty much the same message Diana had gotten. He hung up, shaking his head.

"No luck."

"Hmmm." Diana traced the numbers, looking thoughtful.

"What about your mom?" he asked. "I mean, it's kind of funny that you call your manager first." He hoped that didn't sound as mean as he thought it did.

"Life of a superstar," she quipped halfheartedly. "Actually, I'm trying to remember my uncle's number. She's supposed to be out in Tennessee with him. I mean, last time I—whenever we—whatever. Or I could try our old house in Oregon, but we haven't been back there in so long that we rented it out—I guess they might tell me where she is." She shrugged indecisively and started tapping on the numbers as if she were hoping the right order would come back to her. "I see why guys carry everything in their pockets instead of having a purse. I hate being without my organizer."

"Organizer? I thought superstars had personal assistants for that stuff," he teased her.

She rolled her eyes. "Well, yeah. That's what I *call* my personal assistant. You don't expect me to remember her *name*, do you?" He looked horrified, and she laughed. "I'm kidding, Gus. I'm not really a personal-assistant kind of girl."

"Oh, right," he said. "Uh—do you want to maybe try four-one-one? Maybe they could give you your uncle's number in Tennessee."

"Sure." She brightened. "That's a good idea. Maybe we'll even get an operator who can tell us the date."

Diana hit the speaker-phone button and dialed 411. As the phone rang, she went over to the mirror next to Gus's bed, wrinkling her nose at her reflection. She couldn't have picked a worse end-of-the-world outfit, silly looking *and* uncomfortable. Still, she felt better. Phones still worked. Phones were normal, phones were real. It wasn't the end of the world after all. She pulled back her hair, then let it fall again. Hopeless.

In the corner of the mirror was a photograph of Gus and his brother with two smiling grown-ups. He looked about thirteen years old in it. She studied it out of the corner of her eye, thinking they must have died in the last four years, then. They all seemed so happy. She'd never seen her parents even stand that close to each other.

The phone stopped ringing. There was a silence. Frowning, Gus reached over to pick up the receiver, but before he got to it, a computer voice suddenly barked from the speaker:

WHO ARE YOU WHAT ARE YOU DOING.

Gus froze. Diana spun around and stared at the phone.

WHO ARE YOU WHAT ARE YOU DOING THIS IS NOT ALLOWED.

Diana looked at Gus, wide eyed. Should they respond? This didn't sound normal. Or friendly, for that matter.

WHO ARE YOU WHAT ARE YOU DOING THIS IS NOT ALLOWED. UNAUTHORIZED COMMU-NICATION TO BE TERMINATED. UNAUTHO-RIZED ACTIVITY TO BE INVESTIGATED AND DISCIPLINED. UNAUTHORIZED—

Diana jumped forward, picked up the receiver, and slammed it down. Gus stared at her.

"Shouldn't we have—maybe we should have said something? I mean, maybe that's some new four-one-one thing." She gave a shaky laugh and he shook his head. "Or, I mean, if we explained that we're looking for peo-ple or we don't know what's happening . . ." He trailed off at her expression.

"I don't think so, Gus. Whatever that was, I don't think

it's going to help us. And I think we need to get out of here. Fast."

"Fast? Now? Right away?" He wanted to look for Andrew, but he also felt reluctant to leave his room, the only familiar part of this whole thing.

"Definitely. Don't you get it? Whoever or *what*ever that was, they're going to trace that call. We have to get out of here before they come looking for us."

Alexandria, Egypt

Amon stood on the edge of the sea, arms outstretched. Everything was clean and new. Everything was fresh and open. He threw back his head, lifting his face to the sun.

So it was true. Everyone was gone. A somewhat drastic way of accomplishing the goal, but perhaps he could do something about it, in time. A world without people did him no good, after all. But for now, he could enjoy the silence.

He inhaled, letting the air flow through him. Energy pulsed along his skin. He reached out his hands and gathered the air, summoning the winds. They circled him, lifting and supporting him.

There was time for a tour. The pieces were still moving into place; no reason for him to hurry. His partners sensed something had gone wrong, but whatever it was, it couldn't affect him. Let *them* worry about it. The work he was chosen for was yet to come, once the players were assembled, and then he knew he'd be unstoppable.

He took to the air with a leap. Europe first . . . those crystal hunters sounded too interesting to miss.

NEW YORK CITY

They were still there.

Kali peered around the corner. They didn't seem to be planning on moving anytime soon.

Signs of life: great. Big, spiky, crystal demon things: not so great.

These guys were different from the enormous crystal bird she'd seen two hours ago, but looked related. They were made of glass, too, but they had no wings and were shaped more like human-sized insects—praying mantis types, but with large, pointy teeth.

And they were between her and the Williamsburg Bridge.

In fact, they were *on* the bridge, looking for all the world as if they were guarding it. Big spiky crystal security guards.

She pressed her uninjured hand against her forehead. She needed medication or something. The pain was making her loopy.

Well, she couldn't wait here all day. Her watch claimed that it was nearly 8 A.M., although the sun looked higher in the sky than that, shining down and sparkling off the bad guys.

Maybe they weren't bad guys? After two hours of walking, her arm was throbbing, and she was willing to face anything in order to get home.

She had investigated all the subway stations on the way here; they all had their gates down and water washing gently up the steps, but below street level, as if the tide were going out. She'd also tried three other pay phones, until the last one ate her money and she decided to save the coins and concentrate on walking back to Brooklyn. And she had not seen a single other human being.

Maybe it would be worth it to try and talk to the creatures. Her mom must be panicking by now (surely Brooklyn wasn't like this . . . surely her family was okay). Kali hoped Mom knew that Kali was trying to get home . . . that she hadn't just abandoned them. Kali hadn't run away since Bill died, and she didn't plan to, but sometimes she caught her mother watching her apprehensively, like she might vanish in a puff of smoke at any moment. But she wasn't like that. There was a difference between hating responsibility and neglecting it.

She peeked at the monsters again. Could it possibly get worse if she confronted them? What could they do to her? Best-case scenario: she was imagining them, and she'd be able to walk right through them and go home. Worst-case scenario: probably something she couldn't begin to imagine.

She sighed, picked up her backpack, readjusted her sling, and strode forward. If these guys were typical New Yorkers, they'd ignore her.

STOP.

No such luck. She slowed down, but kept walking toward them. The four of them closed rank, blocking the road.

STOP. The electronic-sounding voice seemed to come from all four of them at once.

"Excuse me. I have to cross this bridge." She got as close as she dared and stopped. The four regarded her impassively, with multifaceted, glittering purple eyes.

STOP.

"I *have* stopped. But I need to get over this bridge, or you'll have to give me a very good reason why not."

STOP.

Kali aimed for the small gap to the left of the creatures and started forward, her face set in the angry-hostile-don't-talk-to-me-or-I'll-rip-your-nose-off mask she usually wore walking down the street.

STOP. Suddenly one of them moved. The one on the end shot out an arm and shoved her forcefully backward into the air. She flew a few feet and crashed to the ground, agony shooting up her injured arm. She let off a volley of curses.

"Hey!" she yelled. "Who do you think you are? Who's in charge of you? What have you done with everyone?"

They didn't respond. Which was at least preferable to hearing "STOP" one more time.

"I demand to speak to your—er—leader," she snarled, climbing painfully to her feet. Now other parts of her hurt too. "I *demand* to know what's going on."

They stared ahead, stone-faced.

Fine. She turned her back on them and stormed away. There were other bridges. Several other bridges. And then there were tunnels and boats and all kinds of options. She would get off this damn island if it killed her.

And there's always your own special methods, she thought. *I'd like to see their faces as they burst into smithereens of shattered glass.* But if there was even a chance she might have caused . . . well, she didn't want to risk playing games with her unwelcome "power," not now.

WEST! the voice clamored in her head again, as it had

been doing for much of the day. She continued to ignore it. Now she was more determined than ever to go anywhere but west. If she *was* going crazy, she wasn't going to let the voices in her head decide how.

For the moment, there was at least one thing she could fix. Her stomach had been growling since she woke up. Food would make her feel better.

She turned up a street, out of sight of the crystal things, which were making no move to follow her. On the corner was an average little convenience store with the door propped open and the grille rolled up like it was an ordinary business day. This was something she didn't understand. The fact that there were no cars and no bodies suggested that however everyone had disappeared, they had had time to leave properly. But most of the stores were open, without gates down over the entrances like she would have expected. She could walk right in to almost every building in Manhattan.

A bell jingled as she stepped over the threshold, making her jump. Inside the store the lights were off, but the refrigerators were humming along just fine, neon bottles of drinks glowing in the darkness. It was creepy and dusty, with a long-abandoned air and a musty, rotting smell.

This felt wrong, like she was trespassing. Well, okay, she was. But Kali would have given anything to have someone—a human someone—barge out and yell at her about it.

She edged inside, past shelves of candy, stacks of old fading newspapers, racks of bright crinkly bags of chips. Where to begin? Well, it was sort of breakfast time. Milk, perhaps? She eyed the cartons behind the glass doors dubiously. They looked dusty and wrinkled. There was something suspicious about milk in New York anyway. She didn't like the way cartons had a special expiration date "In NYC" that was three days earlier than the regular expiration date.

Perhaps she'd stick with something nonperishable. Something in a can.

She scanned the aisles with a sigh. There were enough cans in all the grocery stores in Manhattan to last one person five thousand lifetimes, if she were alone for all that time. But a girl could really get sick of soup for one.

That wasn't going to happen, though. She would get off this island and find her mom and the girls by tomorrow at the latest. She picked a can of black beans and a small bag of rice off the shelves, juggling them perilously in one hand. Now she just had to find a way to boil the rice . . . and she'd need a place to sleep, too. She still ached from the previous night's concrete bed. Plus she didn't know why the crystal things had left her alone before, but she didn't want to risk sleeping outside with them around.

Okay. She admitted to herself that she would have to break into someone's apartment. Just to use the stove and to sleep. After all, *she* didn't make the people disappear (*did I?*), so one could hardly blame her for doing what she had to do. If only she knew anyone who lived in Manhattan—she minded less if it was someplace she knew—but she'd been careful not to make any friends at school or her various jobs. Friends might ask questions or notice unusual behavior, and she'd seen how friends could make a person more angry than anyone else could, which she didn't want to risk. Especially because then friends might turn you in to the police, which you could at least trust family not to do.

So, a stranger's place it would have to be.

Above the store was a complex of apartments. She stuffed the beans and rice and a Gatorade, plus several bottles of water, into her backpack, and grabbed a bottle of Advil from behind the counter. A door at the back of the store led directly into the apartment hallway, and that was standing open as well.

She crept up the stairs. Sunlight peeked in under doors and through the skylight several floors above her, illuminating clouds of dust particles that scattered around her as she moved. She sneezed, froze, and had to remind herself that there was no need for silence. But she moved quietly anyway, feeling like an invader in an ancient house of worship.

Kali strode down the carpeted floors, rickety wood creaking underneath her, and checked each door. Most of them were locked; even in an emergency evacuation, Kali figured, a New Yorker would automatically leave her home locked up securely.

But on the fourth floor, a doorknob turned smoothly under her hand and the door swung open. She held her breath for a second. Silence, outside and in. She peeked around the door: no signs of movement or alarms going off.

The apartment was small, of course, as New York apartments tended to be, although it was probably still more expensive than the three-bedroom her family rented in Brooklyn. The floors were wooden and worn smooth. There were a few large, mismatched pieces of furniture: a sagging flowery couch; an empty white bookshelf across one wall; a heavy, dark wooden coffee table.

Kali stepped inside and shut the door behind her, the click of the latch sounding loud in the stillness. To her right was the kitchen, with plain white-and-yellow tiles and faded chrome. It wasn't the cleanest place she had ever seen, but it would do. It looked like it had been abandoned for a while.

That thought made her feel better about intruding, although she wondered why there were still a couple of pots and a number of bowls, plates, and cups in the cabinets. Another question mark in a day of mysteries, and no one to ask anyway. She took down a pot and moved on to the refrigerator.

This, again, was not as empty as she had expected, although there wasn't anything useful in it—mostly typical things like mustard and soy sauce, plus some white Chinese food cartons. Judging from the layers of dust on this place, she figured she *really* didn't want to know how long those had been there, or what was in them. Still, that meant it wasn't just an empty apartment: someone had been living here, and left. But he had to have left long before last night, so it couldn't be anything to do with her . . . with the current strange situation, that is.

Okay, time to stop thinking and start making food.

Miraculously, the water still worked. She had half expected the whole water supply to be cut off or damaged, but after a few splutters and some disturbingly rust-colored spurts, the faucet produced a stream of normal-looking water. The stove still worked too, although she had to dig out some matches from a drawer and light the pilot. She filled the pot with water and set it to boil, awkwardly wrestling with everything one-handed, then went to check out the rest of the apartment.

There wasn't much: a shabby bathroom, and a bedroom that wonderfully, fabulously, actually had a bed in it. No sheets, but there was a mattress, and that was enough for her at this point.

Best of all, there was a television. Even if something had happened to Manhattan, she could probably get some sort of news. She found the remote control on the bedside table and flopped across the mattress, switching it on. Hooray for the twenty-first century and its obsession with communication.

The TV buzzed to life. Static. She flipped the channel. Static. With a groan of dismay, she scanned through all of them. Static on every channel. Sighing, she flicked it off again and went back to the kitchen.

Whoever lived here before must have taken their computer with them when they left. Too bad—an Internet connection featuring Yahoo News headlines like NEW YORK CITY PEACEFULLY EVACUATED FOR MOVIE FILMING; DON'T WORRY, EVERYONE WILL BE BACK TOMORROW would have been nice. Maybe after eating she could go searching for a working computer.

She stirred the rice into the boiling water with one of the two spoons she could find, and covered it. What she needed was a plan. How to get out of here, where to go, what to do first.

WEST! demanded the voice.

"Yeah, yeah," she muttered. First she would eat, then she would go back outside and scout some more. Check some other bridges, maybe "borrow" some sheets from a department store, see if she could figure out anything else about the crystal things.

She glanced at the window to check the sun's position. Her gaze fell to the street and she jumped back, dropping the spoon.

There was someone down there.

A *real* someone, a person.

He moved slowly, shambling along the sides of the buildings, his eyes darting anxiously to the sky every few seconds. His hair was shaggy and white, and his skin was several shades paler than any she had ever seen before. He crouched in the shadows opposite the building she was in and stared at the grocery store she had entered. Uneasily, she wondered about footprints she might have left in the dust. Should she go down and talk to him? He looked a little crazy, but he *was* the first human she'd seen all day. Normally she wasn't a big fan of humanity, but . . .

His eyes traveled up the building, studying each of the windows. Instinctively Kali ducked, crouching out of sight. At the same time she heard the chimes sound that heralded the approach of the flying crystal bird. Did he know about them? Would he be safe?

She swore softly under her breath. Whoever this guy was, he might know something. And she couldn't let anything happen to the only other human around. She jumped up and sprinted out of the apartment.

As she pounded down the stairs two at a time, she could hear the wind rising outside. The whole building shook with it. She cleared the last few stairs with a jarring thud that shot needles up her arm, and shoved open the front door.

The creature shot overhead with an unearthly shriek. Kali staggered into the sunshine, blinking in the sudden light.

The man was gone.

The crystal pterodactyl pivoted above her, scanning the street with each glowing purple eye. Kali glared up at it.

"What are you?" she shouted. "What is going on? Answer me!"

It gave her the same cold look the crystal insect creatures had, then swooped away in a gust of wind that knocked her to her knees.

At least now she knew there was someone else out here. All she had to do was find him.

A BEACH IN CHILE

That's better.

Sunshine poured over Tigre, waking him up. He squinted in the bright light as Quetzie lifted her wing and hopped back into the water, which had come farther up the beach and now appeared to be going out again. From the position of the sun in the sky, he guessed it was about midmorning.

See? Isn't everything happier with sunshine?

Tigre sat up, blinking at the giant bird.

"Um," he mumbled.

So, I've been thinking, and I've had some brilliant ideas, as I frequently dooo, about where we could go, but it occuuuurred to me that you might need *to go to these other huumans, and it might be far, but neoquetzals never say never! and we'll just travel carefully and rest sometimes and—*

"Quetzie," Tigre croaked, "could you give me a second to wake up?"

Sure, she agreed happily. There was a pause as he rubbed his eyes. She submerged herself in the water and then leaped out, shaking sparkling droplets from her tail feathers. *Was that enough? Are you ready to go?*

"Ha. Yeah, right." He wobbled to his feet, testing his legs gingerly. They seemed much better than he would have expected; he could actually stand without falling over. He didn't want to think too much about walking, though. In fact, he didn't want to think too much about anything. Maybe if he just shut off his brain, events would sort themselves out.

But he was achingly thirsty. How much time had passed since he tore out of school? No way to know exactly—he never wore a watch since losing two on his storm-crazy runs. He hadn't had anything to eat or drink since his interrupted lunch the day before.

"Quetzie? Is there any water around here?" he asked.

Plenty of water! Water everywhere! As far as you can see! Look at all this loovely water!

"No, I mean, you know, fresh water. Something I can drink."

Well, are you ever in luck! You happen to be traveling with the smartest, the cleverest, the most thoughtful neoquetzal in the knooown world. She fluffed out her feathers. *I was lying there, thinking, loooook at all this lovely rain Tigre is making.*

And then I think, well, I bet he'd like some of this for himself when he wakes up.

"You saved me some rainwater?" Tigre said.

Well, I tried. I could oonly work with what I could reach, you know. She waved a wing at the sand.

Arranged in a half circle were three large shells, set on their backs to collect the rain. Gratefully, Tigre lowered himself back down and took a drink.

Sooooooo? Traveling? Fun? Faraway places?

"Okay, tell me something first," Tigre said. "You said there are humans out there somewhere, up north. Do you know where exactly?"

Up! Far! Where it was cold but is no more. Where the sea has taken back parts of the city and shining giants rule. Where huumans hide and scuttle and cannot leave and all is dark and glittering.

Tigre stared at her. She looked momentarily bashful.

It's poooetry! She gave a long, dreamy sigh full of bubbles. *Yes, I'm a poet. I am the art and soooul of this dying world.* Quetzie giggled suddenly and splashed a huge wave at him. *Get it? Art and soul!*

"That's very clever," Tigre said, shaking water out of his ears.

Of course, I've had nooooo one to share it with, she said wistfully. *My species is so rare and wooondrous that it's quite difficult to find any of us. So I have to make doooo with the occasional wandering pterodolphin. They're nothing like me—much smaller, less friendly, noooowhere near as smart, some attitude problems. I oonly talk to them when I get bored.* She splashed him with her tail. *Like now, mister. Aren't we gooing somewhere?*

"All right, okay." He smiled, despite the situation. Apart from the fact that she could communicate telepathically, Quetzie reminded him of the dogs he took care of at the Harris Animal Clinic and how excited they got about going outside.

He finished off the last shellful of water and stood up unsteadily. "That place doesn't sound like anywhere I've heard of, but if you can get there, I'm all for it." *I need to find Mom and Dad. I need answers.*

Quetzie shook out her feathers gleefully. *Okay! Up you go!*

Tigre inched over and surveyed the neoquetzal. Hmmm. Tigre was tall, but not *that* tall.

"Um . . . you're a little . . . big—I mean, I'm not sure how to—maybe if you were farther out in the water?"

Suuuure, she said, hopping back into the ocean. Tigre waded out after her until they were both floating about fifteen feet from shore. Here he could climb directly onto her back, although her feathers were slippery and sleek, and he had to brace his knees against her shoulder blades so he wouldn't slide off. There was a ridge of stiff feathers at the back of her neck, where the bright green fluff of her head met the smooth turquoise of her back. He buried his hands in the ridge and held on for dear life.

Hee-hee! That tickles! Up up and away!

Quetzie's wings unfolded completely and started beating the air, like a waterbird about to take off. Tigre closed his eyes and leaned closer to her. *What am I doing?* he thought. *Why am I letting a strange animal take me somewhere completely unknown?* Honestly, because it was easier than coming up with his own plan.

In any case, it was too late to change his mind. Quetzie rose majestically out of the water, and they sailed into the sky.

North, huh? he thought. *Well, north, here I come. I guess Fate is in charge now.*

LOS ANGELES, CALIFORNIA

Can I bring her CDs? Will she notice; will she mind? Gus fingered them anxiously, then shoved his three favorites into the small duffel bag he had unearthed from the back of his closet. He'd already packed his photos of Mom and Dad and the little stuffed gorilla they'd given him after their trip to Africa; he didn't care if Diana thought it was a stupid thing to bring, although he suspected she wouldn't.

He was so tired. It had to be somewhere near three o'clock in the morning and he'd been up early that day (*today? how many years ago?*) to help with the lights. He never functioned well on less than ten hours of sleep. And he was starting to get really hungry, too—the pizza they'd ordered backstage would normally have been followed by a giant bowl of ice cream when he got home, perhaps with some carrot sticks in between if Andrew had anything to do with it.

He piled in some shirts, his spare pair of glasses, a few other clothes. What was the weather like in Kansas? Should he bring warmer clothes or—*aaargh*. He *had* to stop overthinking. There wasn't time for indecision. Diana would be furious if he wasn't packed when she got back.

The front door slammed and he jumped about ten feet.

"No luck," Diana said, barging into his room. "There are a few cars left in the parking lot, but they're all clunkers—deflated tires, dead batteries, rust everywhere. Is there a mechanic's place around here?"

"I think so," Gus said, instinctively turning to his computer to look it up before remembering his computer was gone. How did anyone accomplish anything without the Internet?

"Well, let's go find it," she said, picking up his backpack and putting it on, the tools inside clanking together.

"I should warn you I don't know anything about cars," he said.

"Well, you're lucky you got stuck with me, then," she said, and he thought *yes, I am* as she went on. "My dad's a mechanic, so I picked up some stuff from watching him—you know, before he ditched us. It's not my strongest skill set, but hopefully I can figure it out."

"Okay, I'm impressed." He shoved a few pairs of socks into his duffel and zipped it shut. "I feel like I'm forgetting something."

"All you need is a toothbrush, right?" she joked. "I'm kidding," she added quickly as he started for the bathroom. "Even if Andrew did leave your toothbrush here, think about it—ew. We'll get stuff like that on the way."

"I suppose." He stood indecisively for a moment, wondering what else he'd forgotten.

"Believe me, the minute we see a mall, I'm replacing this monstrosity I'm wearing. If I can keep borrowing your shirts until then, that'd be awesome. Oh, sleeping bag—good idea," she said, picking it up.

"You never know," he said, feeling oddly embarrassed. "Diana, do you have any idea where we're going? Or what we're running from?"

Suddenly all the lights in the apartment went out. Diana and Gus were plunged into total darkness. For a heartbeat, Gus couldn't breathe.

"They're here," Diana whispered, and it was so much like a scene from a horror movie that Gus nearly laughed. He could feel a hysterical panic clawing its way up from his stomach into his throat, and the rolling anger rose along with it. If anything tried to hurt Diana, he would tear them into pieces with his own—

A hand brushed against his shoulder, then seized his shirtsleeve, and he nearly lashed out with his fists before he smelled lilacs and realized it was Diana.

"Is there a fire escape?" she whispered.

"Out the window in Andrew's room," he whispered back.

"Okay. Grab your duffel and lead the way." She slid her hand down his arm and laced her fingers in his. He took a deep breath and the anger stilled, like a bell she had silenced.

With his free hand, he fumbled for the duffel bag and slung it over his shoulder. He had just started for the door when there was an enormous crash from downstairs. Diana squeezed his hand and they both froze.

Thump thump thump thump thump.

Crash.

"Footsteps," she whispered. "Several of them."

"They're knocking down the apartment doors."

"And they're not even trying to be quiet," she said, her voice shaky with fright. "It's like they know we can't escape."

"Come on," he said, pulling her quickly out into the hall and across to Andrew's room. With five apartments on each floor, and two floors to cover before they got to his, there might still be enough time to get away before they smashed in his door.

Diana hurried over to the window as he closed the door behind them. "Come *on*," she whispered, dropping the sleeping bag and shoving at the old wooden frame. "*Open*, you stupid thing."

Another crash sounded, this one closer than before, and Gus guessed the intruders were on the second floor now. He added his weight to Diana's and together they yanked on the window frame.

With a horrendous squealing noise, it slid up.

The noises from below stopped. *They heard us* shot through Gus's head in the moment of silence before the footsteps sounded again, this time clearly pounding up the stairs toward them.

Diana kicked out the screen in one swift motion and clambered out, hauling the sleeping bag after her. She was halfway down the shaky stairs before Gus was out the window, and by the time he caught up, she was wrestling with the iron ladder that was supposed to slide down to the street.

"It's rusted solid," she panted. "Gus, we're going to have to jump."

HALT.

Diana looked up and shrieked before she could stop herself. In the light from the moon they could see two heads sticking out of Andrew's window, looking down at them. They were triangular and smooth, like snake's heads, and made of glass so she could see the wall behind them. They both had glowing purple eyes.

HALT AND BE TERMINATED. The voice seemed to come from both of them at the same time and sounded electronic, like the one on the phone.

"Yeah, right," Gus muttered, grabbing the sleeping bag from Diana and unrolling it with a tug. "Here." He flung one end over the side and sat on the other, bracing himself against the railing. "Slide down this, so you can get closer to the street before you drop. If you jump from here, you'll probably break both ankles in those boots."

"What about you?"

"I'll be right behind you. Go!"

She didn't argue. Sliding between the bars, she wrapped her arms around the sleeping bag and lowered herself over the edge. Despite his terror, Gus felt a weird thrill at how easily she trusted him with her life. She was light, but he still felt the strain through all his muscles as he held on ferociously to his end.

The weight on the end of the sleeping bag dropped away just as he felt a jarring thud shake the fire escape. He didn't dare look up before tossing the sleeping bag down, slinging his own body over the edge, and dropping the last several feet to the ground.

"Oof!" He felt the sleeping bag below him as he landed and his legs slipped out from under him. Diana's hands found his arm instantly and yanked him up.

He reached for the sleeping bag and she hissed "*Leave it*," and then they were running, dodging unidentifiable shapes in the alley as more crashing noises behind them signaled the descent of the two creatures.

Diana ran swiftly and without hesitation, as if she could sense everything in the path ahead of them. Gus almost felt like he could close his eyes and let her lead him. It seemed like only a few pulse-pounding minutes they were running, in a blur of moonlight and shadows, when suddenly she pulled him through a doorway and shoved him down behind a counter of some sort. She crouched next to him and he noticed with surprise that her breathing was even and quiet, while he was gasping for air.

"Shhhh," she said, resting one hand lightly on his lips. He held his breath, wondering if you could die from terror and suffocation simultaneously.

There were clanking and crashing sounds outside, but they sounded far away and getting farther.

After a moment Diana whispered: "I think we lost them. What on earth *were* those things?"

Gus let out the air in his lungs with a whoosh. "I don't know, and I'm not sure I want to." He lay down on the tile floor, listening to his heart trying to gallop its way out of his chest.

"That was amazing," he whispered after a moment. "Can you see in the dark or something?"

"Yeah, I'm actually Catwoman," she whispered back. "Venus is my secret identity."

"Why doesn't that surprise me?" he said. "It figures I'd

fall for a superstar who's also a superhero." The words were out before he realized what he was saying, and he instantly felt like the world's biggest idiot.

Diana was glad the darkness hid her smile. The practical side of her brain was crowing *I told you so, you shouldn't have encouraged him, look what you did* but the other half felt like it was filling up with iridescent bubbles, and, at the end of the world, that half seemed to be winning. She reached out and let her fingers rest on the side of his face for a moment in a gesture that she hoped said *thank you* and *don't feel stupid* without also saying *now do something about it*, because she wasn't ready for that.

Gus cleared his throat, and she pulled her hand back quickly and sat on it.

"I think we should hide out here for a few hours, in case they're lurking around the area," she said, talking fast so he wouldn't say anything else. "I can see if there's anything I can work with to get us a ride, and you can get some sleep. Hopefully by morning those creatures will be gone and we can head out." *EAST*, said that voice in her head again.

Gus sat up slowly and looked around, but the moonlight didn't penetrate very far into the room.

"Wait—where are we?" he asked.

"The garage you mentioned," she said.

"I didn't tell you where it was, though," he said, pushing his glasses up his nose. "*I* didn't even know. How did you find it?"

"Luck," she said with a shrug. "I probably followed the smell of engine oil." To be honest, she wasn't sure what had just happened. As soon as they got outside, she had known where to go and how to get there as quickly as possible. She guessed it was one of those situations where adrenaline took over and made you capable of things you couldn't normally even imagine.

"Maybe you *are* Catwoman," he said, and she didn't like the tone of awe in his voice.

"Shut up," she said, punching his shoulder. "Let's see if there are any cars out back, and maybe you can crash in a backseat for a few hours."

"Don't you want to get some sleep too?" he asked as they climbed to their feet.

"I'm not tired," she said, and it was true. She was the definition of a night person, and usually couldn't fall sleep until the early hours of the morning, if then. This particularly sucked when her mother was on an early-morning calisthenics kick, or when "Venus" had to go on one of those morning talk shows, but for the most part it worked with her performance schedule. She liked being awake late at night when nobody else was.

Gus dug a flashlight out of his backpack and they went through the door in the back wall, closing the door behind them before turning the flashlight on, so that it wouldn't be seen from the street.

Dust swirled through the beam of light as they edged into an echoing space that smelled of grease and metal, setting off memories like time bombs in Diana's mind— of watching her father at work, climbing under cars with him, holding tools while he tinkered, their hands getting sticky and black so her mother would wrinkle her nose and exile them straight to the kitchen when they got home.

There were six cars scattered around the interior, in different stages of repair. One was a large SUV. Diana would be pinioned by the media and her fans if she ever drove anything that environmentally unfriendly, but the enormous backseat was probably the most comfortable place to sleep that they would find.

Gus hesitated before climbing in. "Are you sure about this?" he asked. "You'll be okay on your own if I go to sleep?"

"I'm always okay," she said. "I'm more used to being on my own than you'd think."

"But with those things out there . . ."

"Don't worry. If they come this way, I think you'll hear about it." She smiled and turned away, taking the flashlight with her, as he started arranging his duffel bag as a pillow.

She wished she could see better, but it was probably safer not to turn on the overhead light. There were windows up near the ceiling, and any light bigger than the flashlight would almost certainly be visible from the outside.

Whatever those things were that had chased them, she did not want to be found again.

SOMETHING IS VERY WRONG.

LOST CONTROL ALREADY, HAVE YOU?

THERE HAVE BEEN . . . UNFORESEEN DEVELOPMENTS.

AND OURS IS BEING DIFFICULT. SHE IS FIRMLY RESISTING OUR SUGGESTIONS. WE MAY HAVE TROUBLE GUIDING HER TO THE GATHERING POINT.

THAT CAN BE COMPENSATED FOR. I KNOW MINE IS WILLING TO GO ANYWHERE. THE GATHERING PLACE CAN BE CHANGED. OTHER OPINIONS?

OURS CAN BE . . . PERSUADED.

OURS ALSO.

ALLOWANCES CAN BE MADE. FOR NOW.

IS THAT ALL?

WE HAVE GRAVE SUSPICIONS THAT SOMEONE IS CHEATING.

YOU ALWAYS THINK SO—

THAT'S ABSURD—

AND WHAT IF THEY WERE? . . .

~∴ JOURNEY ∴~

NEW YORK CITY

Sunset in New York after a full day of accomplishing nothing.

Kali was tempted to walk down Fifth Avenue smashing the flat, smug faces of the store windows to smithereens. Maybe the sound of shattering glass would bring those crystal monsters out to investigate. She'd love to make them mad. She'd love to make them react at *all*. So far the only thing she'd discovered, in the day since everyone disappeared, was that the monsters seemed determined to ignore her.

At first she had avoided them, but as her search for people became more and more pointless and annoying, she had tried again to get past the insect creatures at the bridges. It was like arguing with walls. They refused to respond, but they refused to let her by, either. As for the bird creatures, she'd seen several of them go by overhead, although most were smaller than the first one she'd seen. Even when she stood out in the middle of the street, they barely glanced at her before swooping on.

This city had made her feel tiny, furious, anonymous, and insignificant before, but it had never made her feel so powerless.

It made her want to smash things.

She pressed the knuckles of her right hand against the empty store window, watching the setting sun reflect off the tops of buildings. Night was falling, and she had seen no sign of the old man, or anyone but crystal birds and insects. The only bridge she hadn't tried was the George Washington, which was a serious hike through Harlem, and went west in any case, where she refused to go as long as the voice in her head was insisting on it.

"All right, I'll spare you for now," she muttered at the glass. "But you try looking at me like that tomorrow—"

Was she talking to windows now? She turned abruptly, and her breath caught in her throat.

He was here.

They were here.

Somehow they had crept up on her, five of them. All were incredibly old, although it was hard for Kali to tell exactly how old because she generally considered anyone over thirty to be too ancient to think about. Their long, white, matted hair gathered in clumps around their pale, sickly faces. They moved in a sort of shambling way, like the man she'd seen earlier, staying close to walls and swaying vaguely. It was hard to focus on them, as if they were fuzzy around the edges. The only thing about them that was sharp was their eyes. The pupils were enormously dilated so their eyes looked almost completely black, and they were all staring piercingly at her. They looked like homeless people, but with the craziness level multiplied several times.

Despite having spent the entire day searching for humans, Kali was horrified.

"her"

"she-who"

"creates-destroys"

She recognized the whisper-voices that had woken her up that morning. Here they were. People. And she had no idea what to say to them.

The old man she had seen earlier shuffled forward and bobbed up and down at her. After a minute she realized he was bowing.

"How," he attempted, then broke off in a fit of nasty coughing. The others didn't even look at him; they kept staring at Kali and swaying from side to side. She felt torn between wanting to help him and wanting to run away. Instead, she kept her back against the window and watched him warily. Gradually he recovered and tried again.

"How escape stairs flood where from how young how hunters create-destroy young you how" he rattled off all in one breath. Then he paused and looked at her expectantly. The others shuffled forward, eager expressions on their faces.

"Don't come any closer," Kali snapped. They stopped, still looking hopeful. "Okay. You. Was that a question? Or what?"

The man squinted like he was thinking hard, inhaled, and swung into the exact same speech: *"How escape stairs flood where from how young how hunters create-destroy young you how."*

Toothless grin.

Expectant expression.

Man, old people were weird.

"Okay. Let's try that again. *Wait.* One bit at a time. Do any of the rest of you speak English?"

The old man looked offended. The rest nodded.

"Okay. Anyone else want to tell me what's going on here?"

"She-who" began one woman.

"Creates-destroys" interrupted a man. The woman shoved him so he nearly overbalanced.

"Creates-destroys walls," she managed triumphantly.

"Who creates and destroys walls? What are you talking about?"

The original old man cleared his throat with a huge, horrible hacking sound. He pointed at Kali and insisted: *"You. Young. How?"* Clearly proud of this effort, he glanced around the circle. The others nodded approvingly.

Kali raised her eyebrows. How was she young? What kind of question was that?

A woman reached out and plucked at the air near Kali, as if afraid to touch her.

"Hunters. You. Escape. How?" she quavered.

"What hunters?" Kali asked. Had some sort of hunters come through last night? Had they taken all the other people?

The old woman looked disappointed.

"Look," Kali said. "I don't understand. Do you know what's going on? What happened to all the people?" She met a wall of confused expressions. "Okay. I'm not sure how to communicate this. *People.* What *happened* to them. You know? Overnight? Disappearing?" She stopped, frustrated. Shouting at old people was not going to get her any answers.

Clink-clank. A new sound echoed up from underground. The eyes around her went wide as saucers. Their faces lit up with anticipation, and they shuffled around to stare at the nearest subway entrance.

Clink-clank. Clink-clank. It sounded like someone climbing the stairs with metal feet. *Clink-clank.* It was definitely getting closer.

The old people shuffled backward to clear the way to her. She realized that the water in the subway had subsided and the stairs were clear. And there was someone coming up them, slowly but surely.

It was another old man, but not so old—maybe closer to sixty-five or seventy, if she had to guess. He had a pale gray buzz cut, and his eyes were as sharp and dark as the others. But he moved more confidently, although with the help of a cane. As he came toward her, she realized it was more than a cane: it was a steel pipe, that he held as if it could be either a crutch or a weapon at a moment's notice.

He stopped at the head of the stairs, gazing at her. The others bobbed and swayed with ghoulish grins.

"Forgive them," he said in a deep bass voice. "They are old enough to remember the Before, and it has addled their brains somewhat. That, and a life of constant persecution and darkness."

Kali sighed with relief. "You can talk!"

"Yes. I told them not to speak to you until I came, but they get excited. You understand."

"Um. Sure." His skin was pale too, with deep wrinkles etched under and around his eyes that made him look exhausted. The other men had shaggy beards, but he was clean shaven, more or less—he'd missed a few spots.

"I apologize; I should start with introductions. I am General Pepper."

"General Pepper?" She laughed. "What, you got promoted?"

He looked blank, like he'd never heard of either Sergeant Pepper or the Beatles, or possibly even the concept of humor.

"You know . . . okay, never mind. I'm Kali."

"Kali, Kali," the old people repeated in their whisper-voices.

"Kali. I must ask you to come with me," the general said.

"With you? Where?" Kali asked, instantly on guard.

"To see the Miracle, of course," he explained as if it were obvious.

"The Miracle, the Miracle," the others whispered, louder now.

"What miracle?" Kali demanded. "I'm not going anywhere until someone tells me what's going on."

"The Miracle will explain all."

"Well, why don't you give it a start, at least."

He studied her, eyes darkening. The sun was entirely

down now. She didn't know when, but the streetlights had come on, what few were still working, and they bathed General Pepper and the whisperers in an eerie orange glow.

"It is not safe aboveground. You should come with us."

"Why isn't it safe?"

"The crystal hunters rule the city, but they avoid the underground tunnels. Come with us, and you will be safe there."

"In the subways? Are you kidding? I nearly drowned down there!"

"Ah, but you didn't. You created an exit where there wasn't one before, tore down walls like paper, found stairs long buried in the earth. The Miracle would like to know how you did that," he said.

"She who creates-destroys . . ." Kali looked around at the whisperers in disbelief, feeling a twinge of anxiety. She had hoped no one would find out about that.

"How do you know what happened?" she asked. "If you were watching me, why didn't you help me?" Add that to the Don't Trust Them column.

"You handled the situation without our help."

"Listen, I didn't create anything. Those stairs were there—I just broke through the wall to get to them. They were only blocked off a few days ago. And the wall was flimsy to begin with. I'm not saying it was easy busting out of a flooded tunnel, but it wasn't any kind of magic mojo, if that's what you're saying."

General Pepper looked stern. "Do not toy with us."

"I wouldn't. Unless you were bendier and came with neat accessories."

"Do you have an equally glib explanation for how you have managed to elude the crystal hunters?"

"Oh—the birds, you mean? Or the insects? I'm not sure they're interested in people. They just ignored me all day. It was *really* irritating—" She broke off, disturbed by the weirdly worshipful looks the others were giving her. "Okay. I think you should answer some of *my* questions now. Like, for instance, where everyone is."

"Everyone?"

"Yeah . . . you know, the people of New York. The swarming masses of humanity. The ones who live here? Usually? As of twenty-four hours ago?"

"We are the only people of New York. We stayed when all the rest evacuated to escape the hunters and the flooding. We survive in the tunnels by day, while the crystal hunters roam, and we come out at night when they rest and recharge. But it is not safe; even in darkness they can rise if they choose to."

Kali could feel her pulse speeding up. None of this made sense.

"But what about all the people who work here? The, like, ten million normal people who were here yesterday?"

General Pepper clanked a step toward her, his eyes narrowing. "There are only we few, in the tunnels. So it has been for years. Yesterday was much like today, and the day before that. Nothing changes. The crystal hunters hunt us and keep us here, and we survive and wait for the Miracle to save us. Nothing changes. Until you came."

Kali stared at him. The others swayed more violently, whispering her name.

"No." She shook her head. "No. You're crazy."

"You must come with us." He reached for her injured arm and she jerked away, trying not to show that it hurt.

"I don't think so, psychopath," she growled. She wanted to bring a building crashing down on all of them. If she didn't get out of there, they might find out they were right about her—in the worst possible way. With a powerful kick, she knocked the pipe out from under him so he stumbled. The others gasped and moved closer, but she shoved them aside and stalked away down the street.

They didn't try to follow, but General Pepper called after her:

"You cannot be alone forever. You need us, too. The Miracle wants to see you."

Kali shoved her fists in her pockets, hunched her shoulders, and kept walking.

LOS ANGELES

The sound of shattering glass brought Gus out of the SUV in a hurry, his glasses crooked and his hair standing up in all directions.

"I'm sorry!" Diana called from across the room, trying not to laugh at the panic-stricken look on his face. Pale light seeped in from the windows up above, casting strange mechanical shadows. "It was just me. I didn't realize how loud that would be."

"What did you do?" he asked, still a little wild eyed. "How long did I sleep for?"

"Almost the whole day, and I'm *starving*," she said ruefully. "So I thought I'd break into the vending machine."

She came over and unloaded an armful of snack food and bottled water onto the floor between them. He noticed that she had smudges on her face and her hair was tied back with a piece of rope from his backpack. Even in her leather pants, she looked like someone he might work with backstage—someone he could safely have a crush on. "I figure if anything is still edible after however many years it's been, it's probably vending machine food," she added.

"Wow," Gus said as his stomach growled loud enough to wake the dead. "I don't think I've ever been so happy to see honey mustard–flavored pretzel bits in my life."

"Don't forget the fake chocolate cupcakes," Diana said, sitting cross-legged on the concrete floor. "Or the Life Savers."

"I hope there's crackers with peanut butter."

"With trail mix on the side." She threw a raisin that bounced off his nose, and they smiled at each other. *Nice reaction to the end of the world,* Diana's brain complained. *Everything is falling apart and here you are flirting with a fan.* The memory of the creatures from the night before came back, and her smile faded. She watched Gus stretch and take a seat next to her.

"Gus, how far in the future do you think we are? I mean, how much time has—gone by—do you think?"

He shook his head, ripping open a box of Swedish fish. "I don't know. The only hint is Andrew mentioned 'months' in his letter. Maybe . . . maybe a year? Or two?"

She gave him a look.

"Okay, maybe a little longer."

"Gus, do you really think all this could have happened

in a year? People evacuating Los Angeles, all this destruction, weird glass monsters appearing?"

"All right, I know. So maybe a little longer."

She was silent, resting her head on her hand and picking peanuts out of the bag of trail mix.

"What do you think happened, Diana? Why did they all leave?"

"Well, like your brother said, earthquakes and monsters. I guess he was talking about those things that chased us." She shuddered.

"So where did they come from? Outer space?"

"Yeah, right. Or maybe they were created by some evil genius scientist and loosed on the world by accident. Now all we need is a couple of superheroes—me Catwoman, you . . . hmmm. Robin?"

"Seriously, Diana. What if this is the aftermath of an alien invasion?"

She rolled her eyes. "If Earth had been invaded by aliens, don't you think Andrew would have mentioned that in his letter? I think it's more complicated. Honestly, I'm afraid this is something we did to ourselves."

"We? You mean humans? You think humans made the crystal things and chased everybody out of Los Angeles?" He glanced at her. "I don't know. I never bought those we-destroy-ourselves scenarios. Humans are all about survival of the species, deep down. I always figured that no matter what happened, we'd find a way to get through it. I can't imagine anything so bad that people would just give up and die."

"I know," she said. "Neither can I."

The gutted cars around them seemed to get bigger in

the silence, watching them like skeletal sentinels in a mechanical graveyard.

"It's nearly dark," Diana said.

"You should have woken me earlier."

"I couldn't get any of the cars working until now. I had to find new tires, replace the battery"—*teach myself a few things out of manuals in the back office*—"but I think the little blue one over there will get us out of town, and hopefully at least as far as Kansas."

"You're coming to Kansas with me?" he asked with a grin.

"Of course. I mean, not permanently," she added hurriedly. "But since I can't call my mom, and there's no one in Los Angeles, and as long as you're going that way, I might as well. Maybe I can look for my uncle in Tennessee." A huge yawn caught her off guard.

"You haven't slept in hours and hours," Gus said, sounding concerned.

"Or possibly years and years," she said. "Well, I can't drive anyway, so I'll sleep while you get us out of here." She stood up, brushing crumbs off her shirt.

"You can change a car battery, but you can't drive?"

"Life of a rock star," she said. "No time to learn normal teenage things."

While Gus gathered his stuff and the rest of the vending machine food, Diana told him about the staircase she'd found early that morning, which led to the roof. From there the view stretched surprisingly far, partly because many of the nearby tall buildings were no longer standing. She had climbed out when the sun came up and spotted a horde of the glass creatures, maybe twenty or thirty of them. They were arranged in a zigzag formation around Gus's apartment building, standing with their heads bowed, perfectly motionless.

In the growing light she'd been able to see a lot more detail than she had the previous night. Their snakelike heads were perched on thin, elongated bodies with two sets of multi-jointed arms, which they held folded in front of them and close to their sides like a praying mantis. Her impression that they were made of glass was sort of right, but not complete enough: they looked more like crystal than plain glass, with lots of tiny particles inside set at different angles to catch the light and bounce it around. Their legs ended in four hooked claws like vulture's feet.

She had stretched out on the roof as the sun came up, lifting her eyes just above the edge to watch them. They had the apartment surrounded, although they had to know she and Gus had escaped. Why were they still there, and why weren't they moving?

The answer came with the sunrise. As the light snaked through the streets and hit them, one by one they came to life. A neon purple glow would start wherever the sun first hit and then spread, jaggedly, like electricity, to the rest of their bodies. By the time they were all in full sunlight, their eyes had flamed to life and they were standing at attention, like soldiers waiting to be inspected.

Then there was a thud, and another, and another, and Diana realized that something very, very large was coming. She didn't have time to run back inside, so she pressed herself to the roof, hoping it wouldn't notice her.

The newcomer loomed up between two buildings. Like the insect creatures, it glittered with corners of sunlight and a web of purple lightning. Unlike the insects, it was as tall as a four-story building and shaped like a weight-lifting bear. It was carrying something long and cylindrical that looked like a giant concrete pipe.

She didn't tell Gus the rest of it—about how the creature had lumbered up to Gus's apartment building, reared back an enormous paw, and smashed the pipe through the bricks and mortar and cement like it was clubbing a sand castle with a bat.

Smash went the club. *Smash smash.* The building began to crumble, and Diana couldn't watch anymore. She had crawled back inside, shaking, and decided not to tell Gus. He'd be happier thinking his room was still back here waiting for him.

"Should we check if the creatures are still out there?" Gus asked, interrupting her thoughts.

"I did," Diana said. "I went up before I woke you, to see how we could get to the highway."

The giant bear was gone, and so were most of the crystal insects, although two were poking through the rubble where Gus's building had been. She had seen no other signs of life between here and the highway.

EAST, whispered the voice in her head. *YOU'RE WASTING TIME.*

Don't worry, she thought. *Whatever you are, I'm on my way.*

MEXICO

Tigre was convinced he was about to die of hunger by the time Quetzie finally agreed to land. They had flown all day and through the next night, but she refused to let him down anywhere in South America, insisting that it was *"noooot safe"* and that there wasn't anything he could eat there anyway. He nearly nodded off a few times, comfortable in the soft fluff of Quetzie's feathers, but always snapped awake in terror that he was about to slide off her back.

At last, in the late morning a day after kidnapping him, she spiraled down onto a beach somewhere along the coast of Central America. Tigre's family had taken a trip to Cancun once, for a weekend, and he thought they might be near there, although now the jungle had grown up beyond the beach into an impenetrable tangle of vines and trees.

This must be what it looked like when the Spanish conquistadors first arrived in Mexico, he thought. *An untamed wilderness.*

A new world.

He shivered.

Don't be looong, Quetzie burbled nervously. *I dooon't like this area. The pterodolphins spend moooost of their time in these trooopic waters. Nasty bruuuutes.* She shook her head rapidly so her feathers stood out in a shocked halo.

"I'll be quick," Tigre promised, testing his legs gingerly. They had mostly recovered from the run two days earlier, but now he felt wobbly with hunger. "Fresh water and some fruit, and I'll be the happiest guy this side of the apocalypse."

He was lucky; a stream led back from the beach into a

less overgrown area, where he soon found a pool fresh enough to drink from, a cluster of ripe bananas, and another fruit he didn't recognize that looked like large yellow plums but tasted a bit like pineapples. He ate as fast as he could, knowing he'd probably be punished with a stomachache soon but unable to stop himself.

He wanted to get out of here quickly. The noises around him were unsettling—shrieks and caws that might have been birds, but also, given what he'd seen in the last couple of days, just might be toothy monsters.

Tigre knelt to splash water on his face, keeping a close eye on the bushes around him. It didn't occur to him to look across the pool.

"Whoa." A voice came out of the air. "I want the name of *your* guy!"

Tigre jumped and lost his balance, nearly landing in the water. He struggled upright to see a guy standing across from him, nearly hidden in the shadows of the trees opposite. A person! A real person, after two days of seeing nobody but peculiar animals. Tigre was so relieved he nearly burst into tears.

"Oh thank God," he said, speaking English since the stranger had, too. "I've been so confused—I couldn't find anyone—I need help, I need a phone or—can you tell me what's going on? I—" He broke off, realizing that the stranger was bobbing up and down oddly, as if he had a permanent calypso orchestra going in his head.

"Seriously, man," the stranger said in a fuzzy voice. "That's like, the best job I've ever seen. Man, you don't look a day over seventeen." He waggled his head slowly back and forth.

"I am seventeen," Tigre said, bewildered.

"Sure, dude." The stranger laughed. "And I'm a zybrid. You don't go to anyone around here, right? I've tried them all, and like, none of them is as good as that. I'm, like, totally blown away, man."

"I'm not from around here, no," Tigre said slowly. Something was not right with this guy. "I'm sorry, I'm not sure what's going on."

"That's okay, that's okay," the other man said, bobbing and weaving now. His face slipped into the light for a minute and then back into shadow. Tigre squinted. What . . . what was wrong with his face?

"We welcome visitors here, man," the stranger said. "It gets kinda boring, know what I mean? You can only do so much free-mind before you're like, dude, I'd like to talk to a real new person once in a while, instead of all these pink goats or whatever."

"Pink . . . goats?" Tigre repeated.

"Come on back to Party Central," the other man said. "Hey, we'll roast a llama! There's plenty of free-mind to go around. And you can stay in Rudy's complex, he, like, died the other day, man, what a downer. So his place is free and he totally wouldn't mind if you borrowed it. Come on back with me." He leaned forward, extending his hand across the pool, and Tigre stepped back involuntarily.

The man's face was a mass of tiny seams and taut, orange skin. His eyes were wide and glazed, like they'd been propped open and left that way for too long. His mouth was stretched wide like a cartoon villain's, and his hair was a thatch of obvious plugs, brown synthetic fibers planted across his skull like new grass, burned to a wriggly crisp at the ends. His body looked like sagging flour sacks had been propped up with balloons that were slowly deflating. He was horrifying.

Tigre didn't know what to do. It was just his luck that the only human he'd seen in days was a freaky-looking lunatic. What if he was lying about "Party Central"? What was "free-mind"? And did he say some guy had died? Tigre found himself wanting to run back to Quetzie.

Typical, Tigre, he thought to himself, *choosing the company of animals over other humans.* He could almost hear Vicky in his head, mocking him.

Well, if he had to follow this guy to prove her wrong, then he would. Plus he'd said something about roasting a llama. Tigre felt about ready to kill one with his own hands if it meant he could have some meat.

"Okay, I'll come with you," Tigre said. "I just have to go back and let my friend know where I'm going."

"Friend, huh?" the stranger said. "If it's your doc, I want to meet him."

"My . . . doctor?" Tigre said. "No, Quetzie's just a friend." He backed away, toward the beach, and the guy followed him, splashing through the water like he didn't even notice he was getting wet.

"All right, all right," the man said, wagging his head from side to side with a loony grin. "Keep him a secret as long as you want. But I'm pretty convincing when I want to be, dude. You'll fork over the info sooner or later."

"I'm Tigre, by the way," Tigre said, trying to steer this conversation into normal channels.

"The name's Honking Buffalo," the stranger said. "But you can call me Honk."

Tigre stared at him, wondering if he was supposed to laugh. But Honk just kept waggling his head with the same vague expression; he sure didn't look like he was joking. They traipsed through the trees in silence until they reached the beach.

"It's so quiet," Tigre said as they came out onto the sand. "I keep expecting to hear airplanes overhead, at least."

"What're you talking about, man?" Honk asked. "You know all the advanced stuff was wiped out in the Great Wipeout of year forty. We've got the automated wiring that runs the electricity and water and all, so the old folks would always have that stuff when they got too old to run it themselves, but it's specially designed so it can't ever get too smart or be messed with. No more computers, yeah, no more smart guys fiddling with viruses and chips, ha-ha . . ." Honk's voice trailed down into a mutter and he started kicking the sand.

Tigre squinted at him, puzzled but not sure whether it was safe to pursue this line of questioning. "Year forty?" he said cautiously. "And . . . what year is it now?"

"Who knows, man," Honk said, his cheerful grin returning. "We live for the *moment*, you know? If we had to think about how many years it's been, we'd have to think about ourselves being, like, old and stuff, which goes against the entire Forever Young philosophy."

"Forever Young is a philosophy?" Tigre said. "I thought it was a song."

"Actually, it's a person," Honk said. "Forever founded this community. I can't believe you didn't know that. You must be a forever youngerman, though—otherwise you wouldn't look like you do. Man, I *so* want to know your secret! Is it something you eat? It's salmon, isn't it? Everyone says eating salmon will help get rid of the wrinkles, man, but it's too slimy and pink for me."

Tiger boy? Quetzie's voice bubbled up in Tigre's head. He looked toward the sea and saw a flash of shimmering green feathers break the waves several yards out. *Whoooo is that with youu?* Her voice was anxious.

Tigre cupped his hands over his mouth and yelled as loud as he could. "It's okay, Quetzie! He's a human, like me!" Honk laced his hands behind his head and gazed around with wide eyes, but didn't seem to notice the neoquetzal. Tigre wasn't even sure the man was looking for anything; rather, he seemed to be waiting for something to flit across his field of vision.

I am tooo beautiful to be seen by any mere huuuuman, Quetzie burbled. *Youu were blessed, but I cannot reveal myself to this creature. Get rid of him, and we'll keep going.*

"Get rid of him?" Tigre shouted. "This is what I was looking for, remember? Other humans?"

Noot these huumans.

"Why?" Tigre called. "What's wrong with them?" He glanced at Honk, who was now spinning slowly in place, his eyes riveted on his hands, which he held straight out in front of him. He didn't seem to care that Tigre was apparently having a one-sided conversation with the ocean.

They are not right, Quetzie said. *The northern ones have some sense-speakers still. These have none.*

Tigre could feel it too—a wrongness about this place. This was not where the voice in his head wanted him to be.

That in itself was almost enough to make him stay and investigate, but more than anything, it was the image of Vicky laughing scornfully. "You finally find a human, and what do you do? Run away!"

Even now, the idea of people made him nervous. He couldn't afford to listen to his fears right now, when he needed any information he could get, plus food and if possible a shower and change of clothes.

"I'm just going to go see, okay?" he called to Quetzie. "I'll come back soon. Wait for me?"

She made a sound like a series of large fat bubbles wafting through his head.

All right. Youu have five hours. Then I will have to gooo on.

He waved a thank-you and turned back to Honk, who was wrinkling his nose at the horizon.

"Sorry about that," Tigre said.

"Sorry about what?" Honk asked. "Say, man, does the edge of the sky look kind of wavy to you?"

Tigre looked in the direction he was pointing, at where the sky met the ocean waves.

"Uh. Sure, Honk."

"Ready to go?" Honk beamed at him. "Party Central will be hopping tonight! It'll be alpacatastic! Wait till you meet the others. Forever will love you, man. You are so the best forever youngerman spokesperson. If there were still TV, we would totally put you in our ads."

"There's no more TV?" Tigre said, feeling slightly faint. Not that the loss of *Law and Order* repeats was so upsetting—but a world without TV was a world where something had gone seriously, globally wrong.

"No worries, man," Honk said, clapping him on the

back. The blow felt surprisingly weak, like being slapped with a slice of pizza. "We make our *own* fun here."

Half snorting, half cackling, he headed off along the beach, still bobbing up and down in that funny, seasick way.

Tigre glanced at the ocean, already regretting his decision. He would come back soon, and then he and Quetzie could get out of here.

But first, he had to check out Party Central.

New York City

Kali figured out fast that the old people emerged only at night, and even then they tended to stay out of the streets and stick to the shadows. Hopefully this would make them easy to avoid, as long as they didn't know where she was. On day two of empty New York, while they hid underground, Kali headed uptown and found herself a new apartment. She was careful not to leave tracks, and she chose a nicer building—after all, if she had the whole city to herself, she might as well stay somewhere out of her price range. Even in the swankiest neighborhoods, she had no trouble finding an apartment that wasn't locked.

It was hard for her to understand why she felt so hostile toward the whisperers. They seemed harmless, except for General Pepper, and yet every time she saw them she felt guilty and defensive. She couldn't bring herself to talk to them, and although she wanted answers, she didn't trust General Pepper to give them to her.

She spent the rest of the second day foraging for

supplies in department stores, gathering piles of canned food that seemed edible, choosing clothes with prices she would normally laugh at from stark, haunted-looking racks, although none of them were as trendy and stylish as she'd hoped—fashion sense had apparently been abducted along with all the people. Everything was covered with dust, but some laundry machines in the new apartment building were still working, and she managed to find quarters in broken cash registers.

Her arm ached with pain every time she moved it, and she considered going into a hospital to find a real sling and maybe some medicine. But the first one she found had a sickly, rotten stench wafting out the doors, and something told her she didn't want to find the source. More stolen Advil and strips of torn cloth firmly bandaged around her arm would do until she found her way home.

She also walked up to the George Washington Bridge, but she didn't approach the insect creatures there, partly because the voice in her head was so insistent that she should go that way. She watched them for a while, but they never left, never seemed even to communicate with each other.

She also discovered that more crystal sentries, looking equally unpleasant, were posted at the entrances to the Lincoln and Holland Tunnels.

The strangest thing was that not only were no phones working anywhere, but she couldn't even *find* any computers to try e-mail or check the Internet—not even in the libraries or office buildings she broke into. She couldn't understand it. Shouldn't there be computers everywhere? Where would they have gone? Why would computers disappear when people did? People depended on computers; the world practically couldn't exist without them.

Well, perhaps this didn't qualify as "existing."

Toward the end of the day she started to get really angry. She had to get to Brooklyn. She needed to find her mother and sisters. They wouldn't have evacuated without her. They wouldn't have been *able* to evacuate without her—Mom could barely do anything on her own since Bill died. Kali needed to get home and make sure they were all right.

And if it really was safe in the subways, like the crazy people said, maybe she could get there via a subway tunnel.

She chose the First Avenue stop on the L train, knowing the tunnel there led directly into Williamsburg, Brooklyn. It took almost twenty minutes to convince herself to descend the steps; they were clear of water, but still damp, like the ocean had been through recently, and she kept picturing huge waves suddenly sweeping up and sucking her down into the black depths.

When she finally worked up enough nerve to edge carefully down the stairs, she discovered that the gate at the bottom had been closed and locked, but someone— presumably the underground dwellers—had broken open the chains and left them hanging there.

Kali squeezed through cautiously, holding the gate still so it wouldn't squeak. Beyond were the turnstiles, another set of stairs, and darkness. All the lights were broken at this station, but luckily she had thought to bring a flashlight. She clicked it on and ventured forward, climbing over the turnstile and trying to muffle the sound of her boots squish-clopping through the thin layer of water and mud on the stairs.

The tracks were hidden by a river of dark, sinister water flowing slowly just below the edge of the platform, illuminated by the thin beam of her flashlight.

Kali shone her flashlight up the tunnel toward Brooklyn—nothing—and down the tunnel back into Manhattan. She nearly had a heart attack as the light struck a shape looming out of the darkness. A subway— an L train—sat just beyond the edge of the tunnel, half submerged in water, placid and eerie, like it was waiting for something. It was like seeing a ghost rise out of the ocean. She covered her flashlight and closed her eyes, breathing deeply. Okay. Calm. She could be calm about this.

Clink-clank.

Her eyes flew open.

Clink-clank.

The stifling darkness, the ominous sounds of the water, and the thought of confronting General Pepper down here, alone, were too much for her. She fled back up the stairs as fast as she could.

Later that evening, as the sun was setting and she was heading back to the apartment to avoid the old people, she had what she thought might be her first bright idea in days. A way to prove the general wrong, she hoped.

She stopped at the grocery store on the corner by her building. Yes, there they were, in a pile right inside the door—why hadn't she thought of this before? Because she didn't read newspapers, never read newspapers; she got her news on the Internet or from her mom.

Newspapers were antiquated and awkward, and they got ink and that chalky papery feeling all over your hands. Not to mention she didn't really trust them to be "objective" in this day and age.

But if somehow a lot of time *had* passed, as General Pepper seemed to think, then maybe the newspapers' date would provide a clue. Or else she was right and they would all be dated two days ago, when everyone disappeared.

It certainly wasn't promising that the paper was yellow and the type was faded. They also looked much thinner than normal newspapers, with an old-fashioned, hand-set look to them. She slid off the top one and it made a rustle like a shower of moths.

She looked at the date.

She looked at it again.

She checked the other newspapers in the pile. It wasn't a mistake.

Then she read the headlines.

She walked home, a deep hollow fear opening up inside her, and crawled into bed. Even the shining glass pterodactyls didn't see her again for two whole days.

ON THE ROAD IN NEVADA

"Diana?"

She didn't respond. Gus took his eyes off the road to glance at her and realized that she was sleeping, curled up on the seat with her head resting against the window, a small smile on her face. Did anyone really smile in her sleep like that? It seemed like something that only happened in movies. He thought for a moment about how strange this was—that in the course of two days he could meet a girl he liked so much, discover she was a celebrity beyond his reach, and then get thrown forward in time to an apocalyptic world where he was traveling across the country with her. He wasn't sure this qualified as "lucky," but he couldn't be entirely unhappy about it either, as long as he found Andrew soon.

He hated to wake her, but he'd been driving almost all night and if he didn't rest soon, he was guaranteed to crash the car. Plus the violent tornado inside him actually seemed to be getting worse, not better, spreading to his stomach and his chest.

"Diana?" He reached out hesitantly and touched her shoulder.

Instantly she was awake, jerking up out of sleep and pulling away, lines of stress falling into place on her forehead.

"Ready. Onstage. What's—who—oh." She blinked a couple of times, registering him, the car, the darkness outside. "Oh."

"Sorry. I think I need to stop and like, sleep or something. Just for a little bit."

She yawned and stretched, her leather outfit creaking under his shirt. "Of course." Turning, she checked out the back window. "No sign of any more weird monster things, right? How long have we been driving?"

"I'd guess eight hours, but my watch has stopped and the car clock is all wrong. We're definitely a ways from Los Angeles by now, though. I think we're almost to the other side of Nevada, although a lot of the road signs have fallen down or are too faded to read, so it's hard to tell." There weren't any lights on the road either, so Gus hadn't been able to see much beyond the cone of the headlights. This highway went through a fairly empty swathe of Nevada, but still he had hoped to find more signs of civilization.

"So it's probably some crazy early hour of the morning. Yeah, you should definitely sleep." She hesitated. "Has there . . . have you seen any . . . signs of people?"

He shook his head. There were no other cars on the road. They were on a highway now, but even the rest stops and gas stations along the way were closed and dark, as if they had been abandoned for a while.

"Okay." She sighed. "Maybe we could find a motel and break in or something. Just for the night. And we can look for gas first thing tomorrow."

"We could leave money at the front desk," he suggested. "I have some cash in my wallet. I mean, I feel bad just . . . taking stuff."

"I know, me too. But maybe a better idea would be to write it all down and like, keep track of what we take, so later I can send checks. I mean, you know, to save our cash, and stuff." He heard the unspoken message—she had money to spare and he didn't—but couldn't really argue with that.

"Makes sense. I'll pull off when I see something."

"Okay." She curled up in the car seat, wrapping her arms around her legs, and stared out the window. The highway flashed by, dark and unwelcoming, with no lights anywhere as far as they could see. Gus wondered how far into the country people had fled, and how soon they'd find someone.

"There's one," Diana said, pointing. A bright yellow sign loomed out of the darkness ahead of them, lit up by their headlights. Gus switched into the exit lane—using his indicator automatically, although he knew it was stupid—and pulled off onto the road leading to the motel's parking lot.

"Think they have any vacancies?" Diana joked nervously as they parked. It was an average-looking place; Gus found himself wondering again what "Venus" thought of the shabby surroundings, but she acted like she didn't even notice.

She led the way into the lobby. "Hello?" she called. It was dark and dusty and looked like it had been abandoned for eons. The counter was bare, and the door to the area behind it was locked.

"Blech," she said, grinning. "I bet they don't even have a continental breakfast."

"You seem bizarrely cheerful about this end-of-the-world situation," Gus remarked. He tried to smile, but a stab of pain in his chest made him stop and catch his breath instead. Diana didn't notice.

"I guess that nap made me feel better. And, you know, being gloomy won't get us anywhere. I say look on the bright side: at least the total annihilation of the human species means I can walk around without being mobbed by crazy fans." She saw his expression and rolled her eyes. "I'm *kidding*, Gus."

He wondered if he'd find it funnier if it didn't feel like angry lobsters with pickaxes were trying to claw their way out of his chest.

Diana hopped up on the counter and slid over it, leaving a swathe through the dust. To her left was a wall of numbered hooks with keys hanging from every one. She scanned them and shrugged. "I guess we could just take a few and try rooms until we find something we like, right?"

Gus nodded, swallowing, his pulse speeding up. *Gus, don't even begin to think about staying in a motel room with her or about only the two of you being left on the planet. There is nothing romantic about the end of the world. Stop thinking about it right now.*

"Gus?" Diana was giving him a weird look. "Come on."

They avoided the elevator, taking the stairs and walking slowly down the halls, trying doors. The first room they found was a disaster: sheets torn, pillows ripped up and tossed about the room, the TV overturned and smashed, lightbulbs broken. It looked like the aftermath of a giant temper tantrum.

The next room was orderly and neat under its layer of dust. Right in the center was one large king-sized bed. Diana and Gus both blushed at the sight of it.

"I think we can find a better room," she said hurriedly, and shut the door again.

A few doors down, they found a room that seemed a little less dusty than the others. To their relief, it contained two queen beds.

"Great," Diana said.

"Yeah," said Gus.

"It's perfect," she said.

"Right," said Gus. They both paused in the doorway.

"I'll go see if there are any clean sheets in a cupboard

somewhere," Diana said, "while you, um, wash up, or something." She backed away and took off down the hallway.

Gus dropped his bag inside and looked around. He wandered into the faded, fluorescent-lit bathroom and used a hand towel to clear a space in the dusty mirror. He looked tired. His glasses were crooked, and his hair was rioting every which way. He also looked older, like he had suddenly become an adult in the last day and a half, although he certainly didn't feel any more mature. In fact, he still felt ill, like something was boiling inside him. He rubbed his face vigorously and splashed water on it, but he was too exhausted to do more than that.

By the time Diana came back upstairs, he was fast asleep on top of one of the beds.

She closed the door softly behind her and arrayed her "purchases" on the desktop—things she'd managed to find in the storage/linen closets and the small, virtually empty drugstore downstairs. Gus didn't stir, even when she accidentally dropped the toothbrushes.

She hesitated, then picked up his bag and slid it over to her bed. Surely he wouldn't mind if she borrowed something to sleep in. Tomorrow perhaps they could stop somewhere and find her some clothes of her own. But in the meanwhile, one of his oversized T-shirts (advertising a science fiction movie she'd never heard of) would have to do.

Diana watched Gus sleep for a minute. He looked like a complete stranger without his glasses on, his fidgety shyness stilled into tranquility. *He is a complete stranger,* she reminded herself. *You don't know anything about him.*

Except that he looked safe and reliable, like the only familiar thing in a sea of confusion.

But that was ridiculous. Doug would be appalled at this friendship with a nobody fan. Staying in a hotel with someone she'd just met! The stories in the tabloids! She could hear his high-pitched yap scolding her about it, and she lay down and buried her head in one of the pillows to block it out.

Perhaps things would make more sense in the morning.

Maybe she would wake up and everything would be back to normal.

MEXICO

If the apocalypse were coming tomorrow, some people would fight it. Some people would cry. Some people would lie down and give up.

And some people would party.

Apparently, Tigre discovered, they would do it in Mexico.

Tigre followed Honk over a ridge of sand and there, laid out before them, was the strangest and yet most normal sight he'd seen since leaving school two days ago.

All along the beach, brightly colored umbrellas bloomed, reminding him of the pill bottles lined up in his mother's bathroom cabinet. Farther back, at the tree line, was a giant resort complex, glittering windows reflecting the sea, aquamarine pools set into artificial shapes.

And everywhere there were people—lying under umbrellas, splashing through the waves, sitting on the edges of the pools, smoking. On the surface, it looked like an ordinary day at an ordinary beach resort.

Until you looked more carefully at the people.

Like Honk, there was something not quite right about them. Their skin was leathery, orange, pulled, pressed, and peeled in a hundred different ways. All of their eyes were just a bit too wide; their hair was just a bit too blond.

As Tigre and Honk slid through the sand down the hill, a few of those eyes turned toward them, and then more and more. By the time they reached the edge of the umbrella area, a small group had gathered to stare.

"That is fantastic work!" said one woman with gigantic puffy lips. "Where did you *come* from?" She reached out and poked one of Tigre's arms, then whistled, or tried to until her lips got in the way.

"Get Forever," Honk said, beaming. "We have a new youngerman."

"Awesome," said one of the men, whose hair was long and stringy and reddish. He galloped away toward the resort.

"And some free-mind for our guest!" Honk bellowed after him. "Only the best!" He turned to Tigre and grinned. "Hey, that rhymed. Come on, take a load off, you got your pick of chairs because Rudy and Zappi and Pink all kicked it this month and nobody wanted any of theirs." He ushered Tigre into one of the lounge chairs under a green-and-white-striped umbrella.

"Who are you people?" Tigre said. "What is this place?"

"We're the ones you've been looking for, man," Honk said. "This is the holy center of Forever Youngdom. This is where the grand pooh-bah lives, where all the free-mind is handed out, where all the doctors are trained. Yours must have come through here at some point. Did he send you to us? Where are you traveling from?"

"Santiago," Tigre said. "In Chile."

The crowd's stares ranged from incredulous to hostile.

"Whooooooa," said a lanky man with a Michael Jackson nose. "It is not cool to lie to us, friend. This is a moral community."

"I'm not lying," Tigre protested. "I woke up a few days ago and everyone was gone. I have no idea what's happening."

"Ahhhhh," several of them said simultaneously, nodding like that sounded familiar.

"Yeah," Honk said, wagging his head, "I've had some pretty bad free-mind experiences myself. It's like the whole world goes away, man. That's the point, right? You need the good stuff; it doesn't mess with you so much."

"There's no point in killing ourselves," said Puffy Lips. "Since we are the last generation and all."

"Skate," said a voice that was pleasant and grandmotherly, but sent chills up and down Tigre's spine. "You know we don't talk about that."

Tigre swiveled around on the plastic slats to see a new woman standing behind him, dressed from head to toe in sky blue robes that matched her luminous eyes. Her hair was a dark, warm brown and cut in a short bob, and her skin was several shades paler than everyone else's. She looked almost normal, except that her face was smooth and completely expressionless. A man stood behind her holding a large white parasol over her head.

"Sorry, Forever," Puffy Lips said, dropping to her knees and wincing as she did. "My bad."

Forever's eyes shifted to Tigre and she smiled at him without showing her teeth, barely moving the corners of her mouth. Tigre was suddenly uncomfortably aware that he'd been wearing the same clothes for two days. He probably smelled like a racehorse.

"So this is our guest. I see why everyone is so excited."

"We want his doctor!" said Michael Jackson Nose. "Whoever he is, wherever he works, we should get him here!"

"Perhaps our visitor can be persuaded to share his secret with us," Forever said. "Come inside for some refreshments." She moved her arm in a long, slow gesture toward the resort, then turned and started to glide away up the beach, without waiting to see if he would follow.

Tigre looked at Honk, who grinned and bobbed a few times. "I knew she'd like you, man. Come on."

Forever's building was the closest to the beach, with a view of the sparkling Gulf of Mexico out the tall glass windows. As they entered, Tigre noticed that she stayed in the far corners of the room, avoiding the sunshine, and placed him and Honk on a low white couch where she could face them without the sun getting in her eyes. He sat down gingerly, wishing his jeans weren't so fish-smelling and crusted with salt from the ocean.

Forever seated herself daintily on a large rubber exercise ball. She sat perfectly upright, back straight and head raised, staring at them. Tigre was starting to feel really unsettled by the blank look on her face. He couldn't tell how she felt at all; she could have been ecstatic, furious, scheming, bored, or despairing, but not a clue appeared on her pale face.

Honk started twisting around the moment he sat down, peering eagerly at the doors.

"Is something wrong, Honk?" Forever inquired, keeping her eyes on Tigre.

"No, ma'am, you just said something about refreshments—didn't you?"

She inclined her head slightly and a woman with a wrinkled tattoo of Chinese characters on her shoulder appeared through a bead curtain carrying a tray of drinks and skewers of meat.

"Of course. I hope you will partake as well, Mister . . . ?"

"Montenegro," Tigre said. "Please, call me Tigre."

"Ha!" Honk brayed, as if he'd forgotten that Tigre had introduced himself back on the beach. "That's a funny name, dude!"

Tigre restrained himself. "It's Spanish for 'tiger.' It's a nickname." Claudia had started calling him that because of the way all the wild cats in their neighborhood adored him. He only had to walk outside, and they'd run up purring and launch themselves at his legs. Tigre counted himself lucky that his sister had been generous enough to pick the word for tiger, as, knowing her, she could easily have chosen the word for "cat food" instead. But he decided not to explain all that. He took a few of the skewers and discovered that the meat had an odd smoky herbal flavor to it, but he was too hungry to care.

"This is liquid free-mind," Honk said, grabbing one of the glasses. "You'll love it, man. Keeps you sharp, you know? Keeps you connected to the *universe*. Forever has the best stuff around."

Tigre could smell the alcohol as if it were rising in waves off the tray.

"That's okay," he said. "I don't drink."

The serving woman turned and gave him an astonished look. Honk's jaw dropped. Even Forever's eyebrows twitched a little bit.

"Why not?" Forever asked.

"Well, for one thing, I'm not old enough," Tigre said.

Honk burst into laughter. "Haw haw haw," he cried. "That's a good one, man! Way to play the part! I love it!"

Forever just stared at him. Tigre shifted uncomfortably in his seat.

"Nella," Forever said, "please take Honk downstairs and let him choose a bottle from my cellar."

"Rockin'!" Honk said, leaping to his feet. "Thanks very much, Forever. That's real sweet. Hey, dude, I'll catch you later. Party tonight on the beach, man! We'll build a bonfire! It'll be awesome! Cool! Terrific!" He was still hollering synonyms for "awesome" as his voice faded away down the hall.

Tigre was left alone, facing Forever, and now that Honk wasn't here to balance him out, he felt like he was sinking into the enveloping softness of the couch. The long hours of traveling on Quetzie's back sank in, and exhaustion hit him hard.

"Here," Forever said, leaning forward and nudging a glass toward him. "Take mine. It's just lemonade."

"It is?" Tigre sniffed it, and she seemed to be telling the truth. "Why weren't you having—" He waved a hand at the alcoholic drinks, uncertain about the name "free-mind."

"Alcohol and drugs are bad for your skin," she said. "Not to mention your internal organs. They age you faster than anything else. I tried telling these fools that at first, but no one believed me, or at least, no one cared to give up the one thing that helped them forget, and now it's too late for them to bother quitting anyway. Same with the sunlight." Another slow gesture toward the window. Tigre took a sip of the lemonade, which was sweet in a minty way. "It causes wrinkles and skin cancer and other outward signs of aging. But try convincing the 'last generation' to stay out of the sun. None of them has any self-discipline." She tilted her head very slightly to the left. "But surely you know all this."

Tigre shook his head. "No, ma'am." When she didn't react, he added: "But it sounds like good advice."

She folded her hands in her lap and watched him take another sip of the lemonade. She reminded him of a small garden snake the clinic had rescued from someone's porch two years ago. In contrast to the friendly dogs and cats they worked with every day, the snake was cold, and silent, and inscrutable, and mostly just stared at them through the glass like it was planning something.

Forever leaned forward.

"Tigre, why do you think I look like I do, and everyone else here does not?"

"To be honest with you," Tigre said, "I have no idea what's wrong with those people out there. I don't mean to be rude, but they seem kind of deranged."

"Yes." Something flickered in her eyes. "They are

imperfect followers of my philosophy. My husband and I are the only true forever youngermen, and even he would not have done so well without me watching him carefully."

"I don't understand," Tigre said. "Why are they like that?"

"They're trying to cling to their youth, but they never understood what it really takes to stay young. They think it's about being blonder, more tan, sucking out all the fat. They don't realize it's about watching what you eat, what you do, how you move, how you look, every second of the day. They spend their money on surgeons and chemicals to keep themselves as they remember being, when we were all golden and carefree. They spend their days high on whatever the latest drug is, so they don't have to think about being the last people on Earth."

Tigre felt a chill run down his spine.

"The—last people on Earth?" he said.

"You really don't know," she said softly. "Tigre, how old do you think I am?"

He stared at her, taken aback. Perhaps she was as crazy as the rest of them. He had to play along, but he couldn't begin to guess how old she was. She was one of those ambiguous-looking people, and besides, he'd never been a good guesser. He finished the rest of his lemonade, trying to stall as he searched for an answer.

Maybe she was forty? She could be forty-five, about his mom's age. But women liked it when you guessed that they were younger than they really were. He'd picked that up from conversations in the waiting room at the veterinary clinic. So he should guess low.

"Thirty-two?" he hazarded.

"Hmmm," she said. "That's quite charming. And how old are you?"

Tigre hoped this wasn't going to a really creepy place. "I'm seventeen."

"You really are, aren't you?" she murmured. "What a marvel."

A clatter from the next room made him jump.

"Way?" Forever called. For the first time he saw a real, though unidentifiable, emotion move briefly across her face. She got up and crossed to the curtain, lifting it aside. "Come on out and meet our guest, dear."

A man appeared beside her, clutching the door frame for support. He looked a bit like Forever—same pale skin, same dark brown hair, same bright blue eyes. But his face was contorted in agony and he was half bent over, as if trying to contain the pain in one place. Forever smoothed her hand across his forehead gently, then again a little more firmly, as if trying to press out the wrinkles.

"Stop it," he spat. "I can't help frowning and I don't want to."

"My husband, Always," Forever said as if he hadn't spoken. The man groaned and hobbled over to an armchair, collapsing into it. Forever followed him and perched on the arm, continuing to stroke his forehead until he leaned back and closed his eyes, letting his face fall into repose.

"He is not well," Forever explained to Tigre, expressionless. "But we will find a way to make him better again."

"I'd rather you just let me die!" Always opened his eyes and snarled. "If you had ever experienced a moment of pain in your life, you might understand what I'm going through here."

"I have experienced pain, Way," Forever said calmly. "I have simply never let it control me."

"If you think for one second that I have any control over this—" His face was turning red.

"Don't get yourself excited, Way. You know it's bad for your heart."

He fell back in the chair, closing his eyes again with a defeated sigh. "It's like arguing with the moon."

Tigre was starting to feel a bit woozy. The strangeness of the situation, the comfort of the couch, and his general exhaustion were wearing him down, and he felt his eyes drooping. But the last thing he wanted was to fall asleep and leave himself in the hands of these nut jobs.

He noticed Forever watching him keenly.

"I'm sorry," he said, trying to push himself up. "I should get some fresh air, walk around a bit." His legs gave out and he landed back on the cushions. That was unsettling. He was normally only this tired after one of his running blackouts.

"Nonsense, dear," Forever said. "You should rest for a little while. We're having a big party in your honor tonight, didn't you hear?"

She was starting to swim in and out. "I have to—get back—Quetzie—" he mumbled. But why fight it? He was tired . . . might as well give in and sleep . . . so tired. . . .

"I'm glad I thought to have Nella do the lemonade, too, just in case," Forever said conversationally to her husband, as if Tigre weren't there. "Way, darling, pay attention. I want you to meet your new liver."

Those were the last words Tigre heard before everything went black.

NEVADA

Diana felt herself floating, and knew she was having the dream again. She struggled against it for a moment, but it pulled her down, relentlessly, like it had every time she'd fallen asleep since the earthquake. It was the same dream she'd been having for a year, and she used to look forward to it, but the end of the world had changed it in ways she wasn't sure she liked.

Like this: here she was in a familiar-looking park. Trees and grass stretched around her, but it was still a park, only a park—she could see buildings all around the edges, like giant spectators, watching her.

In her earlier dreams, this used to be a forest, untouched and alone. Once or twice it had been a desert, but that hadn't worried her like this park did. At least the desert was wild. The desert and the forest represented freedom. These buildings made her worry about who might see her, what they would think, her reputation, her career, everything she wanted to escape. She felt trapped and claustrophobic.

But here he came, right on schedule, gliding across the grass toward her as if he were on airborne roller skates. She used to feel that graceful too, in this dream, but now she felt awkwardly self-conscious. He seemed to move on sunbeams, skimming lightly through the air like he had a host of clouds behind him for an entourage.

Her golden stranger.

"I wait for you," he whispered.

"You say that as if you're real," she replied softly.

"I have always been real."

"Maybe you shouldn't be."

"You are coming to me." He took her hands and started dancing her in a circle to music only he could hear.

"I don't even know where I'm going."

"I know where you're going, Venus."

She stiffened in his arms and pulled back. He studied her face, his intent brown eyes familiar and foreign at the same time.

"That's not my name," she said.

"It's one of them." He shrugged, too casual.

"You've never called me that before." He'd never called her anything before, and she liked it that way.

"Things are changing, Venus. Haven't you noticed? Our time is coming."

"Stop calling me that." She stepped away from him, and he let his arms drop to his sides. A ghost of a smile flitted over his face.

"You can't deny her. She's part of you too."

"She's not really me. I thought you understood."

"Shhhh. We'll be together soon, Venus." He reached for her again, and she moved back another step.

"It's me or Venus. You can't have both." She turned and started walking across the grass.

"We'll see about that," he called after her.

The grass brushed against her feet, dissolving into mist as she walked.

For the last year, Diana had looked forward to being with this mystery "guy of her dreams" at night. He was tall and handsome and confident and charming . . . but now something was different. Not just about the dream—about her. When she was dancing with him, she felt like he was a little *too* confident, a little *too* charming.

She wished he would occasionally shrug and look away with a shy smile. She wished he wore glasses and fiddled with them when he was nervous. She wished he made her laugh and took her offbeat ramblings seriously. She wished he cared about her music.

Basically, she wished he were Gus.

She could never hook up with Gus in real life, but that's where he was, while her "dream guy" lived only in her dreams.

It was just as well; she couldn't be romantically involved with either of them, real or not. She shouldn't even think about this. It was time to wake up.

Diana blinked slowly, lifting up and out of the park, the mist, the dream world. The motel room was filled with sunlight. Gus was still asleep on the other queen-sized bed, tossing restlessly from side to side with strange sounds coming from deep in his throat. Diana sat up and stretched, wondering if she should wake him.

Let him sleep. Once he's awake, everything becomes complicated again.

I like him awake. And I want someone to talk to. Besides, he might be having a nightmare.

"Gus?" she said tentatively, reaching out and touching his shoulder.

"NO!" he yelled, rocketing out of sleep so suddenly

that she shrieked and would have fled across the room, except that his hand shot out and seized her arm with a grip of steel. A blast of heat poured through her. Gus's eyes opened and something flickered in them . . . something not Gus at all.

Gus blinked, his nightmare fading, but the emotions still strong within him. He realized with a start that he was sitting up in bed, gripping one of Diana's arms as she half knelt beside him. Her eyes were shocked, and she looked like she had just woken up herself. She was wearing one of his T-shirts over her leather pants.

Gus struggled to control the anger still surging inside him. Where had this come from? He'd always had really boring dreams, about school supplies and being late—never anything that had affected him this strongly. The violent, sick feeling in his chest was still there, although it ebbed to a dull roar as he held her arm and breathed deeply.

"What is *wrong* with you?" Diana exclaimed, shoving his hands away. She started to stand up, but he took her hand and stopped her.

"Wait," he said, and something about his expression made her pause. She looked down at him as he closed his eyes and shook his head. "I'm sorry. It was just a dream." He turned her arm over and brushed his fingers over the spot he had been clutching. "I hope it won't bruise," he said contritely.

She let him hold her arm a little longer, liking the sensation of his hands on her skin, but knowing she shouldn't encourage anything.

Finally she pulled back and stood up, rubbing her forearms. "Well," she said ruefully. "I never thought I'd meet anyone who's scarier in the morning than I am." She smiled at him.

"That's never happened to me before," Gus said, rubbing his face. "Although I've never exactly been a morning person."

"To be honest, I suspect it's a little later than morning," Diana said, with a gesture toward the window. The sun peeking through the curtains was very bright and seemed high in the sky. They had probably slept past noon. Or at least, he had. He looked back at Diana.

"Have you been up for a while?" he asked. He was alarmed at the idea of her watching him sleep. Did he snore? What if he looked totally stupid, or drooled or something? Not everyone could look perfect even in their sleep, the way she did.

"Nope," she said. "I guess my brain didn't think the end of the world was reason enough to wake me." She hopped back onto her bed, still keeping a wary eye on him. "I woke up, I don't know, a few minutes ago, and I noticed you were sort of shaking and . . ." She trailed off and cocked her head at him.

"And what?"

"And sort of . . . growling. And then you started flailing around, and I figured it was a nightmare, so I should wake you up." She touched her arm gingerly. "I didn't realize you were quite so strong."

He gave her a repentant look. "I do a lot of heavy lifting in the theater. I'm really really sorry."

"No worries." She shrugged. "I had some pretty weird

dreams last night too." *That's an understatement,* she thought. He looked at her sharply. Let him wonder; there was no way she was telling him about her golden stranger. The magazines would have a heyday psychoanalyzing *that.*

Well, time to deal with the reality of their situation. She brought over one of the maps she'd been looking at the night before.

"I think I've figured out the best route to where we're going, assuming nothing major has changed since these maps were left downstairs."

Gus sighed dramatically. "Can't a guy have a chance to wake up before he has to talk roads?"

"Sure, of course. I'd just like to get going, you know— it could take us days to get to Kansas." She fidgeted restlessly with the corner of the map. "I know; I can go look for breakfast while you get dressed." She jumped up, pulled on her boots, and was out the door while he was still hunting for his glasses.

Gus yawned, threw off the covers, and frowned at his reflection in the mirror. Okay. Shower. Maybe that would help him feel less ill. She was wearing his spare T-shirt, so he'd need a new one from the car. He hunted around a bit until he found the car keys, then headed down to the parking lot.

As he emerged into the bright midday sunlight, blinking rapidly, he noticed the stillness again. No cars honking. No people talking. He couldn't even hear any birds. It was just . . . quiet.

And yet, as he headed across the pavement to the car,

he had a sudden intense feeling that he was being watched. He paused and looked around.

"Hello?" he called hesitantly. No response. "Diana?"

Silence.

"Ohhhkay," he muttered to himself, unlocking the trunk.

EEEEEEEEEEEEEEEIIIIIIIIIIIIIIIIIIIII-IYYYYYYYYYAAA!

An earsplitting screech suddenly ripped through the sky. Gus jumped, barking his shins on the car and crashing to the ground a split second before a huge, dazzling shape swooped through the space where he had just been. With a frightened yell, Gus scrambled away as the monster shot up and veered around for another try. It gleamed in the light, almost blinding him, but what he could see looked like some sort of giant pterodactyl made of ice. It was the size of a refrigerator and about as menacing as a refrigerator would be if it were plummeting from the sky at your head.

Gus zigzagged through the abandoned lot. He'd have to circle around, maybe find another entrance. The pterodactyl shrieked angrily and folded itself into a dive straight at him.

"GUS!" He glanced over his shoulder and threw himself to the ground as the monster narrowly missed once again.

"Diana, get out of here!" She ignored him, racing across the parking lot toward them. "Go back! Get inside!" If anything happened to her, he'd never forgive himself.

As she ran, she reached into the plastic bag she was carrying, pulling something out and lobbing it at the creature with impressive aim. It shied away from the missile, cawing and hissing.

"Let's go!" Diana cried, pulling Gus to his feet. They turned to run for the door, but the monster landed to block their way, chattering its glassy teeth. Its eyes glowed the same phosphorescent purple color of the glass insect creatures that had chased them in Los Angeles. It hissed again and shuffled toward them, crystal claws glittering menacingly.

"Okay, new plan," she said. "We'll split up and distract it, and try to get around it that way." Without waiting for his response, she shoved him to the right and turned to run left.

The crystal creature lifted off into the sky, spun, and headed directly for Gus.

Fabulous, he thought, *time to be a hero. Lucky me.*

All the rage left over from his dream came roaring back along with the volcanic pain and he abruptly stopped in the middle of the parking lot, facing the pterodactyl. He would not be chased around by this glass thing. He would fight to stay alive, or he would die so Diana could live.

EEEEEEEEEEEEEEEIIIIIIIIIIIIIIIIIIIII-IYYYYYYYYYAAA!

Diana looked over her shoulder and saw the monster circling around to come at Gus again, who was for some lunatic reason now standing still. *That is so not the plan!* She skidded to a stop and raced back.

"Gus, *run,* you idiot!" she yelled.

He bellowed something unintelligible at the creature, puffing up like an angry cobra, but this had no apparent effect. The monster was heading straight for him, and there was no way Diana could get there in time.

"*GUS!*" she screamed.

At the last minute, Gus leaped out of the way, but the pterodactyl flung open its mouth and a sharp ridge of serrated, sparking teeth sliced across Gus's back as he rolled away. It felt like a line of fire seared across his skin, like someone was starting to saw him in two. He yelped in pain and tried to get to his knees, but now electric shocks seemed to be shooting out of the cut and paralyzing him in place. He was still pulsing with anger, but it didn't help make him stronger.

"Hey!" Diana yelled at the pterodactyl, running up alongside Gus. "There are *two* of us here, you know!"

It continued circling as if it hadn't heard her.

"Are you *ignoring* me, you transparent evolutionary leftover?" She reached into her bag again. "*Nobody* ignores me!" She hurled the object in her hand with all her strength just as the monster swooped at Gus once more. The missile crashed into the side of the creature's head with a splintering sound, and a flash of deep purple electricity surged through the glass. The monster shrieked again, a furious, agonized noise, and swerved away, gliding unsteadily.

Diana grabbed Gus's hand and yanked him to his feet, throwing one of his arms over her shoulder and practically dragging him back to the motel. They staggered through the motel doors and kept running past the lobby and up the stairs. As they rounded the bend, they heard a furious pounding behind them, like blocks of ice ramming into a glass door.

"That should buy us a minute," Diana said. "If we can get to our room, it might give up looking for us, with all these rooms to choose from."

"Sure," Gus agreed, concentrating on keeping his legs moving despite the wild arcs of pain leaping across his back. They skidded into their room and slammed the door, bolting it shut. There they waited, breathing as quietly as possible, leaning against the door and listening for sounds of pursuit.

Silence. Even the pounding had stopped.

Gus and Diana exchanged shaken looks.

"That was kinda unpleasant," she said.

"I'll say," Gus replied. "Let's keep the curtains closed."

"Agreed." His knees buckled, and she jumped forward to catch him and support him over to the bed. "Gus, what were you thinking?"

"I was protecting you," he mumbled, gingerly lying down on his side.

"Gus," she said, sounding exasperated. "It wasn't even attacking me! That thing might have killed you, and then where would I be? Stranded in a roadside motel, maybe the last person left on earth. I'd have had to teach myself to drive. And I wouldn't have anyone to talk to." She touched his shoulder lightly, and he flinched. "I can take care of myself, Gus. I'd appreciate it if you'd stay alive."

His whole body was shaking, and he wondered if he was going into shock. "Something's h-happening to me," he managed through chattering teeth. "I feel s-sick and I k-keep wanting to attack things. That's n-not me."

Diana was holding his hand in both of hers, watching him worriedly. The warmth she normally felt emanating from him seemed to be fading.

"Gus, you need medical help. I don't know anything about that stuff."

"I'll be—be fine," he choked out.

"I'm taking off your shirt," she said, dropping his hand. She lifted the fabric of his T-shirt, which was slashed nearly in half and already soaked with blood, and peeled it slowly away from his back. Gus scrunched his eyes shut, an expression of agony crossing his face. He lifted his chest just enough for her to tug the shirt over his head and arms, and then, with a small sound of pain, he passed out.

Oh God, Diana thought. Blood was seeping from the wound, which slashed diagonally across his back from the lower left hip to the bottom of his right shoulder blade, where she noticed he had a tattoo, which surprised her. Small blue sparks of lightning jumped around the edges of the cut, giving his back a weird glow like the black light scenes in her "Rule the World" music video.

She didn't even know where to begin. Maybe if he'd been a car, she could have fixed him, but this. . . .

I guess I should wash it, right? she thought, climbing to her feet and heading for the bathroom. She soaked a washcloth in cool water and brought it back to the bed, kneeling next to Gus.

But as she leaned over to apply it to the wound . . .

No!

Diana jumped, nearly dropping the washcloth.

Don't.

A voice was speaking in her head.

This wasn't like the arguments her brain was always having with itself. And it wasn't the voice that had been commanding her to go east, either, although it was close to that . . . but subtler, like it was whispering where the other was shouting. One voice in her head was bad enough, but two—were they connected?

"Who's there?" she whispered.

DON'T SPEAK. PRETEND TO BE HAVING SECOND THOUGHTS.

She sat for a moment, waiting for something else to happen. *Any other people in my head that would like to share their opinions?* At length she shook her head and leaned toward Gus again.

"I'm sure I'm supposed to clean it," she said out loud, in case it was still listening.

THAT'S TRUE OF MOST WOUNDS.

She stopped.

BUT THIS ONE CONTAINS THE SEA-COLORED LIGHTNING-FIRE.

Diana looked down at Gus's back. Lightning—was the voice talking about electricity?

"Oh," she said, realizing. "Water and electricity—oh my God." She scrambled back, moving the wet washcloth as far from Gus as possible. "I nearly electrocuted him!"

There was no response. Diana felt like crying. She didn't know what to do with a normal cut, let alone one inflicted by a giant glass bird and infected with electricity. She pushed back her hair and rubbed her forehead, breathing deeply.

DO NOT REACT TO MY VOICE. FOLLOW MY INSTRUCTIONS, BUT DO SO AS IF YOU ARE COMING UP WITH EVERYTHING YOURSELF.

Am I being watched? Diana tried thinking as loud as she

could. *Who are we hiding from? How do I know I can trust you?* But either the telepathy thing did not work both ways, or her mysterious helper chose not to answer.

YOU WILL NEED DRY TOWELS. A NEEDLE AND THREAD. WIRES. AND SOMETHING TO CONSUME THE LIGHTNING-FIRE.

Diana thought through the list as she collected all the towels in the bathroom. There were a couple of sewing kits in the motel supplies she had brought upstairs last night. As for wires . . . she looked around the bathroom and spotted a hair dryer hooked into the wall. Perhaps she could dismantle that.

And then—something to consume the electricity?

She piled most of the towels at the bottom of the bed and took one over to Gus, whose breathing was getting shallower. Carefully she pressed the towel against the wound, and a dark spreading red stain instantly soaked through the white terrycloth. Wincing, she looked up and her eyes fell on the bedside table, which contained a clock radio and a desk lamp.

"Maybe I can drain the electricity into one of those," she murmured, hoping her mysterious helper was listening.

YES. THEY WILL DO. NOW LISTEN.

NEW YORK CITY

It was the shrieking that finally drove Kali outside again.

She wasn't sure how much longer she could have stayed in bed anyway—her granola bar supply was running low and she needed more sugar for the tea she was chain drinking. Plus she was getting restless, now that her arm had switched from hurting to itching. All she'd done for two days was lie in bed and concentrate on the pain, imagining the muscles and bones knitting together neatly and smoothly. Maybe she was delusional for thinking this had an effect; perhaps it would have healed just as well on its own. But when she woke up on the fifth morning after everyone disappeared, she could finally clench her fingers into a fist again, and it made her want to get up and punch somebody.

Then the shrieking had started. *EEEEEEEEEE EEEEEEEEEEEEEEEEEEEEEEEEEEEEEEEE EEEEEEEEEEEEEEEEEEEEEEEEE* like the world's loudest, most annoying smoke alarm. She could tell it wasn't human; there was an edge of mechanical whine to it that made her eyeballs hurt, and it went on far longer than any person could have lasted.

At first she tried to bury her head under her pillows, but after about ten incessant, ear-shattering minutes, she threw off the covers, flung open the window, and began shouting obscenities. People in her part of Brooklyn did this all time, but she guessed it was a first for the Upper West Side.

The largest, airplane-sized creature was zooming overhead, followed by a V-shaped formation of the smaller crystal pterodactyls. Kali wondered if anyone had bothered to give a name to groups of crystal hunters—like a pride of lions or a gaggle of geese or an exaltation of larks. If it were up to her, she'd call them an aggravation of glass pterodactyls, and then she'd exterminate the crap out of them.

This seemed to be a ritual of some sort: the boss would

shriek *EEEEEEEEEEE* and then the rest of the aggravation would chorus *EEEEEEEEEE* and then the boss would loop around to fly back in the other direction and shriek again *EEEEEEEEEEE* and then the others would follow suit *EEEEEEEEEE* and it reminded Kali of Josephine's Girl Scout troop singing never-ending rounds of "Row, Row, Row Your Boat" in the living room, only Kali felt much less guilty about wanting to kill the pterodactyls.

She slammed the window shut and stomped off to take a shower, which at least muffled the noise a bit. By the time she returned to the bedroom, wringing out her hair like a rope, the aggravation had moved farther downtown and was circling over a different area. Kali decided that the shrieking would be easier to tolerate if she were at least out doing something, rather than trapped in here with nothing to do but listen. And the sun was climbing up the sky, so all the whisperers should be underground. She had the city to herself, essentially.

Should she try to get to Brooklyn again? Now that her arm was healed, she felt more than strong enough to take on the underground tunnels or the insects. But would it do any good to go back to her house now? If she forced herself to face the truth, she knew—her whole family would be long gone.

She realized, with a weird flicker of emotion that was both fear and excitement, that all her responsibilities had vanished. She was really free for the first time in her whole life—free of work, free of family, free of the hordes of humanity she hated so much. *Just like you always wanted. Suspicious, isn't it?*

Not like this. I didn't mean for it to be like this. I would never have done this . . .

. . . intentionally.

Kali banged open the apartment door and took the stairs down two at a time, trying to shut her brain up with action. What she needed was more information. If she could find out how all of this had happened, she could prove that it wasn't her fault. Surely the world was perfectly capable of screwing itself up without her.

There was no more Internet, so old-fashioned methods would be necessary. She'd start at the public library, the big one on Forty-second Street that she'd always wanted to spend time in, if she'd ever had any spare time. She liked the smell of books and the peace of imposed quiet. Nobody needed the records anymore, so if she found any articles, she could take them with her. Maybe she should put them in her Notebook of Strange Events . . . but that would mean she agreed that this *was* her fault . . . so maybe she'd keep them separate for now.

Kali swung herself over the wall into Central Park, which was no longer the manicured, open park she remembered. The Ramble, for instance, was normally a labyrinth of paths through wooded, hilly terrain, which Kali had sometimes let herself get lost in when people were driving her crazy. But now it was an overgrown thicket of brambles, branches obscuring the closest entrance so you couldn't get in without a machete. Elsewhere there were still some paved paths visible through the trees, but grass was swarming up through cracks in the pavement, and here and there fences had been knocked down by enthusiastic bushes.

She didn't recognize anything until she hit the Great Lawn—a vast oval of grass in the center of the park that was still open to the sky and still as large as she remembered it, although the grass was nearly knee-height now and she wondered if she could figure out from that what time of year it was.

As she crossed the lawn heading east, a faint new sound joined the distant shrieking. Kali paused and scanned the area, sure she couldn't be hearing what she thought she was hearing. It sounded . . . well, it sounded like her Aunt Callista's house, where three small, incorrigible Chihuahuas were constantly freaking out about noises nobody else could hear and intruders nobody else could see. This sounded like the same, high-pitched yapping, only multiplied by ten.

A movement to her left caught her eye and she turned to see what looked like a wave of fur rippling through the grass. As it got closer and the noise grew louder, she realized she was right—it *was* yapping. It was, in fact, a pack of maybe thirty or so small dogs, none taller than the grass, all barking their heads off. At their head was something tiny and white that looked like a Maltese, followed by everything from Yorkshire terrier mixes to miniature poodles, brown and white spanielesque dogs, and a couple that looked related to dachshunds.

Normally Kali was pretty fond of dogs. Normally if she met one with no human attached, for instance waiting outside a store for its owner to return, she would probably stop and say hi to it. But something about this baying pack of fierce little creatures made her think they weren't exactly looking for belly rubs and biscuits. Better safe than turned into puppy kibble. She ran for the trees.

It was lucky she had a fair head start, because even with their short legs, some of the dogs were definitely faster than she was. Kali crashed into the bushes about a bus length in front of them, narrowly avoiding decapitation by a tree branch. She shoved her way through the thicket of leaves, trying to remember how far it was to the street from here. All she could see in front of her was more leaves, more bushes, more . . . was that a wall?

She stopped short, feeling a solid glass wall in front of her. What the heck? The reflections from outside made it impossible to see in. Bushes came all the way up to it and then climbed upward, obscuring the sky above her. She felt like she was stuck in one of her jungle dreams, surrounded by wilderness on all sides, only to find something as crazy as a wall right in the middle of it.

Perhaps she could break through it, but then the dogs would be able to get through, too. Better than that would be a door, a door she could close in their yipping faces. She was already working her way along the wall as she thought this, hearing the sounds of snuffling and scrambling and snarling behind her and feeling more than a little ridiculous at being chased by a herd of Yorkies. Perhaps they'd be friendly if she tried talking to them, but she didn't want to take that chance.

Suddenly she felt a hinge beneath her hands, and then a handle, and she tore at the vines and ivy covering the door until she could yank it open, leap inside, and slam it shut behind her.

Whoa.

She was standing in a quiet stone courtyard, surrounded by marble columns and dotted with sculptures here and there. It was as neat and orderly as a model kitchen and as different from the wilderness outside as toothpaste from tigers. A serene fountain bubbled off to her right and big, square planters full of ivy sat in each corner, while a second floor balcony ran around the top of the room with hallways branching off in all directions.

As the echoes of the door slamming faded away, Kali thought she heard someone whisper "*shhhhhhh,*" and she suddenly recognized where she was:

The Metropolitan Museum of Art.

She had been here once on a school field trip, in seventh grade. Thirty-five bored twelve-year-olds had trailed apathetically through rooms of Impressionists and boring, stodgy American portraits, but Kali had managed to "get lost" briefly, and this sculpture garden was one of the places she had wandered into before an angry parental chaperone had caught her and shepherded her back to the others.

But it was so pristine—so carefully perfect, as if it hadn't been touched by the years of neglect and ruin outside. It looked exactly the way it had when Kali first saw it, down to the ivy pruned back into its planters and the blue sky visible through the glass ceiling overhead.

She moved forward cautiously, hesitant to break the silence. Was there someone else here? Did somebody still take care of the museum? The whisperers didn't seem sane enough, but perhaps this was a strange priority of General Pepper's.

She took the antique wooden staircase to her right and walked along the far side of the balcony. She remembered there being glass cases up here, filled with Tiffany vases and silver spoons. A couple of cases still stood, the glass knocked out of them and their contents missing, but there was no shattered glass on the floor, and the interiors of the cases were swept clean.

Through the doors at the end of the balcony, Kali found herself in a long hallway lined with grandfather clocks. Following a trace of memory she hadn't known was there, she took the next doorway to the right and found herself in the Asian art wing, where painted folding screens and smiling Buddhas glowed under small spotlights in the near darkness.

She was looking at a slab-of-rock fountain perched on a pile of pebbles, the water barely moving enough to be visible, when she glanced up and saw, with a shock that was close to terror, a face staring at her where she had thought there was a mirror.

Kali caught a glimpse of dark hair and startled, almond-shaped eyes, and then the face was gone.

"Hey!" Kali yelled, and winced at how loud her voice sounded in the solemn halls. "Wait," she called more softly, and ran to the side of the fountain—only there was a wall, and she had to run nearly around the whole exhibit before reaching the other side, by which point the person, whoever it was, had vanished.

A door was standing partly ajar at one end of the room. Kali yanked it open and found herself in an upper hallway. Stairs led down to her right and doorways led off in all directions—to the Japanese Zen garden, to South Asian art, back to the American wing. There was no sign that anyone had come through here, or which way they might have gone.

Kali scowled. No way would she chase down someone who didn't want to be found. She knew what *that* was like. So she fought her natural impulse to stay and investigate, and instead headed down the stairs in search of an exit. Perhaps she could come back later and try again when the person might be less startled.

In the Egyptian wing she saw more signs of disruption than upstairs; very few small pieces were left in their cases, and many of the labels that were left behind said the missing things were made of gold. She let herself touch the dark, smooth heads of the sphinxes and wondered what kind of person would think to loot a museum during an apocalypse.

Soon the maze of rooms let her out into the sepulchral quiet of the enormous entrance lobby. The gift shop doors were closed but she could see empty shelves through the glass. A small lamp glowed on top of a circular counter in the center of the hall, where a sign hung that read: INFORMATION.

"Ha-ha," Kali said, idly picking up one of the museum maps. "If only you had any information I actually . . ." Her voice trailed off as she spotted several stacks of papers on the desk behind the counter. They looked like articles clipped from newspapers and magazines, all at least as old and strange looking as the one she'd looked at two days ago, with rubber bands separating the stacks from one another.

She circled the counter and touched the papers warily, afraid they would disintegrate under her fingers, but they were printed on something stronger than paper, like a cross between plastic and fabric. Each pile seemed to be sorted by subject, and most of them covered the catastrophes of the last few decades. One pile was all about the crystal hunters; the top article didn't say where they came from, but it outlined their pack structure, and how each flock had a leader that apparently controlled them—the giant boss hunter pterodactyl, Kali guessed, was the local leader. Another pile was about a company called Eternally Me that offered cyber upgrades for aging humans, and yet another covered mysterious happenings in Africa.

A muffled sneeze came from overhead, and Kali looked up in time to see two dark heads disappearing around the edge of the big staircase. So there were at least two of them.

"Hey, I won't hurt you," she called.

Nothing but echoes.

She looked down at the stacks of articles. This was exactly what she needed.

"Hey," she called again. "Since you won't talk to me, do you mind if I take these?"

Still no response, although she thought she heard whispers.

"I'll bring them back," she said, unzipping her backpack and starting to put the articles inside. "I just need to know what's going on." If the mystery people cared so much about this stuff, they'd come down and talk to her. If not, she'd still get to find some of the answers she was looking for.

Nobody came to stop her before she'd packed away everything on the desk. She felt a twinge of guilt at how empty it looked when she was done, but all this information wasn't doing anyone any good sitting here in the dark.

"Thank you," she called up the stairs. "Maybe we can talk when I bring them back."

She shouldered her backpack and unbolted one of the exit doors that led to the street. With any luck, the shrieking would be over and the wild, small, fluffy dog pack would have retreated back into the woods—although she'd take the long way home, just to be safe.

MEXICO

It had never occurred to Tigre that there might be something more alarming than waking up alone, lost, in the dark, and miles from home—until he woke up alone, lost, in the dark, miles from home, and tied down to a cold, flat surface.

He lay still for a minute, feeling consciousness return slowly, trying to figure out where he was. It felt like wild animals were trying to claw their way out of his head. Some sort of webbing was biting into his arms, and he realized his shirt was gone. His jeans had been replaced with pants that felt softer and looser, and he felt cleaner than he had been before, which didn't cheer him up very much. He didn't want to imagine how that had happened.

Gradually he started noticing details. The surface underneath him was strangely textured—hard, but with a velvety overlay. A lot of smells mixed together in the air: something chemical, like Dr. Harris's operating room, and along with that something like the aftermath of a party, mingled stale beer and sweat. And, very faintly, the salty smell of the ocean.

He also realized that there was someone else in the room with him.

Tigre held his breath, keeping as still as possible. After a minute there was a soft moan, then a sniffling sound from several feet away. Then silence again.

Tigre tried straining against his bonds. He seemed to be pinned down with a mass of netting wound around his whole body and the surface below him. There was no way to break free, although he pulled and twisted and struggled. He gave up on staying quiet, and the other person in the room didn't react to his presence.

Perhaps if he tried to make himself smaller, he could wriggle out from under the netting. Tigre sucked in his breath and rolled to the side. It did seem to work a little—he moved slightly—but not very much.

He gave up and let all his breath out. There wasn't anything he could do. He'd have to lie here and wait to see what they had planned for him. Maybe this was part of their celebration, like the free-mind and the plastic surgery. This was some peculiar colony he'd stumbled into. He wondered why he'd never heard of this cult. They couldn't be that dangerous, could they? They seemed wacked out, but mostly harmless, except maybe for Forever. But Honk would never hurt him—right?

Tigre, you've been drugged and strapped to a table. Does that seem harmless to you?

He wished he'd listened to Quetzie. His heart sank as he realized he must have missed her five-hour deadline. She'd flown away without him, thinking he'd picked these people over her. That thought added a layer of guilt to his regret.

"Hurts," whispered a voice in the dark. "I feel like killing somebody."

Tigre felt a cold shiver run down his body. He tried to will his heart to slow down, his breathing to be quieter. Every sound brought him closer to panic. He wondered if a storm was coming outside, and wished that he had a more useful power, like, say, super-strength, or being invulnerable to kidnapping by freaks.

All at once he heard footsteps—brisk, even footsteps coming closer, clicking on a tile floor. Then there was the sound of a door opening, and a fluorescent light suddenly blazed on overhead. Tigre flinched and slammed his eyes shut.

"Ho, ho, patients," an unfamiliar male voice said. "I love new patients."

"I want this done quickly, Slice." Forever's voice joined it. "Way doesn't have much time."

"You don't often call on my services, Ms. Young," said the first voice, coming closer to Tigre.

"But when I do, I know you can be counted on to be professional, skillful, and above all, discreet," Forever said with a hint of warning in her voice.

"Of course, of course, but I don't think you can possibly—" The voice stopped with a gasp. Tigre desperately wanted to open his eyes and see what was happening, but he was at an advantage as long as they thought he was still unconscious. It was hard to keep pretending, though, when a set of bony fingers starting prodding and pinching at him. He steeled himself to ignore it.

"Hmmm," said the man called Slice. "Most fascinating. Also unbelievable and entirely impossible."

"You see, I told you the truth," Forever said. "He has been sent to us to save Always."

"There could be many uses for one such as this," Slice mused. "It would be a subject worthy of my research. A great study."

"You can do what you like with the rest of him," Forever said. "I'm only interested in the parts Always needs."

Tigre stiffened involuntarily. Parts? He was going to be used for *parts*? Like an old car? How could they do this to him—to anyone?

"Hmmm," Slice said again. The prodding stopped and his voice moved away from Tigre. "Your husband does seem poorly."

"Of course I seem poorly," a third voice spat suddenly from across the room. Tigre realized that Always had been the voice in the dark. "I'm eighty-seven years old, I've had a perfectly miserable life, and now I'm dying of a disease that feels like my insides are being ripped apart by jaguars, and what does my wife do? Tie me to a pool table so she can keep me alive for one more unpleasant, boring day and one more suicide-inducing interaction with her stupid robot face."

"That's the pain talking," Forever said calmly. "It makes him act a bit strangely sometimes. Always, dear, you know the Forever Young philosophy rejects the heresy of robotic upgrades. We don't want any nasty electronic things taking over our bodies like those Eternally Me lunatics, isn't that right, Slice?"

"Agreed," said Slice. "Anyway, if people started going cyber instead of getting plastic surgery, I'd be out of a job! Heh heh heh."

"It was a metaphor, you psychopath," Always snarled. "What I'm trying to say is *let me die already.*"

"I'd better get to work," said Slice. "It sounds like a storm is coming."

"How unexpected," said Forever. "It was so clear this morning. The youngermen will be disappointed to have their bonfire rained out." Her footsteps crossed the room and Tigre felt a cool sea breeze brush over his forehead, as if she had pushed a window open. He could distinctly hear the sound of the ocean. They must still be near the beach. The ocean, and people's voices . . . the normal world, or more normal than this room, anyway . . . he felt a tear slide down his cheek before he could stop it. Right now he would give anything to be back in his hot, stifling English classroom, stuck to a plastic chair.

I don't want to die, he thought.

So what are you going to do about it? argued his brain.

What can *I* do about it? *I'm tied to a pool table and a mad plastic surgeon is preparing to cut me up for spare parts.* He could hear steel instruments clinking together, and it terrified him so much he couldn't keep his eyes shut anymore. He risked a peek and saw that Forever and the man called Slice both had their backs to him.

Slice was small and knobbly and old, with thinning blondish hair. He was wearing a pastel pink lab coat and pale pink rubber gloves, and he was bending over a rolling cart, examining some wicked-looking scalpels. Forever was standing at a window only a few feet away from Tigre, staring out at the night sky. Now that she had pulled aside the curtain, Tigre could see the flicker of a bonfire in the distance.

Tigre rolled his head to the other side and saw that he was in a sort of rec room, filled with pool tables, couches, a TV, a stack of DVDs, and assorted board games. Always was across the room; like Tigre, he was tied down to a pool table with what appeared to be a volleyball net. The man still had an agonized grimace on his face, and he was snarling up at the ceiling.

"You know, Forever, if you gave me a bit more time, I could do this more tidily," Slice said. "There are parts I could take while he was still alive and freeze them, which would make them last longer. If I go straight for the liver, as you asked, it could be quite a waste of the other organs, and you never know who might need them later."

"Something is happening out there," Forever said thoughtfully. "Something new."

Slice paused in his arrangements and looked up, head cocked to listen. "Is that . . . *screaming* I hear?" he asked uneasily.

"Yes," Forever answered. "The pterodolphins must have been attracted by the light of the fire. They don't normally attack in groups like that. I wonder who they will eat this time." She watched for a few more moments, expressionless as ever. Finally she turned back to the surgeon. "Do it now. We cannot risk interruption."

"Wait!" Tigre blurted. "Please, don't do this!"

"Ah, the donor awakes!" Slice exclaimed. "That's quite unfortunate for you, I'm afraid. We don't really have enough anesthetic left to waste on someone who's about to die."

"*Please!*" Tigre begged. "I'm just a kid!"

"Exactly," Forever said. "It's rather astonishing. I would

have so much to ask you, if your internal workings weren't so urgently needed."

"Give me a break," Always growled. "I don't need some loon's liver, Forever. I need to *die*."

Slice brandished a long, thin, curved knife. "I wish I could say this won't hurt much, kid," he said, "but at least it'll be over . . . well, eventually."

"God, I hope this idiot accidentally kills me," Always muttered.

"What if I could tell you the secret to staying young?" Tigre cried, lying desperately. "What if I could tell you about a whole city full of people my age?"

An earsplitting screech tore through the air, sounding like it was right outside the window. Slice jumped nearly a foot in the air and dropped his knife. Before anyone else could react, a hand reached out, grabbed it, and stabbed Slice in the chest.

The surgeon shrieked in surprise and pain. Dumbfounded, Tigre watched Always stand up and wrench the knife out of Slice in a fountain of blood. Slice collapsed to the floor, where the volleyball net lay in pieces. Always must have found a way to escape from it while they were lying there in the dark, and had been pretending to stay trapped until the right moment.

"Oh, Way." Forever sighed. "He was a perfectly good doctor, too. Now I'm going to have to get Saw to fix you, and you know he hasn't been quite right in the head since that pterodolphin bit off his leg."

"You deranged Barbie doll," Always hissed. "I refuse to let you do this to me. I refuse to let you keep me alive against my will." He raised the knife to his neck.

Hey, don't you want to free me first? Tigre thought wildly. *Before slitting your own throat, or whatever you're about to do?* But before he could say anything, there was another loud screech outside the window and a thud as something hit the side of the building.

Tiger boy? a familiar voice suddenly popped into his head. *Are you in there?*

"QUETZIE!" Tigre yelled at the top of his lungs, relief exploding through him. "HELP ME!" He began struggling against his bonds again.

There was a blur of movement and suddenly Forever was across the room, trying to wrestle the knife out of Always's hand. He fought back, and they slipped and slid in the pool of blood, staining the hem of Forever's robes. Her face was still an impassive mask, but all the edges seemed sharper somehow, like an expression was straining to get out.

With a crash, the window, window frame, and some of the wall around it fell into the room. Quetzie's head appeared in the hole.

I think it's time to gooooooo, she burbled. *Those pterodolphins always ruin people's fun. Party pooooooopers.*

"I can't move!" Tigre yelled. "Quetzie, I'm tied down!"

With a few sharp clicks of her beak, Quetzie sliced through the net. Tigre scrambled off the pool table, disentangling himself and thanking heaven he was still wearing his sneakers. He threw his arms as far around Quetzie's neck as he could reach and she swished her tail feathers in a delighted spiral.

It's loooovely to see you, too! she said. *When you didn't come back, I thought perhaps youuuu didn't like me. I nearly kept goooing alone, but I missed you.*

"Of course I like you, Quetzie," Tigre said. "I like you much more than any human I've ever met. I'm so glad you came back for me."

Well, she preened, *I am much more beauuuutiful and uuu-useful than you huumans, aren't I?*

Tigre turned to look at Forever and Always, who were now kneeling in the blood, their hands wrapped around the knife, trying to force it one way or the other with brute strength. Neither of them was paying attention to Tigre or to the large bird that had hopped into their operating theater.

"You're more trustworthy, too," he said. "I'm sorry, Quetzie; I should have listened to you."

Quetzie lowered her bright green head, and Tigre used the pool table to clamber onto her back.

I'm also smarter, she observed. *And funnier. And a better poet. And did I mention more beauuutiful?*

"Yes, you did," Tigre said, lying flat on her back as she carefully edged out of the wreckage. "And you are."

Outside, Quetzie unfurled her tail, flapped her wings once, twice, and with a heavy beating sound and a cloud of sand they rose into the air, which felt heavy with coming rain. She spiraled over the bonfire so he could see it before they left.

Seeee? she burbled. *Pretty!*

Tigre looked down at the roaring fire, around which the horrifying orange figures of Honk and his friends were dancing, singing, smoking, and hooting. Winged, unnatural animal shapes roared and screeched in the shadows around them, darting in to pull screaming people into the darkness and tear them apart.

But the youngermen kept dancing.

SOMEWHERE IN COLORADO

Gus was running, bare feet sure and silent, through the bracken on the forest floor. A low, menacing howl tore through the trees. He leaped over a fallen tree trunk, his body concentrated into motion, energy, a surging life force. The forest was almost dark around him, in that haunted time between day and night where shadows came alive. He felt like a shadow himself, calm inside yet driven forward with a pounding urgency.

He could sense others around him, spread through the trees and fanning out behind, waiting for his signal. They followed him, these others, and he knew they were *his*, his warriors. He felt exultation rush through him and ran even faster, feeling the others speed and turn and weave in response to his every movement. He was seeking something, and they would be there when he found it.

There! Through the trees he glimpsed a foreign light, shining white and unreal in the dusk. He slowed to a lope, keeping himself hidden as he approached. They were there in the clearing: his enemies. He had come to destroy them.

He crouched behind a large fern, eyes bright in the darkness. They were before him: a man and a woman. She had her back to him, but the man was facing in his direction. The light was coming from them: hers a silvery shimmer, his a golden blaze. It was bright enough to dazzle, obscuring their features. But it did not matter. He knew who they were. Anger was building in him now, fighting the stillness inside, ready to take over.

The golden man reached out and took the silver woman's hands in his, pulling her in. She took a step toward him but resisted going any closer, placing one hand lightly on his bare chest and letting out a laugh like sleigh bells. They seemed totally absorbed in each other, oblivious to the darkness, the warriors, the eyes watching them.

Gus tensed, suddenly aware of the wooden spear he clutched, a sharp, cruel-looking whalebone knife lashed to the end. This was the moment. He rose to his feet, hefting the spear, and suddenly the couple looked up and stared straight at him.

The man's eyes were mocking, like he'd known Gus was there all along, and this scene had all been a show for his benefit. The woman's expression was puzzled, as if she had seen him somewhere before and was searching her memory for his name.

Pain and rage sizzled through him as he recognized her.

It was Diana. Diana ensnared by this shining man, Diana so captivated that she didn't know who Gus was.

Fury swelled up from somewhere very deep inside and catapulted him forward, roaring, spear aloft. It was time for action, time for death. The golden stranger pulled Diana close and lifted one hand, palm out, toward Gus, as if to stop him, but Gus thought he saw a flicker of fear in his eyes.

This had happened before. He had come this close and failed. He had tried to save Diana and . . . something had happened . . . something like waking up.

He woke up.

He was lying on his side, on a sleeping bag, facing a soft, gray, fabric-covered surface. There were towels and sheets stuffed all around him, keeping him in place, although the world seemed to be vibrating slightly. He tried to roll over, and the stabbing pain in his back unfolded his memory.

He was not a spear-carrying warrior in a forest. He was an idiot who'd tried to fight a large, toothy, glass bird.

"Ow," he said.

"You're awake!" Diana's voice came from above him, and suddenly the surface under him swerved to the right and came to a stop.

Oh. He was in the backseat of the car.

Which Diana was driving.

She parked in the middle of the highway and knelt in the driver's seat, peering at him over the headrest.

"How do you feel?" she asked.

"Like a monster tried to eat me," he mumbled.

"I'm so glad you're finally awake," she said. "You've been asleep for like a day and a half. We're practically to Kansas already. Are you thirsty?"

"Yes," he said.

She produced a water bottle and his glasses from the front passenger seat and opened her door, coming around to the backseat to help him sit up. As she climbed in next to him, scooting towels aside, he realized with intense embarrassment that he wasn't wearing a shirt. Then again, enough bandages were wrapped around his chest that he hardly needed one.

"Here," Diana said, propping him up against her shoulder and opening the water bottle. "Don't drink it too fast." She unfolded his glasses and gently slid them onto his nose as he fumbled with the bottle.

He let the liquid slide down his throat for a moment before speaking again.

"You fixed me," he said. "I thought you didn't know how."

"I'm a very capable girl, Gus," she said with a wink.

"And you taught yourself to drive." *I guess she really doesn't need me at all.*

"Not very well," she said ruefully. "We're lucky that there aren't any other cars on the road. But I did do one clever thing." She grinned. "I snuck into a Home Depot and found a gasoline siphon pump so I could fill the tank." She poked his thigh, not very hard. "Wasn't that clever of me?"

"Very clever," he agreed. That probably wouldn't have occurred to him before the gas tank ran out. He took another look at her as he drank another swallow of water.

"What on earth are you wearing?" he asked.

"Isn't it ridiculous?" she said, spreading her arms to show off the enormous topaz-blue cotton sweater she had on. He'd probably think it was too warm outside for sweaters, but she was constantly freezing, so she liked wearing sweaters all year long, even back in California.

She'd driven the car right into an abandoned mall so she could keep Gus close by as she searched for something to replace her stupid leather outfit. But it was the strangest mall she'd ever been to. She couldn't find a teen department anywhere, and all the clothes looked like they'd been made by and for old people with no fashion sense whatsoever.

She'd had to settle for a few floppy sweaters and shirts, and two pairs of jeans that were comfortable but would certainly have catapulted her onto *Entertainment Watch's* Fashion Disaster list for the rest of her career, had any of their gurus been around to see her wearing them.

On the plus side, she'd found two sleeping bags and plenty of towels and sheets still in their plastic wrapping. She'd also liberated some toiletries, although she hadn't found any of her usual brands and had had to settle for some odd shampoo that smelled like her grandmother.

"I was worried the movement of the car might hurt you," she said, changing the subject, "but I thought we should get out of that motel before the creepy thing found its way in." *Plus I had to keep going east,* she thought guiltily. The soft voice that had helped her fix up Gus hadn't come back, but the loud one proclaiming *"EAST EAST EAST"* seemed almost constant now.

"How did you get past the creature?"

She shrugged. "It didn't care about me. And I snuck you out while it was dark—I figured it was shut off then, since it didn't seem to notice us arriving."

"Unless it followed us from Los Angeles."

"No, it was sitting up on the roof the whole time. I saw it when we got there."

He gave her an astounded look. "And you didn't feel that that might be worth mentioning? Killer bird monster hanging out over our heads?"

"How was I supposed to know it was one of those things?" she protested. "I didn't see it move at all until you came out of the motel. I thought it was some sort of weird artsy statue. I had no idea it was *alive.* I went in and out a couple of times, and it never bothered me." She paused and thought for a second. "Hey, maybe you offended it."

"I didn't do anything!" he retorted, feeling his strength coming back.

"Maybe it didn't like your hair," she suggested, and started laughing.

"Oh man—" He reached up and felt the tangled mess on his head. He couldn't help grinning back at her. He felt light-headed and giddy, and thoroughly amazed to be alive. "Well, I'm glad you came along with your little hand grenades."

"Hand grenades?" she repeated.

"You know, the weapons you were chucking at that thing. They must have been pretty serious objects to dent its head like that."

"Oh." She looked sheepish. "Ah—actually, those weren't weapons."

"What were they?"

"Breakfast," she confessed, digging a white paper bag up from the floor. "I found a tree out behind the motel." Inside the bag were five apples. Gus's stomach growled loudly the minute he saw them.

"Yes, you may have one," she said, still laughing.

"I bet that thing has never been taken down by produce before," Gus said, accepting an apple. "Catwoman's secret weapon: Red Delicious!"

"Hey, you're not supposed to be making fun of me," Diana protested. "You're supposed to be overcome with gratitude and awe."

"I am," he said.

"Hmmm," she said.

"I *am*," he said, seriously. "Thank you."

"Well, don't make me do it again," she said, deciding not to mention the voice that had helped her. She didn't want to talk about the "go east" message either, in case Gus tried to stop her. It'd be best to keep quiet about both of them, and act like his injury had been no big deal. "Blood is icky. Not to mention your tattoo kind of freaked me out. I didn't think you were a body art kind of guy."

Gus blinked.

"I'm not. I mean—I don't have any tattoos."

"Yeah, you do. On your back, remember?"

They stared at each other for a moment. Confused, Gus reached over his shoulder, then tried to twist around to catch a glimpse of it in the rearview mirror. What was she talking about?

"You really don't know you have a tattoo on your back?" she asked.

"I don't. It must be a scratch or something."

She shook her head. "It's a shape. It's really clear."

"What does it look like?" Gus felt panicked. What kind of weird end-of-the-world phenomenon was this?

"It's kind of a spiral, but not just concentric circles— it's like interwoven circles, you know? I don't know how to describe it. Like waves, maybe? Inside circles?"

Gus leaned his elbows on his knees and propped his head in his hands, trying to breathe normally. This scared him even more than the pterodactyl. A mark on his body that just appeared? The pain in his back was joined by a fizzing wave of anger in his chest, a surge of the sick feeling that had been so quiet when he awoke that he'd hoped it was gone.

"It's like, right *here*," Diana said thoughtfully, reaching out and touching his right shoulder blade. "That's where it starts. And then it spirals in, like this." She drew her finger lightly in wavelike circles across his shoulder, apparently oblivious to the effect of her touch on his bare skin. Gus felt like fainting. He could suddenly feel what she was describing, as clearly as if it were right in front of him—dark green (*how did he know that?*) lines etched into his back, circling ridges that echoed with distant, half-remembered pain as her fingertip brushed them gently. He didn't want her to stop, but as she reached the center, agony shot through him, from his shoulders to the tornado in his chest and then back again, and he flinched before he could stop himself. She jumped back instantly.

"I'm sorry—does it hurt? It looks new."

"It hurts a little, yeah." Gus twisted again to try and see it in the mirror, even though he was sure he knew what it looked like now. Where had he seen that shape before? Somewhere recently ... hadn't he drawn it in the dust on his dresser at home? Why would that be in his head?

"How'd you get such a big tattoo without noticing?" she asked.

"I don't know," he said. "What about you?"

"What about me what?" she said warily.

"Do you have any new tattoos? Maybe it's an effect of the whole end-of-the-world thing. Wouldn't that make sense?"

"Not particularly," she said. "But trust me, I don't have any." *And a good thing, too, or Doug would have kicked my ass.* "Not even on my back," she said quickly, before he could ask.

Gus's face was utterly dismayed. She gave him a sideways, one-armed hug and then pulled back. "Gus, don't worry about it. I'm sure there's a natural explanation. Maybe it was a practical joke that you didn't know about. We don't know that it has anything to do with the end of the world."

Gus rubbed his arms, running through the last few days in his mind. This wasn't natural. If nothing else, he was sure of that.

Over North America

It wasn't that Tigre didn't appreciate the lift. He really did. It would have been impossible on his own. But the journey north from Party Central seemed to take a lot longer than it should have, as if Quetzie was afraid of losing him again, and he couldn't help suspecting that she was dragging it out.

Perhaps it was the all-too-frequent stops for him to eat and rest, scavenging food from deserted cities or overgrown orchards. He took a couple of plain white T-shirts from an American mall, but couldn't find any jeans his size anywhere, so he stuck with the loose dark green pants from the surgery.

Perhaps it was the way she kept taking detours to "show him things," like herds of bizarre grazing creatures with horns like buffalo, shaggy brown feathers, and long whiplash tails, or the hundred lakes in the middle of the American South that he was pretty sure weren't supposed to be there, if he remembered his geography lessons correctly.

Perhaps it was the way she kept avoiding his questions about people.

His patience was starting to wear thin. Lightning crackled in the corners of the sky as they flew, and every time he accidentally conjured a storm, Quetzie insisted on taking shelter to wait it out. Then she would act pointedly unaware of his aggravation, pretending that they were normal storms. And he couldn't bring himself to confront her about it. He didn't want to scare off the one creature he'd found who didn't seem to want to kill him.

As far as he could tell, they were heading northeast in a vague, zigzagging way. He'd never been to the U.S. before, but they flew over something he thought might be the Washington Monument, and sometimes he glimpsed large highway signs for Virginia or Tennessee. The coastline didn't match the maps he remembered, though; there seemed to be more water than there should be.

Finally, about four days after his escape from Party Central, Quetzie spiraled down over an island Tigre recognized from images in movies and on the news: Manhattan. As he finally realized where they were going, he felt a rush of hope—this was where his sister attended law school. Maybe he could find her here! He'd always wanted to visit New York City, although this wasn't how he had pictured arriving. And the city looked different than he'd imagined . . . none of the hustle and bustle, the constant flurry of action and rushing he'd expected. Like Santiago, it was deserted and quiet, the streets vast and empty.

Quetzie circled the skyscrapers, warbling her city poem and flourishing her long tail, as Tigre searched for any sign of life. It was the middle of the day, bright sunlight illuminating the whole city, but he couldn't see anyone anywhere. After about half an hour, Tigre was getting really sick of hearing: *The land where it was cold but is no more. Where the sea has taken back parts of the city and shining giants rule. Where huumans hide and scuttle and cannot leave and all is dark and glittering.*

"Quetzie, are you *sure* there are people here?" he asked.

Of coooourse. I did say they hide and scuttle.

"Yeah, I know," he muttered. "And they're okay people? They're not scary?"

What could be scary about huuuumans? Quetzie said. *If you mean dooo these have knives, then nooo, not like the nooonsense-speakers.*

Tigre sighed. "I guess the best place to start would be Columbia University. I can look for my sister there."

Uuuuuniversity? Where's that?

He realized he had no idea.

Sooo we keep circling, Quetzie said contentedly. *You're nooot in a hurry to leave me, are you?*

"No, no," Tigre said. "Aren't you going to stay?"

Nooooo, tiger boy, I cannoooot. It is dangerous here for neo-quetzals. She waggled her head, nearly shaking Tigre loose. *They dooon't mind me flying throuuugh, but once I land, I will have to gooo immediately.*

"Who doesn't mind?" Tigre said. "The people here?"

Noo, not the people. The not-animals. The coold bad sparkling things. I don't like them. They doon't like me. We mostly keep our distance.

Suddenly Tigre jumped and lunged forward, nearly catapulting off Quetzie's back. Was that a shape moving down there? He craned over and saw a tiny figure moving up the street two blocks away . . . a tiny figure that might be human. Quetzie's words about the danger and not-animals flew straight out of his head. Even after his experience at Party Central, he was still overjoyed at the thought of seeing another person. They couldn't *all* be part of a crazy organ-stealing cult.

"There!" he yelled. "Quetzie, there's somebody!"

All right, Quetzie said, sounding disappointed. They trailed the figure for a couple of blocks. He or she seemed to be walking slowly down the middle of an avenue.

"Can't we land down there?" Tigre said, frustrated. "What if I lose him?"

I shouldn't go so low, but doon't fret, tiger boy, Quetzie said. *I'll drop you at the nearest roooof. Youu can be on the street in no time.*

Tigre breathed a sigh of relief as the neoquetzal drifted down toward a rooftop pool on a tall apartment building. A few blocks to the west, Tigre could see an expanse of green that he assumed was Central Park.

The neoquetzal seemed nervous as soon as she touched down, splashing her wings about and watching the sky.

Well, here you are, in the city of sparkling, glittering bad things and danger but people, yes, huumans here, hiding, skulking, struggling. If you want them, you can find them, althooough why you would want to, I'm not really sure, when you could be traveling with meeeee instead. She dipped her beak in the water and sent it showering in all directions as she spun her tail feathers.

Tigre tried to reach the side of the pool without getting wet, but ended up floundering through the shallow end. He climbed out, shook off the excess water, and ran to the edge of the roof. The figure was still there, only a block away.

I should gooo. Tigre turned as Quetzie started to surge up out of the water.

"Do you really have to?" he said. "Can't you stay even a little while—until I find out if this person wants to kill me too?"

Soooorry, tiger boy. The not-animals will be angry.

"I won't ask you to stay if it isn't safe," Tigre said. "I don't—I don't really know how to thank you for bringing me here. And for saving my life. You're a very noble neoquetzal."

Quetzie fluffed out her feathers and unfurled her tail.

It was my pleasure, tiger boy.

"Will I see you again? Can you come back sometime?"

Maybe. I will try. If you find a way tooo call me, I will come. You can always try to send a message with a pterodolphin, if they dooon't eat you first. They come around here sometimes, looooking for scraps. They like the whoole worship element, although as I said, they're noot very friendly at all. Perhaps the best thing to dooo—

She was interrupted by an inhumanly loud, electronic-sounding voice that seemed to be coming from every corner of the sky.

YOU ARE NOT ALLOWED HERE. YOU HAVE BEEN WARNED BEFORE, BIRD.

Bright rays lanced across the rooftop. With a frightened

cry, Quetzie launched herself into the sky, weaving and twisting to avoid the beams of light. She shot away south without a backward glance.

Tigre threw himself behind the parapet and covered his head with his arms. The beams continued to dance across the pool, sharp spotlights like lasers.

After a few minutes, the lights abruptly shut off. The whirring sound dropped to a hum and then retreated into the distance. Tentatively, Tigre poked his head up and saw their attacker soaring away, but all he could make out in the dazzling sunlight was a flash of crystal, teeth, and wings.

He remained crouching for a minute longer, but the creature seemed to have overlooked him, so he finally clambered to his feet and leaned over the edge of the roof.

The human figure was three blocks away. As he watched, it turned the corner and vanished in the direction of Central Park. He was going to have to run to catch up before it was gone.

He took a quick mental picture of the streets below, then headed for the stairs.

KANSAS

Diana wondered whether it would be a bad idea to try and prop open her eyelids with toothpicks. Hadn't she read a story where people stayed awake that way? She hadn't let herself sleep when they'd last stopped to rest, yesterday at dawn. She was sick of being visited by her golden stranger and his new insistence on calling her

Venus. Jerk. It was *her* dream; shouldn't he do what she wanted him to?

Instead she had done all the exercises she could think of to keep herself awake: sit-ups, push-ups, yoga, pilates. And watched Gus, who was still tossing restlessly and growling in his sleep. When she'd changed his bandages that evening, as they got ready to start driving again, she noticed with bewilderment that his tattoo looked ... bigger. As if it had grown somehow, spreading across his shoulder blade toward his spine, nearly intersecting with his wound. She was sure the tattoo had been only the size of a CD before, and now it looked closer to the size of an old-fashioned vinyl record. But surely that was impossible. Probably an effect of her sleep deprivation.

So toothpicks. Hmmm. It sure didn't sound like a terrific idea. She'd probably end up impaling one of her eyeballs.

At least the squickiness of *that* image woke her up a bit. She blinked rapidly, shifting to sit up straighter.

"Are you sure you don't want me to drive?" Gus said for about the nine hundredth time. He kept clutching the armrest every time she turned a corner or went even a teeny bit over 70 mph. Sheesh.

"Hey, at least I'm not going to faint at the wheel," she said, peering at the map that was laid out on the seat between them. "Besides, we're almost there." She looked up at the road again, where a gigantic tumbleweed had appeared out of nowhere.

Gus made a strangled sound as she swerved wildly around it. "*I'll* read the map," he said. "And I haven't fainted since that first time."

"It's only been a day since you woke up," she pointed out. "Let's not risk it." She was deliberately tuning out the half of her brain that said he would feel more manly and like her better if she let him drive. The other half of her loved being the driver. She liked being the one in control of where she was going, instead of getting driven everywhere all the time. She'd always thought those road trip movies looked stupendously boring, but it turned out there was something exhilarating about the wind whipping through her increasingly disastrous-looking hair. If her stylists could see her now—they'd probably choose the eye impaling.

The car was now rolling through a small, abandoned prairie town; the map Andrew had left indicated that the address was a farmhouse on the outskirts. It was nearly sunrise, and the world was that silvery-pearl almost-dawn color. The landscape around them was bleak, as it had been for days.

On the edge of town they drove past a cemetery, where Gus noticed several holes that hadn't been filled in. He wondered if people had dug them, anticipating they'd need them later, or if they'd been interrupted while digging.

Gus couldn't help thinking of his parents' funeral: the flowers, the solemn people in black, the gravediggers standing off to the side with their heads bowed, the matching dark varnished wood of their coffins, the headstones Andrew had had to pick out. He wondered morbidly who would be around to bury him when he died, and he thought of all the people who'd lived here who must have wondered the same thing.

They drove in silence along the winding gravel road out of town, turning off at a signpost that said: VILLA SWEET VILLA in faded red letters.

Finally they rolled to a stop in front of a building that looked like an ordinary farmhouse. In fact, Diana thought, it looked an awful lot like something out of *The Wizard of Oz*—pre-Oz, of course. Scraggly bushes clung desperately to the hard ground, resisting the wind that seemed intent on carrying off anything that wasn't tied down. A loose shutter on the house thumped back and forth, back and forth. The place looked deserted.

"Gus . . ." she whispered, suddenly frightened. There was something wrong about this place. And this wasn't her destination; she could feel it under her skin. She needed to go farther east, and she needed to go now. Stopping here was dangerous.

"Let's go," Gus said, wrenching open his door.

"Gus, wait—" She reached over and caught his arm. "What if—what if he isn't here? What if it's not safe . . . I mean. . . ."

"He will be here," Gus promised, his dark green eyes bright with hope. "Or he'll have left me a message. He's like that. I'm sure of it." And he was sure of it, Diana realized. He believed in his brother that much. She wondered what it must be like to trust someone so completely.

Gus got out of the car and bounded toward the porch. She had no choice but to follow him or be left alone in the car.

The screen door was torn and warped nearly off its hinges. Diana held it open while Gus knocked firmly on the faded red wooden door.

They waited.

Nothing happened.

Diana let out a breath she hadn't realized she was holding and said, "Okay, let's get out of here."

"Didn't you hear that?" Gus said. "There's someone in there."

"Hear what? I didn't hear anything."

"Movement." He pressed his ear to the door, listening, then turned the doorknob. The door creaked open gently, sending up a cloud of dust.

"Gus . . ."

He stepped inside. Casting an anxious glance at the brightening sky, Diana slipped in after him.

They were standing in a dark hallway that led off to either side of them. On the right was a large, cold-looking dining room, illuminated by pale light squeaking through grimy windows, with a giant wooden table and long dusty benches, a few iron pots hanging from the walls, and not much else. A pair of mice sat up on the table as they came in, then scampered off to a corner. To the left was a darker room, where all the windows were shuttered and shadows seemed to be boiling up out of the corners. Instinctively, Gus reached back, and Diana took his hand.

As her eyes adjusted, Diana could see that the walls in the dark room were lined with couches, all facing the center of the room, where there was a low stool. The walls above the couches were covered with rugs and blankets, but not artistically—it looked like they had been tacked there any which way, to cover as much space as possible, perhaps to keep the room warmer. Pinned to one of the blankets were two faded posters, advertising *The Return of the King* and *X-Men 5*. Gus inhaled sharply when he saw them.

He pointed to the door at the far end of the room, which was slightly ajar. Diana held her breath and listened.

Definitely sounds.

Coming from behind that door.

It sounded like . . . breathing, but jagged and labored.

Gus stepped hesitantly toward the door.

I so do not want to go in there, Diana thought. *But I can't let him go alone.* She had too many nightmare images rushing through her head of exactly what he might find in the next room.

They crept past the couches. They could hear the breathing clearly now. Gus reached up and pushed the door open slowly, the only sign of his tension evident in how tightly he held her hand.

The room faced east, and the window was open, letting in a few colorless beams of sunrise. In the room was a desk, a chair, and a camp cot.

And a man.

At first, even though she could hear him breathing, Diana thought he must be dead. He looked older than anyone she had ever seen before, with matted white-gray hair and spiderwebs of wrinkles all over his face. He was huddled in a corner of the cot and wrapped in a blanket, facing the sun with his eyes closed, taking those horrible slow breaths.

Gus approached the man, pulling Diana with him. As their footsteps creaked across the room, the man opened his eyes and stared straight at them. His eyes were a pale, pale brown and seemed weak, as if they weren't often used. They widened at the sight of Gus and Diana.

"How—" he croaked.

"I'm looking for my brother," said Gus. "Do you know if he's here?"

The man reached toward them, his face crumpling. Diana suddenly found herself wanting to wrap her arms around him and take care of him.

"It's okay," she said, stepping forward and taking one of his hands in both of hers. "It's okay, don't worry, we're here now. Can we get you something? Are you all right?"

The stranger stared at her, then moved his eyes to Gus as he came up behind her.

"Yes," Gus said contritely. "I'm sorry. Is there anything we can do to help?"

"It's you," the man whispered.

Oh God, Diana thought, moments before the realization hit Gus.

Not a stranger. Andrew.

Gus's fingers dug into her shoulder, then pulled her aside as he knelt next to his brother.

"Andrew?" he said, his voice breaking. The old man reached out and touched his hand.

"Gus-Gus," he whispered. "I knew you'd come."

NEW YORK CITY

It was a girl.

Tigre crouched behind the wall of a dry fountain and

swallowed nervously. Well, what had he expected? He came looking for people, and here he'd found one, and now he had to talk to her. That was the inevitable consequence of finding people.

But why did it have to be a girl? And a pretty one, too, if you liked them kind of scary looking. He generally avoided all girls except his sister, Claudia—and Vicky, of course, but the last conversation he'd had with *her* had pretty much cancelled out any positive effects of that relationship.

He peeked over the wall again. This girl was much taller than Vicky, only an inch or two shorter than he was. She looked more solid, too, wiry and grounded, like she had sprouted up out of the earth. Her dark, wavy hair swung down to her waist in a no-nonsense ponytail. She had dark gold-brown skin and a vinelike tattoo around her upper arm, plus piercings in her ears, nose, and belly button, which he could see flashing between her black tank top and cargo pants. She moved like a giant cat, commanding the street, her midnight-black eyes darting around her.

As he was thinking this, she stopped with her back to him, a few feet away. She lifted her head to the sun, closing her eyes and spreading her arms as if offering herself up, absorbing the sunshine as morning filled in the spaces between the empty buildings of Manhattan.

Well. He couldn't sit here staring all day. Bracing himself for conversation, he climbed to his feet and hopped over the wall onto the stairs behind her.

"Excuse me—" he said in English.

She whipped around instantly, her eyes dazzled by the

sunlight, barely glanced at him, and took off running. Which was not exactly the reaction he'd expected.

"Hey! HEY!" he yelled, then jumped down to chase after her. He was surprised at how fast she was. He almost lost her flying around a corner, then caught sight of her disappearing over the wall into the park. What was the matter with this girl? Maybe she'd had an encounter with some liver thieves, too. He catapulted over the wall and up a hill. Hopefully she'd tire quickly; otherwise it would be easy to lose her in here.

He tore through a stand of trees, then realized he couldn't see her anywhere. He jogged to a stop, peering ahead. Where did she . . .

A twig snapped, and he spun around just in time to see her leap toward him. He threw his arms up with a yell but couldn't sidestep fast enough. She crashed into him, and her momentum carried them both rolling downhill, heads colliding, skin tingling electric with the shock of human contact.

They finally slid to a stop in a pile of leaves at the bottom of the hill, with Tigre pinned to the ground. He forced himself to stop struggling, determined not to frighten her off again. She stared down at him.

"Well, hallelujah," she said. "You're real."

He nodded, hoping that was the right answer. He was finding it hard to concentrate; it felt like she was emitting sparks that were flying all around him, creating a tingling electricity shooting up and down his skin.

"Are you the one from the museum?" she demanded.

"No," he said, confused. "What museum?"

"How old are you?"

"Uh—seventeen," he managed. "Why do people keep asking me that?"

"Because it's impossible," she said, standing up in a fluid motion like a lion springing to its paws.

"Why? How old are you?" He decided to stay on the ground for a minute.

"Eighteen, but I'm an anomaly."

"Maybe I am too."

She studied him suspiciously.

"I'm Kali," she finally said, offering him her hand. He took it, and she pulled him to his feet. The strange energy pulsed between their palms, and she dropped his hand quickly, stepping back.

"I'm Tigre," he said.

"Oh," she replied. There was an awkward pause.

"So. Do you live here?" he asked, trying to break the silence.

"I guess . . . I normally live in Brooklyn"—she gestured vaguely to the east—"but I can't get there right now. Why? Do you come from somewhere else?"

"Yeah—Santiago, in Chile."

"Really?" Kali's face lit up. "How did you get here? How did you get past the crystal hunters?"

He explained to her about Quetzie and the strange monster that had driven off the neoquetzal. Kali nodded as he described it.

"Yeah, that's one of the pterodactyl things. Huh." She tilted her head back. "I never thought about trying to go *over* them." She dropped her eyes back to him and shrugged grimly. "Not that it makes much difference, anyway."

"What do you mean?"

"You know, with the catastrophe and the hunters and the chaos ..." She trailed off at his expression. "You mean you *don't* know?"

"All I know is a week ago I was in school, and then I woke up and everything was different. Oh, and there's a cult of plastic-surgery-obsessed lunatics occupying a resort in Mexico. Do you know what's going on?" She nodded, and he felt a colossal weight lift off his shoulders as he realized that at last here was someone who could actually give him an explanation.

"*What* perhaps ... although I have no idea *why*." She paused. "It's kind of hard to explain. Come on, I'll show you."

KANSAS

Diana left Gus and Andrew alone, closing the door gently behind her as she slipped out. Farther back in the house she found a cavernous stone kitchen and a set of creaky wooden stairs leading to the second floor. Past those, down another narrow dark hallway, was a screen door into the backyard.

She hesitated, glancing behind her. Would it be idiotic to go out in the daylight, while Gus was preoccupied? She was fairly certain the crystal creatures weren't interested in her; they only seemed to attack when Gus was around. Plus, she really needed some sunshine.

She pushed through the door, wincing at the squeal its hinges made. The backyard was as dismal as the front, with the same sad, determined bushes and dusty earth. An abandoned wheelbarrow leaned against a fence that darted crookedly around the yard. Diana circled the perimeter, keeping one eye on the sky in case one of the creatures appeared. In a back corner was an overgrown square that must have once been a vegetable garden. Farther along she found an old stone well, but the pulley was so rusty it was useless, and the wooden bucket next to it had a hole rotted through the bottom. Diana hoped they still had supplies in the car from their last supermarket raid, since she suspected they wouldn't be leaving this house today.

She turned her face to the rising sun and tried to ignore the tugging inside her, telling her to go east. It was almost like an ache that she had to stretch out by constantly moving. While they were driving it was okay, but now it flooded over her. She sat down on the back steps, dropping her head in her hands.

This answered the question of how much time had passed, anyway. About seventy-five years, Andrew said, making him nearly ninety-seven.

Which meant—her breath caught in her throat—that her mom would be close to a hundred and twenty. What it really meant, she knew, was that Mom was dead. And so was Dad. And Doug. And probably that dopey, self-absorbed TV star Kenneth that Mom had always wanted her to date, and all the celebrities she had pretended to be friends with at parties, and all the techies who had worked on her albums and all the people who had come to her concerts. However it had happened, she was now in a world where anyone who knew her was gone.

But there was so much she had meant to do. All those

e-mails from old friends that she had meant to send serious, thoughtful answers to just as soon as she had a free minute. The guy from junior high who'd confessed his crush on her, and whom she'd always planned to dedicate a song to, to say sorry for not being a better friend after she got famous. The songs she'd wanted to write, about love and fear and letting people in and trying to understand them, the songs that were going to change the world and make everyone who heard them into better, happier people. All the people she'd ever wanted to apologize to, all the people she'd secretly admired, and all the people who never knew how much they meant to her. All gone, and now she would never get to tell any of them.

Most of all, she wished she could have seen her dad one more time. She remembered what he was like when she was little, when he'd taken her everywhere. Back then her mother was still trying to pursue her own music career, so it was usually just her and Dad, watching hockey and eating spaghetti on the couch together. He'd liked her once upon a time, before she became a superstar and changed her name and he decided he didn't want to have anything to do with her. She wished she could have told him she would have given it all up to spend one more day fixing cars with him. She wished she'd known that herself, back then.

Diana stood up, brushing away tears, and pulled her hair back from her face. She could spend all day swimming in regret if she didn't snap herself out of it. But that wouldn't help Gus and Andrew, and it wouldn't get her farther east, and it wouldn't answer any of her questions.

She went back inside and paused at the door to Andrew's room, listening to the murmur of voices. She heard Andrew say: "I know you didn't get to say good-bye to Mom and Dad so . . . I wanted to wait . . . just in case." It sounded like Gus was crying, and, feeling like an intruder, Diana turned away.

The only part she hadn't explored was upstairs, so she gingerly climbed the old staircase, testing the wood at each step. She found herself in a dim hallway balcony overlooking the dining room. There were six doors along the hall, three on each side, all of them closed.

Taking a deep breath, she opened the first one to the left and found an empty bedroom, with a queen-sized bed neatly made under a thin coat of dust that swirled up as she stepped in and made her cough. She crossed to the window and shoved it open, letting in the pale sun and the fresh air. On the bedside table was a faded paperback she'd never heard of: *Earth Abides*, by someone called George R. Stewart.

The next door led to a bathroom, green and yellow tiles matching the ones in the smaller bathroom downstairs. To her surprise, the water still worked—in sputters with a rusty tinge, but she ran her hands under it anyway and smoothed down her hair, which was acting crazier and crazier every day she was away from her stylists. On the other hand, she noticed that the dark circles under her eyes were gone. She'd begun to think those were permanent, after the last three years. It wasn't like the end of the world was *less* stressful than being a pop star, she thought wryly, but she did seem to be getting more sleep.

The final door on this side of the hall was stuck, and

she had to ram her shoulder into it a few times before it finally scraped open and she saw what was inside.

Diana was staring at the neon blue of the gas fire on the stove, waiting for the water to boil, when somebody grabbed the mug on the counter beside her and flung it into the wall with a crash.

Diana spun around as Gus seized a plate and dashed it to the floor. In his eyes there was something otherworldly and raging that was nothing like the Gus she knew.

"What are you *doing*?" she shouted.

"It doesn't matter," he growled. "Nothing *matters* anymore." He picked up the other mug she'd set out and threw it with all his might into the wall behind her. "Hey GOD!" he yelled at the ceiling. "You forgot one! Don't you want a complete set? Can't forget the little brother!" He grabbed another plate, but Diana yanked it out of his hands and shoved him backward.

"Stop it," she said firmly. "You need to keep it together for Andrew."

"Diana, he's *dying*," Gus said. "I got here just in time to watch him *die*."

"At least you got here in time to say good-bye," she said.

He closed his eyes and stepped away from her, covering his face with his hands.

"We need to get him out of here," Diana said. "This place is depressing and horrifying and ... and ... unsanitary. We have to take him somewhere where he can die with dignity, and then we can bury him properly, which is more than most people of his generation got."

"We?" he said. "What about Tennessee, and your uncle?"

"Come on, Gus. You know as well as I do what we'd find there."

"But where can we go? Those creatures . . ."

She wanted to say *east*, but instead she shrugged.

"Ask Andrew. There might be somewhere he wants to go before he dies. Go ask him now, while I make tea. We should leave as soon as possible."

He nodded, pushing himself away from the counter, and then paused, looking down at her. His eyes were back to normal—sad, but not dangerous.

"You saw something, didn't you?" he said. "You want to get out of here because you found something."

Diana tried to stop the image in her head, but it came before she could prevent it and she pushed past him out into the garden and vomited, again.

He was waiting with a wet washcloth and a concerned expression when she came back inside.

"There's a couple in a room upstairs," Diana said quietly, taking the washcloth. "They're dead. They've been dead for a while. I guess Andrew was too weak to bury them by the time they . . . The room is full of mothballs, but the smell—" She felt like she'd be smelling it for the rest of her life, like it had seeped into her skin in the twenty seconds she'd stood there, feeling the world spin around her.

Gus touched her shoulder, tentatively, and she pulled his arms around her and leaned into him, closing her eyes. The towering rage inside him rippled away into stillness, and he rested his head against hers, letting himself focus on the feeling of her hair spilling over his arms, her face buried in his chest.

"It's horrible," she whispered. "We have to get your brother out of here."

"Yes," he said. "We will."

NEW YORK

Tigre lowered the newspaper and looked at Kali in disbelief. They were sitting in the living room of the apartment she'd co-opted, which was covered in articles and magazines, all arranged into categorized piles. Most of them looked strange and were printed on an odd, durable paper he'd never seen before.

"So we *are* in the future," he said.

"Looks like it. A twisted, hopeless kind of future."

"How is this—" He stopped. "How could this have happened?"

"Nobody seems to know," Kali replied. She leaned back into the couch and drew her bare feet up under her. "Apparently people just . . . stopped being born. No more babies, no more kids, all over the world, all of a sudden. Like, farewell to reproduction. And sayonara to survival of the species." She shrugged, her face a mask of indifference that Tigre found hard to believe. "Guess the planet just gave up on us."

"All right. So people realized what was happening and then . . ." He looked again at the newspaper in front of him.

"And then a lot of things," she said. "People went a bit nuts trying to find a solution."

"Cloning?" he suggested.

She gave him a withering look. "Do you remember how many anti-cloning laws were in place by 2012?"

"Sure, but this was an emergency," he said.

"Tell that to a certain half of America," she said. "Oh wait, you can't—they're all dead. I guess there is a bright side to all this."

"You're telling me they didn't even try it?"

"Some people did, illegally, and in other countries, but it didn't work."

Could've told me that without the lecture, he thought.

"All right," he went on, lifting another article off a different stack. "So the crystal creatures . . . they were made by scientists?"

"Yup. The original idea was to create advanced computer brains that would be smart and powerful enough to hold all our memories."

"To replace us after we were gone," he said softly.

"But of course they screwed it up," Kali said. "The creatures took on a life of their own. They started building more powerful animal versions, like the birds and the insect guards, and enhancing themselves, growing stronger. A lot of them are networked—not all together, but in packs, each with its own leader. People got paranoid that they'd be able to patch in to our regular computers and destroy us that way, so there was this big smashdown in 2052. Everyone got rid of their personal computers, and all the automated systems that run important stuff like electricity were locked down, so they couldn't be changed or affected by viruses.

"In the end, the hunters turned on their creators. Now

they roam around, preying on what humans are left, out of boredom or spite or something. The good news is that they're solar powered, so they prefer not to come out at night, although they can if they've stored up enough energy in their sun-catchers—those crystals they're made of. So far they seem to be ignoring me, unless I directly confront them." She looked at him thoughtfully. "I wonder how they'd react to you."

He shuddered. "Not sure I want to find out. So, these crystal hunters have more or less taken over North America?"

"And Europe, according to the papers I found."

"What about South America? I didn't see any glass animals there—just scary mutant hybrids."

"That's exactly what they are, although most people call them zybrids because we made them," Kali said, pointing to a stack of articles in the corner. "You can read about it yourself. A different group of scientists thought studying the animals would help them find a solution for us. They went a little overboard on the genetic experimentation, trying to figure out what happened and develop some kind of super-animal that could take our place."

"Maybe that's what neoquetzals are," Tigre said. Maybe Quetzie was right about being the culmination of evolution—a super-animal with all the intelligence of a human but none of humanity's bad characteristics.

"I'm guessing the scientists didn't think so," Kali answered. "They didn't consider themselves very successful. They wound up leaving most of their mistakes in South America . . . the ones that would stay there."

"You got all that from the papers?"

"Sort of. I'm guessing some of it."

Tigre sat down on the floor, frustrated. There was nothing here but more questions, and he wasn't much of a reader.

"Where did you find this stuff?"

She looked shifty for a moment, and he could tell before she spoke that she was about to lie to him. "Oh, you know, here and there, the library," she said. He wondered why she would lie about that, and what she was not telling him.

"So how far ahead in time are we? Are there any people left besides us?"

"The last newspapers I've found are dated about sixty years after our time, early 2072, when New York was officially evacuated because of the subway flooding and the Boss Hunter moving in."

"Boss Hun—"Tigre began.

"Really *really* large angry glass bird thing," Kali interrupted. "The leader of New York's pack, and *so* annoying. You'll see it because it does this irritating shrieking ritual every third day or so. Anyway, my guess is it's been at least ten years since the evacuation, probably more. A lot of the canned or super-preservative-stuffed food is still okay, but you have to be careful. As for whether there are any people here—more or less. Well, mostly less." Kali knelt on the couch and peered out the window. "They won't come out while the sun's up, because they're afraid of the hunters, but there are some really old people living in the subway tunnels. They're the classic New Yorkers, the ones who refused to leave in the evacuation, and now they're trapped here. Like me." She smiled humorlessly.

"Most of them are more than half crazy, and they can't talk very well. The only one I've met who can communicate is *seriously* scary, and he kept going on about this 'miracle.' He wanted me to go into the tunnels with them, but I told him I'd rather feed myself to psychotic tigers."

"Why?" He looked at her curiously. "Couldn't they have explained all this to you?"

"They could also have tied me down and stolen my kidneys," she said pointedly. Tigre flushed, wishing he hadn't shared *all* of that story.

"It was my liver," he muttered. "But maybe these guys know something we need to know. Now that you've got me to back you up. . . ."

Kali snorted. "You're right, I do feel much safer," she said.

"Just think about it," he said.

"There's one more thing you should see," she said, changing the subject. "Look at the dates the last few babies were born." She rifled through another stack of articles and pulled out a handwritten list. Handing it to him, she said: "Notice anything?"

He scanned down it. The answer struck him at once.

"Wow," he said faintly.

"Yeah. Nine months after we 'disappeared,' or whatever you want to call it."

"What does it mean?" he asked.

"Think about it. If something happened to stop anyone from having children, but all the women who were already pregnant went ahead and had their babies . . . that means that *something* must have happened about nine months earlier. Exactly about the time something was happening to us."

"You think they're connected?"

"Don't you?" She stopped, clearly having thoughts she didn't feel like sharing.

"So maybe whatever sent us forward in time also caused this worldwide no-more-babies thing," he said. "I don't know. That sounds kind of . . . unlikely."

"More unlikely than anything else about the last week?" She got up, went into the kitchen, and started clattering dishes around.

"True." Tigre spotted a spiral-bound notebook lying under the glass coffee table. The cover was black with a border of orange flames, and the pages were stuffed with articles, newspaper corners sticking out of the edges. "What's this?" he called, reaching for it.

"What?" her voice came from the kitchen.

He flipped through the first few pages, puzzled. These articles didn't seem related to their end-of-the-world situation. They were from earlier days, before the leap in time.

NEW JERSEY DEPARTMENT STORE MYSTERIOUSLY COLLAPSES, read one headline. THIRTEEN KILLED; FOUR-YEAR-OLD GIRL AND MOTHER MIRACULOUSLY SURVIVE.

UNSUSPECTED SINKHOLE OPENS IN SCHOOL PLAYGROUND, said another. SEVEN CHILDREN INJURED.

Perplexed, he flipped ahead and found several pages of medical reports. The patient, Bill Nichols, evidently had rapidly deteriorating lung cancer. Tigre was tilting his head to read the doctor's handwritten notes when the notebook was suddenly ripped out of his hands.

"Don't you *ever* touch this again," Kali snarled.

"What is it?" Tigre asked, mystified and more than a little alarmed at the fierce expression on her face.

"It's none of your business, that's what," she snapped, storming back into the kitchen with the notebook.

"Sorry," he said. "I didn't know."

There was no response except angry clattering. He got to his feet to follow her and noticed a photograph lying on the floor. It must have fluttered loose from the book.

Did he dare pick it up? Would she kill him if she caught him looking at it? His curiosity got the better of him and he palmed it quickly, watching the kitchen door.

The photo was of three small blond girls who looked like they were giggling hard enough to fall off the couch they were sitting on. Above them, behind the couch, leaned a figure with long draping dark hair, whose face was covered up by an X of black tape. Tigre knew before he pried up the tape that it was Kali. Kali with an actual smile on her face, which was something he hadn't seen yet.

This time he heard the clattering stop in time to shove the photo in one of his pockets and look innocent. Kali appeared in the kitchen door and scowled at him suspiciously.

"What's up?" he said, trying to act nonchalant.

"Do you want tea?" she asked abruptly.

"Uh—sure." He followed her into the kitchen as she seized a kettle and shoved it onto the stove.

"You know what the dumbest thing I miss is?" she said. "Milk. There's plenty of stuff to eat that hasn't gone bad, but I hate condensed milk, and of course there's no real milk, and no way of getting any, unless I get off this island and hunt down a stupid cow." She stopped talking and concentrated on getting out sugar and cups. He guessed that this was her way of making peace and moving on.

"Do you think there's anyone else like us?" he asked.

"How would I know? Until you showed up, I thought I was the only one."

"Well, do you think there's a reason we're here?" he asked. "Something particularly special about us?" She didn't reply. "I mean, is this a bizarre accident or part of a plan, and is there anything we can do about it? If we could come forward in time, couldn't we also go back? Is there a way to fix all this?"

"I don't *know*, Tigre—" She started to snap, then stopped mid-sentence, her hands going to her temples. The voice boomed in her head, louder than ever:

ALL YOUR QUESTIONS SHALL BE ANSWERED.
THE TIME DRAWS NEAR.

"Oh, buzz *off*," she barked. She looked up to find Tigre looking shocked.

"You heard that too?" he asked. She stared at him. "The voice—about our questions being answered?"

"It's not just me," she said.

"I guess not."

"Unless we're both crazy." She shrugged. "Or I'm imagining you." She turned back to the stove.

"Well, if you are, you have a pretty boring imagination," he tried to joke. "I'd have imagined me a bit more handsome."

She snorted. "Okay. So you're real and the voices are real. What happens next?"

"I don't know." He leaned against the table and stared out the window. "I guess we wait."

A BEACH IN NEW JERSEY

> At the end of the world
> At the edge of the world
> When there's nothing but stars
> Will I be there?
> Will you?

No, that wasn't right. The sound of the Atlantic Ocean and the quiet, star-splattered night filled Diana's head with music, but all her lyrics kept veering back into love songs, which wasn't at all what she wanted. She let out a frustrated sound.

"What on earth is going on in that head of yours?" Gus asked. "You haven't said a word in about half an hour."

"Sorry," Diana said. "It's nothing." Grains of sand slid over her arms as Gus rose onto his elbows beside her, peering at her through the darkness. They'd been out on the beach for hours, ever since sunset, and it was peaceful after the two nights of nonstop driving they'd done since Kansas.

"You're writing a song, aren't you?"

"Maybe," she admitted reluctantly.

"Sing it for us," Andrew's voice creaked from the other side of Gus.

"Oh, it isn't finished," she said. "Maybe later."

They were silent for another moment, and Diana wondered if she'd been rude. She wasn't really used to old people, since all her grandparents had died when she was fairly young. Moreover, Andrew treated her like she was still a pop star—he couldn't stop calling her Venus, for instance—and it made her feel very strange. With Gus she'd gotten used to being just a normal teenager, and to have someone behave like she was a superstar again was unsettling.

"I think I'm going to take a walk," she said softly.

"Okay," Gus said. "Don't go far."

She scrambled to her feet and slid away down the dunes, toward the ocean.

As the sound of her footsteps faded, Andrew said, "You are head over heels, little brother."

"Me?" Gus said. "No, we're just friends—I mean, it's all weird, with the end of the world and everything—it's not like that." He crumpled up a granola bar wrapper and distractedly put it in his pocket, wincing as the wound in his back complained. They'd been lucky to find canned juices, granola bars, and beef jerky in one of the convenience stores in town, so they could eat without worrying about lighting a fire.

"She's not what I expected," Andrew said. "She's much more normal than I thought."

"Didn't I tell you that?" Gus said. *Seventy-five years ago.*

Andrew was quiet for a moment, running sand through stiff fingers. "Thank you for bringing me here. I did miss the ocean. I never realized how much I loved it until I left California."

"Sorry it's a different ocean," Gus said, "but we figured this one was closer."

"Man, I've been in Kansas for the last forty years,"

Andrew said. "A large puddle would have made me happy. And the part I like best is the sound of the waves anyway."

Gus stared up at the stars, wondering how far away Diana had gone and if she'd be okay out there in the dark by herself. Should he go after her? Or would that make her mad? He couldn't leave Andrew alone anyway.

"I thought I would hate her," Andrew said in a low voice. "I mean—I did hate her, until you guys showed up. I've spent the last seventy-five years blaming her for your disappearance, you know? She got all the attention, all the hype, all the drama and tragedy, and nobody said word one about you. You should have seen the way her mother carried on for the reporters. She accused you of kidnapping her, Gus—*you*. The police interrogated me as if you were the villain, not a missing person yourself."

"That's not Diana's fault, Andrew."

"Diana," Andrew said. "You know, I always knew no one would really name their baby Venus, not even that psychotic witch." He sighed. "Well, you're right. I'd forgotten what she's like in person. It's pretty much impossible to hate her, isn't it?"

"Pretty much," Gus said with a grin.

> *I always thought*
> *the end of the world*
> *would be fast*
> *would be sudden*
> *would take no time at all*
> *And there would be no one*
> *not me*
> *and not you*

Aaargh. There she went again. She turned her face into the ocean spray and closed her eyes.

It was weird seeing Gus with Andrew. He seemed so comfortable with himself now, like he'd rediscovered who he really was.

Diana had always felt lucky to be an only child. She hated watching her aunts and uncles fight. Her mother had been one of five siblings who quarreled all the time, trying to grab the spotlight from one another. Even as adults, they all seemed to be watching for a chance to humiliate their brothers and sisters and regain the center of attention.

Andrew and Gus, on the other hand, interacted like a comedy routine. Even now, with an eighty-year age gap between them, they bantered easily, remembering old inside jokes. Andrew was 2,000 percent more alive than he had been when they found him, as if Gus were some sort of energy drink for his soul.

The strangest part, to her, was how easily Andrew had accepted the idea that she and Gus had jumped forward in time. She clearly hadn't seen enough science fiction in her life. The brothers had been speculating about why and how the time travel had happened for the whole drive here. They kept saying how strange it was that there weren't any aliens or nuclear accidents involved. Diana was starting to feel guilty that she hadn't told Gus about the voices, since it sounded like something they'd love to work into their theories, but she didn't quite know how to bring it up now.

Diana stared north, wondering how far it was to New York City. Now that she had gone as far east as she could without a boat, the tugging feeling had become sharper and more defined, like a thick, pounding headache suddenly narrowing down to a vicious needle. She thought it might be trying to direct her north.

Was she just imagining that she could see lights off in the distance? Perhaps she should keep walking along the beach, swing inland farther up, and try to find another car she could tinker into life so she could set off on her own.

After all, Gus had Andrew now. He didn't need her. And being around Andrew had reminded her of all the reasons she couldn't let herself fall for Gus. Yes, it was the end of the world, and there weren't any tabloids here. But what if they could find a way back to their own time? (This was a central theme of many of the brothers' theories.) Then it would just be cruel, telling him he could be with her only when no one else was around.

Besides, there was still a strong part of her that didn't want anything to do with relationships. The idea of relying on someone, even someone she trusted as much as Gus . . . of giving up her independence . . . surely she should walk away now, while she still could without hurting anyone.

Do it, said the voice in her head. *Go that way. Go now. These two don't want you here. Your place is elsewhere. Go.*

"So what did people do? Just spend their lives waiting for the end? Didn't they try to do anything about it?" Gus said. He dug his hands into the sand and heaped it into a pile, burying his feet.

"Sure they did, Gus," Andrew said. "But no one could

figure out what happened."

"I guess I can't imagine what I would have done," Gus said. "I bet people our age didn't think it was such a big deal at first. I mean, we weren't intending to have kids for a while anyway, and I'd have figured they would find a cure by the time I did."

"Yeah, that was me," Andrew said. "I didn't think it affected me. All I cared about back then was finding you. Then I met Ella—I told you about her, right, Gus-Gus?"

"Gee, let me think," Gus joked. "Ella, Ella . . . doesn't ring a bell . . . although the words 'ad nauseum' are springing to mind."

"All right, all right," Andrew said. "But she was the *one*, you know?"

"Yes. Like Neo," Gus said solemnly. Andrew thwacked him and he ducked away, glad that in the dark Andrew couldn't see Gus's reaction to how weak and thin his brother's arms were.

"*No,* more like . . . Arwen," Andrew said dreamily. "She was a police officer in the missing persons unit. She was the only one who believed you hadn't kidnapped Venus. For months she helped me follow every hopeless lead. Finally one day she asked me to dinner and forced me to talk about something besides you.

"A year later I asked her to marry me. But by then it was obvious something was very wrong with the world, and she wanted to wait until things were more stable. We made all these plans for when everything went back to normal. We both wanted two kids, one boy and one girl." He sighed.

"Did you pick names?" Gus asked, trying to keep Andrew from slipping into sad memories. The wound in his back was hurting again, and he lifted his shirt to let the cool ocean air drift over it.

"We argued about that a lot," Andrew said, smiling again. "Something about knowing we couldn't have any made us talk about kids all the time. Of course we were going to call the boy Gus." His voice faltered a little, then returned. "But for the girl, she really wanted Margaret or Rachel, and nothing I could say would get her to even *consider* Kara or Leia." He frowned. "Kara . . . I don't remember why I liked that name. . . ."

"That was Starbuck's first name on *Battlestar Galactica*," Gus said. "Andrew, that was your favorite show. We watched all the DVDs at least once a year."

"Oh yeah," Andrew said, but Gus couldn't tell if he really remembered or not.

"You are still a geek, right?" Gus joked.

"That was such a long time ago," Andrew said wistfully. "I've had no one to talk to about our favorite shows for . . . it must be decades."

Andrew and Gus had had a Friday night ritual, going back to when their parents were still alive, of making tacos and watching the Sci-Fi Channel together. Gus realized the last time had only been a week ago for him, but it had been three-quarters of a century for Andrew.

He hated thinking of all the Friday nights they could have spent together, all the nights that were gone now.

"Explain to me again what happened to the other continents." Gus looked along the moonlit beach, listening to the waves and hoping Diana was okay out there. She'd been gone a long time.

"Africa went dark early on, around 2025," Andrew said

with a wheezing cough. "It became too dangerous to go there; anyone who tried disappeared and was never heard from again. Nobody knows why. In other places there were enormous natural disasters, which the environmentalists said was only to be expected considering the crazy climate changes going on. But nobody could have expected what happened to the Polynesian islands. New Zealand, Hawaii, Tahiti, even Australia—all destroyed by massive earthquakes and tidal waves." He passed his wrinkled hands over his face, as if he were wiping away the memory of tears. "The sea just swallowed them up."

Gus shuddered. "Like the myth in reverse," he said.

"What myth?" Andrew asked.

"The Maori one about the demigod Maui. He was fishing and caught his hook on an underwater world, and ended up pulling all of New Zealand out of the sea. So it's like the sea took it back."

"You have some weird trivia in that head of yours," Andrew croaked.

Gus shrugged, half frowning. "Yeah, don't ask me where that came from." He leaned over and squeezed Andrew's paper-thin hand. "Maybe we should take a break from the doom and gloom talk."

"You can go find her," Andrew said. "I'll be okay here. It won't be daylight for a while yet, and the hunters almost never come out at night."

"Nah, she'll be fine. You should have seen her fight off the last thing that attacked us," Gus said. He was starting to worry about her, but he didn't want to leave Andrew alone. "I'm sure she'll come back soon."

New York

"This is a bad idea," Kali said for the hundredth time. Didn't this guy know anything about weirdos? Where did he get this bizarre ability to trust people? Just because *she* didn't knife him instantly didn't mean anyone else in this city was safe. Especially the creepy old people.

And this plan about actually going down into the tunnels? In the dark, where who knew what might be lurking? And floods might come up at any second? She felt her chest constrict just thinking about it. She was glad she hadn't told him about the secret museum people. He'd probably want to barge in there and bother them, too. Besides, she liked having something that nobody else knew.

"It's the only way we can figure out what's going on," Tigre insisted. "Don't you want to know whether anything has changed since those last articles?"

"Not particularly," Kali growled. She gestured to the empty streets around them. "Looks pretty unchanged to me."

"Well, we'll find out," he said, coming to a stop outside a subway entrance. He glanced up at the sky, shot through with gold and pink as the sun set behind them. The buildings looming around them looked cold and forbidding, except at the very top where the sun lit the glass windows into a blaze of orange light. A distant screech signaled the retreating presence of the crystal hunters.

"So what do you propose, smart guy?" Kali asked, leaning against the stair railing and crossing her arms. "We wander around underground shouting 'Hey, miracle, we're ready to see you now!'?"

Tigre gave her a thoughtful look, flicked on the flashlight she'd given him, and headed down the stairs. With an exasperated sigh, Kali followed him. *Who made* him *boss, anyway?* she thought grumpily. *And why am I agreeing to this?* But she continued on, sticking close to Tigre.

The stairs opened up into a wide underground space. To their right was the token booth, the dust on the windows so thick they couldn't see inside, and a Metrocard machine tipped on its side, its screen cracked and wires twisting out of the back.

To their left were the turnstiles. The black iron gate that would have blocked their way was shoved to the side, the lock broken. More of the silver fish were painted on the columns and walls, with messages like the ones Kali had seen in the tunnel where she nearly drowned: THIS IS THE END, JUDGMENT IS UPON US, stuff like that. Kali saw Tigre's eyes widen as he saw them, but he said nothing.

They clambered easily over the turnstiles. Tigre offered his hand to help Kali, but she shoved it away. He shrugged and surveyed the choices in front of them. There were more stairs, down to the platform; two staircases on either side of them. He hesitated, suddenly uncertain.

"Downtown," Kali said. "I bet they're downtown." He looked at her quizzically. "Well, if *I* were a mad end-of-the-world underground cult living in the subway tunnels, I'd probably want my headquarters to be where all the tunnels come together, right? That way it's easier for my crazy old people to get back to the center, no matter how old and crazy they are. So, obvious: Times Square.

Downtown from here." She headed purposefully for the staircases on the left. Tigre paused for a second, then sprinted after her.

"That's pretty smart," he said. She rolled her eyes. They descended the steps in silence for a few seconds.

Suddenly Tigre chuckled.

"What?" Kali snapped.

"It's just funny . . . I mean, you know, we could use any of these tunnels to walk downtown. But you instinctively head for the downtown platform." He trailed off at her expression. "It's just . . . funny. . . ."

"Hmph," she acknowledged.

"So, which way is downtown?" he asked.

"Remind me why I even considered letting you be leader." She seized the flashlight and pushed past him to the end of the platform, where the tunnel disappeared into an ominous darkness. The Do Not Enter gate was tied back to a nail driven into the wall, and the passageway stretched ahead of them, running parallel to the submerged tracks.

She'd often looked at the narrow walkways along the subway walls, imagining the workers tramping down here, inches away from the trains. But it was a little unnerving to be standing here, about to walk along them herself. She wondered if there were as many rats down here as there used to be. She hadn't seen any aboveground, which surprised her—she would have thought animals like that would take over the city in the absence of people. But perhaps they'd needed the people to survive . . . or perhaps they were all deep underground, waiting for her to step into the dark so they could crawl over her feet and chew off her toes and spread diseases and whatever else the creepy things did.

The sound of Tigre approaching propelled her forward, one hand touching the wall as she edged into the darkness. She would not let him realize how nervous she felt, especially with the water lapping along the tracks just below her.

They walked for a few minutes in the dark, Tigre close behind her. The darker it got, the harder it was for Kali to breathe. She kept imagining the water rushing at them, and her ears strained for sounds of waves. What would they do if a flood came now? Would they have time to run? Would it sweep them up and crush them against the walls? She closed her eyes for a second and tried to slow down her heart.

"Kali? You okay?"

"Yeah. Kinda claustrophobic down here," she tossed over her shoulder, and kept walking.

They passed another dark, empty platform, with stairs at either end leading up to the street. Kali breathed a little easier as they went through it; at least here there was a way out.

A few minutes into the next tunnel, she said, "This was stupid."

Tigre sighed. "I know, you've said—"

Kali interrupted him. "No, I mean, we should have walked to Times Square aboveground, and gone into the subway there."

"Hmmm," Tigre said. "I was hoping someone would find us if we were underground long enough. We can get out at the next station and walk from there, if you like."

"The next station *is* Times Square, dumbass."

"Oh."

Kali stopped suddenly and grabbed his arm. "Did you hear that?"

"What?"

She listened intently for a second. "That! Water rushing. And wind. Don't you hear it?"

"It's been doing that all along, hasn't it?"

"Not like this. We have to get out of here." She shoved him back the way they'd come.

"Back that way? Shouldn't we go forward?"

"We don't know what's ahead of us, or how far it is," she snapped.

"But the sound is coming from back there—we have more chance of outrunning it if we go forward," he insisted, shoving her back.

"Fine." She turned and took off down the tunnel, running as fast as she dared on the slippery, narrow edge. Tigre swore and chased after her, watching the light bobbing ahead of him. She was right; the sound of waves was getting louder, echoing off the walls around them. And the water on the tracks below them was swirling, eddying back and forth ominously.

Kali gave a muffled shriek, and the light disappeared.

NEW JERSEY

"We'll give her five more minutes," Gus said desperately.

"Gus, man, she's been gone for hours. She's not coming back. And we *have* to get inside before the hunters come out. They're not a joke, Gus."

"I know that—you've seen my back, Andrew." His wound was healing more rapidly than seemed normal, but the tattoo was worrying him. He'd shown it to Andrew, but his brother hadn't recognized it either. "But it's not like the crystal hunters *eat* people or anything," Gus said. "They're machines, for crying out loud. We're smarter than they are."

"If my arthritis would let me, I would smack you over the head right now," Andrew said.

Gus squinted at the rays of light that were starting to creep across the ocean, glittering on the waves. Diana was nowhere to be seen in either direction, and this beach stretched for miles. But surely she hadn't just *left* them. Had she been planning this all along?

"Wait," he said. "What's that out there?" He pointed at something advancing from the far horizon. From this distance it looked like a long, thin mirror, as long as twelve houses and the height of a person. The light caught on it in fits and starts and sent reflections back like Morse code.

Andrew's face turned an even more deathly shade of pale, and he seized Gus's hand in one wrinkled claw.

"Run, Gus," he said. "Run as fast as you can and don't look back."

"What is it?" Gus asked.

"Just *go!*"

"And leave you here?" Gus yelled. The unfamiliar anger and sick, boiling feelings, which he hadn't felt since his meltdown in the kitchen in Kansas, surged back to the surface again. "Are you crazy? Get up and run with me, you jerk!"

"I'll slow you down," Andrew cried, resisting as Gus

tugged him to his feet. "Get out of here. You have to keep yourself safe."

"What's the point?" Gus bellowed. He threw one of Andrew's stick-thin arms over his shoulder, ignoring the blaze of pain that sent through his back, and started dragging him up the beach to the car. He stumbled in the sand and gritted his teeth. "There's nothing here for me without you, Andrew. You *have* to stay alive."

"No, *you* have to stay alive," Andrew said. "You must be here for a reason, Gus. However it happened, whoever or whatever is behind your time traveling, it must mean something, right? You know how these stories work. You're like Frodo or Quadrillion or Angel."

"Or Bill and Ted," Gus muttered. He glanced back and saw that the mirror was much closer. Now he could see that it was really many smaller mirrors arranged in formation like geese or military bombers, and then he realized that it was the flying crystal hunters, *lots* of them, like the one at the motel but multiplied seventy, eighty, ninety times over.

Swearing loudly, he started running faster, trying to keep Andrew's frail body upright as the sand tugged at them. The car was still several feet away, in the cracked and weather-beaten parking lot.

"You're here to make a difference," Andrew insisted, "and I will not let you die saving an old guy like me." He tried to pull away, but Gus clung to him stubbornly.

"Andrew, I'm nobody!" Gus yelled. "This is not a science fiction movie—this is the universe's idea of a terrible joke, okay? So suck it up and run!"

They hit the parking lot just as the first wave of

hunters reached the edge of the beach. Thanking the gods he hadn't locked the car the way he normally, instinctively did, Gus yanked open the back door and shoved Andrew inside. An ear-shattering shriek rang out as he dove into the driver's seat and slammed the door behind him, and a winged glass pterodactyl only a bit smaller than the car itself landed with a thud on the hood. It glared malevolently at him with glittering purple eyes, electricity sparking through its wings like veins, and reared back to plunge its beak through the windshield.

Just in time, Gus managed to start the car and slam into reverse, knocking the creature backward onto the asphalt with a sickening crashing sound. Andrew let out a small huff of breath and lay down across the backseat, clinging to the seat belts. Gus peeled out of the parking lot and down the street as fast as the car would go, but the hunters kept up, tilting their wings like fighter planes to swerve around the buildings.

"Hang on, Andrew!" Gus shouted. He glanced at his rearview mirror and saw one of the hunters dip straight down toward the car. With a squeal of tires, Gus spun around a corner and the hunter smashed into the road behind them, sending shards of glass in all directions.

"Yeah!" Andrew yelled. "Take that, birdbrain!"

"Two down," Gus said grimly, "ninety-eight to go. Any suggestions, Andrew? What do people normally do in this situation?"

"I've never seen this many before," Andrew wheezed. "It usually takes only five or six to destroy a whole battalion of soldiers."

"Oh, thanks. That's very comforting."

Gus spun the wheel again, following the signs to the highway. It would be more exposed there, but then he could also go a lot faster without worrying about crashing into anything. He had no idea what to do besides try and outrun them. His eyes darted to the gas gauge and he swore. They weren't going to get far on what was in the tank.

The churning angry feeling in his chest was telling him to turn and fight them, to rage and battle and kill, but he remembered what Diana had said about running away and staying alive. For her and for Andrew, he had to try.

A thud shook the car as a hunter flew into it from the left. Another hunter promptly came from the right, smashing its head against the door and sending the car skidding across the road.

"Gus, watch out!" Andrew yelled, twisting around to look out the back window. Gus glanced up in time to see three of the hunters drop into a dive together. If all three of them hit the car at once, there would be nothing left except tiny pieces of Gus, Andrew, and glass.

Rubber screamed as he slammed on the brakes. The three hunters shot overhead, two of them crashing into the street in an explosion of glittering light. The third managed to stop at the last second and soared back into the sky.

"HA-HA!" Andrew yelled. "You're no match for my little brother! He is the Chosen One!"

"What in the name of all the gods are you so excited about?" Gus yelled, hitting the gas pedal again.

"We're fighting back!"

"Actually, most people would call this running away," Gus shouted. The ramp onto the highway was just ahead. He could see at least twenty of the hunters already there, circling above it like vultures.

"That's not the right way to look at it," Andrew said. "This is bigger than you or me, Gus. You must accept your destiny."

"Okay, Yoda," Gus said, trying to sound calm for his brother's sake. "I just hope my great power doesn't come with great responsibility or anything." Should he take the highway? He didn't know these streets, and at least the highway was big and open. But then twenty hunters could dive-bomb him at once, or just a couple of them together could easily knock the car over the edge. What should he do? His hands were shaking on the wheel.

"I'm not kidding, Gus," Andrew said. "You have to—"

"SHUT UP AND LET ME DRIVE!" Gus exploded.

Shocked silence from the backseat.

The highway was too risky. Gus's eyes flicked back and forth, and just as he was about to spin the car to the right, he caught a flash of movement as something leaped out in front of him.

A crystal pterodactyl? He swerved wildly across the road before realizing that it was another car. A small yellow Beetle, going as fast as he was, and it was flashing its hazards at him. As they zoomed up the road, he realized it was leading him to the highway.

"Andrew, these crystal hunters can't drive cars, can they?" he shouted.

"Nope. They don't need to," Andrew said.

"Good enough for me," Gus said, and he stayed close

behind the other car as they burst onto the highway, sending a pack of pterodactyls wheeling and shrieking above them. Immediately two of them folded their wings and dove at the car, but here there was enough space for him to dodge at the last minute, and one plummeted to the ground in a shower of glass.

The crystal hunters above them beat their wings faster, and purple electricity seemed to jump between them. Then three separated off from the others, soaring higher. They spun and dove one after the other toward him, leaving enough time between each dive to see where he would turn.

"Why aren't they attacking that guy?" Gus yelled, seizing the wheel and swinging the car wildly from one side of the road to the other. The yellow Beetle was shooting ahead, and the hunters were ignoring it completely.

"Do you think it's Venus?" Andrew asked, leaning forward as far as the seat belt would let him. "She said the hunters don't go after her, didn't she?"

Gus shook his head. "No way. She definitely can't drive like *that*." He had been trying not to think of what might have happened to Diana, but he couldn't stop imagining that she had been attacked out there on the beach, alone in the dark.

"His indicator! His indicator!" Andrew shouted. "He's taking the next exit!"

Gus hit the brakes and let one of the pterodactyls crash past him. As he turned to follow the Beetle down the exit ramp, he felt a horrible popping, crunching sound below the car, and then one of the tires blew out with a dramatic bang that sent them wobbling nearly into the guardrail.

With ferocious effort, Gus managed to stay on the road, but the hunters sensed his weakness and came on even faster, surrounding the car so he could barely see out the front. He let out a volley of curses.

"Where is he?" Gus shouted.

"That way!" Andrew shouted, pointing down a side street that led back in the direction of the beach.

At the end of the street was an enormous building that Gus guessed was a warehouse. A large garage door in the side was rolling up as they raced down the street toward it.

"We'll never get in there and get that door shut again before the hunters get in," Gus said.

"Maybe that's not his plan," Andrew said, pointing. The yellow car was pulling up to the curb next to the warehouse.

"Does he seriously want me to *park* with these *things* after us?"

"You are the one who must decide," Andrew said, sounding like a half-mad Obi-Wan Kenobi. "The fate of humanity lies in your hands." He broke off in a fit of coughing, but his eyes were bright with excitement.

The driver's side door of the Beetle popped open and a person leaped out: tall, gangly, and wearing large goggles, an aviator helmet, a saffron jumpsuit, and about twelve scarves of different autumn colors. As Gus rolled to a stop behind the Beetle, the driver reached in, pulled out a gigantic shotgun, and pointed it straight at them.

"AAAAAAAAAAAAAAAAAAAAAAAAAAAH!!!" Gus screamed, throwing himself to the floor of the car.

BLAM BLAM BLAM BLAM BLAM!

A chaos of noise erupted outside. Pterodactyl screeches mingled with shotgun blasts and the sound of someone yelling.

Through the ringing in his ears, Gus could barely hear the tinkling of glass pouring down around them. He kept his eyes tightly shut and prayed that if he had to die, it would be over quickly.

All of a sudden his door was wrenched open and arms encircled his waist, pulling him out. He started to fight back, then realized the hands clutching him were Diana's.

"What—how—what are you *doing*?" he yelled.

"Help me grab Andrew," she shouted. He struggled out of the car in time to catch his brother's other arm, and together Diana and Gus half carried, half dragged Andrew toward a small door in the side of the warehouse.

"What's going on?" Gus yelled. He looked back and thought he caught a glimpse of strange rainbow-colored monsters in the air, fighting the crystal hunters. Then Diana yanked him through the door behind Andrew and slammed it shut, and suddenly he was standing in a square brown office, furnished with a heavy wooden desk, three folding chairs, and a ceiling fan with only one functioning lightbulb.

Diana lowered Andrew into one of the chairs and Gus leaned against the door, waiting for his heart to stop pounding. The room was so ordinary, so calm. It looked boring and functional, a place to file and type and crunch numbers every day and nothing more. The blades of the fan swooped slowly around and around, as if there were no monsters, nothing trying to kill anybody, no crazy world of death outside. He almost felt as if he had jumped through time again.

"That was phenomenal!" Andrew cried. "That was astonishing! I've never seen anything like it! After the first ten years of trying to fight back, most people just gave up and died," he explained to Diana.

"Not Gus," she said.

"Not Gus," he repeated proudly.

Gus finally managed to catch his breath. "Diana, where were you? Who was that out there?"

She handed a glass of water to Andrew before answering, and he took it with shaking hands.

"I—went for a walk," she said awkwardly. "And I ended up farther away than I thought. I was about to turn around and come back when I met Justin." She gestured to the far corner of the office and Gus nearly leaped out of his skin when he realized there was a person standing there.

This one was as tall and gangly as the one with the shotgun, with the same goggles and helmet, but his jumpsuit was navy, his scarves were different shades of blue, and he seemed more hunched and stiff than the other. He was peering through something that looked like a mounted pair of binoculars, pressed against a large, dark mirror on the wall. Shaggy white hair stuck out from under the helmet.

"He's monitoring the pterodolphins. I'll introduce you in a minute," Diana said.

"Pterowhats?" Gus said. Andrew's eyes widened.

"Justin and Treasure run a pterodolphin study center. They specialize in capturing and retraining them."

"Correction, my dear!" said the man in the corner, flinging his scarves over his shoulders as he turned around. He had a strange accent that sounded somewhere between South African and Scottish. "We specialize in capturing and *attempting* to retrain them. They're much more intractable than regular dolphins, I'm afraid. The pterodactyl part is rather nasty, not to mention the teeth!" He waggled his left hand, encased in a leather glove from which two fingers were missing. "Not very good planning on somebody's part, I must say, eh?"

The door behind Gus burst open and slammed shut again almost immediately behind a figure in a whirl of saffron and orange.

"Treasure!" Justin bellowed, crossing the room in two strides. "Another fantastic operation!" The two of them pulled off their goggles and helmets, revealing dark skin and matching shocks of unruly white hair, then threw their arms around each other, kissing as if they had been separated for years.

Gus gave Diana a quizzical look, and she shrugged.

"Treasure is Justin's wife. She was the very last human born on Earth—hence the name. Justin, Treasure," she said, raising her voice, "this is Gus and Andrew."

"Oh, *hello*," the saffron-clothed figure said, disentangling herself from Justin's embrace. She had a beaming, wrinkle-lined face that reminded Gus of grandmothers on TV. "It's so lovely to meet you. Excellent driving, young man."

"Wasn't he amazing?" Andrew said. "Thank you for saving us, by the way, not that he wasn't doing a great job on his own." He shakily tried to get to his feet, but Diana gently pushed him back down. Treasure waved her hands in the air. Gus noticed that she was missing a couple of fingers as well.

"Think nothing of it, my dears! We haven't had an opportunity like this in positively ages—such a lovely crowd of crystal hunters to try our new batch of pteris on."

"We've been trying to train them to fight the crystal hunters," Justin said excitedly. "Initially, we thought they could be like guard dogs, trained to protect humans, but they don't like us very much, oh ho, no."

"So instead we focused on making them hate crystal hunters, and that seems to be working brilliantly," Treasure jumped in. "Every time they see one, they attack, even with plenty of yummy human prey around."

"It's the most fantastic defense system anyone has ever come up with!" Justin enthused. "We're working *with* humanity's mistakes to create a better world of tomorrow for future generations!"

Gus saw Diana shaking her head at him, but the words were out of his mouth before he could stop himself.

"But—there *are* no future generations," he said.

"What?" said Treasure.

"Wot's that, my boy?" said Justin.

"No world of tomorrow," Gus said. "No more kids, no one left to appreciate your experiments." Diana threw up her hands and scowled.

Treasure and Justin stared at him with puzzled frowns for a minute. Then identical smiles spread across their faces.

"Oh!" said Treasure.

"Oh ho!" said Justin.

"You mean *us*," Treasure said. "Well, yes, my dear, of course *we've* decided not to have any children. Our work is our life, and, really, we don't need anyone besides each other. We're happy to devote ourselves to the benefit of all."

"Now come have some tea and cookies!" Justin declared cheerily, and the two of them swept through the room's other door in a flurry of colorful scarves.

Diana gripped Gus's arm with a steely expression and hissed: "Do *not* talk to them about the end of the world. They don't believe it's happening."

"How?" he whispered back. "Can't they see what's going on outside?"

"Their minds can't accept it, so they don't believe in it," she said. "And if you haven't noticed, they're quite happy this way. So let them be, would you?"

"But it can't be safe for them to live like this."

"Hey, seventy-five years of survival is nothing to sneeze at," she replied. "I think they're doing better than most people."

Andrew was nodding. "A lot of folks ended up like that, completely in denial. And there were others who never planned to have kids anyway, who were happy the way they were. Especially the ones born last—they grew up without expecting kids, so a lot of them were actually pretty stable about it . . . not like us 'before' people. All they had to deal with was the crystal hunters, the natural disasters, the rioting, the destruction of computers . . . okay, maybe there weren't that many stable ones. I lived with a couple of them, though—Zachary and Fiona.

Perfectly content to just be with each other."

Diana had a pained expression on her face and Gus guessed that she was remembering the couple she'd found upstairs, and wondering if they were Zachary and Fiona. He suddenly thought of something.

"If they don't believe it's happening, how do you know Treasure was the last person born?"

"She got a plaque," Diana said. "No, seriously. It's on the floor of the car, under a bunch of graphs. I guess they just pretend it isn't there."

She knelt to put Andrew's arm around her, and Gus helped her guide his brother into the next room, which was also dimly lit. Diana lowered Andrew into an over-stuffed armchair. Justin and Treasure were bustling about, setting out cracked tea cups and Twinkies still in their plastic packaging. Gus could make out several beanbags and armchairs scattered around, plus a long workbench covered with sheaves and sheaves of scribbled-on notepa-per. More notepaper was scattered around the floor, and large graphs and charts and diagrams were pinned to all the walls except for one long one, which was empty.

He discovered why as Treasure strode to the far wall and flicked a switch. A light blazed on in the room on the other side of the wall, which was actually a window. Gus and Andrew both gasped.

The space beyond was cavernous. It looked like a cage in a zoo, but blown up a thousand times. Droppings and rotting food were scattered around the floor, and one quarter of the room was occupied by a huge tank of water. All along the walls and up to the ceiling were twisting branches, like in a monkey house, but the creatures clinging to them or swimming in the tank were not remotely cute or funny.

They looked like misshapen dolphins, horribly endowed with pterodactyl wings, stunted legs, enormous claws, and flipper tails. Their beaks were longer than normal pterodactyl beaks and bristled with hundreds of fierce teeth. Instead of the pinkish gray of regular dolphins, they were mottled green and blue and yellow and red, like fish or parrots. They were as big as the crystal hunters.

There had to be more than a hundred of them. As the light flicked on, most of them threw their heads back, opened their beaks as wide as they would go, and started screaming. Others began to beat their wings together and hiss angrily, shuffling from side to side on their perches.

In the left wall of the room, Gus could see a door of iron bars through which one creature could probably fit at a time. He guessed Justin and Treasure must use that door to let out as many pterodolphins as they wished to use. The next room probably led to the garage door they opened to release those few into the world. He wondered how the fight with the crystal hunters was going. He also wondered if Justin and Treasure were planning to get their specially trained pterodolphins back, and if so, how.

His head was already throbbing from the din. Treasure flicked the switch off again, and the darkness plunged the room back into silence.

"The fruits of our labor!" Justin said. "Aren't they lovely, lovely animals?"

"Lovely" was not the word Gus would have picked, but he nodded politely.

"They're a little peeved at the moment," Treasure explained. "They know their comrades got to go out and have a real knock-down drag-out tussle, and my goodness are they jealous. It's really quite sweet, isn't it?"

"How many did you let out to fight?" Diana asked.

"Twenty-three," Justin said, beaming at her. "A glorious expenditure of resources, but if we don't use them now, when will we? And it looked like they were holding their own well enough—what did you think, dear?"

"They were absolutely smashing," Treasure said. "Only Periwinkle was looking a bit bruised by the time I scurried back indoors."

"Periwinkle?" Andrew managed. He looked tired, but his eyes were bright and he was grinning. "They have names?"

"Of course!" Treasure said. "How else would we tell them apart?"

Gus and Andrew exchanged glances.

"Tea?" said Justin.

"Twinkie?" said Treasure.

Diana studied Andrew, wondering if he was really okay. He looked excited, almost too much so, and he was breathing faster than seemed normal for such an old guy. Surely being chased through the streets by flying glass pterodactyls wasn't very good for a ninety-seven-year-old heart.

She turned her eyes to Gus as he gingerly settled into a beanbag chair with his tea. She wondered if he suspected that she had not exactly "gone for a walk." She wasn't lying about the last part, though. She had been about to turn around and come back. At least, she thought that was true.

But then she had nearly stepped on Justin. He'd been lying on the beach, covered entirely in sand, with only the top of his head to the tip of his nose sticking out. She'd nearly had a heart attack when he surged up out of the sand at her, waving his arms frantically.

"STOP! DON'T MOVE!" he bellowed.

She froze, and immediately wondered if this wasn't actually a turn-and-run-as-fast-as-you-can situation instead. But he looked harmless, and it was heart-stoppingly thrilling to see another person. She realized what he was yelling about when he darted over and brushed away a thin layer of sand on the ground in front of her.

She had been about to step on a pterodolphin nest.

Justin had explained the biology of the nest in a rapid patter of delighted words, pulling her down to lie on the sand next to him and peer in. The nest was a transparent shell encasing three nestled eggs. The shell felt solid and hard like plastic, but as the hatching time drew near it would become permeable, and that was when the baby pterodolphins were most at risk from predators and unwary intruders.

It was fascinating, not least because it was a reproductive process that still worked, unlike humans'. Of course, mentioning that had earned Diana some odd looks and some "wot, wot"s, which was how she realized that Justin had shut out the apocalypse around him. That, plus his complete lack of surprise at her appearance.

Then Treasure had come bounding up, having spotted them through the telescope they kept trained on the beach. It was as introductions were being made and information exchanged and hands shaken that suddenly a loud siren started wailing from the warehouse. Treasure and Justin both lit up like Rockefeller Center Christmas trees.

"An attack!" Treasure squealed gleefully. Diana chased after them as they sprinted up the beach at an uncanny speed for such old folks. Treasure was already loading the shotgun in the car when Diana caught up.

"Justin says they're attacking farther along toward the point," Treasure said, gesturing in the direction Diana had come from. "We'll have to lure them over this way to try our pteris on them. Guess they must have found some live folks in the area."

Diana blanched. *Gus.* "My—my friends," she stammered. "Oh my God, my friend, I left him there, and the crystal hunters have been trying to kill him for days—I have to go back."

"Well, saddle up, darling, and let's go hunter hunting!"

It was hard to believe that anyone would actually go in search of the creatures, but at least they had found Gus and Andrew. She wondered if Gus found this as strange as she did, the two of them perching on beanbags in the lab of a pair of mad scientists, with a crystal hunter–pterodolphin battle raging outside.

"I don't—" Andrew said. "I don't feel so well."

Gus and Diana both sprang up instantly.

"No, I'm sure I'm—fine—it's just my—the old ticker acting up." He rested his hands on his chest, tried to take a deep breath, and toppled off the chair.

"Andrew!" Gus cried, leaping across the room and kneeling to prop his brother against a beanbag. "Are you okay?"

"I don't think he is, my boy," Treasure said, peering over Gus's shoulder with a concerned expression. Andrew's face was turning gray, and he clutched at Gus's hands convulsively.

"This is my fault." Tears began rolling down Gus's face. "If I hadn't brought you here—if I hadn't made us stay on the beach after sunrise—if I hadn't forced you into that stupid car chase—"

Andrew hushed him. "If you hadn't, then my last day on this Earth wouldn't have been the most fun I've had in years."

"Fun?" Gus cried. "We were nearly killed by giant monsters!"

"Exactly!" Andrew said. "It was just like Frodo and Sam against the Nazgul on the Fell Beasts at Minas Tirith."

Gus choked out a laugh. "Even when you're dying, you're a big dork."

"Takes one to know one," Andrew said softly.

"Don't go," Gus begged. "I don't know what to do without you."

"Sure you do," Andrew wheezed. "You got all the way to Kansas to find me. And you have Diana to help you save the world."

"Even if I could, which I can't, I don't want to save a world that doesn't have you in it," Gus said.

"Now, Gus," Andrew whispered. "Would Frodo or Angel say something like that?"

Gus was sobbing now. Diana stood, wiping away her own tears, and beckoned to Justin and Treasure. They nodded and followed her out of the room, and she shut the door to give the brothers a last moment of peace.

OVER SWITZERLAND

WHAT ARE YOU DOING?

Amon rolled lazily onto his back and drifted, facing the sky.

"What does it look like I'm doing?" he said.

IT LOOKS LIKE YOU HAVE FORGOTTEN YOUR MISSION. AND KEEP YOUR VOICE DOWN. THIS IS NOT OUR TERRITORY. ANYONE COULD BE LISTENING.

"Doubtful." Amon spun into a more vertical position, adjusting the winds around him. "This place is totally deserted."

TO YOU, PERHAPS.

"I haven't even seen one of your sparkling crystal toys around lately. I thought they were supposed to be all over Europe."

THEY ARE NOT OUR TOYS. HUMANS CREATED THE CREATURES ON THEIR OWN. FORTUNATELY, THEY HAVE PROVEN USEFUL. . . . WE FIND THEM MUCH EASIER TO CONTROL THAN YOU DO.

"Oh, I didn't have any trouble with them," Amon said. He was floating over what he suspected might once have been Switzerland, fascinated by the folded look of the Alps below him.

A sudden gust of wind punched him forcefully in the stomach, and he gasped in pain.

YOU DID NOT HAVE TROUBLE BECAUSE WE ORDERED THEM TO LEAVE YOU ALONE. DO NOT OVERESTIMATE YOUR ABILITIES.

"I think I can handle a few see-through robots," Amon hissed furiously.

CALLING THEM ROBOTS IS YOUR FIRST MISTAKE. THEY ARE MORE EVOLVED THAN THAT, THOUGH NOT YET SENTIENT. WE HAVE PROGRAMMED THEM TO THINK THEY ARE, IN SUCH A WAY THAT HUMAN SCIENTISTS COULD NOT UNDERSTAND OR REVERSE THE PROCESS. BUT IN TRUTH, THEY SERVE US.

Another gust of wind knocked Amon flat on his back.

AND IF WE SO CHOOSE, THEY WILL ATTACK ANYONE WE WANT. EVEN YOU.

Amon struggled upright, seething. This was no way for someone of his stature to be treated. But there would be time later for punishment, and revenge.

"So what is your point, O Gracious Benefactors?" he sniped.

YOU HAVE SOMEWHERE TO BE. WE SUGGEST YOU GO THERE. NOW.

"Are the others even there yet? I'm saving myself for a grand entrance." Amon settled back smugly.

BE WARY OF ALIENATING YOURSELF, AMON. ANYTHING COULD HAPPEN WITHOUT YOU THERE. NEW ALLIANCES COULD BE FORMED.

"New alliances?" Amon asked, suddenly alarmed. "What about ours? They won't break it, will they? They can't. I was promised—"

PROMISES MEAN LITTLE IN THIS BATTLE. WINNING IS ALL. WHO KNOWS WHAT OUR ALLY MIGHT RESORT TO IN UNUSUAL CIRCUMSTANCES.

"What unusual circumstances?" Amon said suspiciously. "Something specific?"

YES. THERE IS A NEW CONTENDER, OR POSSIBLY JUST
AN ANOMALY. HIS NATURE IS UNCLEAR TO US AS YET.
BUT HE JOURNEYS TO THE DESTINATION AS WELL. AND
WE BELIEVE HE IS MORE OF A THREAT THAN ONE
MIGHT THINK.

"He?" Amon spread his arms, gathering the winds. "I
don't think so. There will be no interference. I want what
was promised me. And don't worry; you'll get what you
want too. I'll take care of this interloper." He lifted grimly
into the air currents, speeding west. "I think the time has
come for my dramatic entrance."

THEY ARE NEARLY ALL GATHERED. THE TRAINERS MAY CONTACT THEM SOON.

WE INSIST THAT THE ANOMALY BE DEALT WITH. HE IS A DISTRACTION, A DELAY, AND A NUISANCE.

YOU ARE STRANGELY INTERESTED IN THIS ANOMALY, CONSIDERING THAT HE HAS YET TO CROSS PATHS WITH YOUR REPRESENTATIVE.

NONE OF US CAN AFFORD A DEPARTURE FROM PLAN AT THIS POINT. THIS IS FOR THE GOOD OF ALL.

EXCEPT HIMSELF, OF COURSE.

PERHAPS IT IS TIME FOR A MORE DETERMINED ATTEMPT.

THAT LAST WAS NOT PRECISELY A FEEBLE EFFORT.

YES, BUT THIS TIME WE WILL NOT FAIL. NO MISTAKES, NO SURPRISES. THESE ARE THE RULES WE AGREED UPON.

IT IS TRUE. WE MUST BE FAIR.

IT MATTERS LITTLE TO OUR SIDE. DEAL WITH HIM AS YOU WISH.

WE ARE AGREED, THEN. IF THE ANOMALY REACHES THE GATHERING PLACE . . .

HE WILL BE ELIMINATED ONCE AND FOR ALL.

GATHERING

NEW YORK

"KALI!" Tigre yelled, and suddenly there were hands on him, grappling with him, pinning his arms—*where did they come from*—hands out of nowhere in the darkness that wrestled his arms behind him as he struggled, nearly slipping into the water, and then they pulled him back, yanking him into the wall, or where he thought the wall had been moments before. He kept yelling Kali's name. The hands didn't bother to muffle him, as if they knew his yelling was futile.

He was thrown to the floor, concrete scraping his knees. He heard clanks and bangs and a rolling, creaking groan. Then, to his relief, he heard Kali's voice swearing and hissing as she was, evidently, carried into the room and dumped next to him in the dark.

"The Miracle *insists* on seeing you now," intoned a grim voice. "There will be no more evasion."

"For God's sake, what do you think we're doing down here?" Kali spat furiously. "Sightseeing? Going for a swim?"

A light flickered to life off to Tigre's right. A white-haired woman with a tired slant to her shoulders shuffled forward with an old-fashioned oil lamp and offered it to Kali, then backed away, bobbing up and down.

Kali held up the light and they surveyed the room: small, concrete, bare, with more silver fish painted on the walls. Tigre realized that they had come through a door in the tunnel, made of reinforced steel and fitted tightly into the wall. Another doorway in the left wall led to more darkness, but not empty darkness—he could hear shuffling and whispering now, and see eyes reflected in the light. The tunnel dwellers crowded closer, but stopped short of crossing the threshold.

In the room with him and Kali were three men in military outfits that looked cobbled together from various uniform stores. One of the men was leaning on a metal pipe, glaring sternly at Kali; Tigre assumed that was General Pepper. She glared right back.

"So, all right already," she said. "We're here. Take us to see your damn miracle."

"Who is this?" General Pepper asked, pointing at Tigre. "Did you create him also?"

"*No,*" Kali yelled. "I can't create things! You need a new obsession already!"

"Forgive our queries, creator-destroyer. We have seen your power. It does not seem unlikely to us that you might create yourself a companion."

Tigre gave Kali a baffled look. She had carefully neglected

to mention anything about potential superpowers. She looked back at him with fury in her eyes.

"You didn't create me. She didn't," he said hastily.

"See?" she challenged them. She reached down and hauled Tigre to his feet, ignoring the energy that sparked through them as their hands touched. "So, come on, miracle ahoy."

General Pepper indicated the doorway in the left wall. One of the other men led the way through it, and Kali and Tigre followed him, with a second man bringing up the rear.

"Creator-destroyer?" Tigre muttered as they crossed through the next room.

"Crazy people, remember?" she hissed. "Delusions come with the territory."

He dropped it for the time being and concentrated on watching where he walked. The ceiling was low, and both he and Kali had to duck to keep from hitting it. Kali's eyes darted from side to side as they traveled, as if she were checking for exits, but the only doors were the ones connecting the series of rooms they were walking through. Some of the rooms were little more than hallways. Their rough, jagged walls looked to Tigre as if they'd been chiseled out of the concrete by hand.

At length they came to a room with no more doors. In the center was an iron ladder leading up to a hole in the roof. The man leading them went straight up it. Kali paused and regarded the light she was carrying.

"How am I supposed to take this—" She glanced back up at the disappearing feet of their guide, who had plunged ahead without any light source. The other man stood in the doorway, watching them without speaking. Tigre noticed that General Pepper wasn't with them, as he had thought.

"You know," Kali yelled up the ladder, "this would be a lot easier if you hadn't made me drop my flashlight in the underground river back there!"

No response.

Kali gave an exasperated sigh and pulled the elastic band out of her hair. She twisted it around the handle of the lamp, snapping the circle over her wrist so the lamp hung off her arm, and swung herself onto the ladder. Tigre followed right behind her.

Up they climbed, up and up, through what appeared to be a large pipe. Soon they couldn't hear the man above them at all. Tigre could feel the man below him moving swiftly and pausing every so often to wait for Kali and Tigre to climb on.

Finally they saw light flickering above them, glittering and silvery. They climbed out into an open, tiled space, about ten feet square. Tigre was panting.

"Those old people must be pretty spry," he said breathlessly to Kali. When she didn't respond, he looked up, and saw what she was staring at.

At the other end of the room was a raised dais, surrounded by tiny lights of all kinds—candles, lamps, even a few battery-operated night-lights. They glowed and flashed off the tiles lining the walls, ceiling, and floor, some of which were painted silver and some of which were bits of mirrors, seizing and reflecting back the lights in a glittering dance. There were also broken bits of mosaics carefully arranged here and there: a lizard, a hat,

Alice in Wonderland. Tigre wondered if they came from other subway stations.

In the far corner, in front of a wall-length black curtain, stood General Pepper, staring intently at the dais, which was surrounded by strange offerings: piles of coins, toys still in their packages, faded books, ribbons and jewelry and beads of all kinds, arranged artfully around the edges.

In the center of the dais sat a small person, cross-legged. It was impossible to tell whether it was male or female. Huge dark eyes gazed out of a pure white face, with perfect, symmetrical features. He or she was completely bald, and his or her head glowed like the full moon in the darkness. A robe of deep purple covered everything from the shoulders down, except for two small hands extending from the sleeves and resting gently on its knees.

Male or female, it was most unmistakably young—even younger than they were, perhaps twelve or thirteen.

"The Miracle," General Pepper said in a reverent whisper. "Show your respect."

"It's all right," the Miracle said in a high, pure voice that sounded female. "They are not my subjects. They do not know our ways." It—she?—regarded them with wondering eyes.

"But, Miracle—" General Pepper protested.

"Leave us, General," the Miracle said softly.

The general stiffened, then gestured to the other two men. All three disappeared behind the curtain. The Miracle closed her eyes, as if listening.

Tigre glanced nervously at Kali, who couldn't seem to tear her eyes away from the Miracle.

"Alone now," Miracle said, opening her eyes. "You may sit." She spread her hands toward a couple of cushions on the floor below the dais.

"What is this?" Kali demanded. "How are you ... possible?"

"I might ask you the same thing," Miracle replied with a tranquil smile, but Tigre thought he could detect an edge to her voice. He folded himself onto a cushion, and Kali grudgingly followed suit.

"We're here by accident," Kali began. The Miracle's smile cracked wider.

"One person's accident is another's miracle," she murmured.

"We're not miracles," Kali retorted quickly. "*I'm* a regular person."

"Hey, so am I," Tigre objected.

"We came from the year 2012," Kali explained, ignoring him. "We seem to have time traveled somehow."

The Miracle's eyes were huge as saucers now.

"2012?" she breathed. "From the future?"

"What? No, the past—what are you talking about? What year is this?" Kali sputtered, her voice rising. The Miracle smiled.

"You are in the Year of our Miracle 13 A.B."

"A.B.?" Tigre asked.

"After Birth. Mine."

Kali snorted. "These people measure time by when you were born?"

"I thought—" Miracle shifted slightly, looking unsettled for the first time. "I was given to understand that all people did. I am *the Miracle*."

"Oh, I see," Tigre said suddenly. "Kali, we're idiots. The Miracle—born after everybody thought no more children would ever be born. It wasn't in the newspapers we saw, so it must have happened after the evacuation, more than sixty years after our time."

"Then who were your parents?" Kali asked her. "They must have been ancient when they had you."

"My mother died bearing me," the Miracle said, "and yes, she was very old at the time. She said I was a gift."

"What about your father? Is it General Pepper?" Tigre asked.

The Miracle smiled slightly. "I wish he were. General Pepper is almost the only man who never claimed to be my father."

"*Claimed* to be?"

"Of course. It could have been a number of people; my mother never knew herself. But many of her partners leaped at the opportunity to be known as the only man on the planet capable of fathering a child. Such a one would be in high demand."

"You mean—" Tigre said.

"*Ew*," Kali said.

"You are truly from the Before Time?" the Miracle asked. "You do not know any of this?"

"We are," Tigre said. "We don't know how we got here."

"Are there any others like you?" Kali broke in. "Other people our age?"

"I am the only," Miracle said with dignity. "I am the salvation of our race."

"Wow," Tigre said. Kali and Miracle looked at him.

"That's—I mean—Kali, imagine being the only kid on the *planet*. With nobody else under sixty years old to talk to or play with. It's sad."

"I am never sad," Miracle said sharply. "It does not befit a miracle to feel sorrow. I am the hope of all humanity."

Yada yada yada, Kali thought. "So *you* can have kids?" she asked.

Miracle's face fell and her large eyes closed. A strained pause followed. Finally Miracle took a breath and opened her eyes again.

"No. It is uncertain as yet how I am to save our species. The doctors say I am not . . . physically equipped to conceive, but I may have other useful properties. I must. I am the Miracle." She leaned forward, suddenly passionate. "There *must* be a reason for me."

"I'm sure there is," Tigre hastened to agree. Kali looked skeptical, but kept her mouth shut.

Miracle pulled back and regarded them. "There might be a reason for you as well."

"I'm not the salvation of humanity, or any of that mumbo jumbo," Kali declared firmly.

Tigre could picture Vicky's reaction to that idea. Someone who created thunderstorms when he was angry . . . didn't sound like what humanity needed right now. Images that he'd been able to suppress for days suddenly popped into his head—blood, rain, an old brown trench coat shredded beyond recognition—and he winced. "Me neither," he said softly.

Suddenly the Miracle gasped. She doubled over as if she'd been stabbed, jerking and contorting on the dais. Kali and Tigre leaped to their feet, but as they started forward

Miracle's head snapped up. The dark eyes were gone, replaced with a glittering iridescent film that seemed to glare at them. Kali and Tigre froze, transfixed.

A new voice came from the Miracle's mouth, impossibly deep, inhumanly forbidding, resonating around the room.

"HUMANITY," it boomed mockingly. Miracle threw her arms up and rose to her feet, somehow towering over them despite her tiny size. *"HUMANITY IS NOT WORTH SAVING."* She pointed menacingly at each of them. *"YOU SHOULD NOT BE CONCERNING YOURSELVES WITH THESE TRIFLING MORTALS."*

Tigre was too shocked to speak, but Kali snapped back: "Well, what *should* we be doing? Sitting around waiting for the voices in our heads to order us off a bridge?"

"THE OTHERS ARE CLOSE. THEY WILL BE HERE BY SUNRISE. FIND THEM AND PREPARE; THE BATTLE WILL BE SOON. NOW LEAVE THIS PLACE. YOU HAVE NO NEED OF THIS VESSEL."

"What do you want her for?" Tigre asked, his voice cracking. "Do you know why she was born? What is her purpose?"

There was a pause. Light seemed to ripple along the Miracle's pale arms. Finally the voice came again:

"SHE IS HERE FOR OUR AMUSEMENT." It chuckled harshly. *"DESPAIR IS AN ENTERTAINING EMOTION, BUT MIXED WITH FRUITLESS HOPE—"* It laughed. The iridescent glaze glittered from the Miracle's eyes, then started glowing, as if burning from the inside. Light poured out, illuminating the room. Kali and Tigre covered their eyes

as the light intensified, and then, just as it got to the point of being unbearable, it suddenly flared out. At the same moment Miracle screamed, and they dropped their hands to see her collapse to the dais.

Tigre jumped forward, swept the clutter off the platform, and lifted Miracle's head onto his lap. Kali knelt beside him as he checked the Miracle's pulse. It was fast, but not abnormal. He rubbed her wrists and looked at Kali. She was staring at Miracle with a mixture of confusion, pity, and anger.

The Miracle moaned softly. Her eyes, back to their usual darkness, fluttered open, and she blinked at Tigre and Kali.

"I—" She reached up and touched her forehead, then sat up quickly. "A visitation! I had another visitation, didn't I?" She turned and looked at them, excitement transforming her into a much younger child. "Did I prophesize? Was there a message for me from the gods? Did they allow you a glimpse of your purpose?" She seized Tigre's hand. "Did they say anything about mine?" She smiled proudly. "They speak only through me. I am their chosen vessel."

"They . . . um . . ." Tigre didn't know quite what to say. He opened his mouth to stammer out what they'd heard, when Kali interrupted.

"They said your purpose is still a secret," she said. "But that they needed you to give us a message." She gave Tigre a look, and he nodded.

"I told you I was necessary," she whispered, beaming. "What was the message for you?"

"Uh—it was pretty mysterious," Kali said.

"The gods often are." Miracle nodded sagely.

"We have to go find someone, and fight some sort of battle, sometime soon," Tigre puzzled out.

"Are there any other people like us, that just appeared?" Kali asked. "Do you know of anyone else?"

"That has not been revealed to me," said the Miracle. "I am sure General Pepper would have told me if he knew of any. Perhaps they have yet to arrive in this time."

"Perhaps," Tigre said doubtfully. Kali stood and seemed about to speak when they heard pounding from behind the curtain.

"Miracle! Exalted One!" General Pepper's voice called. "Are you safe? Please allow us into your gracious presence!"

The Miracle sighed and almost rolled her eyes. She rearranged herself on the dais and gestured Tigre and Kali back to the cushions on the floor. With a flick of her hand she activated something, and they heard the sounds of a door rolling open.

The three men burst through the curtain, brandishing pipes. They stopped when they saw the Miracle gazing serenely at them.

"We thought we heard screaming," General Pepper grunted, eyeing the debris that had been swept off the dais.

Miracle rose to her feet and turned toward him. "The gods have spoken. They have blessed our visitors with a glimpse of their glory." She spread her hands, palms up, lifting her head toward the ceiling. "Thanks must be offered for their munificence."

The three men dropped to their knees and lowered

their heads to the ground. Kali and Tigre exchanged glances. Miracle lifted one hand toward the two of them.

"I give you leave to depart," she said. "May your sacred mission be successful and may your presence bring new glory to us all. Go in hope."

Go in hope. Her words echoed mockingly behind them as they descended the ladder, back into the darkness of the tunnels.

Diana peered at the sky, then glanced back at Gus. He drove mechanically, as he had all night. He hardly seemed to notice where they were going and followed her directions without question. They'd been driving for hours, and not once had he stopped for a rest.

They had buried Andrew in a park adjoining the beach, surrounded by trees. They had even been able to do it in the middle of the day, the day he died—yesterday—because Justin and Treasure's pterodolphins had driven off the crystal hunters. Once Treasure was able to lasso the surviving sixteen pterodolphins back inside, she declared it was safe to go outdoors for at least a few hours.

Gus had been very quiet since then. Diana had been tempted to leave him with Justin and Treasure, but the voice in her mind was getting stronger every minute, and she wanted Gus with her when she confronted whatever it was. Besides, surely activity would be better for Gus than mourning by his brother's grave. She was a little worried about the idea of leaving him with kooky pterodolphin trainers anyway.

He didn't even argue with her. He had slept for the rest of the day after they buried Andrew, but crawled obediently out of his sleeping bag after the sun set, when Diana came to wake him. He numbly accepted the keys to the yellow Beetle and stood without speaking while Diana said good-bye to Treasure and Justin. Treasure assured them it was all right to take the Beetle rather than try to repair the damage their car had received during the chase. Justin wished them luck in their "expedition" and told them to come back and visit anytime. He and Treasure both promised to visit Andrew's grave as often as they could.

It wasn't until the two of them had been driving for an hour that Gus had finally spoken. "Where are we going?" he said flatly.

"New York City," she said, feeling something click into place inside her, as if that was the right decision.

She hoped their destination would inspire some sort of reaction from him, maybe even a conversation, but he just nodded and kept driving.

And now here they were, miles and hours later, with the George Washington Bridge looming in front of them, and he still hadn't asked her why they were here.

She glanced at the sky again. It was getting lighter, but how long until the sun came up? Did they have time to make it into the city? *We can get there before dawn,* she thought. *At least there's no traffic.* She started to smile, then stopped, wishing she could share the joke with Gus.

"Let's take the West Side Highway down," she said, studying one of the maps Justin had given them. *You couldn't be a bit more specific than "New York City"?* she thought at the voice in her head. "We can turn into the city around midtown. Okay?"

He shrugged, barely.

"Gus, don't give up," Diana said. "Remember what Andrew said. There has to be a reason we're here. And I think we'll be able to figure it out in New York. Maybe by the time we go to sleep tonight, we'll have a million answers and we'll know exactly how to fix everything. Imagine that, okay?"

He looked at her sideways.

"Perhaps there's a secret colony of super-smart scientists hiding out in New York," she continued, trying to remember some of Andrew's wild theories. "Maybe they found out how to pull us through time and they know that we can be helpful. Maybe there's something we can do about the crystal hunters, stop them somehow, or . . . I don't know." She trailed off. Wild speculation was not her forte. There was a pause.

"Maybe we can get back," Gus burst out suddenly, making her jump. "Whoever brought us forward must be able to send us back."

"Back in time?" Diana said. "Maybe. I don't know, Gus. I think whatever we're here for is here."

"You can't explain how they sent us forward, either, can you? There *must* be a way."

"But, Gus, why would you want to? You heard what Andrew said, what it's been like. If we go back, we'd just have to live through it. If we stay, there's a chance we can make things better."

"If we go back," Gus said, "at least I'll have seventy-five more years with my brother, the way I'm supposed to."

Diana sighed. "Well, first let's find out if it's even possible."

They drove in silence over the bridge and down the west side of Manhattan. Diana thought she saw glints of crystal lurking at the edges of her vision, but every time she turned they seemed to disappear. Gus was quiet, but at least he finally looked alive.

The sun was peeking over the horizon as they reached the Seventy-ninth Street exit.

"Here, you think?" Gus asked.

"Sure. We need a place to hole up for the day, anyhow, so we might as well start looking around here. Or hey, we could stay at the Four Seasons." She laughed a little. "Doug was always glad the Plaza Hotel had closed. I think he was afraid if I stayed there I'd become even more like Eloise than I already am."

Gus gave her a blank look.

"Eloise? The little girl who lives in the Plaza Hotel? Famous children's book?" Gus's puzzled look remained. "Wow, you're officially hopeless. Eloise is one of my favorite characters ever. The point is, she's a teeny bit bratty and very independent."

"You seem pretty independent," Gus said, maneuvering around potholes.

"Sure. And changing my name was *my* idea."

"It wasn't?"

"No way. I wanted to go the whole Diana/goddess of the moon and the hunt and deer and stuff route. I thought it would be much cooler, and more in line with my kind of music, you know?" She felt strange admitting all this, but she kept going, relieved that Gus was finally talking. "But, you know, I was like twelve when they came up with my superstar persona. Not even my mom would listen to me, let alone all the big honcho producers. We had this 'image meeting' when the record label signed me, and within two hours I was gone. They replaced me with something else. Some*one* else, this goddess of love person." She shivered. "That's not really who I am. Or what I'm like. But it sells albums."

"I guess you're not exactly what I expected," Gus admitted.

She gave him a wry look. "Nothing like getting to know someone's dark side."

"No, I—I think you're even more interesting now."

That can't possibly be true, Diana thought. Gus had now seen her grumpy, mean, bossy, sleepy, cranky, frustrated, and completely stylist free. He had to think she was the least likable person on the planet, especially compared to sweet, charming, perfect Venus.

She looked out the window and noticed that they were driving south along Central Park. She had never seen New York City like this. It felt like a quiet country town that just happened to have enormously oversized buildings and wide, empty streets. Central Park itself looked alive and hopeful, unlike the desolate surroundings they'd been through so far. It was overgrown, but in a wild, exuberant way. She felt suddenly optimistic.

"That way," she pointed. "The Plaza's on the opposite corner, on the south side of the park."

"Think we'll be able to find parking?" Gus remarked, deadpan.

"Hey, that's *my* joke," she protested, punching him lightly on the arm.

"What the—" Gus suddenly slammed on the brakes. "Did you see that?"

"See what?" Diana glanced around, but nothing seemed unusual.

"I could have sworn I saw a person," he said, twisting around in his seat. "Someone moving in the park."

"Really?" She studied the trees, orange and yellow and green leaves igniting in the growing sunlight. An uneasy feeling stirred in her chest. "I don't know, Gus. Maybe we should get inside now and then look for people once it's dark."

"I don't want to wait that long," he insisted. "Besides, you have more of those apple missiles, right?" He grinned. Diana worried that he was able to be cheerful so quickly after his brother's death, but relief overrode her concern, and she smiled back.

"True; Justin gave me some from his orchard. Although I wouldn't have said no to a shotgun if Treasure had had any extras."

Gus was already pulling over. They climbed out into the silent street, and Diana shivered. She wondered for the first time what month it was, and how much the weather had changed in the last seventy-five years, and whether it was going to get colder or warmer from here. The colors of the leaves suggested it was early fall, but it didn't seem chilly enough for that. She'd always been bad at gauging temperature, since she was cold all year long.

"Hello?" Gus called. "Is anyone there?" He shielded his eyes with one hand and squinted into the park. Branches creaked overhead as the wind sidled through the trees, the only sound they heard.

Diana's uneasiness came creeping back.

"Maybe we shouldn't be shouting," she whispered. "Maybe we should go."

"Yeah, I know," Gus agreed, but he stood still, watching the park. A hint of a new sound twinkled in the air, at the edge of hearing. Diana glanced at the sky.

"Gus, did you hear something?" she said.

"Like what?" He was walking away from her, toward the park.

"Like—like wind chimes, kind of."

"Maybe," he said, tilting his head. Before she could stop him, he had scrambled up to stand on top of the park wall.

"Gus, get down," she hissed frantically.

The sound of wind chimes was getting louder. Wind chimes—or crystal.

"The hunters!" Diana cried. "Gus!"

An enormous gust of wind surged down the street, smashing into Diana and blowing handfuls of dirt into her face. She shut her eyes for a moment and staggered forward. The bag of apples was torn from her grasp. When she could open her eyes again, a vast crystal pterodactyl was swooping down toward them. It was unthinkably enormous, huger than her brain could comprehend, the size of a small plane—nine or ten times the size of the ones that had attacked yesterday.

It dove toward Gus, who was crouched on the wall clinging to the stones, his eyes squeezed shut.

Diana felt disconnected from her body, as if she were

watching the scene from far away. The hunter's wings seemed to fill the entire sky. Thin neon-purple lines darted through the creature's body, and its bright, sinister eyes were fastened on Gus.

Although the moment seemed to last ten centuries, there wasn't even time to scream.

Huge crystal talons wrapped around Gus's torso and pulled him aloft. Diana could see him yelling, hanging from the creature's claws, but the roar of the wind and the sound of the chimes drowned him out. The pterodactyl swung into a lazy turn, then beat slowly off into the distance, carrying Gus away.

The wind died down as quickly as it had come up.

Diana was breathless with horror. This couldn't happen. Gus couldn't be gone just like that. The crystal hunters couldn't *win*, not after all their running and hiding and fighting and being careful.

She ran back to the car, which, luckily, Gus had left running. Sending up a brief prayer to any gods who were listening, Diana jerked the gearshift to drive and slammed on the gas pedal. The car peeled forward and she grabbed the steering wheel, shooting down the street in the direction the crystal hunter had gone.

DO NOT BOTHER, the voice in her head suddenly piped up. HE IS NO CONCERN OF YOURS, AND NOW IT IS TOO LATE FOR HIM. PROCEED TO THE GATHERING PLACE AT ONCE.

Sorry, mysterious voice, Diana thought. *You screwed up this time. I'm getting Gus back, whether you like it or not.*

Tigre hadn't said a word since they emerged from the Times Square station into the pale light from the rising sun. He just started walking uptown to Kali's co-opted apartment. The silence suited Kali fine—she had no idea what to say.

She wasn't used to feeling sorry for people. The Miracle reminded her of Beth, her six-year-old half-sister, who liked to act like a princess but was desperately eager for people to love her. Kali thought again about how her family might have reacted to her disappearance so many decades ago. Did Mom have to go back to work? Who looked after the girls? Were they all okay? How had they survived without her? Were any of them still alive? She wondered how the girls had turned out, and what they had been like as teenagers, and what they had decided to do with their lives, and she felt for the first time like she had lost something important.

Tigre's head suddenly jerked up.

"Did you hear that?" he asked.

"Hear what?" Kali yawned hugely, realizing how tired she was.

"I thought I heard a car." He stopped, frowning down at the ground. Kali crossed her arms and waited a moment before speaking.

"You're probably hallucinating. The first couple of days, I was sure I was hearing things everywhere. Turned out to be the creepy old people or the creepy flying things, most of the time. Never a car, though."

"No, I'm sure there was something." He glanced up Fifth Avenue, then started to run.

"Come on!" he called over his shoulder. "We can catch up to it!"

"Catch up to *what*?" Kali said, exasperated. No way

was she running around the city chasing phantom cars.

Tigre slowed down as a gust of wind hurtled along the street. Kali recognized it, and the attendant chiming sound, and she glanced up to watch the Boss Hunter swoop overhead, glad it wasn't shrieking for once. She was used to seeing it by now, and she was curious to see how it reacted to Tigre.

Not at all, as it turned out. The hunter shot by without paying Tigre the slightest bit of attention.

Was it *carrying* something? Kali turned to watch it soar down the street. It looked like it was carrying a person. Had it captured one of the old people? Why would one of them be out in the daytime?

Suddenly there was a screech of brakes behind her. Her New York pedestrian instincts kicked in, and she threw herself onto the sidewalk as a car hurtled past.

A yellow Volkswagen Beetle. An actual, honest-to-goodness *car*. With someone *driving* it. Not very well, but still.

Tigre was now running back toward her with a comically astonished expression.

"She didn't even stop!" he cried. "She must have seen me, but she just kept on going!"

"Smart woman," Kali remarked sardonically, getting to her feet.

"Come on, let's follow her!" He beckoned as he sped past.

"*Or*," Kali said, seizing his arm and jerking him back, "we use our brains, run in the opposite direction, and hope she doesn't find us."

"What?" Tigre stared at her. "Are you crazy? This is

probably one of the people we're supposed to find. Why the heck would you run away from her?"

"So what if she *is* one of the people we're looking for? Remember that little part about a battle once we find them? Maybe they're dangerous. Maybe they're here to kill us."

"I doubt it," he said in an irritatingly soothing voice. "The girl driving that car was tiny. I bet she's harmless. Now come on, before we lose her!"

"We're not going to lose her," Kali said. "She's following the crystal hunter. And I know exactly where it's heading."

Tigre craned his neck in awe, watching the walls of the building soar into the sky above him. He hadn't even thought to look for it as Quetzie flew him in, but here it was: the Empire State Building.

"See," Kali said, pointing. "The flying hunters must have lopped the top off at some point, so it's open to the sky where the viewing area was. And since it's the tallest building in New York, it makes sense that the biggest, most obnoxious crystal hunter would have made its nest up there." She squinted up to the edge where the hunter's wings were barely visible, glinting in the sunlight. "I call it the Boss Hunter because the others act deferential whenever it's around."

"Do you really think it was carrying someone?" he asked again. Predictably, she got annoyed.

"I told you I think so," she snapped.

"What do the hunters do with the people they catch?" He shuddered. "They don't *eat* them, do they?"

"Come on, use your brain. They're machines—they don't need to eat. I have no idea how they kill the people they catch—or what they do with the bodies. The newspapers all cryptically referred to 'disappearances' and 'elimination.' Very coy."

"Very unhelpful," Tigre said, returning his gaze to the street and scanning for signs of the girl in the car.

"Here's the main entrance," Kali said. She kicked aside a pile of glass and crunched forward through the shattered doors. Tigre followed her into the lobby area, which was lined with stained-glass images of the Wonders of the World, most of them curiously still intact. In the front was a metal-relief plaque of the Empire State Building, covered with dust and grime but still shinier than anything else he'd seen so far in this city.

Kali gestured silently to the far corner of the lobby. Tigre could hear it too: a muffled voice. They edged forward until they could see the girl clearly.

She was tiny, only a bit over five feet tall, Tigre guessed, with reddish-gold shoulder-length hair, a dancer's build, and a strikingly pretty face. She was wearing jeans and a dark blue-gray flannel shirt that was much too large for her. She also looked familiar, but Tigre didn't know why.

The girl had found the entrance to the stairs and was wrestling with a locked door, swearing.

Tigre hesitated, remembering Kali's first reaction to him, but Kali stepped forward briskly.

"That's probably not going to work," she said.

The other girl shrieked and whipped around, clutching her heart. Her eyes widened when she saw Kali and Tigre.

"Oh my God! People!" she cried. "*Young* people! I'm Diana. Who are you? Where did you come from?" Her smile was delighted and genuine, and Tigre felt instantly at ease. Even Kali's icy demeanor seemed to thaw a little bit.

"Kali. Tigre. You mean you didn't notice us when you nearly ran us over?" Kali asked, jerking her thumb toward the street.

"No—really, did I do that? I'm sorry. Where did you— no, never mind. I have to get upstairs." She seized the door handle and rattled it furiously. "That *thing* took my friend, and I have to get him back."

"The elevators aren't working?" Tigre asked, and immediately felt stupid as both girls gave him incredulous looks.

"Even if they were, there's no way I'd get into a small box suspended from cables with that creature right over my head," Kali declared.

"Please, we have to hurry," Diana said. "Gus might—it might have—"

"Let me try," Kali said, moving to the door. "You and Tigre look for other ways up." The girl obediently turned and headed down the hall. Tigre started to follow, but something made him glance back over his shoulder.

Kali's eyes were closed. She had planted one foot on the wall next to the door and wrapped both hands around the door handle. As he watched, something seemed to shimmer in the air around her, like a wave of heat rising from a summer sidewalk. With a powerful heave, Kali surged backward and the entire door came roaring free with a clatter of marble cascading from the wall around it.

Tigre's jaw dropped.

"You did it!" Diana cried, running back to Kali. "Thank you, thank you!" She threw her arms around Kali and hugged her briefly. Kali's body tensed, and both girls felt a sharp surge of electricity, like the one Kali had felt earlier with Tigre. Diana jumped back with a startled expression, then turned and started running up the stairs.

So whatever that was, Kali thought, it wasn't unique to any of them. Which was better. Having a special weird electric connection with Tigre would have been . . . weird. She waved to Tigre.

"Come on, this was your idea," she called. "Guess we're stuck being rescuer types now." She took off after the smaller girl, leaping up the stairs two at a time.

Tigre shook off his amazement and went after them. But he couldn't help thinking: *so the old people were right about Kali's powers after all.*

"This is going to take forever!" Diana's voice echoed down the stairs in frustration as she rounded the corner on the twenty-ninth floor. Kali had recognized "Venus" at once, of course, although she wasn't exactly a fan of her music. What were the odds someone this famous would have been transplanted here too? Still, it was definitely her: there was something about the way the girl carried herself, like she was used to being watched, that screamed "superstar." The fake name was interesting, too. Diana. Was she hoping no one would recognize her in this new world? Didn't she know there wasn't anyone left who cared about that kind of thing?

Still, Kali was impressed by the singer's stamina. Despite her longer legs, Kali was having trouble keeping up, and Diana wasn't even breathing heavily yet. At the other extreme, a few floors below them, she could hear Tigre huffing and puffing. He'd said he was a runner, but apparently he wasn't used to multiple long flights of stairs.

"Actually," Kali called up to Diana, trying not to sound too breathless, "the record for running up these stairs is nine minutes, thirty-seven seconds. Or it was seventy-five years ago, anyway."

"Really?" the singer called back. "Okay, we can do that!" And with a patter of sneakers, she surged ahead.

Kali paused a moment, clutching the rail and sucking in air. All her instincts told her not to like this girl, but there was something kind of irresistible about her. Kali actually *wanted* to help her, which was not a feeling she was used to.

"Just doing the right thing," she muttered to herself. "The guy needs rescuing. It's what anyone would do."

Taking a deep breath, she forced herself to start climbing again, trying to ignore the fact that fewer and fewer of the fluorescent lights were working the higher up they went.

It wasn't quite nine minutes and thirty-seven seconds, but Kali guessed that she reached the top of the stairs in about fifteen minutes, although her protesting leg muscles seemed to think it took about three millennia longer.

Diana was waiting for her at the top, crouching by the door. Kali could barely see her outline in the dim light from the last working bulb, two floors down.

"Thanks for coming," Diana said warmly. "I appreciate it *so* much. I don't want to put you guys in danger or anything—"

"It's no problem," Kali said. "The hunters couldn't care less about me. I could probably stroll out there right now and the Boss would just ignore me, the way it always does." She wished she felt as confident as she sounded. She'd never gone tromping through the Boss's nest before, after all.

"I bet it won't keep ignoring you if you try to take away its prey," Diana said. She glanced anxiously through the railing. From several floors down came low, wheezing sounds. "Should we, uh—should we wait for him?"

Kali grinned despite herself. "It does sound like it's going to be a while."

"What are we going to do?" Diana said, spreading her hands as if she were just realizing that she had no weapons. "I had this vague notion I'd just run out there and grab him, but now—" She shivered. "I don't know."

"We can't make a plan without knowing what we're getting into," Kali said. "Let's open the door a crack and see what's going on."

Diana nodded and gingerly turned the door handle. Kali was relieved to see it was unlocked—she suspected the wall-shattering trick might not be the most subtle entrance. She pushed the door open an inch and both girls peered through the crack.

The door opened onto the outer observatory walkway, where an iron fence ran around the top of a low wall so people could look out without falling over the edge.

Opposite the fence was an inner wall of windows that abruptly cut off where the top of the building had been knocked away. A pile of rubble rested where the lightning rod in the center had been, arranged into a grotesque mockery of a bird's nest.

At the far end of the walkway, the Boss Hunter was perched on the outside wall, tearing at the fence with its claws and beak as if to rip open a section. Directly below the pterodactyl, a boy was lying on the walkway, apparently unconscious. Diana gasped when she spotted him.

Instantly the pterodactyl's head whipped up. Kali jerked Diana back and let the door snick shut.

"Do you think it saw us?" Diana whispered.

"I don't know," Kali whispered back. They crouched in the semidarkness, listening, but there was no sound from beyond the door.

"Do you think Gus is dead?" Diana's voice shook a little as she asked.

"No," Kali answered. "I saw him move."

"Really?" Diana said, relieved. "What do you think that thing is going to do with him?"

"I have no idea, but I doubt it'll be fun. For Gus, that is."

"I wish there were a way to destroy that thing," Diana said vehemently. "That would show those crystal hunters. I bet if we could destroy the biggest one, all the others would leave him alone for good."

"It would probably shut down all the ones in this area if we took out their leader," Kali mused. "Maybe then Miracle could at least see some sunshine." Not that it was Kali's problem, of course. Not that she cared what happened to a bunch of loony underground kidnappers.

"Miracle?" Diana repeated, mystified.

"Tell you later," Kali said. "Okay, I have an idea."

Tigre puffed up the last few stairs and collapsed in a heap at the top as Kali was outlining her plan.

"It would help if we had a distraction," she finished. She regarded Tigre's prone, gasping form thoughtfully.

"Nuh-uh," Tigre wheezed, guessing her thoughts. "Can't outrun it. Can't run. Too—tired—breathing is—hard."

"Hmmm," Kali said. "Is there anything you *can* do? Anything you perhaps haven't told us about yet?"

"Anything?" Diana pleaded, practically batting her eyelashes at him.

Tigre closed his eyes. After a moment he said, "Sometimes I . . . create storms."

"Create *storms*?" Diana said. "Are you serious? You mean, like, a rainmaker?"

"I think he's serious," Kali said. Something about him, about his electricity, had made her wonder if he might be like her. She stopped short of thinking "powers," but the word lurked there, in the back of her mind. And if Diana had been brought here too—might she be like them as well? Yeah, that'd be fair, giving someone superstardom *and* superpowers in one lifetime.

"Not helpful anyway," Tigre muttered. He crawled onto the landing next to them.

"Actually, it could be," Kali said. "These hunters feed off solar power, remember? If you could summon a storm and block out the sun—well, it might not stop the Boss Hunter, but it could slow it down, or at least distract it long enough for Venus to grab Gus."

Diana flinched as Kali said her name.

"That's who you look like!" Tigre cried.

"Not looks like, that's who she is," Kali said. "Sorry to blow your cover."

"I'd really prefer it if you called me Diana," she said. "That's my real name, and it feels weird to be Venus in a world that's not buying my albums anymore."

"I can't believe I didn't recognize you," Tigre sputtered. "My sister *loves* your music."

"Thanks," Diana said, touching him on the arm. She pulled her hand back quickly and even in the half-light Kali could see from their expressions that they'd felt the same electric shock.

"Let's do this, then," she said. "Tigre, how long does it take for you to create a storm?"

"Um." He shifted unhappily. "Honestly, I've never done it on purpose. I'm not sure I know how."

Kali frowned.

"I'll—I'll try, though." He closed his eyes. "Just give me a minute."

"I'm not sure we have a minute," Diana said, peering through the door again. "Look."

Gus sat up groggily. His head ached from hitting the walkway when the crystal hunter had dropped him. The sick, furious feeling inside, which had subsided for the three days he'd been with Andrew, had returned in full force now, and he could barely breathe through the constricting pain in his chest and back. He cracked open his eyes, realizing he'd lost his glasses, and saw the enormous crystal hunter watching. A wave of terror swept over him.

YOU ARE NOTHING, BOY.

He clutched his head. Was that a voice he'd just heard? It sounded like it was coming from inside his head, not from the crystal hunter, which hadn't moved. It stared at him with beady purple eyes, perched on the wall in an area where the fence had been bent and torn aside. Beyond was an open view of the eighty-six-story drop.

YOU'RE A POINTLESS WASTE OF SPACE AND ENERGY. YOU MIGHT AS WELL BE DEAD.

Gus squinted around him. He was alone on the walkway with the monster. And yet he was definitely hearing a voice.

PERHAPS YOU SHOULD JOIN YOUR BROTHER.

With an electronic-sounding caw, the crystal hunter hopped up onto the inner mound of rubble and sidled along until it was between him and the doorway. The only way for Gus to go was toward the fence. And down.

YESSSSS, the voice whispered. *DOWN. MAKE THE PAIN STOP. ALL AT ONCE, ALL GONE, FREE OF PAIN. SO EASY.*

"Shut *up!*" Gus yelled. The creature reacted, spreading its wings with an outraged squawk, but the voice continued smoothly in his mind.

YOU KNOW IT'S THE EASIEST WAY. NOBODY CARES ABOUT YOU. THERE'S NOBODY LEFT FOR YOU. YOU SHOULD BE DEAD LIKE ALL THE OTHERS.

"Stop it!" Gus cried, burying his head in his hands. "Just stop it! It's not going to work! I'm not going to jump, no matter what you say!"

I THINK YOU WILL. SOONER OR LATER.

The crystal hunter hopped toward him menacingly,

sharp teeth glinting in its crystal jaw.

"If you want me dead," Gus said to it, "why don't you kill me yourself? You could have dropped me anytime while you were bringing me here."

THIS CREATURE IS NOT SPEAKING TO YOU, FOOL. IT IS NOT SENTIENT ENOUGH FOR THIS LEVEL OF CONVERSATION. IT IS MERELY A TOOL OF OURS. WE COULD EASILY HAVE IT KILL YOU, BUT THAT IS NOT HOW WE PREFER TO WORK. IT'S A MORE POWERFUL SACRIFICE IF IT COMES VOLUNTARILY. WE'D LIKE YOU TO CHOOSE YOUR DEATH—BUT MAKE NO MISTAKE. IF YOU DO NOT, AND WE GET BORED, WE WILL FIND A MUCH MORE HORRIBLE WAY FOR YOU TO DIE.

The hunter's claws flashed in the sun. It leaned toward him, and Gus scrambled away until his back was pressed against the wall, below the broken fence.

Perhaps he was useless. Perhaps he was alone.

But Andrew would want him to fight.

He glanced again at the door on the other end of the walkway and realized with amazement that it was slowly creaking open. And emerging from it was—Diana! She caught his eye and held a finger to her lips, creeping forward.

Gus steeled his face so he wouldn't give her away. "Oh yeah, you hunk of glass," he taunted the pterodactyl, "and how long does it take you to get bored?"

NOT LONG. AND BE WARNED, BOY—WE SEE EVERYTHING.

The crystal hunter whirled around with a roar and spread its wings as wide as they would go, towering over Diana.

Gus barely had time to register that there was someone else behind her before he was up and running forward, trying to dodge around the creature while it was looking away.

The wing came down like a wall of glass, and Gus slammed straight into it.

"Gus!" Diana yelled. The creature had knocked him out, but it didn't seem to notice. It loomed overhead, clacking its jaw at Diana.

Kali darted past her and over to the interior wall. She pressed her hands against the glass windows and closed her eyes, concentrating.

"Come on, Tigre," Diana murmured. "A diversion would be mighty useful right now." She glanced at the sky. A tiny gray cloud that looked more like a puff of smoke was ambling its way toward them, and a breeze was picking up. Off in the distance there were more clouds gathering, but not fast enough.

The pterodactyl's eyes sparked and it turned toward Gus's prone form. A tremor ran through the building.

"Kali!" Diana cried desperately. "I can't get to him!"

Kali glanced over her shoulder and saw the crystal hunter reaching a long claw toward Gus. With a frustrated sound, she took her hands off the building. The trembling stopped.

"Come on!" Kali yelled, running toward the creature.

Diana sent up a silent prayer and dashed after her, weaving in the opposite direction so the hunter's attention was divided between them. The pterodactyl roared.

Suddenly the sun broke through the meager cloud

cover. A bright blaze of light lanced down and struck the crystal hunter.

"That's not helpful, Tigre!" Kali shouted.

"Watch," said a commanding voice from above them.

Diana looked up, and her mouth fell open.

It was the golden stranger from her dreams.

He had appeared from nowhere, standing atop the rubble nest directly in the beam of light, surveying the battle below him.

The pterodactyl's head was raised, facing the light as if drinking it in. As Diana watched, the beam grew brighter and brighter till it hurt her eyes to look at it. The neon purple lines of energy running through the crystal hunter began to glow more and more fiercely, as if its power centers were overloading.

Kali glanced from the stranger to the hunter, then met Diana's eyes. She pointed wordlessly at Gus, strode back to the interior wall, and placed her hands on it again.

Diana edged around the creature, now mesmerized into stillness by the sunlight, and knelt beside Gus. He was breathing shallowly, and a large, angry bruise was already forming on his forehead.

"Gus, wake up," she whispered, trying not to draw the hunter's attention. "We have to get out of here."

His eyes twitched, and a small moan escaped him.

"Come on," she said, reaching an arm around him and tugging him into a sitting position. "We have to get you away from the creature before Kali does whatever it is she's doing."

The building started rumbling again.

"Mmmmfrr," Gus mumbled, reaching up and touching his head. He slowly blinked his eyes open. *"Ow."*

"Well, nobody said running into a glass wall would be painless," Diana said, trying to keep the note of panic out of her voice. "Now come on, stand up. We'll let you rest after the world ends, all right?"

"Thought it already had," he muttered. She wrapped her arms around him and helped him to his feet.

The roof quaked, he staggered, and she caught him. Their eyes met.

"Thanks for coming for me," he whispered.

"Thanks for staying alive until I did," she replied.

Impulsively, she tilted her head up and kissed him. He didn't start or jump back, as she almost expected him to, but tightened his arms around her.

The building shook violently, and Diana pulled back, feeling herself turn bright pink. *Spectacular impulse control, Diana,* she scolded herself. Gus looked dazed. She glanced up and saw, with a feeling of relief, that her stranger was watching the creature instead of them. She took a deep breath and tugged Gus after her, maneuvering around the pterodactyl without any reaction from it.

Tigre hurried toward them and helped her support Gus through the doorway into the stairwell.

"Who *is* that guy?" he said. "I'm sure I only needed a few more minutes to create a storm, but whatever he's doing shut it down right away. I couldn't even begin to fight it."

"The important thing is that it's working," Diana said, and felt guilty at the crushed look on Tigre's face. "His name is Amon," she added.

"You *know* him?" Gus asked.

"Um. Yes and no," she said. "It's complicated." The building gave a violent shudder. "I think we should get downstairs."

"Not without Kali," Tigre said stubbornly. "You guys go ahead and I'll make sure she's okay."

Diana helped Gus to stand as Tigre opened the door again, and all three of them had a clear view of the paralyzed pterodactyl. Kali's hands were pressed against the glass of the interior wall as the building shook around her. Amon stood overhead on the nest, his arms folded, watching calmly.

As the trembling reached a crescendo, Kali pulled her hands back.

"Get out of here!" she shouted at Amon. "It's coming down!"

Pieces of masonry were starting to tumble down from the nest and crash onto the walkway, but he didn't move.

"Come on!" Kali called.

"I'll be fine," he said in the same calm voice, which was still powerful enough to carry to where Diana and the others were. "But you might not be if you stay any longer."

"Suit yourself!" Kali yelled, dodging a block of concrete. She threw her hands over her head and ran for the stairs. Through the dust cloud coming off the falling rocks, Diana could swear she saw Amon rising directly up into the air. A flash of sunlight dazzled her eyes, and when she could see again, he was gone.

With a loud, roaring groan, the entire nest tilted and slid toward the transfixed crystal hunter, gathering speed to crash down upon it with a sound like the smashing of a thousand wind chimes.

Tigre reached out and hauled Kali through the door just as a chunk of wall collapsed behind her.

"Down the stairs," she gasped. "I don't know how much damage there is."

"How did you do that?" Tigre said wonderingly.

"Run now, talk later," Kali said. "Help me with him." She lifted one of Gus's arms over her shoulders. Diana relinquished Gus's other arm to Tigre and followed them as they supported him down the stairs as fast as they could.

They saw large cracks running through the walls on the upper levels, but they managed to make it to the street without anything else crashing down around them. Tigre lowered Gus to the sidewalk in the shadow of a door opposite the Empire State Building and Kali got her first good look at him: ordinary enough, with tired green eyes, and disheveled brown hair. He slouched a little, whether sitting, standing, or walking, and Kali noticed that he maneuvered to keep Diana in sight at all times, even when he was talking to someone else.

"We totally crushed that thing!" Diana said jubilantly. "I bet the crystal hunters won't dare mess with us now!"

"They never messed with me before," Kali said with a shrug. "I'm surprised they went after you."

"Not me—just Gus," Diana said.

"Hey," he protested weakly, giving her a bedazzled smile. "I never agreed with that theory."

"Want to argue about it now?" she said, cocking an eyebrow at him.

"Nah," he replied.

"I bet we've made the world safer for everybody," Diana continued with excitement. "I mean, if we could take down something that size, we could totally destroy the smaller hunters. Maybe that's why we're here. To fight the crystal hunters and give the world back to humanity!"

"We did kick its ass," Kali admitted.

"Well, *you* guys did," Tigre said.

"I didn't do much either," Diana said kindly. "Lots of screaming and yelling for help, if I remember correctly."

"Well, if you hadn't asked for help, we wouldn't have known Gus needed rescuing in the first place," Kali pointed out.

"And your part of the plan would have worked, Tigre," Diana said, "if Amon hadn't shown up."

"You really know him?" Gus asked.

"Sort of," Diana said, embarrassed. "I didn't think he was real. He shows up in my dreams sometimes."

"In your *dreams*?" Gus said. Something poked at the corner of his brain. He hadn't gotten a good look at the guy—but he had noticed the golden light coming off him. Could it be the same guy from *his* dreams? The one he kept trying to kill?

"I think we should get you somewhere safe and, say, indoors," Kali interrupted. "Let's go back to the place where I'm staying uptown."

No. The voice rumbled through Kali's head, louder than it had ever been before. It actually sounded angry. As she flinched, she saw Tigre and Diana reacting too.

YOU WILL PROCEED TO THE GATHERING PLACE. NOW.

"Bite me!" Kali yelled at the sky.

"What gathering place?" Tigre said simultaneously.

Diana was delighted. "You can hear it too? I thought it was only me!"

"Hear what?" Gus asked.

"Bossy know-it-all voices in our heads," Kali snapped.

"You've heard this before? Why didn't you say anything?" Gus asked Diana. "Is that how you knew to come here?"

"Yes," Diana said. "I was afraid you'd think I was crazy if I told you."

A hurt look flashed across Gus's face.

"Does anyone know where we're supposed to go?" Tigre asked.

"Who cares?" Kali snapped. "You don't seriously think we should do what they want, do you?"

"Hey, maybe it's not the cool New York thing to do, but if it'll get us some answers, then yeah, I think it's a good idea."

"Well, excuse me," Kali said, stung. "I'm sorry if the 'cool New York' impulse to *survive* is too 'hip' for you."

"Look, whoever is talking in our heads is obviously controlling this whole thing," Tigre said. "Why would they go to all this trouble just to kill us? Why wouldn't they use a crystal hunter to do it now instead of waiting for us to be in a specific place?"

"That's a lot of assumptions," Kali pointed out. "You have no idea who this voice is or how they're connected to the time jump and the crystal hunters. And if they *are* controlling the situation, then quite frankly that makes me trust them *less*, not more, and I think it's plain idiotic to do what they tell you to like obedient little cows."

"Well, I think it's paranoid not to!" Tigre huffed.

"It's a pointless argument anyway," Gus interrupted. "Since we have no idea where to go."

"Actually—" Diana said hesitantly. "I think I might know. Well, I have an idea," she amended. "Something I realized when I saw Amon. It's not that far from here, if I'm right. We could check it out and leave if it looks like a trap."

"That makes sense," Tigre said, nodding.

"Go ahead," Kali said, folding her arms stubbornly. "I'll meet you back at my place, *if* you survive."

Thunder rumbled in the distance, and they all looked up at the sky, surprised to see dark clouds creeping overhead. Kali shot Tigre a suspicious look, and he fought to stave off the surge of annoyance he was feeling.

"You're really not coming?" Tigre asked.

"I am really not coming, hotshot. I've done my group bonding for the day. Good luck with the crazy voices, and I hope you don't come back possessed or something, because if I think you've all become alien spawn, I'll probably kill you."

Tigre had the uncomfortable feeling that she wasn't kidding.

Diana's car was parked in the middle of the street around the corner. Raindrops started to fall as Tigre got in the backseat and closed the door. Through the windshield he saw Kali shoot an irritated look at the sky and stalk away.

"Are you doing this?" Diana asked Tigre as she started the car. "Is it some sort of delayed reaction?"

"Doing what?" Gus asked.

"Tigre can make storms," Diana answered.

"Huh," Gus said. "Wouldn't *un*making storms be a little

more helpful?" He eyed Tigre in the rearview mirror.

Tigre winced and closed his eyes, concentrating. Quell the anger, batten it down, keep it pinned inside. The storms hadn't sent him mindlessly crazy since the night with the monkeys, but something about this situation was setting him off. Something about Gus and Diana. Which was more than peculiar; it was idiotic. Maybe he was just feeling guilty about how useless he'd been in the rescue. Thunder rumbled outside again.

"Seventy-ninth Street?" Gus asked as Diana pulled over to the curb.

"Yup. We'll walk in from here."

They entered Central Park slowly, glancing around them. The canopy of trees overhead was so thick that the rain barely reached the ground, keeping them mostly dry as they picked their way along the overgrown remnants of a path.

For a moment they walked in silence, surrounded by green. Tigre could almost imagine he was back in the jungle outside Santiago. The stillness was absolute.

"So why here?" Gus asked.

"We're going to the Great Lawn. That's where we've been meeting lately, in my dreams. I know it sounds crazy," Diana added apologetically.

"You and that guy?" Gus said. "But you've never met him before in real life?" He didn't know why this revelation was stirring up so much anger in him.

She shook her head. Just then the trees opened up before them, and Tigre was dazzled by a ray of sunlight.

A ray of sunlight containing the stranger who had saved them.

• • ● • •

It was exactly like her dream.

Only this time it was real.

He floated down onto the open lawn, a path of sunlight blazing through the rain clouds to set him on the grass. The wind swept before him, clearing aside the raindrops and leaving a dry space for them all to stand in.

Her golden stranger.

He was black haired and copper skinned, not as dark as Kali and Tigre, but with deeper, darker, ancient-looking eyes. He was not as tall as Kali or Tigre either, but he had a commanding presence, as if he were accustomed to being obeyed. Two gold bracelets shaped like serpents wound their way up his arms, and a circlet of gold with a sunburst in the center rested on his head. He was wearing a short-sleeved white linen shirt and pants, with gold-covered sandals on his feet.

He touched down and reached his arms out to her.

"Amon," she said. She couldn't believe he was real. She'd been having this dream for a year now, and she'd thought it signified something, but in an esoteric, symbolic kind of a way—certainly not in a prophetic-vision-of-actual-events way.

"Greetings," he said with a brilliant white smile.

"Thanks for your help back there. I'm glad you're okay," she said, walking forward but pausing out of reach of his arms. "Are you really real?" she whispered.

"Of course I am real," he said in a voice like windstorms over the desert. "I have been telling you so, haven't I, Venus?"

"Diana," she said. "I've told you before to stop calling me Venus."

"But Venus is my destiny," Amon said with an edge in his voice. He stepped toward her, but stopped abruptly as Gus planted himself between them. Gus was sure this was the guy from his dreams now. And maybe he didn't want to kill him in real life, but he knew he didn't like him.

"Her name is Diana," Gus growled. "And she's not your destiny."

Amon regarded him like an earwig, his lip curling with disdain.

"You must be the anomaly," he said scathingly. "I can't imagine what *they* were worried about. You're obviously no threat at all."

"We'll see about that," Gus retorted.

"Wait," Diana interrupted. "Who *they*? What they? What anomaly? Do you know what's going on?"

"You mean you don't know?" Amon said with evident surprise, gazing around at them.

"Know what?" Tigre asked.

"Who would have thought the others would have such respect for the rules?" the sun boy replied with amusement. "So I am the only one who knows?"

"Cut it out, Amon," Diana said. "What is it we should know?"

"That we," Amon responded, spreading his arms wide, "are all gods."

You seem to have failed.

It seems he is more than we expected.

It does not matter. Amon will take care of him for us sooner or later.

Now they are assembled. We can allow the trainers to contact them and begin preparations for the battle.

And then our role truly begins.

Yes. Then we six will be the judges of this contest, as we agreed.

And we will see who survives.

Avatars

"Well, except him." Amon pointed to Gus.

"Gods?" Tigre said, thinking of rain and blood. "I doubt it."

"Do you?" Amon said intently. "You don't feel the power inside? You've never wondered about the strange things that happen when you're around?"

Tigre glanced uneasily at Diana and Gus. "Strange things," he repeated slowly.

"I don't understand," Diana said.

"I do," Gus said to Amon. "You're cracked in the head. The end of the world has turned you into a raving lunatic with delusions of superpowers. Or possibly you were born that way." He turned to Diana. "There's no reason for us to trust this guy."

"He *did* just float down out of the sky on a ray of sunshine," Diana pointed out. She frowned at Amon. "Tell us what you mean by 'gods.'"

"We are the avatars of our pantheons." Amon smiled at

the expressions on their faces. "Don't you know what an avatar is? An earthly manifestation of an immortal being? Imagine a pantheon of gods. They are exalted and praised to the heavens; they receive sacrifices and prayers and glory and are worshipped by an entire civilization. They are supreme, omnipotent, and everlasting. That is how gods—all gods—are designed. But then that civilization fades, or transforms. New idols rise . . . monotheism replaces the pantheons, centuries pass, and technology becomes the new all-mighty, the new all-worshipped.

"How do you think that feels?" he hissed, his face darkening. "To be *forgotten?* To be ignored, to be replaced—to be treated as a fairy tale, a fantasy, a bedtime story? Oh, those old myths, weren't they funny, weren't they *amusing.* All those gods cheating on each other, ripping out hearts, battling ancient monsters—how *entertaining.* How creative."

He narrowed his eyes. "But the Egyptian gods, at least, were powerful once. We will be again."

"Egyptian *gods?*" Gus repeated. "Like, the ones with animal heads and all that mummy after-death stuff? They're going to come back and rule the world—that's the master plan?"

"Precisely," Amon said coldly. "Your gods would like it to be them ruling the world instead, but I assure you I will win."

Gus laughed. "That's a new twist. I thought I could imagine all the ways one might go crazy at the end of the world, but this is pretty spectacular."

"Gus," Diana said quietly, "perhaps we should hear him out."

"Diana, you can't be serious!" he flared. "He thinks he's a *god*."

"You wouldn't understand," Amon said. "You can't feel the power the rest of us have." He turned to Tigre. "You know the storms are not a coincidence. You have felt the strength, even if you cannot control it. Somewhere deep inside you, you know you are Catequil, the Incan god of thunder and lightning. You are the representative of the Mesoamerican deities. And you—" He turned to Diana. "Why do you think people always love you? Why do you think you became so famous so young? Why do they worship you?"

Diana felt faint. She wanted to say *Because of my music* or *Because I like them* or *Because I work really hard at it*. She glanced at Gus. She didn't want to think. . . .

"Because you are Venus, goddess of love and beauty herself," Amon pressed on relentlessly. "The star of the Greco-Roman divinities. How could anyone help but love you? That is your power—no one can resist."

Diana had always worried about the question *What if they only love you because you're rich and famous?* It had never occurred to her to wonder . . . *what if they only love you because they have no choice—because your superpower commands it?*

Is that the only reason Gus cares about me?

And by the way . . . thanks for the lamest superpower, universe. I couldn't get flying or invisibility or telepathy? I get "everybody loves you"?

"Oh yeah?" Gus said angrily. "And who are *you* supposed to be?"

The golden boy swept into a low bow. "I am Amon-

Ra, lord, sun god, and warrior of the Egyptian pantheon." He straightened and glanced around at their glittering, sunlit bubble enclosed by pelting rain.

"So you did this?" Diana said. "Why? What was the point? Why destroy humanity?"

"We were *all* part of the decision to do it, even if you can no longer remember it. And why? Revenge," Amon said. "And power. And boredom."

"All noble motivations," Gus said.

"No pantheon alone was strong enough to make this happen, not after millennia of weakness and decay. So the oldest, most powerful pantheons decided to work together—Egyptian, Greek, Mesoamerican, Norse, Indian—to bring the world to this state. And now that humanity has been brought to its knees, it is time for us to fight."

"Fight—each other?" Tigre spoke up for the first time in a while. He looked dazed and uncertain.

"Surely you see that we cannot share rulership of this planet. Who would rule the sea—your god or ours? Who would create the thunder—you, Catequil, or Thor? Who would be the lord of death—Anubis or Hades? There is only one way to decide."

He paused.

"But—" Gus said. "What about God? You know, *the* God, actual God. The one who really, um, rules . . . all that stuff." Diana gave him a surprised look and he shrugged, embarrassed. Nobody he knew ever talked about believing in God, but he'd formed his own opinions, quietly, after his parents died.

Amon sniffed. "You may believe what you like about

an invisible supreme lord—*some* pantheons would even agree with you. But if there is one, he does not interfere in our affairs. We have no more evidence of him than mortals do. He certainly doesn't seem interested in this battle, does he?"

Gus turned red, and Diana took his hand and squeezed it reassuringly. "What kind of battle are you talking about?" she asked Amon.

"We are not all here yet. Once we are assembled, there will be a battle among the avatars to determine which pantheon shall rule in the new age."

"Rule over what?" Gus interrupted. "What's the point of a ruling pantheon without any humans to worship you?"

Amon looked at Gus as if he were an unpleasant bug.

"That will be addressed after the battle," he said.

"So there's a way to bring them back?" Diana said. "To save humanity?"

"We are not interested in 'saving' humanity, but there is a plan in place to ensure we have worshippers."

"But you don't know what it is, do you?" Gus pressed. "You're as clueless as we are."

"I certainly have more clues than *you* do," Amon said. "For instance, I know that the one who wins this battle will absorb the powers of all the other avatar gods, becoming the most powerful immortal in the history of this miserable planet. This will guarantee control over the other immortals of all the other pantheons. The losing avatars, of course, will stay mortal, and so shall die . . . fade away to nothingness." He shuddered, his cool exterior slipping for a moment.

"Imagine," he murmured, "after centuries of immortality, to risk it all on these mortal bodies . . . but it was the only way."

The others stared at him.

"What are you talking about?" Tigre finally said.

Amon rolled his shoulders impatiently. "What use would it be for immortals to fight each other? We can never die. We can barely be wounded. It would be a pointless, eternal battle with no hope of resolution. The only way to create a struggle with any meaning was to become these mortal shells—bodies that can feel pain, suffer injuries, and, ultimately, die."

"Well," Gus said. "That's really charming."

"Each pantheon chose a representative," Amon continued relentlessly. "Each avatar was reborn as a human. With no memories of their immortal life, but fragments of their power still remaining inside them." Diana noticed that his fists clenched unconsciously as he said this, as if he keenly felt the "fragmentary" nature of his powers.

"Why should we believe any of this?" Gus asked.

"My pantheon has been communicating with me for the last year," Amon said, shrugging. "I cannot understand why the others did not choose to prepare you as well, even if it was *technically* against the rules."

"You knew this was coming?" Diana asked. "You knew about all of this? You never said anything to me, in the dreams."

"I hinted, didn't I? Besides, you did not need to know. I thought your deities would fill you in once the change took place. I suppose they are waiting for the last few avatars to arrive. But their weakness only makes us stronger, Venus, you and I."

"There *is no us*," Diana insisted.

"We shall see." Amon smiled, a smug, self-satisfied expression.

"What about me?" Gus asked suddenly. He didn't—couldn't—believe any of this. But perhaps there was a reason for the sickness, the dreams, the tattoo, and maybe this guy had the answers, even if Gus despised him. "Assuming any of this is true—whose avatar am I?"

"Nobody's," Amon replied with contempt. "You are not one of the chosen. You are an accident, nothing more."

Gus felt like he'd been punched in the stomach. Diana was a goddess. This guy was a god. They'd met in their dreams. And he was nothing.

Amon continued, smiling slyly.

"You are merely a common mortal, an accident that should not be here."

THAT IS NOT . . . ENTIRELY CORRECT.

Kali paced through the streets, her sweatshirt hood pulled up over her hair but failing utterly to keep her dry. The rain had soaked her through within two blocks. Stupid Tigre and his stupid too-late thunderstorm. She didn't bother to hurry, figuring she couldn't get much wetter than this.

She hated how much she wanted to run back to the others, to the only normal people left in the world, although "normal" was pushing it a bit. Still, they were real, and sane (if perhaps a little suicidal), and young. And they didn't think she was some kind of destructive she-demon like the old folks did. Of course, they didn't know her very well yet.

KALI . . .

Kali shivered, splashing through a puddle that had already formed in one of the potholes. She refused to go back. She wouldn't go back. No one, whether voices in her head or ancient military dudes or friendly but possibly psycho fellow teenagers, would tell her what to do. She wasn't going to participate in whatever game the universe was playing. Maybe she'd go to the Metropolitan Museum instead and see if she could make some new friends.

KALI . . . IT'S ME. . . .

She stopped and looked around. She could have sworn she'd heard a voice, but not one of the creepy booming ones inside her head. This one sounded like it had come from outside, but so quietly she couldn't be entirely sure.

Glass and steel buildings stretched above her, featureless and wet.

Something flashed at the edge of her sight and she whirled around, instantly alert. Was that a shape darting into the shadow of a building?

Kali shoved her damp hair out of her eyes and squinted through the downpour. It might be one of the crazy old people. Probably not a crystal hunter, if it knew her name. But she should investigate. After all, it might be another lost teenager with voices in his head.

KALI . . .

She scouted around until she found a piece of pipe leaning against a door. It was small, but it was sturdy and she could do damage with it if she needed to. She edged slowly around the side of the building into a small courtyard on the corner. There was a sad-looking modern art sculpture huddled in the center of it, drooping as if it knew it was one of the last pieces of art humanity would ever create.

Beyond the courtyard was a towering glass atrium. Giant windows, most of them smashed, encased a dark interior.

"Yup, this looks like a terrifically smart idea," Kali muttered to herself. "Follow the mysterious figure into the abandoned building. No way *that* plan could end badly."

KALI . . . I WAITED. . . .

The voice again. Coming from the atrium, as far as she could tell, but it whisked by so fast and so lightly she still thought she might be imagining it. Only one way to find out.

She kicked out the few shards of glass left in the door and stepped inside, her boots crunching through the debris. The sound echoed faintly in the vast interior. The clouds outside were massed so thickly that it felt like night, especially in here, where no light penetrated. Kali wished she still had the lantern they'd used in the subway tunnels, but the old people had taken it back. Or rather, she wished she still had the flashlight she'd dropped in the underground river when they grabbed her.

Suddenly a part of the darkness moved, detached itself from the shadows, and stepped toward her. She froze, icy fingers of fear trailing up her spine.

KALI, the voice breathed, louder now, but only barely.

ALWAYS SO REBELLIOUS. ALWAYS SO ALONE.

"Who are you?" Kali growled, keeping her voice low so the figure wouldn't hear it shaking.

THE REAL QUESTION IS . . . WHO ARE YOU?

"No, that sounds nice and poetic and all, but that's not the real question. For instance, you seem to know my name already, which gives you an advantage." She peered at the figure, which seemed to be about her height, but fuzzy and formless, like a man-shaped mist. When it stopped moving, she lost track of where it was as it melted into the shadows around it.

KALI, KALI. DO YOU REALLY NOT KNOW ME?

"Gee, let me think. Tall, dark, and foggy . . . nope, I think I'd remember meeting someone like that."

It actually seemed to chuckle, if that was what the exhalation of air could be called. I THOUGHT YOU WOULD RECOGNIZE MY ESSENCE.

"Sorry. I don't hang out with a lot of 'essences.'"

NO. ONLY MINE.

"Okay, sure. And tell me again . . . you are?"

TIME IS SHORT, KALI. THE COMING BATTLE IS OF THE UTMOST IMPORTANCE. I HAVE RISKED EVERY-THING FOR THIS. I HAVE RISKED YOU, MY SOUL, MY OTHER HALF. The shape stepped forward again and Kali caught a glimpse of eyes and a glint of what looked like moonlight pinned into his hair. It was a him, she decided.

"Yeah, you're the second person today to tell me about an upcoming battle. But nobody's said anything about who I'm fighting or why I should bother. Maybe I'm not interested in this little war."

YOU HAVE NO CHOICE.

"Just watch me!" she retorted angrily.

ONE IS TOO POWERFUL ALREADY; THEIR AVATAR KNOWS TOO MUCH; HE HAS BEEN PREPARED AND IS DANGEROUS. ONE IS SCHEMING BUT WEAK; THEY PLAY GAMES WITH THEIR AVATAR, WHO IS TORN AND WILL NOT UNDERSTAND. ONE IS MEDDLING IN AFFAIRS OF PROPHECY, AND THEY HURTLE TOWARD THEIR OWN DESTRUCTION. ONE IS IMPENETRABLE; CANNOT BE PREDICTED, CANNOT BE SWAYED, CANNOT BE TAMED. ONE IS REDUCED AND ABANDONED; THEY ARE PREPARED TO SACRIFICE THEIR AVATAR AND WAIT AGAIN, BUT IT WILL NOT GO EASILY. THEN THERE IS THE ANOMALY. AND THEN THERE IS YOU.

"That's a lot of ones," Kali said, mentally counting. "You do realize none of that means anything to me, right?"

IT WILL. THERE IS NO TIME FOR LENGTHY EXPLANATIONS. WE MUST ACT AT ONCE, ALTHOUGH IT IS DANGEROUS AND PERHAPS DISHONORABLE. BUT IT IS THE ONLY WAY YOU WILL UNDERSTAND, AND THE ONLY WAY WE CAN WIN. AND WE MUST WIN.

"What do you mean, dangerous and dishonorable?" Kali began warily, when suddenly the darkness split in two and the figure launched itself toward her. With a yell she leaped backward, tripped over the doorway, and fell, the pipe flying out of her hands. Too fast to be possible, the figure was upon her, and she saw it was a young man with long, dark, matted hair, a glittering black serpent twined around his neck, and a third eye in the center of his forehead. He was the most terrifying thing she'd ever seen, and yet at the same time she felt a flash of recognition that frightened her almost as much as the man himself.

"Get off!" she shouted, and shoved at him, scrambling to her knees. But her hands sank into him, like he was a waterfall, letting her in but pounding away at her at the same time. He seized her head in his hands, pulsing against her temples.

REMEMBER. REMEMBER IT ALL.

Tigre started as the voice rang through their heads. Amon and Diana reflexively reached up to touch their temples.

"What?" Gus said, recognizing their reactions. "Was it the voice again? What did it say?"

"Isis, I know that's you. What do you mean 'not entirely correct'?" Amon snarled at the sky. "You said you did not know what he was."

"So you don't know either," Diana pressed. "Maybe he's an avatar too."

"No," Amon said firmly. "I know the pantheons. He is not part of the plan."

NOT PART OF THE PLAN, NO. BUT NOT A COMMON MORTAL, EITHER.

"What are they saying?" Gus demanded.

"Cease these games, Isis," Amon hissed, turning slowly, his eyes darting around the lawn. "I know you can manifest. Show yourselves."

There was an unnerving pause. The rain slowed to a drizzle.

Suddenly Tigre gasped, and Diana seized Gus's hand. Amon narrowed his eyes.

Figures were materializing in a circle around them.

Some began as mist coiling up from the grass; others seemed to coalesce from the rays of the sun. A few appeared to be emerging from the raindrops themselves. They were all glowing, misty, indistinct. As they became solid, they began to glow, obscuring their features.

Tigre and Gus covered their eyes, dazzled. Peering through his hands, Tigre could see Amon striding forward to confront one of the shining figures.

"Explain this," the Egyptian boy demanded, pointing at Gus.

The figure sharpened and cleared, the glow fading. They could see now that it was a woman, tall and imposing, with straight dark hair and enormous dark eyes heavily outlined with black and gold. She wore long white robes and a headdress surmounted by a fierce-looking bird of prey; her arms were folded, and she gave Amon a cold look.

"You are not the Supreme God at present, Amon-Ra," she said in a voice that rang with ancient power. "Do not presume to command us from your position. Remember you chose to be our avatar."

Amon's expression darkened and he drew himself up, although he was still a good few inches shorter than the woman.

"When I am restored—" he hissed.

"Then we shall discuss the situation further," she finished. Her eyes traveled slowly over to Gus, and she blinked once in a slow, catlike motion, as if she were contemplating eating him.

"So you are the interloper."

Tigre felt sorry for Gus. The guy looked paralyzed

with fright. Tigre would not have wanted to be on the receiving end of this woman's stare.

"I guess I am," Gus half stammered. "I didn't mean to be—"

"It was a fortuitous coincidence." Her eyes darted sideways to Amon and back to Gus. "For some." She smiled a smile that made Tigre want to run all the way back to South America.

One of the figures behind the woman moved and began to sharpen, as she had. Tigre caught his breath.

The new figure was also female. She was the most beautiful woman he'd ever seen, and also the strangest. Her skin was the deep velvety blue of a summer evening, and it glimmered as she walked forward as if tiny stars were embedded all over her. Long dark blue hair swung down her back, and when she looked at Tigre, the pupils of her eyes were like small suns in wells of darkness, drawing him into an endless floating dream space.

She smiled slightly, teasingly, when she caught him watching her, then turned to address the first woman, her blue hands reaching for the other woman's arm. As her eyes left him, Tigre felt released, but also like he'd lost something irretrievable. He shook himself, trying to dispel the feeling.

"Isis," the blue woman murmured. "Do not be too cruel. It is not the boy's fault."

"But it is the fault of what is inside him," Isis replied, still gazing at Gus.

"We are partially to blame as well. If we had not tried to exclude them in the first place—"

"They were not welcome, Nut," Isis interrupted.

"They are not strong enough to compete. They should have accepted that."

"Well, it's too late now," said a new voice, which would have been jovial if it weren't so loud and booming. Another figure strode toward them, coalescing as he came. "He made it here. It seems he must be allowed to compete."

"Without a trainer?" Isis responded mockingly. "Without a judge, an earth shaker, an illusion bearer, a leader? Alone? What chance does he have?"

The new speaker reached them, peering down at Gus as he passed. He was the tallest yet, perhaps as tall as eight feet. He moved like a swift storm cloud, flowing and seething with energy. His beard was long and gray, his eyes sharp and murky green like the sky before a tornado.

"What chance does he have? None!" he barked cheerfully. "So what harm can it do? He'll get killed off early, and we can carry on."

Gus's mouth dropped open.

"Killed off?" Diana cried, outraged. "What are you saying? Nobody's killing Gus!" She stepped protectively in front of him and glowered up at the three deities. "You sent those crystal hunters after him, didn't you? You were trying to get rid of him!"

"We did not have to direct the crystal hunters to the boy," the blue-skinned goddess explained. "The rest of you were given special protection by your pantheons. He is alone, so he is not protected. They targeted him naturally, as they would any other human in this world."

"Well, perhaps we gave them a *little* encouragement," Isis said.

"Our darling Venus!" boomed the bearded man, peering down at Diana. "All spunky and warriorlike. How adorable!" He reached down to pinch her cheek, and she leaped back in horror.

"I'm *not* Venus," she protested. "You've made a mistake. That's just an image made up for the public. I'm not some goddess of love. I don't *want* to be."

The tall man peered at her, studying her features. "Diana is still strong in you, then?" he said curiously. "I thought she would have faded back by now. Interesting."

"What?" Diana said.

"Um," Tigre said, drawing the attention of Isis and the male god to him for the first time. "So, wait, you're saying Gus is some sort of accident? But he's a whatchamacallit—an avatar anyway? For who?"

The bearded god regarded him with a faintly puzzled look. He turned to Isis.

"Is this the Incan?" he muttered. Isis narrowed her eyes.

"Yes, Zeus," she said impatiently. "He doesn't exactly look like a Viking, does he?" Tigre recognized the name of the chief of the Greek gods. This guy looked the part, but he acted more like a belligerent drunk uncle than a king thunder god. He wondered why Zeus went by his Greek name while Venus used her Roman name instead of Aphrodite. Perhaps the gods got to choose which name they preferred. Not that these were the most important questions right now.

Nut, the blue goddess, glanced at Tigre again with another faint smile, and he forcibly dragged his eyes away from her.

"Well, you see, my boy," Zeus said, turning back to him, "when we conceived of this contest, of course we couldn't include *all* the pantheons that ever were. Some of them simply aren't strong enough to rule the world in the new age." He nodded at Gus. "We made arrangements with a few of them. Take Africa, for instance. Far, *far* too many gods, not to mention a lot of peculiar things going on there. Extremely dangerous and most confusing. So we made a deal. They get Africa to themselves; we get the rest of the world. We don't bother them; they don't bother us. All very reasonable, insofar as you can get anything sensible out of African gods.

"Then there were others who were not so powerful. In this particular case"—he cast a baleful look at Gus—"the Polynesian gods."

Gus's hand flew to his shoulder. He looked stricken, like he'd just recognized something.

Zeus continued without noticing.

"The Polynesians were scattered among many islands. There were common threads to their pantheon, but it's basically a mishmash of ideas and names and mixed-up myths that vaguely resemble one another. Only natural, as they were so spread out, see? But certainly not cohesive or strong enough to take part in the battle. We dismissed them as unimportant. And to be sure they didn't cause any trouble, we destroyed their home." He winked at Diana in an avuncular way.

There was a pause. Diana looked like she was about to cry, and Tigre felt pretty horrified himself.

"Taken back by the sea," Gus murmured.

"Yes," Zeus said, his voice booming. "My brother

Poseidon is quite good at that sort of thing. A real champion when it comes to island swallowing."

"But the Polynesians were not content to know their place," Isis interjected stonily. "They presumed to send an avatar anyway. They did not have the years of preparation we did. They did not have time to go through the process of rebirthing a deity as a mortal, by the time they uncovered our plan. Instead, they had to take advantage of circumstances during the Change to create *that*." She pointed at Gus.

"An accidental physical connection allowed them to bring him here," Nut added, nodding at Diana. "Since he was touching a true avatar at the time of the Change, the Polynesian pantheon was able to pour all of their combined energy, all of their power, their essences, into sending through one of their gods. They did not choose this mortal. But now he is theirs."

"They had to force their god into a human vessel," Isis observed. "It will be . . . interesting to see what develops as the mortal and immortal souls struggle within him, assuming he lives long enough to be worthy of notice."

Everyone looked at Gus, who was paler than Amon's robes at this point.

"So . . ." he said slowly. "It *was* an accident. But now I'm some kind of god too—a Polynesian one?"

Nut stared down at him.

"The very last," she said softly.

Kali screamed.

Images rushed through her head in a scalding flood.

Vivid emerald green, steaming jungles. Tigers roaring, orange fur rippling. Elephants mourning in misty fields of bones, silently moving their trunks over the remains of their ancestors in elephant graveyards. Stone temples rising out of the trees, ancient carvings twisting over the surfaces. Rubies sparkling in the darkness.

And destruction. Animals dying. Temples crumbling. People fleeing with howls of fear. Demons writhing in the shadows. An ocean of blood pouring over the world.

Over it all, one figure prevailed. She was tall, a hundred feet, a thousand feet tall, with ten arms, weapons in every hand. She wore a necklace of skulls and a belt of dismembered human hands. Her eyes glowed a dangerous blood red, including a third one in the center of her forehead. She was terrifying. She was all-powerful. She was the embodiment of destruction and chaos.

She was Kali.

These were not images. They were memories.

Kali screamed.

"Diana," a voice whispered.

Diana glanced around, startled. One of the shining figures was crouching nearby, beckoning to her. She looked back at Zeus and Isis, but they were absorbed in discussing Gus, and they didn't notice when she stepped away into the throng of shining figures around them.

As she moved toward the one calling her, it began to solidify and sharpen into the shape of a guy who looked about her own age. Bright blue eyes shone out of a familiar bronzed face, framed by a mop of gold hair. He grinned at her with perfect white teeth.

She crouched down next to him and realized why he looked familiar. He looked like *her*.

"Diana," he whispered. "It's so amazing to see you! You look better than I expected—I wondered what the effects would be, but you still look the same, only different, not like her at all, except you look friendlier than usual. Not that you don't usually—well, no, you don't, except to me, of course. Are you okay?" He spoke in a flurry of words that reminded Diana of one of her favorite songs, from her first album, called *Sunlight*, where the musical notes tumbled over one another in rapid succession. Nothing he said made sense, but there was something warm about him that made her move closer.

Glowing outlines of other deities were all around them, the brightness of their light hiding them from sight of the others.

"Who are you?" she whispered back.

"I tried to stop them," he hurried on without answering. "You have to believe me—you know better than anyone that I can only tell the truth. I fought for you; I did everything I could. I told them that it would make us weaker, and I especially told them that I would never, ever let them do this, which is why, in the end, they had to trick me."

"What do you mean?"

"It was Dionysus—you know how he is, all sly and friendly and convincing. I really thought he was on my side, on *our* side, because why wouldn't he be? He always thought you were wonderful, and he should have known you could be relied on, but I guess Venus convinced him. I should have known he'd fall for her wiles. It never occurred to me, I mean, you know how I am, I can never tell when someone is lying. I always figure they must be telling the truth, because I know I am, and I can't begin to fathom why someone wouldn't. You're the other most honest person I know, although who knows what putting that deceitful Venus character in has done to you. Anyway, that's how they did it—Dionysus slipped something into my drink and by the time I woke up, it was done and there was nothing I could do and I can't even tell Athena—our judge—about their cheating because they might disqualify you altogether and then you might die and be gone forever, so I had to just accept it. Forgive me, Diana."

"Stop stop stop," she said finally, interrupting his flow of words. She felt protective, like he needed taking care of and that was her job. It was unsettling, considering that she didn't know him and he seemed to be talking complete nonsense. "I have *no idea* what you're talking about. Start with: who are you?"

"You don't—oh, of course you don't," he said. "That's part of the mortality process, losing all your memories, and so, they said you wouldn't know what had happened and so you wouldn't mind. But I was right, wasn't I? I can tell you know things aren't right. I knew *you* would never want this."

"This what?"

"The melding," he said, catching her hands in his. "When we chose our avatar, we chose you, Diana, goddess of the hunt and the moon, because we all agreed that you are a mighty warrior who could defend us and return us to power. Of our choices, you were the strongest and purest and most devoted, not to mention one of the few willing to take the risk, which certain gods I could mention never would." His eyes flicked in Zeus's direction with a bitter look that seemed out of place on his friendly face.

"But our leaders were afraid," he continued in a lower voice. "I suppose we should have expected that, knowing them. They've never won anything fairly that they could find a way to cheat themselves into instead, so of course when they started thinking we might lose, they came up with a way to sneak by the rules. I think it was Hera's idea, which would be so typical. She hasn't really liked Venus since that whole golden apple/Trojan War disaster, so she'd jump on any way to get rid of her."

"Er," Diana replied, trying frantically to remember her Greek mythology.

"And she's never liked you very much either, as a daughter of Zeus by another woman. In fact, I'm not sure there's anyone she does like," he trailed off reflectively.

"So what happened?"

"Hera convinced Zeus that we should make an alliance—you know how he is, he'll do almost anything she tells him to—except stop sleeping with other women, of course. She pointed out that we shared the world with Egyptian gods once, so why not do so again? I mean, they are not as different from us as, say, the Incans, plus of course they had entered their strongest god as their avatar, which just shocked everybody, that someone like Amon-Ra would take a risk like this, and we had to wonder, could anyone actually beat him? Of course, the Egyptian pantheon knew that too, so there was no chance of an alliance without a bribe." He gave her a meaningful look.

"Me?" she squeaked.

"Not *you* you; Amon-Ra would never be able to tame Diana, our chosen avatar," he said. "The Egyptians agreed to Hera's plan on the condition that he be given Venus, our goddess of love, all flaky blond scheming bit of her. And of course *she* was thrilled at the idea of being the star and the prize simultaneously—you know how she is about being the center of attention, not to mention he is *so* her type, which is to say arrogant enough to think the world revolves around him." He thought for a moment, then added: "Which, technically it does, since he's a sun god, but he's not the only one, and we're not all that full of ourselves, right?"

"I thought," Diana said, dredging something up out of her memory, "I thought that in Greek mythology Venus was married or something."

"To Vulcan? That guy?" The deity snorted contemptuously, nodding toward the other side of the circle. "Everyone knows Venus never took that relationship seriously. He was probably the only one who did." Diana followed his gaze over to a huddled figure that seemed to glow more darkly than the others. As she watched, it swung its head around to face her, and she shivered without knowing exactly why.

"But if I was—am—Diana . . . ?"

"It took a lot of power," he said quietly. "I did not think they could have done it without me, truthfully. But they worked together, Hera and Zeus, Mars, Dionysus, Mercury, Poseidon, Hades, even Demeter—but you remember how she is, she'll agree to anything to keep the peace. The rest thought it was our only hope; they just couldn't believe that our little moon goddess could be strong enough to defeat the king of the whole Egyptian pantheon. So they forced Venus into you. They arranged circumstances so you would accept her without knowing what was happening. And gradually the two parts of you joined together."

Diana's head was swimming with new information. That was how she'd felt for years, torn between her Diana self and the Venus image. Was this really why?

"Amon-Ra hopes, of course, that at the end of the struggle inside you, Venus will be ascendant so he can have his willing partner," he continued. "But you still look like her." He reached out and brushed her hair back from her face, sadly. "My warrior sister."

"Sister," she said again, finally realizing. "Oh my God—you're Apollo."

"God of the sun," he said with another rakish smile. "But a much better one than Amon-Ra; *I* would know better than to try and hook up with a goddess of love. There are much worse gods than me—and the worst of all is Amon-Ra, with his wind floating and ordering people about and thinking he knows everything. You stay away from him, Diana. We don't need an alliance to win this battle, and he will do everything to crush who you really are. But now that I know the real you is still in there, I will help you stay strong."

Diana shivered again and drew her flannel shirt closer around her. "You're the one who helped me," she whispered. "When Gus was hurt by the hunter."

"I *am* the god of medicine, too," he said with a cheerful shrug. "I figured he was important to you, especially when Zeus and Isis wanted to get rid of him so badly. Listen, we don't know who we can trust right now. But if you play along for the moment, you'll find they are easier to fool in the long run. I know the Diana part of you hates this idea, sister, but believe me, if you fight them openly, you may push them into desperate measures. If they can find a way, they might even remove Diana from you entirely."

She shuddered. Remove part of her personality? The part she actually liked?

"Always remember I'm here for you," Apollo whispered, standing and squeezing her hands.

She turned to go back to the others, and caught Amon watching her from the edge of the circle. A sly smile skittered across his face.

"I'm a what now?" Gus asked.

"Oro, Polynesian god of war," the blue woman repeated patiently. "But the change was forced and sudden, so it is impossible to tell what or how much you absorbed."

"Yes. You probably have very limited powers indeed," boomed Zeus merrily.

"Perhaps you should accept your fate and let us kill you now," Isis suggested, peering down her nose at him.

"Shut up," Gus said furiously, clutching his head in his hands. He couldn't think. He wasn't a god, and then he was. But he was still alone, thrown into a battle he couldn't win, possessed by some angry war god from the mythology of a people who didn't even exist anymore.

"I'm not like this," he said. "I'm a regular guy. I'm a *nice* guy. I'm the last person anyone would pick to be somebody's war god." He instinctively turned to find Diana, but she had moved away into the shining forms that surrounded them. The Egyptian guy had stepped to one side as well, keeping an eye on the crowd as if he were watching for her. Gus didn't like the expression on his face.

"*I* certainly would not have picked you," Isis said.

"Nor I," Zeus agreed, looking him up and down with a skeptical expression. "War gods are usually quite a bit taller, for one thing. More muscle definition, of course. Possessed of a commanding self-confidence that makes people want to follow them into battle. Arrogant bastards. Rather annoying, actually. Still, they serve their purpose, eh?"

Isis let out a long exhalation, then reached out and tipped Gus's head back with one finger on his forehead.

"Get off," he snapped, jumping away.

"Yes," she said. "There is no hope for this one. Nor that one," she added, nodding at Tigre, who was looking at his feet with a miserable expression.

"Why should we believe you?" Gus asked. "Where are these other 'pantheon representatives' or whatever? I bet his Incan welcoming committee doesn't think he's hopeless." Although the slump of Tigre's shoulders probably wouldn't give them a whole lot of encouragement, Gus thought to himself.

"I wonder," Isis said. "They have a reputation for giving up easily, and they are weak. As you can see, they couldn't even join us for this meeting."

"It requires much power to manifest as clearly as we are right now," Nut interjected. "They are conserving their strength."

"A sure sign of weakness," Zeus rumbled, winking at Amon-Ra.

"True," Isis agreed. "Their cause is nearly as hopeless as that of the Polynesians." She slanted her eyes toward Gus again, an amused smile flickering on her lips. "You may as well give up now too, Incan."

Tigre kept his eyes on the ground and didn't respond.

"Listen, neither of us is giving up," Gus said, trying to sound braver than he felt. "I think you're just trying to scare us off because you're afraid we'll win."

"*I* am not scared of anything," Isis hissed in a voice that reminded Gus of snakes sliding through the shadows of rocks. "You will die, one way or another."

"And the sooner the better," Zeus added jovially. "All this talk talk talk is making me restless. Let us take our avatars and begin preparations for battle." He spread his arms wide, nearly hitting Diana as she came back into their circle.

"Take your avatars?" Gus repeated, his makeshift courage falling. "Take them where?"

"To our individual training grounds," Isis said silkily. "We chose ours some time ago. *You* don't have any." She beckoned to Amon-Ra.

The Egyptian god looked sullen, but he followed her, only turning back to fix Diana with an intent stare as he walked away.

"You are to walk south along the main way," Nut said to Tigre. "When the sun is higher in the sky, your trainer will be able to manifest, and he will direct you." She nodded graciously to them all and then slowly faded into a blue shimmer in the air, then nothing.

"Come, Venus," Zeus said. "We have a lot of lovely battle planning to do." He gave her a hugely expressive wink.

"I want Gus to come with me," she said stubbornly. "I mean, he has nowhere else to train, right, and no one to tell him what to do?"

"I'm afraid that's out of the question, my dear," the thunder god rumbled. "Alliances are not permitted, as you might recall." He rolled his eyes significantly, then winked at her again, several times in a row. Gus got the distinct impression that the god was trying to tell her something they weren't supposed to know. From the indignant look on Diana's face, he guessed she knew what it was, too.

"But—" she said.

"Now, now. No arguing in front of the other teams. Let's go somewhere and discuss this *privately*." Zeus reached out to take her arm, and she jerked away.

"Diana, you don't have to go with him," Gus said firmly. "We don't have to let them tell us what to do. We're our own people, even if we have super-gods inside us or whatever."

"That's true," she said. "And I'm your avatar, Mister Zeus, so listen up. I need to know that Gus is safe from the crystal hunters."

"This is none of your concern," Zeus said. "Who cares what happens to the Polynesian avatar?"

"I do," she said, crossing her arms. Gus felt a glimmer of warmth in his chest.

The Greek thunder god scowled ferociously. Diana

stood her ground, staring him down.

"Very well," he said. "He can be protected, too. It's a simple enough electricity spell."

"And then he can come with us?" Diana pressed.

"No. Avatars must train separately. Those are the rules." Diana closed her eyes, thinking.

Gus wanted to tell her to forget this guy, to forget the whole thing, to come away with him and forget that any gods had ever tried to tell them what to do or that any-one wanted them to kill one another in order to rule the world. He didn't care if all the bad guys in the world were after him. They could go back to Justin and Treasure and help them fight off crystal hunters for the rest of their lives. Would it really be so terrible being the last people alive in the world, if they could be together?

But he couldn't get the words out. He couldn't tell her what he was feeling, and he didn't know what she was thinking, and he felt like his whole life was hanging in the balance.

"Okay," Diana said finally, opening her eyes again. "I'll come with you, but only on two conditions."

"What are those?" Zeus rumbled, narrowing his eyes.

"First, you give Gus the same protection the rest of us have—it's only fair to level the battlefield at least that much. Second, I want you to call me Diana, not Venus. You know and I know that she's a part of me too, and that's my choice. Got it?"

The Greek god puffed out his cheeks and pulled on his beard for a minute. He darted a sideways look at Gus, then back at Diana, then up at the sky. At length he blew a huge gust of air out of his mouth and nodded.

"Very well. I accept your conditions for the time being, although we might have to discuss them again in the future, my girl."

Sickened, Gus turned away and kicked at a patch of grass. Fine. If she wanted to leave, she could go. He was alone, just like the Egyptian goddesses had said. The angry churning feeling in his chest spasmed and breathing felt difficult.

"Make him safe," Diana said.

Gus tensed to run if the god came anywhere near him, but all Zeus did was raise a commanding hand, making a gesture that looked like shoving air toward him. A wave of nausea hit him, like a thousand shocks all over his body at once, and he fell to his knees, clutching his chest. As the wave passed, he felt the boiling feeling subside a little too.

"Gus?" Diana was standing next to him, a concerned expression on her face. "Are you all right?" She reached out and touched his shoulder. They both jumped as a prickle of electricity ran through them.

"Oh," she said, glancing at Tigre. "I see."

"It is done," Zeus said. "We must go."

"I'll see you soon, okay, Gus?" Diana said. "Stay safe. And you too, Tigre. Tell Kali—I don't know. Tell her at least it isn't aliens."

"Okay," Tigre said. "Good luck, or whatever."

Gus glanced up, hoping to make eye contact with her, but she had already turned away, and within moments she had disappeared into the trees with the bearded thunder god.

The shimmering circle around them was fading now, figures evaporating back into the air or coiling down into the ground like mist. The air was colder and dimmer, and gray clouds were starting to collect again overhead.

Gus pulled himself to his feet, his whole body aching, and turned to Tigre, who was standing with his hands shoved into his pockets, frowning at the sky.

"I guess you'll be going south, then," Gus said. "To find your—trainer person."

"I don't know. I'm not even sure what they mean by 'south along the main way.'" Tigre shook himself, wishing he could talk to Quetzie, who liked him and would never give up on him. He wondered if he could figure out how to call for her. "I think Kali was right, and maybe we should stop following orders. Anyway, I want to know what she thinks of all this before I give up completely. I'm going to go find her and tell her what's going on."

"Okay," Gus said, his spirits rising a little. "I'll come with you."

Wordlessly, the two of them walked together, side by side, out of the park.

Kali lay still, breathing deeply.

Shiva knelt beside her, his eyes studying her face, one hand lightly resting on her wrist. Moments passed.

"Do you remember now, my idol?" he said finally.

Her dark, dark eyes turned slowly toward him. In their depths he could see fires burning.

"I remember," she said.

"Do you understand? Why this was necessary?"

Her eyes moved back to the sky, visible through the glass roof, where gray clouds were scudding away from emerging rays of sunshine.

"I understand," she said quietly.

There was a pause.

"But you were still wrong," Kali said. "It is not yet time for the world to end."

"I know the cycle is not complete," Shiva said, almost pleadingly. "But they would have destroyed us if we did not participate. We had no choice."

"You needed more faith," she said. "We had millions to support us before. It is now that we have no choice."

He watched her cautiously as she curled to her feet, her movements poised like a panther's. She looked down at him where he knelt on the ground and held out her hand.

"Come, husband," she said. "Let us destroy what remains of this world."

...to be continued in Book Two:
SHADOW FALLING